MW01531231

STROKE

A NOVEL

ALSO BY CARLOS LEDSON MILLER

Belize

Panama

STROKE
A NOVEL

Best wishes!

Carlos Ledson Miller

Redbud Publishing
Victoria, Texas

This book is a work of fiction. All incidents and dialogue, and all characters, with the exception of some well-known public figures, are products of the author's imagination and are not to be construed as real. Where real life public figures appear, the situations, incidents, and dialogue concerning those persons are entirely fictional and are not intended to depict actual events or to change the entirely fictional nature of the work. In all other respects, any resemblance to actual events or locales or persons, living or dead, are entirely coincidental.

© 2004 Carlos Ledson Miller

Published by

Redbud Publishing Company
P.O. Box 4402
Victoria, TX 77903

www.redbudpublishing.com

Printed in the United States of America

All rights reserved. No part of this publication may be reproduced, stored in a retrieval system, or transmitted in any form or by any means – electronic, mechanical, photocopy, recording or any other – without the prior written permission of the publisher. The only exception is brief quotations in printed reviews.

ISBN 0-9720293-8-9

For women cueists, everywhere

Part I

Chapter 1

"UNEVEN SHOULDER" cautioned a temporary, orange freeway sign. Sedonia straightened hers, and a sharp twinge near the base of her neck reminded her yet again of her recent surgery. She flipped on her left blinker and maneuvered her black Mazda Miata away from the six-inch drop-off and into the center lane of the Gulf Freeway. Construction barrels bottle-necked the Sunday afternoon traffic, and her lane change drew a horn blast. She glanced into the rearview mirror and saw the pitted grill of a rusty brown pickup truck too close to her bumper.

"GALVESTON 28 MILES" read a green sign. Sedonia grew uneasy; the League City exit would be next. She drew a deep breath, trying to relax. The rusty pickup rumbled past on her left. Sedonia glanced over and caught a glimpse of the redneck driver, turned sideways in his seat and glaring at her. She suppressed the impulse to extend the one-finger salute.

"LEAGUE CITY 1 MILE." She flipped on her right blinker, and a woman in a gray Suburban slowed to let her change lanes. Moments later, Sedonia exited onto the feeder road, then caught the green light and passed through a busy intersection. Ahead she saw a large weathered sign that read "Champ's Billiards." Beneath the sign stood a building that looked like a rundown hunting lodge. It seemed out of place, set in front of an aging freeway strip mall. There were no empty parking places in front, so she pulled around to the rear. That lot also appeared to be full, but she found a place in the far corner that was wide enough for her Miata.

She parked, then sat for a moment, having second thoughts about her mission. A sigh escaped. Three months ago, she'd been the top amateur golfer in the nation and about to join the Ladies Professional Golf Association tour. Just three months ago. Now she was a nobody, looking for a pool hustler named Emilio. Tears of frustration welled unexpectedly, but she blinked and forced them back. There'd been enough of that.

She quickly slid a twenty-dollar bill and her driver's license into a rear jeans pocket, then pushed her purse under the car seat. As she climbed out, she looked around. No one in sight. She started across the potholed asphalt. Parking in remote areas always made her uneasy, and now she glanced from side to side as she hurried through the jumble of dusty vans, pickups, and cars. She made a mental note to be on her way before dark.

At the front of the building, she hesitated, then pushed open the door and stepped inside. She'd expected a large room, filled with pool tables, but instead found herself in a small outer bar, with a baseball game blaring from a big-screen TV. Several men occupied the only table; two others slouched at the bar. They all turned and looked at her with interest.

Through open doorways to the right and left, she saw rooms with pool tables. Uncomfortable under the male scrutiny, she turned and headed through the doorway on the right. Nine pool tables, arranged side by side, filled the rectangular room. The faux lodge decor had been carried into the interior. Several deer heads hung high on the wall; they looked as dusty as the exposed rafters above them. The mixed smell of cigarette smoke and stale beer saturated the air.

Games were in progress on each table, and Sedonia noted that all the players were women. Her foreman had told her that in addition to the main tournament for men, there would be a satellite tournament for the ladies. Spectators lined the walls. She found a good vantage point beside a young man with a sparse growth of facial hair.

At the closest table, a slight woman in her mid twenties, Sedonia's age, was playing a heavyset woman who was at least well into her forties. Both wore faded jeans and T-shirts, and displayed humorless expressions. Sedonia recognized the game: Nine-Ball. It was one she and her father had often played.

The older woman walked around the table to where Sedonia stood, and brusquely gestured for her to move back, so she'd have room to shoot. The young man next to Sedonia gave her a tentative smile, then moved a half step to his left. Sedonia had to crowd against him to get out of the shooter's way. As they waited for the shot, the young man stroked his wispy goatee with one hand. Sedonia felt the back of his other hand resting strategically against her backside. She couldn't risk moving without disturbing the player about to shoot.

The woman lined up on the green 6-ball. With a smooth stroke, she drove it into the gold-striped 9-ball, which in turn rolled into a side pocket for the win.

Sedonia stepped away from the man's hand and gave him an angry glance, then told the player, "Nice shot."

The woman looked over her shoulder with a frown, and responded with a curt nod.

Okay, Sedonia thought, lesson one: no talking.

As the loser racked the balls, Sedonia shifted her gaze to the next table. Two women in their thirties also were engrossed in a serious game. Sedonia's eyes began to sting from the cigarette smoke. A sharp *crack!* like a rifle shot, caused her to jump. The older woman had broken the rack, and balls now scattered about the table. The blue 2-ball slammed into a side pocket and a moment later the maroon 7-ball rolled into a far corner pocket.

"Do you play?" asked a nasal voice behind her. It was Sneaky Hand.

"A little," Sedonia said. "I'm looking for Emilio Sepulveda. Do you know him?"

"I know an 'Emilio', but I don't know if his last name is . . . whatever you just said."

"He's supposed to be a well-known pool player."

"That's probably the guy I know. We just call him 'Emilio'. He's over on the men's side."

Sedonia nodded, and then squeezed past him and worked her way through the spectators. As she passed through the bar, the men at the table again looked up with interest.

The room on the other side of the building was smaller, holding only five pool tables. Spectators circled the perimeter. Men's games were in progress on each table, but none of the players looked Latino. Those waiting to shoot sat perched on stools, focusing on their respective games like birds of prey.

Sedonia found a place beside an elderly man. "Excuse me," she whispered, "I'm trying to find Emilio."

The man tapped the shoulder of the person sitting in a chair in front of him. "She wants to talk to you."

A thin Latino, perhaps thirty, looked back with a frown. "Yes?"

Sedonia leaned forward, so as not to disturb the nearby players. "Are you Emilio, Raul Garcia's nephew?"

The Latino gave a quick nod, then stood and said, "Come." He led her back into the bar area. "What do you want?"

Sedonia again felt uncomfortable under the scrutiny of the men in the bar. She asked Emilio, "Could we talk outside?"

He gave another curt nod, and led her out the front door and around to the side of the building. Traffic roared past on the nearby freeway.

Sedonia took a deep breath. "Whew. It's smoky in there."

Emilio waited. Dressed in a nondescript pair of jeans and a faded sports shirt, he might well have been one of her house painters, reporting for work. Apparently, clothes didn't make the player.

"I'm Sedonia Forbes," she began. "I was talking to Raul at work the other day—"

"I have no time for a long talk," Emilio interrupted in accented English. "In a few minutes, I have to play again."

"Raul told me you'd be here this weekend," Sedonia said quickly. "I want to learn how to play pool. Good pool."

Emilio studied her for a moment. "Your name is Forbes?"

Sedonia nodded.

"Forbes Painting Company?"

"Yes."

"My uncle works for your father?"

"He did. My father passed away."

Emilio's frown indicated he didn't understand.

"My father's dead," Sedonia said. "Heart attack, three months ago. I own and operate the painting service now. Raul's my foreman."

Emilio responded with a look of resignation. "Why do you wish to play pool?"

From his manner, Sedonia sensed he was only continuing the conversation because she was his uncle's employer. "I . . ." she began, but suddenly felt emotion threaten her eyes. She looked over at the freeway for a moment, then turned back and said, "I've been a golfer since I was a little girl. A damned good golfer. I was about to turn pro a couple of months ago, but I hurt my shoulder. I've had surgery on it, but . . . it can't be fixed."

Emilio gave a tentative nod.

"My father also taught me to play pool when I was little," Sedonia said, "and he and I played a lot while I was growing up."

"So," Emilio said with a tolerant smile, "you played pool with your father."

"And also in college, and at . . ." She hesitated, then finished uncomfortably, "the Bay Oaks Country Club."

Emilio responded with a patronizing chuckle.

Sedonia knew how silly she must sound to him, but pressed on. "I need to replace golf. I need something I can do . . . something competitive that I'm good at. It's . . . important to me."

Emilio frowned. "And you want me to show you how to play pool?"

"If not teach me" Sedonia said, "at least see if you think I'm any good."

Emilio hesitated, then said, "There is a poolroom on the NASA Parkway called Buster's. Do you know it?"

"No, but I live in Nassau Bay. I'm sure I can find Buster's."

"I can meet you there tomorrow . . . about three o'clock."

"Tomorrow, I've got appointments all day. But from Tuesday on, I can meet you wherever and whenever you have time."

"*Bueno*," Emilio said. "Tuesday at three o'clock. But right now, I have no more time for you."

Sedonia extended her hand. "I'll see you on Tuesday, then. And thanks." His grip was firm, but his palm was as soft as hers. Professional pool players apparently avoided calluses.

He released her hand, turned, and headed back inside. Sedonia watched him disappear around the corner of the building. "Emilio is one of the best pool players in this area," his uncle had told her. "Everyone knows him by just his first name . . . like Elvis."

Sedonia considered going back in and watching the rest of the matches, but then decided to leave while the ominous parking lot was still bathed in sunlight.

The following morning, Sedonia entered her father's paneled den to wait for the estate liquidator and a prospective buyer who were rummaging about upstairs. The room, having been closed for months, had a musty odor. She opened the heavy drapes that covered the three floor-to-ceiling windows, and midmorning sunlight—diffused through dense shade trees—illuminated the interior. In the backyard, the swing that her father had hung from a gnarled limb, twenty years earlier, oscillated in the breeze, as if still awaiting the little girl's return.

Sedonia heard a door open upstairs, and then the shuffling of the liquidator's and buyer's feet as they perused the master bedroom. Sedonia heaved a sigh; the vultures were circling.

She turned back and looked about the room, which for a quarter-century had been her father's enclave. Shadows of tree branches played across the tan protective cloth that covered the massive billiard table. His five rifles still stood behind the glass door of the oak armoire, and on the wall nearby hung a dozen photographs, depicting him with friends on deer and dove hunts. Shelves on the opposite wall displayed his numerous golf and billiard trophies.

His oak desk lay bare now, except for a gold pen and pencil set, an empty letter holder, and a small unlit lamp. Behind the desk hung his architecture diploma from the University of Houston and several photographs depicting Cougar athletic teams and individual players. Always seeming out of place in this montage of Houston red and white was a picture of quarterback Joe Montana, in his dark blue and gold Notre Dame uniform. He was crouching under center and gazing intently at the Houston defense, a moment before throwing the last-second, game-winning pass in the 1979 Cotton Bowl. "That son of a bitch broke my heart that day," her father had said on more than one occasion. But at the bottom of the picture, he'd added a caption that showed his grudging respect: "Joe Montana — The Look of Eagles."

The top of the long credenza was covered with photographs, trophies, and other memorabilia that depicted Sedonia's transition from little girl into young womanhood: Brownies, Girl Scouts, children's soccer, high school swimming and volleyball, and first place in the Women's National Collegiate Athletic Association golf tournament.

Three crystal trophies stood side by side, reflecting her championships in the last three Bay Oaks Country Club tournaments. And accorded the place of honor in the middle of the credenza was a large silver trophy. The inscription read: "U. S. Women's Amateur Golf Champion."

Shortly after her father's death, Sedonia had accepted the Bay Oaks members' invitation to play in one final amateur tournament before joining the Ladies Professional Golf Association. In prior years, her father had served as tournament committee chairman, and she knew he would have wanted her to try for a record-breaking fourth straight victory. Postponing her debut as a member of the LPGA by one month shouldn't have made a difference. But it had.

Now with a profound sense of loss, she scanned the array of photographs that covered the wall. In most, her proud father posed with her. Conspicuously absent was any sign of her mother.

The estate liquidator and the prospective buyer entered the room, snapping Sedonia out of her sad reverie. She turned and acknowledged them with a curt nod. Then she walked over and opened a window. Dust stirred on the billiard table cover.

At 5:30 on Tuesday morning, Sedonia drove slowly through the still-sleeping community of Seabrook. Her Miata's windshield wipers slapped at the heavy fog on one side of the glass, while the defroster fought the condensation on the other. Ahead, a diffused silver glare was the only indication that the sun was rising from the Gulf of Mexico.

Sedonia cautiously approached a nearly hidden intersection, then turned right, off 2nd Street and onto Todville Road. To her right, the fog shrouded the fifty-foot-high bridge that spanned an inland channel and linked the neighboring coastal communities of Seabrook and Kemah. A twinge in her right shoulder told her she was too tense. She leaned back, but a moment later leaned forward again, peering into the wet, gray morning.

She arrived at Waterfront Street and turned left. The shocking pink paint of Maybellene's Bar penetrated the fog. Sitting high on pilings and overlooking the bay, the ramshackle tavern was a favorite hangout for Johnson Space Center employees. Just four hours earlier, it probably had been a hive of activity. Now it stood like a garish apparition.

Lights glimmered ahead from the small seafood markets that lined both sides of the street. Vietnamese shrimpers and oystermen would already be out on the bay, fog or no fog, making their initial drags, while their wives and children tended the shops and prepared to receive the day's catch. Sedonia's house painting company was the only enterprise on Waterfront Street not dedicated to drinking or eating. A sad smile formed. Once, the Forbes Painting Company also had been a family affair.

Waterfront Street came to a dead-end at the bay. She turned left into her company's parking lot, and the oyster-shell surface crunched beneath her tires. A light shone from the office window. She pulled up beside her foreman's dilapidated panel truck, and climbed out. The smell of rotting fish and other decaying bay creatures permeated the humid air. The office door flew open.

"¡Hola, Sedonia!" her foreman called out.

"Hola, Raul."

He held the door for her as she entered the one-room office. An old wooden conference table stood off to the left, cluttered with blueprints, brochures, and paint samples. Raul's small metal desk was on the right. He avoided it whenever possible, more comfortable when his responsibilities required that he be in the warehouse, or better yet, out on a job site.

Sedonia walked over to a scarred wooden desk behind the conference table, and secured her purse in the top drawer.

"You are here early," Raul said.

"But not as early as you," she said with a smile. "Never as early as you."

Raul responded with a self-effacing nod.

"Coffee smells good," Sedonia said, and went over and poured a cup, then returned to her desk.

Raul limped over to his desk, and perched on the edge. Decades of crawling up and down ladders had aged him more than his 65 years. "Did the . . . house business go okay, yesterday?"

Sedonia gave a resigned nod and took a sip of coffee. "I met with the last of Dad's creditors. His estate's completely settled now."

"Are we . . . okay here?"

"Things will be a little tight, but I think we'll be able to keep going." Sedonia knew she ought to be more encouraging, but signing over the bulk of her father's assets the previous day had left her discouraged.

"Did you find my nephew on Sunday?" Raul said, in an apparent attempt to get off the uncomfortable subject of the company's viability.

"Yeah. He and I are getting together this afternoon."

"You are meeting with him?" Raul said, concern in his voice.

"At 3:00. So, I thought I'd better come in early this morning and get some work done."

"But I just thought you just wanted to watch him play, not . . . spend time with him."

"I want him to see if I'm any good."

"Sedonia . . ." Raul began, then paused, seemingly uncomfortable with what he had to say next. "Emilio is my nephew . . . but . . ."

Sedonia waited.

"He is . . . wild," Raul continued. "He never wants to work, just to play. I don't think you should spend time with him."

"Why not?"

"The way he makes his money."

"Pool hustler."

Raul nodded slowly. "Why is it, you wish to do this?"

Sedonia sighed. "I need something, Raul. Last month, I was in really bad shape . . . emotionally. I hit rock bottom. Dad's passing away . . . my shoulder . . . our financial problems here . . ."

Raul gave an understanding nod.

"I'd assumed I'd be able to make my living playing golf," she continued, "and then this damned shoulder!"

Raul said, "And the doctors can't fix it?"

Sedonia heaved a sigh. "The surgery and the stretching exercises I do every morning allow me to do ordinary things. But for the rest of my life, I won't be able to raise my right arm above shoulder height."

Raul responded with a sympathetic shake of his head. "And now you think maybe you can learn to play pool, instead of golf?"

Sedonia hesitated. For perhaps the thousandth time in the past three months, she felt overwhelmed by her father's absence. She needed to confide in someone. However, she knew it wasn't appropriate to burden her foreman with her despondency. Raul had problems of his own, including what he'd do if her business folded. Finally she said, "It's probably silly, but last week I saw some women playing pool on TV. They were good, and they handled themselves like . . . like professional golfers do."

"Will your shoulder let you play pool?"

"I think so." She stood and simulated a pool stroke on her desk. Then she sat back down. "I need to be able to do something, Raul." Her emotions broke through. "God, how I need to be able to do something!"

Raul gave her a smile and nod. "I will tell my nephew he must try to help you."

"Thanks."

"But, Sedonia," he said, "promise me you won't spend too much time with Emilio."

* * *

Buster's Billiards stood unobtrusively in the middle of a drab strip mall on the NASA Parkway. As Sedonia pulled into the parking lot, it occurred to her that she must have driven past this poolroom hundreds of times without ever noticing it. She found a parking place beside a shiny blue Chevrolet Silverado pickup. As she climbed out and locked her car, she tried to see through the poolroom windows, but the tint was too dark. At the entrance, she drew a quick breath and stepped inside.

"Hello, little lady!" rang out a man's voice. "What can I do for you?"

Her eyes were still adjusting from the abrupt change from the bright afternoon sun to the dimly-lit room. The bartender wore a black T-shirt that covered a muscular frame. His head was shaved, his scalp tanned, and a broad smile beamed from beneath a shaggy black mustache.

"Uh . . . I'm meeting someone," she said, then glanced over her shoulder. "Him." Emilio was shooting on a table in the far corner. He was the only other customer.

"E-mil-io," the man said, his East Texas drawl lingering over the name. "Ya gotta watch that boy. That E-mil-io . . . he's strong!" Something in the man's tone sounded more mocking, than respectful. "What would you like to drink?"

"Uh . . . white zinfandel?"

"Don't carry wine. Beer or mixed drink?"

"Coors Light."

When he returned with her beer, he said, "First time in here?"

Sedonia nodded as she reached for her money.

"First drink's on me, particularly when the customer's as good lookin' as you are. I'm Buster. I own this place."

"Thanks. I'm Sedonia."

"Se-don-ia," Buster said with a smile. "Purty name, purty gal."

Sedonia smiled. Not too subtle in his approach, but this guy would be hard to dislike. She crossed the room to Emilio.

He ignored her and continued to pocket the remaining balls on the table. He apparently was practicing Eight-Ball. He ran through the seven solid-colored balls first, then started on the seven striped balls. She noted his stance. He lined up with his elbow farther away from his body than her father had recommended. But once the stick slid forward and struck the white cue-ball, the stroke was smooth and firm, and the cue-ball wound up in good position for an easy next shot. As the last ball, the black eight, dropped into the pocket, he finally looked over and acknowledged her presence by saying, "I only have half an hour."

Sedonia frowned. Half an hour, and no manners. "What do we do first?"

"You don't have a stick?" he said.

"No. Will I need my own stick?"

"You've got your own golf clubs, don't you? Same thing."

"Where do I buy one?"

"Talk to Buster. I don't sell sticks. Here, use mine for now."

Sedonia accepted his custom cue—dark wood, fancy inlaid ivory points, and a white wrap. Her father had had first-rate pool equipment in his den, but nothing like this work of art.

Emilio spread the balls out on the table. "Show me how you play. Shoot any ball you want."

Any self-consciousness Sedonia might have had was overridden by her annoyance at Emilio's attitude. She lined up on the yellow 1-ball and slammed it into the side pocket. Her right shoulder responded with a sharp warning twinge.

"Don't shoot so hard," Emilio said.

No shit, she thought, rubbing her shoulder. She bent over and lined up to shoot the maroon 7-ball into the far corner. She took a deep breath, then went through the routine her father had taught her: three practice strokes, hesitate and concentrate on the object ball . . . stroke. The 7-ball rolled cleanly into the corner. She lined up on the purple 4-ball in the side pocket. *One, two, three . . . stroke.* The 4-ball dropped into the side. Emilio and the shoulder twinge were now partitioned from her thoughts; her world was reduced to a dark-green rectangle, and the desire to make brightly colored balls disappear. *One, two, three . . . stroke. One, two, three . . . stroke.* She made a long rail shot on the last ball, the orange five, then straightened up and looked at Emilio.

He walked around the table, pulling the balls from the pockets and dropping them at random. Sedonia winced. From the time she'd been a little girl, her father had warned her about dropping balls on the delicate slate that lay beneath the green felt.

"Damn it, Emilio!" yelled Buster from behind the bar. "Quit slammin' those balls on the table!"

"Fuck you," Emilio muttered, but not loud enough for Buster to hear. To Sedonia he said, "You told me your father taught you to play?"

She nodded.

"He taught you that one-two-three shit?"

"Yes," Sedonia said, an edge to her voice.

"It's not bad," he said. "Some people use it, some people don't. But it's not bad. Shoot these balls, but let your chin touch the cue when you shoot."

Sedonia bent over for a shot on the red-striped 11-ball.

"Lower," Emilio said.

Her chin touched the cue stick. "It feels awkward."

"Don't talk. Shoot."

Sedonia shot and missed the corner pocket by at least six inches. She straightened up. "I feel more comfortable not bent over so low."

"You didn't do your one-two-three shit on that shot. Touch the cue with your chin, and don't raise your head until the object ball drops in the pocket. And do your one-two-three shit."

Sedonia gave him an annoyed glance, but then bent low and did as he'd instructed. The blue 2-ball stuttered, but dropped into the side. Next she made the purple 4-ball. She cleared the table without missing again. As the last ball dropped, she straightened up and said, "It still feels awkward."

"That's because you've been shootin' wrong all this time."

"Yeah, but it seems to me—"

"You're right," Emilio interrupted. "What do I know. Maybe if your father had taught me, I'd know somethin' too. I gotta go." He took his stick from her, unscrewed it, and slipped the two pieces into a hand-tooled leather case.

Sedonia took a deep breath, trying to quell her annoyance. "Listen, I appreciate your teaching me, but—"

"Lesson's over, *chica*. Refinery day shifts get off in twenty minutes, and today is payday. Payday for them is payday for me."

"You'll be playing for money?"

He started toward the bar. "Yeah, gonna be playin' for money."

Emilio paid his tab, and as he waited for Buster to bring him his change, Sedonia said, "I'd like to come along and watch."

He frowned, then said, "Do you know where Wayne's Icehouse is on Highway 225?"

She shook her head.

"Follow me then."

As they headed out the door, she heard Buster call out, "Come back and see us again . . . Se-don-ia."

Emilio's blue Silverado pickup raced east on Highway 225, with Sedonia's black Miata in pursuit. Traffic on the four-lane freeway consisted primarily of tractor-trailer rigs, servicing the miles of oil refineries and chemical plants that sprawled off to the right. This industrial row always reminded Sedonia of a scene from the futuristic movie, *Mad Max.* Rusty cyclone fences, topped with barbed wire, enclosed the employee parking areas. A grayish dust covered the on-duty shift's pickups, vans, and cars. Uncut weeds occasionally fought their way through the gravel expanses to provide the only touch of green. A maze of piping, seemingly bent at random, covered hundreds of acres; corrosion showed on the joints and valves. Signage on enormous storage tanks encouraged Productivity, Quality, and

Safety. And high above the scene, vent pipes released yellow flames and leaked dark smoke into the sky, which wafted over the nearby blue-collar community, with the poignant name: Deer Park.

Emilio's pickup swerved from the center lane to the right, then down an exit ramp. Sedonia glanced into her review mirror—*clear*—then followed. A half-mile down the service road, they turned right into a gravel-covered parking lot. A faded rusting Lone Star Beer sign indicated they'd arrived at Wayne's Icehouse.

Sedonia pulled up beside Emilio's truck and climbed out. The acrid smell from the surrounding refineries and chemical plants seemed to caution against breathing too deeply. She glanced back as they started toward the icehouse. Emilio's shiny Silverado stood out among the dust-covered pickups and vans that filled the parking lot. And her spiffy two-seat sports car clearly came from another world.

The front of the building consisted of four garage doors, open in deference to the ninety-degree temperature outside. Two fans, six feet in diameter, roared in the doorway and blasted the hot, humid air through the building and out an open garage door at the rear. Sedonia was aware that conversations trailed off as she and Emilio entered the room and walked toward a makeshift bar that had been fashioned from unpainted sheets of half-inch plywood. A glance to her right confirmed the two dozen male patrons were more interested in her than they were the pool hustler. The only other woman in the place was a buxom barmaid in her fifties, who was pulling a beer from a cooler. Sedonia and Emilio drew up a couple of rickety wooden barstools.

Two grizzled old-timers sat across the bar from them, and one said to Emilio, "Back again, huh, meskin?"

Sedonia gave Emilio a worried look. They both seemed out of place here. Emilio, however, gazed at the man for a moment, then said, "Fuck the Alamo. Remember Santa Anna."

Sedonia felt her stomach tighten. She frowned at Emilio, trying to convey her concern.

The old man gazed back at Emilio and slowly shook his head, then broke into a rasping laugh, which abruptly turned into a hacking cough. He lit an unfiltered Lucky Strike to quell his spasms.

To Sedonia's relief, the incident seemed to have passed. She looked about the room. A few of the men were still observing her, but most had returned to their beer and their conversations. Anglos, Latinos, and blacks shared the half-dozen mismatched, Formica and chrome tables. Nearby, an older white worker sat with his back to her and sounded off, something about a "cat' cracker." The other men all nodded in respectful agreement, as if he might be their supervisor. Sedonia had heard the term "cat' cracker" before, but just knew it was slang for a catalytic cracking unit, which had something to do with refining crude oil. The men in this icehouse apparently worked together, and they obviously drank together. From their appearance and demeanor, she suspected they also fought together.

The heavyset barmaid came over. "What can I get you, honey?"

Sedonia said, "Uh . . . Lone Star?"

"We don't carry that here. That's an old sign out front." Without asking Emilio for his order, she reached down into the cooler, pulled out a Coors Light, and set it in front of him. "Don't start any shit in here this afternoon," she told him. Her tone left no doubt that she was in charge, and she meant what she said.

"I'll have a Coors Light too," Sedonia said.

After they'd each had a chance to take a drink, Sedonia said so only Emilio could hear, "There are hustlers on golf courses too, but to win money, they have to play with people who don't know them. But here, you're obviously well known."

Emilio turned on his bar stool and gazed out at Highway 225, so his response couldn't be heard by the others. "I give them 'weight'. It's . . . how you call it . . . a 'handicap'. They think I give them enough weight so they have a chance to beat me. But I just give them enough so they keep coming back. They ain't seen my best game here. They ain't seen nothin' like my best game."

Sedonia looked back at the men in the room. No one fit her preconceived notion of a pool player. Two faded and stained tables stood nearby, unoccupied. "The pool tables here aren't very big," she said, "and they look like they're in pretty bad shape."

"Bar-boxes," Emilio replied. "You gotta put quarters in 'em. They get fucked up because the icehouse doors are always open. You gotta shoot hard, or the ball don't go straight."

"Hey, hoss," said a voice behind them. A young refinery worker had entered the icehouse and now stood behind them. He wore grimy jeans, a stained T-shirt, and a hardhat with a Shell Oil logo across the front. He carried a soft vinyl cue case. "I reckon you're here to play pool," he said to Emilio.

"I reckon so," Emilio said, with a sarcastic imitation of the worker's nasal twang.

Sedonia frowned. Emilio seemed to go out of his way to antagonize people. Didn't he realize that he and she were outsiders here?

"What kind of weight you gonna gimme?" the man said.

"I ain't givin' you shit," Emilio replied.

"Gimme two games on the wire," the worker drawled, "and I'll play you race-to-5 for $25."

"Two on the wire!" Emilio said. "Fuck that. I'll play you even."

"Two games," the worker said firmly.

"Shit," Emilio said, "if you want somebody to give you money, go to the welfare office."

"Yeah, you'd know about welfare, wouldn't you?" the worker said, then joined the men at the nearby table, who earlier had been discussing cat' crackers. The older man asked why he was late, and the worker told him he'd had to get his check cashed, and then take some money home to his wife.

Emilio turned his back on the man and ordered another beer. In an aside, he told Sedonia, "He'll be back."

She whispered, "Sounds like you're trying to start a fight, not get a pool game."

"Sometimes you gotta piss people off to get 'em to gamble."

"What's 'race-to-5'?"

"First one to win five games, wins the bet. And he's askin' for 'two games on the wire'. That means I gotta give him two games before we start. Which means, I'll have to win five before he wins three."

"Is that too much . . . 'weight'?"

"Nah, I could give him three on the wire, easy. But I want more than $25 from him. This guy's got no gamble. Didn't you hear? He takes his money home to his wife. He'll only play me once, then he's gonna quit on me."

"Hey, hoss," the worker called out. "We gonna play?"

Without turning around, Emilio called back, "I'll give you one on the wire."

"That's what you gave me last time. That ain't enough."

"You almost beat me," Emilio said, still facing away.

"'Almost' only counts in horseshoes and hand grenades," the worker retorted.

Emilio finally turned around. "I'll give you two on the wire, race-to-5, for $100."

"Fifty," the man said.

Emilio started to turn away again, but the older man at the table said, "I'll put twenty with his fifty." The other three men chimed in with $10 each.

The worker handed the $100 to the barmaid. "Hold the stakes, Nell."

Emilio handed her five twenties, then flipped a quarter toward the table.

"Heads!" the worker called.

The coin landed in the middle of the felt, and Emilio stepped over to take a look at it. "Rack 'em."

The worker fed three quarters into the table. As he started racking for Eight-Ball, Emilio sauntered over to where a dozen cue sticks stood in a disorderly stack against the far wall. He picked one up, glanced at the tip—as if to be sure it had one—and then returned to the bar. Sedonia's father had showed her how to roll cue sticks on a pool table to be sure they weren't warped, but Emilio didn't bother doing that. Apparently, he didn't need a straight stick for this match. If he did, he'd have gotten the fancy one out of his pickup.

The worker pulled his personal cue stick from the vinyl case and screwed it together. Sedonia noted that bright decals of some sort decorated the butt.

"A gimme stick," Emilio said with a snort, "from Camel cigarettes."

The worker removed his hardhat and told Emilio, "Break!"

"I'll dump a couple of games," Emilio said under his breath to Sedonia, "and still take him 5 to 4."

Emilio's break was weak, but the red 3-ball slowly found its way into a side pocket. He disinterestedly applied chalk to the tip of his cue, then went to work on the remaining six solid-colored balls. He didn't look like the same player Sedonia had seen an hour earlier at Buster's. His stance was straighter—not the chin-on-the-stick technique he'd showed her—and he tended to raise his head in mid stroke, a no-no in any sport that involved hitting balls. He also shot softly, not hard as he'd told her was necessary on tables in this poor condition. Three of his balls barely found their way into nearby pockets, then a long shot drifted well off target.

The worker painstakingly chalked his cue as he studied several makeable possibilities. Finally he decided on the green-striped 14-ball. He shot hard and missed the pocket by at least four inches. "Fuckin' table!"

Emilio's turn. He made a ball, then declined to take a straight-in corner shot, and attempted and missed a cross-table bank in the side. The worker hurried back, and this time pocketed four stripes before missing. Emilio again shot easy and the ball drifted away from the pocket. The worker managed to make the remaining three stripes, and then the black 8-ball to win the game. His coworkers responded with triumphant shouts.

"Rack!" he told Emilio. Including the two-game weight Emilio had given, the score was now 3 to 0, in the race-to-5.

The next game got underway. The workers were quiet when their man shot, but grew vocal when Emilio stepped up, either talking directly to him, "Don't miss now!" or talking about him to each other, "I think this ol' boy's 'bout done! Whatcha think?"

Sedonia frowned. Although gambling on golf was not uncommon at the Bay Oaks Country Club, harassing people while they were playing was unacceptable.

Emilio kept the game close and won, making the match score 3 to 1. The next game was similarly close, making the score 3 to 2. When Emilio was shooting, the clamor from the workers was now nonstop. Emilio came over to the bar to get a drink of beer while the worker racked for the next game.

Sedonia said, "Do you have to put up with this?"

Emilio frowned. "Put up with what?"

"All their . . . talking."

Emilio chuckled. "They're trying to 'shark' me, but they're wasting their time."

"Then it's allowed?"

"If you're gonna play pool, you better get used to it."

Sedonia didn't reply. She couldn't imagine trying to perform under this level of verbal abuse and animosity.

Emilio told her, "I'm gonna give him one more game, then I'm gonna come off my stall."

Sedonia surmised "come off a stall" meant he'd stop missing on purpose.

Emilio returned to the table, broke weakly, and failed to make a ball. The worker lined up on the orange 5-ball and fired hard. He missed, and as the 5-ball caromed down the table, it tapped the black 8-ball into the side pocket. In the game of Eight-Ball, pocketing the 8-ball prematurely was an automatic loss. The match score was now tied, 3 to 3.

Sedonia waited to see if Emilio would "stay on a stall" one more game. He did. The game went back and forth until both players had made all the balls in their respective suits. Then Emilio missed an easy shot on the 8-ball, and left it in perfect position for his opponent to tap it in for the win.

The score was now 4 to 3 in the worker's favor. He just needed one more game to win the $100, and his backers now stepped up the verbal abuse on Emilio. "You dogged that last 8-ball, man!" and, "He choked on the eight! I seen him do it!"

The worker looked confident as he stood at the break end of the table and waited for Emilio to rack the balls. He looked over at Sedonia and said, "Is he your boyfriend?"

Sedonia ignored him.

"Hey, honey! I said, is he your boyfriend?"

Emilio came over to the bar. The worker waited for a response to his question. Finally, Sedonia just gave a quick shake of her head.

"I didn't think so," the man said. He looked at Emilio with contempt. "What the hell would a gal like you be doin' with a guy like him?"

Sedonia saw Emilio react for the first time to something that had been said. He glared at the worker for a moment, then snapped, "Break, motherfucker!"

The worker seemed momentarily taken aback. When he broke, he miscued, and only three balls moved any distance. Emilio, still standing at the bar, flipped his cue stick upside down, so the tip rested on the concrete floor. He took the butt between his palms and rapidly twisted the stick back and forth, like a Boy Scout starting a fire. Then he flipped the stick to its regular position, butt on the floor, and with a piece of blue chalk he meticulously dressed the freshly roughed tip. The workers all watched, quiet now, their expressions seeming to indicate they anticipated what was about to happen.

Emilio strode to the table. He rested his chin on the cue stick and slammed the blue-striped 10-ball into the corner pocket, and with the same shot sent the other fourteen balls scattering about the table. Firing fast and loose, he cleared the stripes from the table, then slammed the black 8-ball into a corner pocket. Score: 4 to 4.

The worker racked for the match-deciding game. Emilio walked down to the break end of the table. "Loose rack!" he snapped.

Sullen-faced, the worker re-racked the balls, this time making sure they were tight. Emilio returned to the other end of the table. His break had the rifle-shot sound Sedonia had heard at Champ's Billiards on Sunday. Balls scattered and seemed to be fighting to get into the pockets. Three solids and a stripe were down. Emilio, still firing fast and loose, rapidly pocketed the remaining four solids, and then the black 8-ball to win the match. He'd run the table, not giving his opponent a single shot in the deciding game.

"Gimme my money," he told the barmaid.

She pulled the $200 from her jeans pocket, then hesitated, looking for confirmation from the workers.

"Give it to me!" Emilio demanded.

She handed it over, and Emilio told Sedonia, "C'mon. Now!"

Sedonia heard the ominous sound of chairs scraping on the concrete floor as they hurried through the open garage doors.

"¡Aya carajo!" Emilio swore as they quickly made their way across the gravel parking lot.

They arrived at their vehicles and looked back. The workers stood in the icehouse doorway. The barmaid's angry voice carried across the parking lot. Sedonia couldn't distinguish the woman's words, but her threatening tone apparently was preventing bloodshed in her parking lot.

"They know me now," Emilio said as he unlocked his pickup, "thanks to you."

"Thanks to me!" Sedonia protested, unlocking her Miata.

Emilio glowered at her for a moment, then replied. "That guy was right. What's a country club girl like you, doin' with a guy like me?" He climbed into his truck, slammed the door, and a moment later showered gravel as he roared out of the parking lot.

Sedonia jumped in her car and followed him onto the Highway 225 feeder road. He entered the freeway at the next ramp, heading east. She made a U-turn at the next intersection, then got on the freeway and headed toward home.

She checked her rearview mirror. No one had followed her from the icehouse. She set the speedometer on 70 and took a deep breath. What the hell *was* she doing running around with someone like Emilio? Then she smiled. Winning golf tournaments had given her the same adrenaline surge that she still felt right now. And she hadn't even been the person playing. Yet.

Chapter 2

"Do you have Emilio's phone number?" Sedonia asked Raul. Her foreman had kept himself busy in the warehouse all morning, but finally had come into the office for coffee. Sedonia suspected he had been avoiding her.

Raul stirred his coffee, avoiding eye contact, and responded with a noncommittal, "Uh . . . he stays with his girlfriend."

"Do you know about yesterday at the icehouse?"

Raul looked at her and responded with a worried nod. "I told you, he . . ."

"Does he still blame me for what happened?"

"He knows he . . . behaved bad. He called me last night. He was afraid . . ."

"Yes?"

"Afraid that he had made a problem for me . . . here at work."

Sedonia shook her head. "Good grief, Raul. Did he think I might fire *you*, just because *he* behaved like a jerk?"

"Well . . ."

Sedonia realized this was a serious matter to Raul. "I couldn't run this place without you."

He didn't respond.

Sedonia continued, "You ran this business before I was born."

A hint of a smile formed. "I didn't run it then," he said. "I was just a painter."

"But you've run it the last several years."

"Only because your father was busy with his construction company."

Sedonia appreciated Raul's continuing loyalty to her late father.

The telephone rang, and Raul hurried over to his desk to answer it. "Forbes Painting Company." He listened a moment. "Would you like to talk to Miss Forbes?" He looked at Sedonia and shook his head, then dropped into his chair and began scribbling notes on a yellow legal pad.

Sedonia hoped the phone call meant new business. Two house painting jobs had concluded the previous week, and her entire eight-person staff now was working on a church in San Leon. Unless she could line up another job within the next few days, she'd have to lay off everyone except Raul. She hated this part of the business. Not only were the missed paychecks hard on the people who worked for her, but usually one or two would have found employment elsewhere by the time she had another job for them.

"Yes, sir," Raul said into the phone, then nodded toward Sedonia. "Sherwin Williams Classic neutral ground for the base and tumbleweed trim for the exterior. I will have the cost estimates when you get here."

Sedonia smiled. Good! A job. She walked over to the front window. The two Vietnamese-owned seafood markets across the street already had customers' cars in their parking lots. A large, dilapidated trawler usually was moored behind the buildings. This morning, however, it must be out dragging the bay for shrimp. Sedonia had an unobstructed view across the narrow channel that separated the neighboring communities of Seabrook and Kemah. The latter's restaurant row had not yet come to life. It would be another hour before the first lunch patrons arrived.

"Yes, sir, Mr. Landry," Raul said. "I'll tell Miss Forbes. Thank you." He hung up.

Sedonia turned. "Good news?"

"That was Mr. Landry, from Coastal Construction. He was in his truck and his phone battery was low. He has a remodeling job and he's coming over this afternoon to—"

The telephone interrupted them again. Raul answered it, glanced at Sedonia, and said into the phone, *"¡No, Sobrino!"* He lowered his voice and continued for a moment in rapid Spanish.

Sedonia had taken two years of high school Spanish and spent her summers on her father's predominantly Latino painting crews. She knew *"sobrino"* meant "nephew." She said, "Is that Emilio?"

Raul grimaced. "Yes."

"Let me talk to him." She picked up the receiver on her desk and punched the lit call button. "Emilio, this is Sedonia."

There was a moment of silence, then he said, "I am sorry . . . I got mad last night."

"Forget it," she said. "Where are you playing tonight?"

Raul was listening on the other phone. "Sedonia, no," he interjected.

"Would you mind if I watched you play again?" Sedonia asked Emilio. "My uncle . . ."

"Yeah, I know," Sedonia said. "He's afraid you'll be a bad influence. Can I watch you play again?"

"If my uncle says it is okay."

Raul frowned and vigorously shook his head no.

"He says it's okay," Sedonia told Emilio.

"I'll be at Chug's Lounge on Highway 3," Emilio said. "Do you know it?"

"I've driven by there," she said. She'd been curious about the name. "What time?"

"About 9:00."

"Can you coach me at Buster's this afternoon?"

"I guess—"

"Sedonia!" Raul interrupted. "Mr. Landry will be here at 1:30 to talk about his job. You should be here too."

She was tempted to tell Raul to handle the meeting by himself, but she saw her presence was important to him. "Okay," she said with a sigh. Then she told Emilio, "I'll see you at Chug's Lounge at 9:00."

Buster looked up from his newspaper as Sedonia entered the poolroom. "Se-don-ia," he said. He seemed pleased to see her.

"I wasn't sure you'd be open this early," she said.

"Just got here. Open at 11:00 a.m. and close at 2:00 a.m., unless I've got a couple of serious gamblers matched up."

Sedonia looked around; she was the only customer.

"Let's see," Buster said, "you drink Coors Light, don't you?"

"Too early for me," Sedonia said. "Emilio told me you sell cue sticks."

"What kind you lookin' for?"

"I don't know. I was hoping you'd be able to fit me."

"You hoped I'd 'fit' you?" Buster said, a leer forming.

Sedonia flashed a look of annoyance. "That's a golf term. You 'fit' clubs to people. I don't know what the pool term is, or what kind of stick I need. Can you help me, or not?"

The leer vanished. "C'mon over here."

They walked to a tall display case with glass doors, and Buster unlocked it.

Sedonia said, "Do they come in different sizes?"

"Same length, about fifty-eight inches. But different weights, from sixteen ounces to about twenty-one. Do you like a light or a heavy stick?"

"I don't know. What do professionals use?"

"It varies. Most men prefer nineteen ounces. Some women go lighter . . . eighteen or even seventeen."

"What do you have in nineteens?"

"Any idea what cue maker you want?"

Sedonia shook her head. "And what's the price range?"

"Depends on who makes it and what you want. But in general, you can get a purty good cue for $300. A *real* good one for $600. Or, you can pay $2,000 for a top of the line." He paused, awaiting her response.

"Like golf," she said finally. "When my dad fit me with clubs, he said the important thing was to spend just enough, so that whenever I had problems, I'd know the clubs weren't to blame."

"Your old man sounds like a purty smart feller."

Sedonia wished her father were around right now to help her chose a cue stick. Of course, he probably wouldn't want her in a pool hall in the first place.

Buster took a cue stick out of the display case. "This here's a nineteen-ounce Jerry Olivier. He's a local guy who makes cues." He handed it to her.

Sedonia felt an unexpected surge of excitement, similar to when she'd first seen her Miata on the showroom floor. Unlike Emilio's cue stick, this one had no fancy inlays. This stick's beauty lay in its simple elegance. The lacquered wood butt was stained a dark green, accentuated by the even darker highlights of its swirling grain. The black wrap felt like satin in Sedonia's hand. She walked over to a nearby pool table, and rolled the stick on the surface, as her father had taught her.

Buster said with a laugh, "I ain't gonna sell you no warped cue, honey."

"The green color," she said, "does that mean it's a woman's stick?"

Buster laughed again. "There ain't no 'his' and 'hers' in cue sticks. Most of 'em are made out of birds-eye maple. Cue makers just stain 'em different colors to make 'em purty. Same thing with the inlays you see in some of these others. That stuff don't help you shoot. Just looks purty."

"How much for this stick?"

"It's used," Buster said, "but Jerry's refinished it, so it's good as new. If it *was* new, it would cost you $350. I'll let you have it for . . . $225."

Sedonia had no idea what the stick was actually worth, and she was tempted to tell him she'd think about it, then do some comparative shopping somewhere else. She checked her watch. She needed to get back to the shop so Raul could go to lunch before the contractor arrived at 1:30. "Does it come with a carrying case?"

"Se-don-ia," Buster said in a mock whine, "you don't want me to make *no* money, do you." He sighed. "Okay, I got a gen-u-wine Naugahide case I'll throw in with it."

They walked back to the display cabinet, and Buster reached for a non-descript vinyl case. A hand-tooled leather case stood next to it.

Sedonia said, "How about the other one?"

"I'd have to charge you $175, just for the case."

Sedonia pulled out her checkbook. "Naugahide will do just fine."

A few minutes later, as she pulled out of Buster's parking lot, she experienced the same sense of discomfort she usually felt when she had to deal with a car mechanic. Had Buster taken advantage of her, just because she was a woman?

* * *

The office door opened, and Sedonia looked up from the accounting ledger on her desk. *This* was Mr. Landry? A smile parted his rugged features as he strode across the room.

"Hello, Sedonia. Remember me?"

Sedonia stood up, slightly flustered. As they shook hands, she said, "When Raul told me we were meeting with a 'Mr. Landry', I didn't make the connection."

"It's been a while, hasn't it? You were still in high school."

Sedonia nodded, well remembering that particular summer between the ninth and tenth grades. Her mother had divorced her father, then promptly remarried a petroleum company manager and moved to Saudi Arabia. Sedonia had stayed in Texas with her father. And in the midst of the family turmoil that summer, she'd formed a schoolgirl crush on a handsome University of Houston student who worked on one of her father's construction crews. Brad Landry was ten years older now, but still handsome.

"Please, have a seat," Sedonia said, then sat back down behind her desk.

Brad pulled up a guest chair and assumed a comfortable slouch, crossing his legs so that the side of an engineer boot rested across one knee. He set a battered briefcase on the floor beside him. "I was saddened to hear about your dad," he said. "I was down in Mexico when he died, and didn't learn about it until I got back. Sorry I missed his funeral."

Sedonia nodded. "It all happened . . . very quickly."

There was a pause, then Brad said, "He was a hell of man, your dad. I learned an awful lot from him. Not just about the contracting business, but about life in general. By the end of that summer, I felt like he was my second father. Nowadays, they'd call him a 'role model'. He was a good one."

"Thanks, Brad." She felt more comfortable in his presence now, no longer like a flustered schoolgirl. "Raul's at lunch, but he ought to be back in a minute. We weren't expecting you until 1:30."

"I'm early," he said. "So you're running Forbes Contractors now."

"Forbes Painting," Sedonia corrected. "I had to sell the rest of the business to settle my father's estate."

"I just heard about that the other day," Brad said. "That's part of the reason I'm here. What happened?"

Sedonia sighed. "When my parents divorced, my mother deferred taking her half of the business. Then when Dad died, she decided she wanted her share. Dad also had other creditors, so I had to liquidate the general contracting business, the house, and everything else he owned to pay everybody off." Sedonia stopped, realizing she was confiding personal matters to a man she hardly knew.

"That's what I figured," Brad said with a nod. "Divorces can be tough. I went through one myself, a couple of years back."

Sedonia stole a glance to this left hand. No ring.

Brad looked at her with a wry smile. "Guess marriage was the one thing your dad didn't know how to teach me."

"Me either," Sedonia said with a laugh. Five months earlier, she'd broken off a two-year relationship with the drummer in a local band, and since then she'd felt no desire even to date, much less attempt another romantic attachment.

The office door opened, interrupting them. "I'm sorry I'm late," Raul said, with a worried check of his watch.

Brad stood up and the two men shook hands. "No problem, Raul," Brad said. "I'm running early this afternoon."

Raul pulled up another chair and joined them.

Brad's manner turned businesslike. He asked Sedonia, "Are you in the painting business to stay?"

She was momentarily taken aback. "Well . . . yes."

Brad nodded. "I'm a general contractor, just like your dad taught me. Since I didn't want to compete with him, I've kept my territory on the other side of the Gulf Freeway. Most of my projects have been in Friendswood. Now your dad's gone, and I've got no such loyalties to the people who bought you out. I'm going to be moving into this area. I've primarily been doing private homes—new construction and remodeling—but now I'm also getting into commercial work."

Sedonia chuckled, and Brad stopped talking and looked at her with a quizzical expression.

"I'm sorry," she said, smiling. "You just reminded me of Dad. Okay, you're expanding and coming this way. Where do we fit in?"

"I need more sub-contractors who I can count on. I know Raul from the old days. I couldn't ask for better. How large a crew do you have, and how stable are they?"

Sedonia hesitated, then decided that with Brad, candor would be her best option. "I've currently got eight people," she said, "plus Raul and me. It's a struggle. When we're between jobs, I sometimes have to lay workers off. And sometimes, they don't come back."

"What's your job status now?"

"We're finishing a project this week, and I've got nothing else lined up," she admitted. "We need business."

Brad turned to Raul. "You got anybody who can hang and float sheetrock?"

"Yes, sir. Jesse and Marta."

"How about cut and install molding?"

"Yes, sir. They can do that too."

Brad turned back to Sedonia. "I'm finishing out a 3,800 square-foot house I've built in Friendswood. I've got about three weeks of drywall, trim, and paint work left. A sub-contractor, who's worked for me for the past couple of years, has given me his preliminary proposal. But I want to use his crew on a shopping center remodeling job that I'm about to start."

Brad reached down and withdrew a manila folder from his briefcase. He handed it to Sedonia, then continued, "I'd like for you to go over their proposal and note any changes you think would be necessary. At the time it was drawn up, the customer hadn't settled on her paint requirements. I've got that information now, and I discussed it with Raul over the phone this morning. So, you'll need to add in that expense too."

"I have those paint costs," Raul interjected. He handed a sheet of paper to Brad, who looked at it, nodded, and passed it to Sedonia.

Sedonia read through the other sub-contractor's proposal, line by line. Finally she looked up and said, "We'll get our written proposal to you tomorrow morning. But these figures look reasonable, and I can tell you right now, we accept the job." She extended her hand across the desk. "My crew will be on your job site, bright and early Monday morning."

Brad smiled as they shook hands. "It'll be nice to be working with the Forbes family again."

She returned his smile. "Thanks, Brad. Only this time, *we're* working for *you*."

Sedonia accompanied him outside. He started to get into his white Dodge Ram pickup, then turned and walked back to her. "I usually make it a point not to mix my business and social lives, but would you be interested in having dinner with me tonight?"

"I'm . . . sorry," she said. "I've . . . made other plans."

Disappointment showed on his face. "Are you seeing someone?"

"Uh . . . yes." She wasn't "seeing someone" the way he meant it; however, it was better to not lead him on, since she knew she wasn't available emotionally.

"Too bad," Brad said with a wry smile. "Well, hopefully, this Friendswood job will just be the first of many we'll be doing together."

"I certainly hope so. And, Brad, thanks again."

She watched him pull out of the parking lot and disappear down Waterfront Street. Then she turned and gazed in the other direction, toward the bay. The shrimp trawler from the seafood market across the street was returning from the day's drag. Two sailboats knifed through the choppy water. Despite having just received relief from her immediate business problem, she couldn't shake the undercurrent of melancholy that had begun with her father's death and had been compounded by her shoulder injury. Would she always feel this way?

Purchasing the cue stick this morning had briefly lifted the pall. She walked over to her Miata, opened the trunk, and withdrew the stick from its case. She screwed the two pieces together, and again admired its simple elegance. Simple elegance, like the perfect golf swing. The thought brought to mind the feature article that had appeared in the *Houston Chronicle*, shortly after she'd won the U. S. Women's Amateur Golf Championship. The city's leading sportswriter had reported her dramatic victory and had enumerated her intercollegiate and club titles. He referred to her as "an up-and-coming, female Tiger Woods" and showed the parallels between the two golfers, including the active role each of their fathers had played in their early development. The article concluded with the announcement that after playing in one final amateur tournament at her late father's country club, Sedonia would turn professional. The sportswriter had predicted immediate success for her on the LPGA tour, describing her skill as "world class."

Returning her gaze to the bay, Sedonia recalled that last amateur tournament. On the 17th hole of the final round, she'd stood under a shedding pine tree, just off the right side of the fairway, waiting while her opponent searched for a drive she'd hooked into the left rough. The stifling Gulf Coast heat and humidity made it difficult to breathe, and Sedonia simply wanted to get this round of golf over with. Spectators lined the back of the putting green, awaiting her approach shot, and a tournament official stood nearby to ensure she didn't illegally ground her club on the pine needles.

Sedonia led the tournament by five strokes, with only this hole and one more to play. There was no way her opponent was going to catch her. Finally the woman emerged from the rough and signaled she was dropping a ball. The penalty now gave Sedonia a six-stroke lead. The woman hit a perfect fairway wood, which bounced once and rolled onto the putting surface.

Sedonia responded with a grudging nod, then lined up her own shot. The ball rested on a shallow bed of pine needles. The putting green was less than 200 yards away, but the first 10 yards were beneath low tree limbs. Her 2-iron would keep the trajectory low enough to avoid the tree, but she'd need to hit the ball hard to reach the green.

She took a deep breath and reassured herself that there was no pressure on this shot, not with a six-stroke lead. Then she addressed the ball, eyeing the pine needles immediately behind it and reminding herself that she needed to take a slight divot. She took another deep breath, and began her slow, deliberate backswing. She hesitated momentarily at the top of her swing, then started the club downward, her lips pressed together. *Hit it hard!* At the instant of impact, the clubface slammed into something immobile, and the shaft twisted violently in her hands and wrenched her right shoulder with a blinding stab of pain. Sedonia had cried out and dropped to her knees.

Now, gazing out at the bay with the cue stick clutched against her breast, her vision blurred as she whispered, "World class."

Sedonia glanced down at the digital clock on her dashboard: 8:54. Chug's Lounge was less than a mile away, so she should arrive right on time. Nighttime traffic along Highway 3 was light. On her left, a succession of strip malls, storage sheds, auto parts stores, and other small businesses flashed by. Most had closed for the day, and only a scattering of vehicles remained in the parking lots. On her right, a railroad track ran alongside the highway. Far ahead, she saw the searching beam of an oncoming train.

Sedonia rotated her head slightly to relieve the tension in her neck and shoulder muscles. What kind of people frequented a place with a name like "Chug's?" She'd find out shortly; the roadside sign had come into view. The neon "C" flickered as if it were about to extinguish. Would Chug's patrons return when the sign renamed the lounge "hugs"?

Sedonia slowed, then turned left off the highway and into Chug's parking lot. She recalled that the brown, wooden building previously had been a barbecue restaurant. Emilio was leaning against his pickup, arms crossed, waiting for her. She pulled in beside him and climbed out.

"Hi," she said. "I bought a cue stick this afternoon." She walked around to the back of her car and opened the trunk. "Take a look at it and see what you—"

A warning blast from the approaching train cut her off.

"C'mon," Emilio said. "We need to get inside."

"Take a look at my stick first."

"Bring it with you," he said impatiently, then grabbed her elbow and pulled her toward the lounge.

The locomotive rumbled past, preventing her reply. She yanked her arm from his grasp as she followed him into the lounge.

"Train beer!" Emilio shouted, then hurried toward the rear of the room.

Sedonia slowed to get her bearings. There were only a half-dozen customers, all men. Two coin-operated pool tables stood off to the right— "bar-boxes" she remembered Emilio had called them. A long counter separated the pool area from the dance floor and general seating area. Two men wearing slacks, dress shirts, and loosened ties were playing on one table; the other table wasn't in use. The men interrupted their game and looked at her with interest.

She caught up with Emilio and discovered he was already engaged in a heated discussion with the middle-aged man working behind the bar.

The bartender said, "You gotta already be in here when the train goes by."

"I *am* in here," Emilio protested. "The fuckin' train's still goin' by."

"I mean you gotta be in here when the train *starts* by."

"Bullshit! I know the rules."

The bartender glared at Emilio for a moment, then shook a finger at him. "I'll give you a train beer this time. But next time, you gotta already be in here when the train *starts* by."

"Her too," Emilio said, gesturing toward Sedonia.

"She just got here!" the bartender said.

"Bullshit! We came in together. She's with me."

The bartender turned to Sedonia. "That right? You with him?"

Sedonia hesitated. She not only didn't know what these two men were arguing about, but she was reluctant to be linked to Emilio, who seemed to inflame tempers wherever he went. But finally she said, "Yeah, we . . . came in together."

Now the bartender wagged his finger at Sedonia. "I'm gonna give *you* a free beer too," he said, "but don't ask me next time."

"I didn't ask you—," Sedonia began, but the bartender ignored her, and turned and stalked to a cooler at the other end of the bar. Sedonia turned to Emilio. "What's the problem this time?"

"Train beer," he said. "When a train goes by, they gotta give you a free beer. That's the rule."

The bartender came back with two Coors Lights. He slammed them down on the counter, then walked back to the other end of the bar.

Emilio looked at Sedonia and grinned. "C'mon," he said, and grabbed his beer and headed across the room. Sedonia took a deep breath, trying to quell her annoyance, then picked up her beer and followed him.

A counter ran along the far wall. Emilio set his beer on it and walked over to the unoccupied pool table. "You got some quarters?"

Sedonia shook her head. Emilio gave her a suspicious glance, then reached into his pocket and pulled out three quarters. As he racked the balls, Sedonia took her cue stick from its case and screwed it together. She was aware that she and Emilio had drawn the interest of the two men who were playing on the other table.

Emilio walked over to her. "You buy that stick from Buster?"

She nodded.

"Lemme see how bad he screwed you."

She handed him the stick. He held it under the pool table light and checked the signature on the butt. "Jerry Olivier," he said noncommittally. He shot the cue-ball the length of the table a couple of times, then straightened. "How much did Buster charge you for it?"

"Two hundred and twenty-five dollars," she said, expecting him to scoff at what she'd paid.

"It's used," Emilio said.

"He told me."

Emilio shrugged. "Okay, let's see how you shoot with it. You break."

Sedonia didn't move. "Did he screw me?"

Emilio shook his head. "That stick's worth three, maybe four hundred dollars. Buster must like you."

Sedonia smiled as she walked down to the break end of the table.

Emilio said, "Wait a minute," then went over and rummaged through several house cues that were lined up against the wall. He returned with two, and handed one to Sedonia. "Don't use your stick to break."

Sedonia leaned her stick against the counter. It slid sideways and, before she could grab it, crashed into a stool and onto the tile floor.

Emilio picked it up and shook his head. "You put a ding in it. This stick ain't gonna last you a week."

One of the men nearby laughed.

Emilio and the two men were watching, and Sedonia felt flustered as she leaned over the table in her accustomed stance. *One, two, three . . .* An instant before she drove the stick forward, she remembered Emilio's admonition that her chin should touch the cue. The last-moment change of position threw off her stroke and she struck the cue-ball too low. It flew off the surface and slammed into the other pool table.

"*¡Cuidado, chica!*" Emilio said. "We playin' on this table, not that one."

One of the men picked up the ball off the floor and threw it back to Emilio; the other pulled out his handkerchief and waved it in mock surrender. All three were laughing at her.

"You gotta chalk your break cue too," Emilio told her. "Chalk up, and try again."

Sedonia stood immobile at the break end of the table, feeling blood rush to her face. What the hell was she doing here! With these . . . laughing hyenas.

Emilio walked up, handed her cue stick to her, and nudged her out of the way. "I'll break," he said, and then drove the cue-ball hard into the rack. Balls flew wildly about the table, but none fell into a pocket. He straightened up and said, "Your shot."

Sedonia felt tears of frustration forming. She turned to the side, so the men couldn't see her face, and began unscrewing her cue stick.

Emilio moved around in front of her, so she had no choice but look at him. "Table's open," he said. "Your shot."

Sedonia's embarrassment turned to anger. She screwed her stick back together and pushed past him. As she applied chalk to the tip of her cue, she felt the small ding from when it had fallen. Damn it!

She appraised the layout. The cue-ball was near the middle of the table; the solid colors looked like the easier suit. The orange 5-ball was first to feel her wrath. *One, two, three . . . stroke!* She slammed it into the near side pocket. The maroon 7-ball was next, followed by the green 6-ball. Then she missed a tough bank shot on the yellow 1-ball.

Emilio walked to the table. He gave her an appraising look, then began shooting his suit: the striped balls. At the icehouse the previous evening, Sedonia had seen him purposely miss—"on a stall" he'd called it—and then come off the stall and play his best game. Now, as he rapidly walked around the table, pocketing stripes, he clearly was not on a stall. He wound up with perfect position on the black 8-ball, and pocketed it for the win. "Rack," he said.

Sedonia laid her cue stick on the table and walked over to the bar. She handed the bartender a $20 bill and said, "I need $5 worth of quarters." He responded with a pained expression, as if making change were an imposition, then went over to the cash register. Sedonia turned back to the pool tables. Emilio was talking to the other two players. Probably about to piss them off, she thought, but at that moment they all turned toward her, laughing.

The bartender came back with her change and slapped it down on the bar. She returned to the pool table area, just in time to hear Emilio say, "Race-to-5 for $100?"

Both men declined, and one unscrewed his stick. "I gotta get goin'," he said. Before he left, he peeled off two twenties and a ten, and handed them to the other man. "My old lady's gonna be pissed."

As the one player headed for the door, Emilio asked the other, "How about it? Race-to-five for $100."

The man smiled and shook his head.

Emilio said, "I'll give you two games on the wire."

The man shook his head again.

"Three games on the wire," Emilio said.

The man seemed to consider the bet for a moment, then declined again, saying, "I've seen you play."

"Shit, man," Emilio said with contempt in his voice, "I thought you had gamble. My girlfriend here could beat me if I give her three games on the wire!"

Sedonia glared at Emilio. Where the hell was he getting this 'girl-friend' stuff!

"Guess you'd better play her, then," the man replied.

"No," Emilio said, "how about *you* play her? You got enough gamble for that? *No* games on the wire, race-to-5, $100."

"Wait a minute," Sedonia said. "I'm not playing for $100. I don't *have* $100."

Emilio waved off her comment. He pulled out his wallet, withdrew five twenties, and slapped them on the table. "How 'bout it, *maricón*?" he asked the man.

"Emilio!" Sedonia protested. '*Maricón*' was a Spanish pejorative, like calling someone a 'faggot'.

Apparently the man spoke no Spanish. Rather than take offense, he simply looked back and forth between Emilio and Sedonia for a moment, then said, "How about . . . $200?"

Emilio pulled out five more twenties. "She gets all the breaks."

The man looked at Sedonia and chuckled, apparently remembering the cue-ball flying off the table. "Okay," he said as he matched the pot. "Race-to-5, $200, and she gets the breaks." Emilio put the money on the light that hung low over the pool table, then walked back to where Sedonia was standing.

"Emilio—," she began.

"Gimme those quarters you got," he said.

"Emilio, I'm not ready to play for money."

He dug into his own pocket, pulled out three quarters, and threw them onto the table. Then he turned his back on her opponent and spoke softly, so only Sedonia could hear. "This guy's a car salesmen. I've seen him in here before. Thinks he's a shark, but he ain't shit."

"But—"

"Two hundred dollars is all I got. Don't lose." He handed her a house cue to use on the break. "Chalk it this time."

Sedonia's fingers shook as she applied the chalk; she hoped the men didn't notice. She took a deep breath, remembering having experienced similar anxiety before teeing off on the first hole of every major golf tournament in which she'd appeared. Nevertheless, she'd successfully played through her nervousness and had won numerous titles, including the U. S. Women's Amateur Championship. Surely she could compose herself and play well enough not to embarrass herself in a Chug's pool match! The thought reassured her. She positioned the cue-ball near the right side rail, and bent low to shoot. *One, two, three . . . stroke!* A sharp *crack!* and the balls scattered across the table. The yellow 1-ball hesitated in front of the far side pocket, then dropped. The match was on.

Sedonia exchanged the house cue stick for her own. As she bent low and lined up on the green 6-ball, she felt the ding rub against her thumb. She twisted the stick slightly, so the mar wasn't so noticeable. *One, two, three . . . stroke.* The ball stuttered in the corner pocket, but finally dropped. The cue-ball didn't stop as she'd intended. She'd struck it low enough that it should have stopped when it struck the 6-ball, but instead it had rolled forward. She lined up on the blue 2-ball and again put "stop" on the cue-ball, but again it rolled forward. Nevertheless, she managed to work her way around the table, making three more balls, before finally missing.

She pulled up a stool beside Emilio as her opponent prepared to shoot. "The cue-ball's acting strange. It doesn't stop the way it should."

"Bar-box cue-ball," Emilio said without taking his eyes off her opponent. "They're heavier."

"Heavier?"

He gave her a look, as if she were a backward child. "Bar-box cue-balls have metal in them. That way the table knows the difference between them and the other balls. When the cue-ball goes in a pocket, the machine gives it back to you. When an object ball goes in, it stays there."

Sedonia turned her attention back to the table. Her opponent missed badly, but left her with an impossible shot on the maroon 7-ball. In desperation, she shot hard. The 7-ball not only didn't come close to a pocket, it also knocked in one of her opponent's balls.

Sedonia again pulled up the stool beside Emilio and waited for her opponent to shoot.

"You should have played a 'safety' on that last shot," Emilio said, "like he did."

"A safety?"

"You don't know what a safety is?"

"I know what the word means, but I don't know what you think I should have done."

"You should have just barely hit the 7-ball, and stopped the cue-ball on the rail behind his 13-ball, so he didn't have a shot. Now you left him where he's probably gonna run out."

Sedonia frowned. She'd never purposely missed a shot in her life. Her opponent, as if to demonstrate Emilio's point, made the orange-striped 13-ball and then rapidly pocketed the other stripes. He called the black 8-ball in the far corner and made it. The score was 1 to 0, his favor.

Sedonia broke. Balls scattered, but none found a pocket. She walked over to the counter and sat down beside Emilio.

"You broke too hard," Emilio said under his breath, pique in his tone.

"What do you mean, I broke too hard?"

"Look what you did," he said. "The balls are all spread out for him. If you're gonna break that hard, you gotta make one."

Sedonia shook her head. Who the hell knew if they were going to make a ball on the break! As it turned out, the break was the only shot she got. Her opponent rapidly pocketed seven solid balls, then the 8-ball for the win. She was behind 2 to 0 in the race-to-5.

Sedonia tried to break more softly the next time, but miscued slightly. The blue 2-ball rolled into the far side pocket; however, all the other balls, except the maroon 7-ball, wound up within inches of where they'd been racked. She glanced over at Emilio.

He shook his head in disgust. "Looks like a One-Pocket break."

Asshole! she thought, then went to work on the table. She lined up on the 7-ball and touched her chin against the cue stick. *One, two, three . . . stroke!* The 7-ball flew into the corner, plus the force with which she'd struck the cue-ball scattered the other balls and left her with good position on the green 6-ball. She began methodically working her way around the table. Her new shooting stance still felt awkward, but the balls were falling, and Emilio had shut up. Finally, she was down to the black 8-ball—easy shot along the end rail. She lined up, touched her chin on the stick, and took a deep breath. *One, two, three . . . stroke.* The 8-ball stuttered in the corner, but finally dropped. She'd won her first competitive game.

She walked back to the counter and took a sip of her beer while her opponent racked the balls.

"You almost dogged the 8-ball," Emilio said.

Sedonia glared at him. "Don't you ever have anything positive to say?"

He gave her a dismissive shake of his head.

Sedonia broke a little harder the next time, and the blue-striped 10-ball rolled around the table, then finally dropped into the near corner pocket. She didn't have an easy next shot, and had to attempt a thin cut on the red-striped 11-ball. She missed it altogether, and the cue-ball hit her opponent's yellow 1-ball. He walked over and picked up the cue-ball.

"What are you doing?" she said.

"Ball-in-hand. You missed the 11-ball."

Sedonia looked over at Emilio, who came over to the table. "She hit the eleven!"

"No I didn't," Sedonia said. "I missed it. But what's he doing with the cue-ball?"

"Shit," Emilio muttered, and returned to his seat at the counter.

"You gotta hit your object ball, lady," her opponent said, "or I get the cue-ball in hand. I get to put it anywhere on the table I want." He placed it behind the orange 5-ball and began pocketing the solid colors.

Sedonia joined Emilio at the counter. "What other rules do I need to know?"

He shook his head. "Too late now, *chica*. You're gonna cost me $200."

Her opponent lined up on the black 8-ball, looked over at Sedonia and grinned. "Eight in the side," he said, then slammed it in, much harder than necessary. The score was now 3 to 1 in his favor.

Emilio turned to Sedonia with a look of disgust. "Next time, you gotta—"

"Shut up."

"Don't tell me—"

"*¡Callate!*" Sedonia snapped. She glared at him until he finally picked up his beer and took a swallow. Then he set the bottle down and gave her a single slow nod. "Shut up" in Spanish, he understood.

Sedonia returned to the table to break for the fifth game. She touched her chin on her stick, then thought, to hell with all of this! She straightened to her normal stance and drove the cue-ball into the pile as hard as she could. The rifle-shot crash of the initial impact coincided with a stab of pain in her right shoulder. The balls caromed about the table; the pain passed. Two stripes and a solid dropped into pockets. The two obnoxious men might as well have been in the parking lot. Her world was the dark-green rectangle. *One, two, three . . . stroke. One, two, three . . . stroke.* Finally she said, "Eight in the corner." The score was 3 to 2.

Another driving break and another stab of pain. Two solids rolled into pockets. *One, two, three . . . stroke. One, two, three . . . stroke.* And finally, "Eight in the side." She'd run two racks in a row without giving her opponent a shot. The match was now tied, 3 to 3.

Her opponent yanked off his already loosened tie before bending over the table to rack the balls.

A dull throb in Sedonia's shoulder warned her against another power break. She held back, but still managed to pocket the red 3-ball in the corner. She made two more balls, then missed a long cut shot. However, the cue-ball rolled down the table and hid behind her maroon 7-ball, leaving her opponent without a shot.

He muttered under his breath, but loud enough that Sedonia heard, "So now you're gonna play safeties, huh, bitch?"

"I didn't—," Sedonia began, but then stopped herself. Who the hell cared if he thought she'd missed on purpose?

He elevated the butt of his stick until it was almost perpendicular to the table. Sedonia wasn't sure what kind of shot he was attempting, but when he drove the stick down, he jumped the cue-ball off the table. "Fuck!" he exploded.

Now Sedonia had ball-in-hand. She placed it behind her toughest shot on the table, made it, and then ran the rest of the balls. Score: 4 to 3, her favor. She just needed one more game.

As her opponent racked, he looked disconsolate, and for a moment Sedonia felt sorry for him. An instant later, however, he looked up and snarled, "Break . . . sandbagger!"

A power break, and this time a *blinding* stab of pain. Two balls of each suit rolled into pockets. *One, two, three . . . stroke. One, two, three . . . stroke.* And finally, "Eight in the corner."

"*¡Chica!*" Emilio shouted as he rushed over, arms open, with a smile on his face.

Sedonia pushed past him, unscrewing her cue stick as she walked. She slammed the two pieces into her cue case, and a moment later banged out the front door.

Sedonia padded barefoot through her Nassau Bay condo, wearing one of the oversized T-shirts she usually used for nightgowns. She stopped in the kitchen and prepared a strong Dewar's and water over ice, then continued into the den, where she saw her red voicemail light blinking.

She picked up the receiver and pushed the "Messages" button. "Hello, Sedonia," a woman said. Sedonia immediately recognized the voice of her surgeon, and she felt a pang of apprehension. "This is Dr. Robinson. I just wanted to see how you're doing. Please call my office and make an appointment. It's time for a follow-up." The doctor hung up.

Sedonia took a deep breath. Everyone had accepted as accidental her overdose of hydrocodone. Everyone that is, except Dr. Robinson, who Sedonia had sensed was suspicious. Was the doctor genuinely concerned for her well being, or was she concerned about possible repercussions over having so casually prescribed such a large amount of the controversial painkiller?

Sedonia punched the "Delete" button. She was past that now.

The next message came up. "Hey, *chica,*" it began. "Why you ran off tonight?"

Sedonia shook her head. During a long shower, in which she'd let hot water soothe her aching shoulder, she'd decided her pool playing days were over. She couldn't believe she'd wasted $225 on that damned cue stick! Maybe Buster would buy it back, even with the ding she'd put in it. She reached for the "Delete" button, just as Emilio's voice said, "You got $100 comin'."

Sedonia hesitated. She was due half the bet?

"Come by Buster's tomorrow," Emilio continued. "I'll be there about 3:00."

Sedonia replayed the message before she deleted it. Then she glanced up at the clock above her desk: almost midnight. She opened the sliding glass door and walked out onto the balcony. A humid breeze rustled the metal wind chimes that hung from the ceiling. Below, the landscaped grounds and the small boat pier were encased in darkness. Across Egret Bay, the beacon from the South Shore Harbor lighthouse went on and off at three-second intervals.

She dropped into a patio chair and took a sip of her scotch and water. Too strong! She took another sip, hoping it would act like Drano and clear the bad taste left by the pool match. What a couple of jerks! But then a wry smile formed. Although she'd embarrassed herself, nevertheless, she'd won $100 in her first pool match.

The deep rumble of a jet boat drew her attention. In the darkness to the left she saw a set of red, green, and white running lights approaching. The waterfront bars and restaurants down the coast probably were beginning to empty. The lighthouse beacon flashed, illuminating a purple and white cigarette boat as it passed in front of her balcony. It threw a ten-foot rooster tail in its wake. Sedonia caught a glimpse of a couple seated at the rear. Fifteen feet of jet engine protruded in front of them. These powerful, impractical boats dominated the local waterways. Her sailboat friends called them "penis extenders."

The boat disappeared and Egret Bay grew quiet again. She'd lost contact with her boating friends when she'd begun dating a musician and had gravitated toward his circle of acquaintances. Now he was history, and they were history. And her golf friends were history . . . and her father was history. She took another sip.

She forced herself to recap the pool match, as she'd always done after a golf match. Her father had taught her: identify one mistake you're going to correct before playing the next time. Jumping the ball off the table on the break? She'd corrected that during the match. Her new stance? It still seemed awkward, but she supposed she'd get used to it. On the other hand, when she'd reverted to her old stance, she'd run off the final four games and won the match. Nervousness? Yeah, she'd been nervous at the beginning of the match, but she'd dealt with that. Playing 'safeties'? She couldn't imagine she'd ever purposely try to miss a shot.

What else? She frowned. Really, there wasn't anything else, at least nothing connected with the game itself. All right, so she'd embarrassed herself. She'd simply been competing in an unfamiliar world. It was a world in which a male fraternity had evolved the rules. It couldn't be that complicated!

She took another sip. All in all, she hadn't done too badly . . . except for the ding she'd put in her cue stick. She had some extra fine sandpaper in a kitchen drawer. Tomorrow, she'd need to sand out the ding before she met Emilio. No, on second thought, she'd take care of that right now.

Chapter 3

No more late-night scotches, Sedonia vowed as she jogged through a Nassau Bay residential neighborhood in predawn haze. The sun hadn't yet risen above the horizon, but both temperature and humidity already approached 90. On her left, a row of houses blocked what little morning breeze stirred off the bay. Perspiration soaked her tank top and shorts. She wiped her eyes with the back of her hand and regretted not having worn a headband.

At the next intersection, private homes gave way to two- and three-story office buildings, occupied by companies associated with the Johnson Space Center. She passed Lockheed's modern blue and gray structure on her right, and saw her reflection in the first-floor windows. She looked like she felt, as if she were running in molten asphalt.

The sound of a car coming up behind her drew her attention. She moved closer to the curb, but the car hung back. Probably enjoying the view, she thought with annoyance. She glanced over her shoulder and saw a balding young man behind the wheel of a red Corvette. The car finally accelerated past, the driver pointedly ignoring her. He turned left into the green and beige Boeing complex and disappeared behind the building. Sedonia shook her head. Men!

Her thoughts switched to pool. Some of her scotch-enhanced confidence of the preceding night had worn off. She liked the game, and possibly was good at it, but she was uncomfortable with the tension her presence generated. Male interest wasn't new; she'd dealt with it since high school. But in the past it had been at a manageable level. In the pool environment, men seemed more threatening. Would they ever accept her as just another player?

She jogged through a hospital complex, then stumbled slightly as she rounded a corner and entered another residential neighborhood. The sun's rays now flashed through the tree branches. Her breathing grew labored, and fatigue pushed pool ruminations from her mind. Ahead lay the neighborhood park that indicated she was one-quarter of the way into her usual four-mile jog. She shook her head and made a U-turn. Two miles would have to do for today. No more late-night scotches!

Buster had a tray of balls waiting on the counter when Sedonia walked into the poolroom. "Saw you pull up," he said. "Want something to drink?"

She picked up the tray. "No thanks. Can I take any table?"

He nodded.

The front door opened, and a Budweiser man wheeled in four cases of beer. Buster turned his attention to the delivery, and Sedonia selected a nine-foot table near the front window. The only other person in the room was the disheveled, elderly janitor wielding a push broom. Sedonia checked her watch as she screwed her stick together. Two o'clock; she'd have an hour to practice on her own before Emilio arrived.

The nine-foot regulation table looked enormous after having played the night before on Chug's six-foot bar-box. She decided to take the opportunity to practice long shots. Bending low, she touched her chin on the cue stick and sent the blue 2-ball down to the other end of the table, missing the corner pocket badly. Her next three shots also were off target, and she shook her head in frustration.

"You're bending over too much," Buster said.

Sedonia jumped. She'd been concentrating and hadn't noticed him pull up a stool nearby. "It feels awkward to me too," she replied, "but Emilio told me my chin should touch the cue stick."

"Lemme see your regular stance."

Sedonia assumed her former stance. Now it too felt awkward.

Buster said, "Spread the balls out on the table and hit some."

As Sedonia pulled the balls from the pockets, the janitor shuffled over. He assumed a vantage point nearby and leaned against his broom. Sedonia frowned, and he responded with a shy, nearly toothless grin.

"Monk," Buster said, "take out the trash, and then go sweep off the sidewalk."

The janitor shuffled away, and Sedonia prepared to shoot. She felt uncomfortable with Buster watching so closely. She missed two of her first five shots, none of which were particularly difficult.

Buster stood up. "Gimme your stick."

Sedonia handed it to him, expecting him to show off his own shooting skill, but instead he said, "There are three things you need to do. The first is, hold your stick right. Don't grip the end." He demonstrated where she'd been holding it, then moved his hand forward. "The middle of the wrap is a good place to start. Grip it there, then slide your hand a couple of inches either way, until it feels comfortable."

Sedonia frowned. That was one of the first things her father had taught her. She must have changed her grip when she started leaning over more.

Buster returned the stick to her. "Show me your regular stance again."

She did so, this time holding the butt of the stick correctly.

"The second thing you need to do," Buster said, "is to get comfortable. Emilio's right; your head's too high, but he's got you overcorrecting. Try to find something comfortable in between."

"Like this?"

He nodded, then walked around behind her. She started to straighten up. "Stay down," he said.

She felt uneasy, leaning over the table, with him standing right behind her. An instant later she felt his hand grab the back of her right knee. She immediately straightened up and demanded, "What are you doing?"

"Your back leg's too straight. Bend that back knee slightly, but don't crouch. Try it."

Sedonia hesitated a moment, then leaned over, and again felt his hand on the back of her knee.

"Right about . . . there," he said.

Sedonia flashed a look of annoyance over her shoulder. "Okay. I've got it."

Buster smiled as he straightened up. He returned to his stool and said, "Hit some more balls."

Sedonia hesitated. Was this guy teaching her, or just playing with her? Golf pros had occasionally positioned her with their hands, but that had been on a country club driving range, not a dimly-lit pool hall. She took a deep breath, then walked around the table and selected a long shot on the yellow-striped 9-ball. She placed her hand on the middle of the wrap and slid it back about four inches. Then she assumed her new stance, slightly bending her back knee. *One, two, three . . . stroke.*

Her awareness of Buster's scrutiny disappeared as soon as the 9-ball rolled dead center into the corner pocket. She quickly lined up another long shot and went through her new ritual: *grip . . . stance . . . one, two, three . . . stroke.* The orange 5-ball disappeared at the other end of the table. She ran the rest of that rack, and then spread the balls back on the table and made all fifteen without missing. Smiling, she looked over at Buster. "What's number three?"

"Number three?"

"You said there were three things I needed to do. Grip, stance, and what else?"

"Don't pay too much attention to what other people tell you."

Sedonia smiled. "You mean rule three is: Don't follow the rules?"

Buster remained serious. "Sometimes I hold classes here. I call it 'pool school,' and I charge $50 an hour. Most of the people I teach are women, who take the class so they can play pool with their boyfriends. Their problem is, they try to do *exactly* what I tell them."

Sedonia frowned. She'd overheard male golf pros, and tennis pros too, make the same observation, as if in their minds, women's conscientious application of technique somehow was a fault.

Buster continued, "A player with *average* natural ability and *good* technique can usually beat a player with *good* natural ability and *poor* technique. However, if you watch the top pool players, you'll see they've got the basics down, but they've always got some variation that works better for them."

Sedonia was still frowning. Where was he going with this?

Buster smiled. "Some of the best players in this part of the country come in here to gamble. Road players call me and have me match 'em up with locals. I can measure a player's speed as good as anybody, better than most."

"Speed?"

"It means how good somebody plays in competition." He studied her for a moment, then added, "You've got a lot of natural ability."

His words triggered the recollection of the *Houston Chronicle* reporter's description of her golf game: "world class." She took a deep breath, lined up on the maroon 7-ball, and sent it down the table into the far corner pocket, dead center. Then she straightened up and said, "So you think I've got good 'speed'?"

Buster shook his head. "I don't know. I said you have natural ability. I can't measure your speed until I see you play for money."

Sedonia nodded. "Emilio's meeting me here in an hour. What's his speed?"

"He's above average, but he's afraid to match up with the really strong players that come through here. He mainly just works the neighborhood lounges. I gotta give ol' E-mil-io credit, though. He's got gamble."

Sedonia said, "I'd like to sign up for your next 'pool school'."

Before Buster could reply, a man's voice rang out from the counter, "Hey! This would be a helluva good place to open up a bar!" Another customer had arrived unnoticed.

Buster rose from his stool. "I could take your $50," he told Sedonia with a smile, "but to be honest with you, I think I've probably just taught you all you can learn from me."

"So I just need to practice?"

"Practice like you're doin' is okay, but to really improve your game, you need actual competition. And, you'd need to play a lot. If you did, you could be good. Damn good."

* * *

Emilio arrived at Buster's 45 minutes late. He acknowledged Sedonia with a curt nod and then, without apology or explanation, screwed his cue stick together.

"Don't you owe me something?" Sedonia said.

Emilio frowned for a moment, as if her share of last night's winnings had slipped his mind. Finally he opened his wallet and handed Sedonia $80. "That's all I've got."

Sedonia kept her hand extended.

He gave a resigned shake of his head, and forked over the missing $20. Then he said, "Can you jump the cue-ball off the table any time you want to?"

"That was an accident."

"I thought so. It worked good, though. That's the reason that guy gave you the breaks."

Sedonia shook her head. Emilio was a con man.

"So," he said, "you want to play more pool like we did last night?"

She hesitated. Emilio wasn't a person she wanted to be associated with, but Buster's comment was still foremost in her mind. If she played a lot, she could be good. Damned good. Still undecided, she said, "Where would we be playing tonight?"

"Can't play tonight. My daughter is havin' her *quienceañera*."

Sedonia was surprised. A *quinceañera* was a celebration of a Latina's fifteenth birthday, and Emilio looked too young to have a teenage daughter. The knowledge that he apparently had a family, in addition to his Uncle Raul, put Sedonia a bit more at ease in his company.

Emilio walked over to the table and began racking the balls. "You shoot good," he said. "We could make some money."

"Like last night? Hustling pool?"

He finished racking the balls, then walked back to Sedonia. "Hustlers are in the movies. I'm just a gambler."

"You make people think you can't play, then you beat them out of their money. That's hustling in my book."

"I don't read books," he said. "But since you do, tell me how this is different than playing cards. When you play poker and you draw three aces, do you tell the other players, 'Oh, look, I have three aces!' No, you bluff. You make them think you have nothing, until the bet is down."

Sedonia smiled at his rationalization. Maybe he had something there.

"Well?" he said. "Do you want to play again, or not?"

Sedonia hesitated. Buster had emphasized that competition was at least as important as practice, if not more so. Finally she said, "Yeah, I'd like to play again."

"Tomorrow night, then. Nine o'clock, at Juan's Beer Garden on Highway 3."

Sedonia nodded. She'd never been inside, but the painters who worked for her occasionally mentioned it.

"But tomorrow," Emilio said, "leave your stick in your car. And if we play against each other, you must let me win. Too many people at Juan's know me, and they won't gamble with me. If they see you beat me, they won't gamble with you either."

Sedonia studied him. That explained why he'd played so hard against her at Chug's the night before. "So I'd have to lose to you on purpose?"

Emilio nodded. "And we'll split the money, fifty-fifty, like last night."

Sedonia mulled over his offer. She must be playing well, since he wasn't confident he could beat her on his own.

"What do you say?" he pressed.

"I don't know if I can throw games," she said.

He responded with a shake of his head and a look of disdain.

"But," she said, "I'll meet you at Juan's tomorrow night, and we'll see how it goes."

He responded with a grudging nod. "Okay, 'we'll see how it goes'."

"One more thing," she said. "When we practice, like right now, I don't want you going on a stall. I want your best game. Okay?"

Emilio didn't respond to her question. Instead he said, "Let's play. Race-to-9. I'll break."

"Uh-uh," she said. "I'm not going to let you break your own rack."

Emilio responded with a look of mock indignation.

Sedonia said, "And I wouldn't trust you to deal yourself a poker hand, either."

Emilio relinquished the break end of the table and said with a chuckle, "You learnin', *chica*. You learnin'."

As Sedonia turned off Waterfront Street and pulled into her company parking lot, Raul was securing the padlock on the warehouse door. Sedonia checked her watch: 6:10. Her paint crew must already have returned from the jobsite.

"How'd it go?" she said as she climbed out of her Miata.

"No problems," Raul said. "We just got back a few minutes ago. Everybody else has gone home."

Sedonia felt a pang of guilt as she preceded him into the office. She should have been back an hour ago, but instead she'd remained at Buster's for a second race-to-9 with Emilio. Good old Raul, though. He always took care of things in her absence, without recrimination.

He'd left a neat pile of unpaid invoices on her desk, and beside them lay two incoming checks. Sedonia switched on her computer and brought up the company accounting system, while Raul busied himself cleaning up the coffee bar. Sedonia heaved a sigh of relief when she discovered one of the checks on her desk was early payment for a recently completed job: $12,300. The other was a $47.93 rebate for returned, unused primer paint. When her father had run the company, they'd simply inventoried unused supplies. Nowadays, they had to operate on a much tighter margin.

She entered the checks into the accounts receivable, then leafed through the pile of invoices and selected six lucky creditors she could afford to pay, while leaving a balance large enough to meet her payroll at week's end. Next week, they'd start work on Brad Landry's project, which should carry them financially through the month. She leaned back in her chair, thinking how handsome Brad had looked when he'd stopped by the office. Then with an impatient shake of her head, she leaned forward again and updated the accounts payable.

After she'd printed and signed the six checks, and paper-clipped them to their respective invoices, she told Raul, "These can go out tomorrow."

He started over to the supply cabinet to get some envelopes. "I'll mail them on my way home."

"Tomorrow," Sedonia snapped.

He responded with a quizzical look.

"I'm sorry, Raul," Sedonia said. "I'm just . . . tired. Tired of living from payday to payday." She didn't mention that she also felt guilty. Guilty of absenting herself from the business, while Raul was putting in 12-hour days. "Please," she said, "go on home. Leave these for tomorrow."

He responded with an uncertain nod. "I'll see you in the morning."

Moments later she heard his old van crunch across the oyster-shell parking lot and head down the street. She walked over to the front window. The two Vietnamese-owned seafood markets were busy. Past the old trawler and across the channel, she saw Kemah's restaurant row coming to life for the evening. She considered driving across the bridge for dinner.

She reached back and massaged the right side of her neck and shoulder muscles. How many games had she and Emilio played? She'd lost the first set, 9 to 7, then the second 9 to 5. Thirty games. She'd been ahead 4 to 0 in the second set, then her shoulder had begun to hurt. Although she hadn't told him of her discomfort, he'd instinctively reacted to it, like a shark to blood. She smiled at the unintended "shark" pun. Discomfort notwithstanding, though, she'd enjoyed the competition that afternoon. Next time, she vowed, I'll beat him.

She turned and looked back at her desk. There were quarterly tax reports that needed to be done; however, she decided she'd follow the advice she'd given Raul and leave it for tomorrow.

As she closed and locked the office door, she decided against driving across the bridge; selecting a place to eat was too much trouble. Maybe instead she'd just grab a hamburger at the Bullfrog Club on Clear Lake. She hadn't been there in months. Perhaps some of her former sail-boating friends had stopped off after work. However, as she settled in to her car seat, a wave of fatigue swept over her. She decided all she wanted was a long hot shower, a heated can of soup, and a good night's sleep.

At 8:45 the next night, Sedonia turned off Highway 3 and pulled into a small parking area. Although Juan's Beer Garden overlooked the railroad tracks, it didn't have quite the blue-collar feel of Wayne's Icehouse on refinery row. The vehicles parked in front were a mix of pickups and cars, some old and some new. There was no sign of Emilio's Silverado. Sedonia withdrew a twenty-dollar bill and her driver's license, then slid her purse under the car seat.

Leaving her custom cue stick locked in the trunk, as Emilio had instructed her, she crossed the parking lot. The garage-type doors at the front of the beer garden were open. As she entered she was hit by a blast of humid night air being circulated by one of three large floor fans. A half-dozen men were playing pool on three bar-boxes that stood off to the right. An older man, waiting to shoot on the middle table, gave Sedonia a friendly nod as she headed over to the U-shaped bar. Open doors at the rear of the beer garden led to a grassy patio. A weathered picnic table stood under a large oak tree.

The far side of the bar was unoccupied, and Sedonia walked around and pulled up a wooden barstool. A sign on the wall read: "NO FIGHTING. WEBSTER POLICE STATION IS ONE BLOCK AWAY." Reassuring, Sedonia thought with a wry smile.

A young, attractive barmaid was leaning across a beer cooler and talking to an older couple. The topic was the weather. Four men with loosened ties sat at a nearby table. Sedonia picked up a fragment of their conversation, something about "the God-damned tracking system." She surmised by their topic, intensity, and slurred speech that they must be Johnson Space Center employees, who probably had been drinking beer since they'd gotten off work.

Sedonia glanced over at two Latinos seated on the opposite side of the bar. One smiled and said, "*Hola, Sedonia.*"

"*Hola . . .*" she replied, struggling to remember the man's name. "I haven't seen you in a while."

"I have been . . . home," he said.

Sedonia thought she remembered her father having told her that "home" for the man was a little town somewhere in Central Mexico.

"I just come back yesterday," he said. "Raul tell me about your father. I am sorry to hear it."

"Thank you."

"Uh . . . do you have work for me?"

"Not right now . . . Paco." His name finally had come to her. Her father had been forced to lay him off in January, when business had declined. "But be sure Raul knows where to reach you, in case something comes up later."

"*Bueno, gracias,*" he said, but disappointment showed on his face. The men picked up their change off the bar. Paco gave Sedonia a wave, then he and his friend left the beer garden and headed down Highway 3, on foot.

"What can I get for you?" the barmaid said.

"Coors Light, please," Sedonia said, then moved over one stool to catch more of the breeze blowing from the nearest fan. She'd had the foresight to wear a sleeveless blouse; however, because of the unwanted attention she'd been receiving lately, she'd decided on jeans rather than shorts.

"A dollar fifty," the barmaid said.

Sedonia was surprised at the price; area bars usually charged twice that amount. She pulled the $20 bill from her jeans pocket. "Let me have three dollars worth of quarters with my change, please."

The barmaid smiled. "Doin' your laundry tonight?"

"No, for the pool tables."

"You're a pool player?"

Sedonia nodded.

"We don't get many women players in here," the barmaid said as she opened the cash register. She gave Sedonia her change, then nodded toward the pool tables. "Do you know those guys over there?"

"No."

"They're all pretty good, particularly the guy playin' on the middle table. The one in the blue shirt."

"Thanks for the warning."

Sedonia saw Emilio's pickup pull into the parking lot. Moments later, he entered the beer garden, but gave her a quick shake of his head and took a seat on the other side of the U-shaped bar. After he received his beer, he gave a head gesture toward the pool tables, apparently indicating that Sedonia should join one of the games. Instead, Sedonia picked up her beer, walked around the bar, and pulled up a stool beside him.

Emilio gave her a look of annoyance. "I didn't want those guys to know we're together."

"So I gathered. And you want me to play them. But I don't know how to get into the game."

"Just put your quarters up." He glanced over at the players, then turned back. "Play on the middle table. I've seen the young guy in here before. He's got some gamble, but he won't play me."

The man pointed out by both the barmaid and Emilio was overweight and appeared to be in his twenties. He was dressed as if he'd just come off a municipal golf course: blue T-shirt, khaki shorts, white sweat socks, and dust-covered loafers. Of the half-dozen men playing on the three tables, he was the only one with a custom cue stick.

"Do I just walk up and ask to play?" Sedonia said.

"Yes," Emilio said, exasperation in his voice.

Sedonia waited until the middle table was between games, then approached. "Uh . . . do you mind if I challenge?"

The older man replied with a friendly smile, "Certainly not."

But the younger man responded in a dismissive tone, "We're playin' for a beer."

"That's okay," Sedonia said. "I'd like to play." She started to turn away.

"Put your quarters on the table," the younger man said impatiently, "so we know you're next."

A strip of dirty adhesive tape near the coin slot had the numbers "1" through "9" handwritten on it. Sedonia put her three quarters on the "1."

The men returned to their next game, and Sedonia walked back over to the bar.

Emilio asked her, "Did he say they were playing for a beer?"

"Yes."

"Shit. He usually plays for money. He must be hustlin' that old man."

After they'd watched the game drag on for a while, Emilio said, "Yeah, he's hustlin'. He's on a stall."

The older man finally pocketed the 8-ball. He turned to Sedonia with a triumphant smile. "You're next, dear."

Before leaving the table, the younger man put three quarters on the "2". Then as he approached the bar, he gave Sedonia an annoyed look, and asked Emilio, "Friend of yours?"

"Just met her," Emilio said.

The man responded with a look of skepticism, and then turned and headed toward the men's room.

Emilio said in a low voice to Sedonia, "You gotta go on a stall against the old guy too. But you gotta win the table."

She turned to him with a frown. "What?"

"I ain't got time to explain it to you. Win the game. Just don't make more than three balls in a row."

Sedonia took a deep breath as she got up from her barstool.

"Would you like me to rack, dear?" her elderly opponent said as she approached.

"No, that's okay," Sedonia said. Damn, he was a nice old guy, too.

Sedonia racked the balls, then selected a house cue from several that were leaning against the wall. She was rolling it on the table to be sure it wasn't warped, when the other man came out of the men's room and took a seat at the bar near Emilio.

"Looks like we got a real pro here," he said, sarcasm in his tone.

The old man broke and failed to make a ball. Sedonia directed her attention to the table. After having spent the past two afternoons practicing on Buster's 9-foot tables, playing on this 6-foot bar-box would be easy. Emilio had told her not to make more than three balls in a row, but she didn't see how anyone could even purposely miss on a table this size.

She chalked her cue stick, lined up on the green-striped 14-ball, and sent it down the side rail. It disappeared into the corner pocket, but she'd forgotten to correct for bar-box cue-balls being heavier and harder to stop. The cue-ball rolled farther down the table than she'd anticipated, and it lodged between the rail and the blue 2-ball, leaving her an impossible next shot.

"Bad luck," her opponent said.

Sedonia drove the cue-ball into the rail in an attempt to kick her red-striped 11-ball, but instead hit her opponent's yellow 1-ball.

"I'm afraid I get ball-in-hand," he said.

Sedonia nodded, then glanced over at Emilio, who gave a barely perceptible nod of approval. He evidently thought she'd misplayed those two shots on purpose.

Her opponent made two balls and then missed. Sedonia ran three balls, then studied the purple-striped 12-ball. She could cut it into the side, but if she did, the cue-ball would roll into the corner pocket. She took a deep breath. *Decision time.* She leaned over the table and shot harder than necessary. The 12-ball rolled into the side pocket and the cue-ball scratched in the corner.

Her opponent gave a sympathetic shake of his head as he retrieved the cue-ball from the return slot. Then he put the ball in the middle of the table, lined up an easy shot on the red 3-ball . . . and missed.

Sedonia returned to the table. She had four balls left, including the 8-ball. *The hell with it.* She quickly pocketed her last three stripes, then called the 8-ball in the corner, and made it.

"Well done!" the old man said. "Are you ready for that beer?"

"Uh . . . not right now," she said, "Thanks." She felt guilty about taking advantage of the polite gentleman, even for a $1.50 beer.

The younger man returned to the table and studied her as he deposited his quarters. Sedonia walked over to the bar and took a sip of her beer. In an aside to Emilio she said, "How much should I play for?"

"Whatever he says. But race-to-5 for $50 is what we want."

Her opponent finished racking the balls, then said, "We playin' for the same beer?"

Emilio said under his breath, "Okay. But go on a stall."

Sedonia told the man, "A beer's fine."

A trace of a smile formed on his face. "How about $5 a game?"

"How about . . . race-to-5 . . . for $50?" Sedonia countered, then wondered where *that* burst of bravado had come from.

The man turned to Emilio. "I figured all the time she was with you."

Emilio shrugged, then stood up and pulled some change out of his pocket. "You don't have enough gamble to play her? Okay, *I'll* play her."

"Bullshit! I got next game."

Emilio approached the table, and the two men faced each other. Sedonia was concerned they were about to fight, and she backed away. The man glared at Emilio for a moment, then walked over and asked the barmaid, "Can I put $50 on my credit card?"

The barmaid glanced at Sedonia and smiled. Apparently she'd been watching the events unfold. She took the man's credit card, and a few moments later returned with his cash.

"Fifty is all we're gonna get out of him," Emilio whispered to Sedonia. "So shoot your best shot. But if you get up by three games, give him one or two."

Sedonia frowned.

"We don't want to scare off the others," Emilio finished quickly, because the man was walking back, cash in hand. The players on the other two tables interrupted their game to watch.

Emilio dropped the pretense that he and Sedonia weren't together. He pulled $50 out of his wallet, and both men put the stakes on the light that hung low over the table.

"Call it!" the man barked.

"Heads," Sedonia said.

The man gave a disgusted shake of his head. "Your break."

Sedonia broke hard and balls flew about the table. No pain from her shoulder. Two striped balls found pockets and the rest were out in the open. Five quick shots, then she said, "Eight in the corner." She'd run the first rack without giving her opponent a shot.

On the surface, her opponent appeared unfazed as he racked the balls for the second game; however, Sedonia sensed he was seething. She broke hard again, but this time received a warning twinge from her shoulder. She made a stripe and a solid, and now had her choice of suits. The table looked so small. She couldn't see how she could possibly miss. She didn't.

Her opponent slammed the balls on the table as he racked for the third game, still without having had the opportunity to shoot. As he lifted the rack, the head ball moved forward slightly. Sedonia decided not to risk making him even angrier by asking for a re-rack. She heeded the previous warning twinge, and this time didn't drive the cue-ball quite so hard. The loose rack and her easy stroke produced a poor break. Only three balls struck a rail, and the rest stayed bunched in the middle of the table.

Her opponent strode forward. He chalked his custom cue, then tapped the tip against the side of the table. He had one clear shot: a slight angle on the blue 2-ball. He slammed it into the side pocket and sent the cue-ball careening about the table. Luckily for him, when it stopped he had good position on the maroon 7-ball. From his intense manner as he re-chalked his cue, Sedonia sensed he was about to shoot hard again and try to break out the other balls. Instinctively, she almost offered a warning. He drove the cue-ball into the 7-ball, missing the shot. The other balls scattered about the table, all except the black 8-ball, which rolled slowly into the corner pocket. It was an automatic loss.

"God damn it!" the man shouted. He glared at Sedonia, then grabbed his custom cue at either end and brought it down hard across his raised thigh, shattering both halves at the metal joint.

"That's enough, Travis!" the barmaid yelled.

"Fuck you!"

The barmaid reached over to a phone mounted on a nearby pole and took down the receiver. "I've told you before about this!"

The man now fixed his glare on her.

"Get out of here right now," she said, "or I'm callin' the cops."

He hesitated, then reached up and grabbed his money off the pool table light. Emilio jumped off his barstool and started toward him.

"You!" the barmaid shouted at Emilio. "Stay out of this!"

Emilio stopped. The man snatched up his empty cue case, then bolted through the front door. Moments later his car broke traction as he roared out of the parking lot and onto Highway 3.

Sedonia turned to the barmaid. "I'm sorry about this."

"It's not your fault. Travis is a hothead. I'd appreciate it, though, if you'd keep your boyfriend away from him in the future."

"He's *not* my boyfriend," Sedonia said through clenched teeth.

Emilio walked over and retrieved his money off the light. "Okay," he said to the men at the nearby table. "Who's got next game?"

Sedonia shook her head. Emilio's constant aggressiveness irked her, and the other guy's testosterone display had been ridiculous. It was just a damned game! She walked over and laid the house cue on the pool table, and then headed toward the open doorway.

"Hey!" Emilio called out. "Where you goin'?"

Sedonia just gave an impatient wave over her shoulder, and didn't look back.

Chapter 4

Sedonia turned left off the NASA Parkway and headed down the long, narrow parking lot that led to the Bullfrog Club, a floating tavern on Clear Lake. Although it was 4:15 in the afternoon, a dozen or so cars already occupied the prime parking spots along the bulkhead. Many Bay Area residents, particularly the boating community, started their weekends early on Friday afternoon.

Sedonia recognized her friend's yellow Volkswagen Beetle and pulled in beside it. Christy had sounded surprised when Sedonia had telephoned that afternoon. Sedonia had distanced herself from her circle of friends after her father's death and her shoulder surgery, and then had disassociated herself from them altogether after her hydrocodone overdose. Her former friends were painful reminders of her previous life, the life she'd taken for granted. However, sitting in her office earlier this afternoon, she'd felt a need for companionship, particularly for the company of another woman.

She climbed out of her car and started across the parking lot. The Bullfrog Club rose two stories from the deck of a rusty steel barge. The upstairs bar wasn't open yet, but through the downstairs windows she could make out silhouettes of customers. As she strolled along the narrow pier, she looked down at three jet boats already moored for the night's revelry. The names were familiar: *Seaducer, Invader, Purple Passion.* How long had it been since she was last here? Only three or four months? It seemed much longer.

Apparently the tide was out in nearby Galveston Bay; Clear Lake was unusually low. Sedonia had to hang onto the side rail of the steep metal gangplank as she made her way down to the entrance. An approaching powerboat caused the tavern to rock as she stepped through the doorway.

"Sedonia!" cried a woman's voice.

Sedonia spotted her friend, seated among three men at the far end of the bar. Christy had cut and bleached her hair since Sedonia had seen her last, and though it was still early summer, she already had a deep tan. Everyone turned as Sedonia approached.

"Hi," she said, forcing a smile. She'd hoped to have the opportunity for a quiet chat. Instead, this group looked as if they'd been drinking for a while, priming for a rowdy weekend.

One of the men said, "Where you been keepin' yourself, sweetheart?"

Sedonia remembered his name was Dave something or the other. Fifties, balding, and overweight, he was the owner of *Purple Passion* docked outside. On weekends, his "crew" usually consisted of women barely out of their teens. If anyone needed a "penis extender," he did.

"Hello, Dave," Sedonia replied, this time unable to force a smile.

The day shift barmaid was new since Sedonia had last been here. Young, brunette, and clad in cutoff jeans and a bikini top, she looked as if she'd arrived on one of the jet boats. "Are you a bullfrog?" she asked.

Sedonia suppressed an internal groan and answered with the obligatory "You bet your sweet ass I am." The reply identified her as a longstanding customer and entitled her to a fifty-cent discount on her beer.

Dave leaned back on his barstool and theatrically eyed the barmaid's backside. The other men laughed, and even Christy smiled.

Sedonia told the barmaid, "I'll have a Coors Light."

Dave got to his feet and started toward the men's room. The other two men turned their attention to the soundless telecast of an Astros baseball game that flickered on an overhead TV set.

The barmaid returned with Sedonia's beer. Sedonia gave her three one-dollar bills, which paid for the beer, and her "bet your sweet ass" reply provided a fifty-cent tip. She'd been here only a few minutes, but already felt the need to get away. However, she'd invited Christy to meet her, so she couldn't just leave. Another approaching boat caused the tavern to rock again. Sedonia felt a headache coming on. "Let's go upstairs," she told Christy.

"Upstairs? The bar's not open yet."

"I know. C'mon, I need some air."

Christy told one of the men where they'd be. He responded with a disinterested grunt.

The upper deck was unoccupied, and the two women took a table shaded by an overhanging roof. Although the afternoon temperature and humidity were still in the 90s, a breeze blowing off the lake made it bearable. Sedonia looked to her left. The fifty-foot-high bridge that spanned the channel between Seabrook and Kemah was already jammed with cars—commuters retuning home from Houston and weekenders heading for the Gulf Coast.

"Did you want to talk about something?" Christy said.

Sedonia sensed her friend was anxious to get back to the guys in the bar. "I just haven't seen you in a while," she said. "What have you been up to?"

Christy brightened and launched into a confidential monologue about having broken up with someone named Al. Sedonia didn't remember ever meeting this Al, but tried to appear interested and nod at the right places.

Finally Christy said, "Do you think I did right?"

Sedonia hadn't been paying attention, but ventured, "I'm sure you did."

"What about you?"

"Me?" Sedonia said. *God, what had they been talking about?*

"Yeah. Are you . . . doing all right?"

Sedonia didn't know if Christy was asking about her love life, her shoulder, or her overdose on pain medication. She chose the safest of the three. "My shoulder's doing much better."

"Oh," Christy said. "Can you play golf again?"

"No . . ."

Christy frowned. "But you said . . ."

"It's better, but . . . I won't ever be able to play golf again."

Christy looked perplexed.

Sedonia felt annoyed with herself that she'd gotten into this conversation. How could she get out of it? Christy was still waiting, so Sedonia rallied with the first thing that came to mind. "I'm playing pool now."

"Pool? I didn't know you played pool. I used to play in college."

Dave and his two friends clumped up the stairs.

Sedonia barely concealed a wince.

"C'mon, girls," Dave said. "We're goin' over to the Blue Mackerel. The Baymen are back in town, and they're playin' there tonight. We gotta get there early to get a good seat."

Christy was already on her feet and looked down at Sedonia with a half smile. "Did you know they were back?"

Sedonia shook her head. The last she'd heard, her former boyfriend's band was in Austin.

Christy said, "Do you and Frankie still keep in touch?"

Sedonia stood up. "No, we don't." Then she told Dave, "Y'all go ahead. Maybe I'll stop by later."

"Okay," he said. "We'll save a place for you."

Sedonia nodded, then followed them down the stairs. She had no intention of seeing them later. She wished she'd never have to see them again. Nor Frankie.

Later at home, the sun disappeared below the horizon and the evening breeze rustled the metal wind chimes that hung from the balcony ceiling. Restless, Sedonia got up from her chair and walked over to the railing. The lighthouse on the other side of Egret Bay began its nightly vigil, flashing on and off at three-second intervals. Two jet skis raced past her balcony, temporarily interrupting the quiet. Then there was only the sound of the bay lapping against the wooden pier.

Sedonia sighed. Friday night, and nothing to do. The Bullfrog had been a disaster. Any of the other singles bars probably would be the same. And the Blue Mackerel was out of the question.

She turned back toward the living room. TV? No, she'd anesthetized herself with too much TV the past few months. Besides, she was too restive. Pool kept coming to mind. This past week it had brought her out of her despondency, at least temporarily. She wished there was somewhere she could play right now. Without an escort, however, the places Emilio had taken her were too threatening. And she wasn't about to call and ask him to meet her some place. What a jerk!

She sighed again, then her expression brightened. Buster's!

Sedonia stepped through the doorway of Buster's Billiards, her cue case slung over one shoulder. She hesitated, feeling as if she'd come to the wrong place. She'd expected the usual afternoon quiet, but instead, music blared from the jukebox and the poolroom overflowed with patrons. The two-dozen tables were all occupied, and the bar was standing room only. She was about to turn and leave, when a door at the rear of the room flew open and Buster charged through.

He hurried behind the bar, and an attractive blond barmaid handed him the telephone. He said something, nodded twice, and then hung up. As he leaned over a beer cooler, he glanced toward the front door. "Se-don-ia!" he said with a smile.

She walked over to the waitress station. "You're busy tonight."

"Every night. If you want a table, I'll have to put you on the list. Probably be an hour or so."

"Uh . . . no thanks." She'd come here intending to practice, but now felt uneasy in the midst of all the intense activity.

Buster pulled three bottles of beer from the cooler, including a Coors Light that he set in front of Sedonia. He told the barmaid, "These are on me." Then he came out from behind the bar and said to Sedonia, "C'mon."

C'mon where? she wondered, but grabbed her beer and followed. They threaded their way through the pool tables and players, and then passed through the doorway at the rear of the room.

Sedonia stopped short, and Buster closed the door behind her. They were in a private room, perhaps 20' x 20'. In the middle stood a nine-foot pool table, and a player leaning over to shoot. He slammed the blue 2-ball into the far corner pocket, then straightened up and looked over at Sedonia with a quizzical expression. Three other men were scattered across a row of wooden, theater-type seats that lined the far wall. Buster's janitor sat off to the side by himself. They also stared at her.

Buster said, "Sedonia, this here's 'French Quarter' Jimmy Dupre."

The player walked around the table. He appeared to be in his early thirties, medium height and build, and dressed in jeans and a dark-blue T-shirt. Intense green eyes bored out of a slightly dissipated face. He accepted one of the beers from Buster and said, "You matched me up with a chick?" He spoke with a strident New Orleans accent, sounding more Bronx than Southern.

Buster looked at Sedonia and grinned. "How about it? You wanna play him?"

Sedonia felt a pang of apprehension, not knowing how to respond. She slid her cue case off her shoulder.

"What's your game?" Jimmy asked her.

"Uh . . . Eight-Ball," Sedonia said.

"*Eight*-Ball?" Jimmy said, then turned to Buster with a frown.

Buster laughed. "She's just a spectator. I gotcha matched up with Darrell Colby. That was him on the phone. He's on his way over from Champ's."

Jimmy nodded, and turned back to the table.

Buster told Sedonia, "I thought you might like to watch a couple of strong players."

"Sure," she said, but still felt uneasy and out of place.

"C'mon over here with the railbirds," Buster said.

Sedonia followed him to the far side of the room. The row of seats stood on a raised platform and offered a good view of the table. Sedonia sat down. The two closest spectators were older men, who acknowledged her with nods, then turned their attention back to Jimmy. The third spectator, young and swarthy, looked like a menacing character from *The Godfather*. Buster walked down and handed him the other beer.

When Buster returned, he took a seat beside Sedonia and waved for the janitor to join them. He shuffled over, took a seat beside Sedonia, and looked up at her with a shy, vacant stare.

"Monk," Buster said, "this is Sedonia."

Monk smiled, exposing a single upper tooth in front. "Hello, Sedonia," he said. His thick, moist speech signaled mental disability.

Buster turned to Sedonia. "Monk's got a special gift for handicapping pool players. Plus, he's a helluva good janitor."

Sedonia smiled at Monk, who again responded with his shy grin. His mannerisms reminded Sedonia of the autistic savant in the movie, *Rain Man*.

"'French Quarter' Jimmy's a road player," Buster continued.

"A road player?"

"Yeah, he travels around the country, gambling on his game. That other guy's his stakehorse. They drove over from New Orleans this afternoon, and called here and asked me to match 'em up."

"Is Jimmy good?"

"Almost as good as he thinks he is," Buster said. He turned to Monk. "How does Jimmy match up with Darrell?"

Monk began to rock and nod. His usually vacant stare seemed to focus on the opposite wall. Abruptly he turned to Buster and said, "'French Quarter' Jimmy needs to give Darrell the eight."

Buster nodded. "That's how I make it, too."

Jimmy was strutting around the table, slamming balls into the pockets much harder than necessary. He fired in a cross-table bank shot, then looked at Sedonia and said with a smirk, "Eight-Ball player, huh?"

Sensing her "Eight-Ball" response had somehow become an inside joke, Sedonia turned to Buster for an explanation.

He responded with a smile. "Serious gamblers play Nine-Ball, One-Pocket, and Bank-Pool. Eight-Ball's for amateurs."

Sedonia suppressed her annoyance. She was tired of men poking fun at her unfamiliarity with pool. Also, she'd played for $200 earlier that week at Chug's. That wasn't exactly chicken feed. She wondered what they'd be playing for here.

The door opened again and a haggard looking man, possibly in his fifties, entered the room, carrying a cue case. He saw Buster and walked over.

Buster called out, "Jimmy, this here's Darrell."

Jimmy gave the newcomer a curt nod, then turned his back on him and continued firing balls into the pockets.

The swarthy man at the end of the row got up and came over. "Whatcha wanna play for?" He too had the strident New Orleans accent.

"You his stakehorse?" Darrell said as he pulled out his cue stick.

The man nodded.

Darrell screwed his stick together. "Race-to-9 for $500. And, he's gotta gimme the eight."

Sedonia watched with interest.

The stakehorse shook his head. "Race-to-9 . . . three set minimum . . . $2,000 each. No weight."

Sedonia's eyes widened. Two thousand dollars! And wasn't gambling illegal? Yet here she was, in a back room, with men talking about $2,000 bets.

Darrell told the stakehorse, "I ain't seen your man play, but I hear he's supposed to be strong. I'll go $1,000, but one set only. And he's gotta give me some weight."

Jimmy finally stopped firing practice balls. "We didn't drive all the way over here from Naw'lins to play for chump change," he said. "Buster told me you had gamble."

The two men glared at each other, and Sedonia shifted uneasily in her seat, wishing she were closer to the door. This "French Quarter" Jimmy character was as obnoxious as Emilio, maybe more so. She glanced over at Buster, who was watching the exchange with an impassive expression. Apparently, his role was simply to get the players together, not to negotiate the stakes.

Finally Darrell said, "I'll play you some One-Pocket for $200 a game."

"Fuck One-Pocket!" Jimmy exploded. He began unscrewing his stick.

"I'll put $1,000 with Darrell's," said a voice to Sedonia's left. She leaned forward. The speaker had been one of the other two older spectators. He appeared to be in his sixties and wore a striped dress shirt, a tie, suit slacks, and fancy suspenders.

Jimmy looked over at his stakehorse, who said, "Three set minimum."

The older man shook his head. "Adjust the weight between sets."

"Fuck!" Jimmy exploded. "There ain't no gamble in this whole fuckin' town!" His stakehorse went over and spoke with him for a moment, then Jimmy said, "Five-ahead . . . for $3,000."

There was a pause, and Sedonia whispered to Buster, "What does that mean?"

"They play 'til somebody pulls ahead by five games."

Darrell and his backer huddled for a moment, and then the other older man joined them. Finally Darrell turned and said, "You gotta gimme the eight."

"Shit, man!" Jimmy said. "I just met you a minute ago, and now already you're beggin' me to give you weight. Fuck you!"

Darrell and his backers huddled again, and then motioned for Buster to join them. After a brief conference, Darrell told Jimmy, "One set . . . ten-ahead . . . for $3,000."

Jimmy gave a disgusted shake of his head, but screwed his stick back together.

Buster returned to his seat next to Sedonia. "Ten-ahead," he muttered. "This'll take a while."

Sedonia had lost track of time, mesmerized by the intense competition. "French Quarter" Jimmy seemed the better shooter of the two. He played with flair—firing fast and loose, attempting bank shots, and once even jumping the cue-ball over another ball to make an object ball. Within the first hour, he'd pulled ahead by six games, but then had seen his early advantage dwindle as the local player, Darrell, countered with a mix of conservative offense, stifling defense, and precision cue-ball positioning.

Now as Jimmy prepared to break, he was ahead by only one game. Sedonia studied his break technique as he placed the cue-ball against the right rail. Several practice strokes, then a full lunge and a resounding *crack!* as the cue-ball slammed into the nine object balls that had been racked in the shape of a diamond. Balls scattered about the table; two found their way into pockets.

Jimmy set his break cue aside, grabbed his regular cue, and strutted back to the table. He began rapidly pocketing the balls in numerical order, seldom slowing to study a shot. Instead, he relied on his shooting skill to overcome occasional poor cue-ball position. It occurred to Sedonia that to have a complete game, a person should combine Jimmy's shot making with Darrell's precision positioning. Jimmy drove the gold-striped 9-ball into the side pocket. Now he was ahead by two.

Buster stood up, and Jimmy gave him an inquiring glance.

"It's quarter to two," Buster said. "I gotta close the bar."

Jimmy nodded, then chalked his break cue for the next game.

As Buster left, Sedonia saw through the open doorway that only a few tables in the main room were still occupied. She wondered if Buster was going to allow this $3,000 match to continue past closing time.

Buster returned, just as Darrell eked out a hard-fought win. After more than four hours of play, Jimmy was now ahead by just one game.

"Told you this would take a while," Buster told Sedonia. "I gotta lock the front door. If you want to get out between now and the end of this set, now's the time to leave."

Sedonia wanted to see the outcome, but obviously it would be hours before one of the players could pull ahead by ten. "I'd better get going," she said.

She and Buster walked through the now dark and deserted poolroom, then stepped outside. The night air was cooler, but still humid. It was almost 2:30 in the morning, and traffic was light along the NASA Parkway.

"Thanks for letting me watch," Sedonia said.

"Learn anything?"

"A lot," she said. "Who do you think is going to win?"

Buster shrugged. "Darrell's a good gambler, but Jimmy's awful strong."

"He also seems like a jerk."

"Intimidator," Buster said.

"Intimidator?"

"The best players make you fear them."

"Fear? Or respect?"

"Fear."

Sedonia didn't reply. His fear hypothesis didn't correlate with her golf experience. She'd respected good players, not feared them.

Buster seemed to sense her resistance. "When I first took you into the back room, did you think I intended for you to play Jimmy?"

She smiled. "Yeah, for a minute there."

"Did you feel fear?"

"Well . . . but that was because—"

"Doesn't matter why. What matters is, you saw an opponent and you felt fear."

"I don't know if I buy that, but what's your point?"

"The best players make you fear them," he said again. "Fear in a race-to-9 can be worth three games on the wire. But good gamblers play despite their fear. They do whatever it takes to win, and to turn things around and make the better player fear *them*. That's what Darrell's doin' in there right now." He gave Sedonia a moment to ponder, then said, "I gotta get back inside." He turned to leave.

"Buster," Sedonia said.

He stopped and turned back.

"Thanks," she said.

He responded with a quick nod, then disappeared through the doorway.

Sedonia hurried across the nearly empty parking lot. Crouched next to her small Miata was a black Camaro Z-28, with Louisiana license plates.

The middle-aged proprietor of *Restaurante Merida* personally brought a pot of coffee over to Sedonia's table. *"¿Mas café, Sedonia?"*

She folded the sports section of the Saturday morning *Houston Chronicle*. *"Si, por favor,"* she said. Then she stretched and said, "I overdid breakfast, Gustavo. Again."

He replenished her coffee. "I am glad you enjoyed it. Again."

Sedonia smiled. Her father had first brought her to this restaurant when she was in grade school, and she'd been a regular customer ever since. She opened her wallet and started to hand Gustavo her corporate American Express card, but then decided not to add further to her company's debt, even $6.50. Instead, she handed him a five and three ones, to cover the bill.

"Gracias," he said with a smile.

"De nada," she replied.

Gustavo left to look after his other patrons, and Sedonia took a sip of coffee. She hoped another cup would wake her up. She'd gone to bed at 3:00, slept six hours, gotten up and done her stretching exercises, and then gone on her morning jog. After a shower, she'd felt invigorated. But now after the restaurant specialty—*huevos ranchero*, fried potatoes, ham, and six soft tortillas—she felt in need of a *siesta*.

She checked her watch: 11:15. Her original plan was to go into her office after breakfast and put in a few hours on the paperwork she'd put off during the past week. Then later in the afternoon, she planned to go by Buster's and practice some of the techniques she'd seen Jimmy and Darrell use the night before.

She finished her coffee, then stood up to leave. On the other hand, Buster's was only two blocks away. And if she went there first, she'd be able to get in some practice before the Saturday evening regulars filled the place.

A half-dozen cars were parked in front of Buster's Billiards, including the black Camaro Z-28, which appeared to be in the same spot as the night before. Sedonia frowned as she got out of her car. Could the match still be going on? Cue case in hand, she headed across the parking lot.

Inside, a young man with a ponytail was working behind the bar. Four other men, late teens or early twenties, occupied two tables nearby. They interrupted their games as Sedonia walked over to the bar.

She asked the bartender. "Is Buster around?"

"He's busy. Can I help you?"

"Are Jimmy and Darrell still playing in back?"

"Yeah . . ." the bartender said.

"I was here last night. Had to leave. Okay if I go back in?"

"Lemme check."

Sedonia followed him, and when he opened the door to the private room, Buster saw her and waved her in. The match was between games, and Darrell was racking the balls. As Sedonia crossed the room, she glanced at the other spectators—same cast as last night, except one of the older men was gone. The one with the dress shirt and tie, who had backed Darrell, was still there and appeared to be dozing. Jimmy's stakehorse was intently focused on the table. Monk was still stationed beside Buster, and smiled as Sedonia took a seat beside him.

"Can't believe they're still playing," Sedonia said.

"Second set. Just playin' five-ahead this time, for $1,000." Buster looked and sounded tired.

"Who won the first set?" Sedonia said.

"Darrell."

Sedonia looked at Darrell with increased respect. The lesser-skilled player had fulfilled Buster's hypothesis and had ground out a victory during the night.

Darrell took a step back from the rack, and Jimmy immediately fired his break ball. "Get in the hole, motherfucker!" he yelled, as the gold-striped 9-ball slowly rolled into the corner pocket for the automatic win.

"Shit," Buster muttered.

"You got money on this?" Sedonia said.

Buster responded with a fatigued nod. "I won $500 on the first set, but now it looks like I'm about to give it back."

"What's the score?"

"Jimmy's already four ahead. I shoulda checked him for speed."

"Speed? You mean like finding out how good he is?"

"No, I mean 'speed' . . . like amphetamines. Look at him."

While Darrell was still sorting the balls into the rack, Jimmy was already practicing his break stroke. The instant Darrell lifted the wooden triangle and took a step back, the cue-ball sent the balls flying about the table. Jimmy attacked the table, and moments later slammed the gold-striped 9-ball into the side pocket.

"Two thousand on the next set!" Jimmy shouted.

Darrell was unscrewing his stick. "I'm done."

"I'll give you some fuckin' weight," Jimmy said. "You can have the eight."

"I told you, I'm done."

"You got $2,000 of my money!" Jimmy shouted. "You can't quit me now!"

"Watch me," Darrell said.

Jimmy rushed over. "You no-gamble son of a bitch!" He continued to rail at Darrell until Buster got up and stepped between them.

"If you ever want to play in here again," Buster told Jimmy in a measured tone, "you'd better knock this shit off."

Jimmy glared at Buster, but finally took a step back. Darrell and the railbird who'd been backing him left the room, and Sedonia decided this was a good time for her to leave too.

Back inside the main room, she got a tray of balls from the bartender and took her favorite table, the nine-foot Brunswick near the front window. She was practicing long shots, when the men emerged from the back room. Jimmy was still griping, loud and profane. Buster, Jimmy, and Jimmy's stakehorse walked over to the bar, and Sedonia heard Buster order double Jack-Cokes for his guests. Then he told the bartender that he was going to drive Monk home. He gave Sedonia a tired wave as he left.

Sedonia resumed practicing and was lost in concentration when a voice said, "What's your name?"

Jimmy had come up and was leaning against the next table. He had a full drink in his hand, and some of it sloshed onto the gray carpet. His green eyes now seemed vacant; evidently, Jack-Coke was overriding the amphetamines.

"Buster introduced us last night," she said. "My name's Sedonia."

"Sedonia. Never heard that name before."

She turned away and lined up her next shot.

"C'mon," he said. "I'll buy you lunch."

"Not interested," she said, then sent the maroon 7-ball into the far corner pocket.

"You got gamble?" he said.

She ignored him and walked around the table for her next shot.

"Play ya for a piece of ass," he said.

Sedonia turned and glared. "Get lost!"

Jimmy's stakehorse hurried over. "C'mon," he told Jimmy. "Let's get outta here." He took Jimmy by the arm and led him away from the table. At the bar, they downed their drinks, then headed for the door. Jimmy yelled something unintelligible over his shoulder at Sedonia as he stepped into the bright midday sunshine.

Sedonia glanced over at the other tables. The four young men were watching her. She turned, lined up on the green 6-ball, and sent it down the table. It dropped into the corner pocket, dead center.

Chapter 5

Sedonia opened the mini blinds, and Sunday morning sunshine streamed into her office. It was a day later than planned, but she was well rested and determined to catch up on the previous week's paperwork. The pot on the coffee bar began to perk.

She pushed the "Messages" button on her telephone and a computerized voice said, "Friday, 4:27 P.M."

Brad Landry's pleasant, deep voice followed. "Hi, Sedonia. This is Brad. I stopped by your office earlier today, but Raul told me you were gone for the afternoon. I left a check with him, to cover the next load of supplies for the Friendswood job. By the way, your crew's off to a good start there."

Sedonia winced. She should have gone by and checked the jobsite herself during the past week.

There was a pause on the recording, then Brad continued, "Uh . . . I also kinda hoped you might want to . . . meet me for a drink after work at the Black Seagull this afternoon." After another pause, he concluded, "Well . . . give me a call when you get a chance: 281-555-3016."

Sedonia replayed the message and jotted down the phone number, then pushed the "Delete" button. She leaned back in her chair and shook her head. She'd wasted Friday afternoon with her friend Christy, when she could have been with Brad Landry. But on the other hand, if she'd have met Brad, she probably wouldn't have seen "French Quarter" Jimmy and Darrell match up at Buster's. She smiled at having thought in terms of "match-ups," realizing she was picking up Buster's pool vernacular.

She rotated her right shoulder. It was still tender from practicing for several hours the previous afternoon. Mimicking Jimmy's style, she'd discovered how to stroke the cue-ball low enough to draw it back, even when the object ball was three to six feet away. However, she was unable to discover the secret of making the cue-ball jump another ball, as Jimmy had done during the match. She suspected that trying to do so was what had aggravated her shoulder.

Not practicing today would be the sensible thing to do. But darn it, she was playing so well! It reminded her of the time when she was 14 and had received a golf tip from a member of the Professional Golf Association, who was practicing on the Bay Oaks Country Club driving range. She already had her handicap down to a five, but she was receptive when the pro suggested she make a significant change to her swing plane. She did exactly as he instructed, and her first shot soared high above the 250-yard marker. Four buckets of balls later, her father discovered her on the driving range, blisters on both hands, still hitting balls and still smiling.

After that, breaking par had become routine; however, she'd never lost the thrill of hitting spectacular drives, particularly during a match. Making long shots on a nine-foot pool table now gave her a similar thrill. But, as Buster had said, she needed to get accustomed to making them in actual competition.

She shook her head, trying to snap out of her pool musings. Leaning forward, she thumbed through the stack of paper that Raul had left on her desk. There it was: Brad's check for $3,000. Good, her company needed the cash infusion. She'd have to apply at least some of it to current bills, and then count on other payments arriving in time to cover Brad's supplies when they came due. She hated juggling cash receivables and payables like this, but felt she had no choice since she was running on such a tight margin. It was ironic that $3,000 was so significant to the operation of her company, while the day before, a couple of pool players like Jimmy and Darrell had played a single set for the same amount.

She stared at the check for a moment, then returned it to the stack, and got up and walked over to Raul's desk. His old-fashioned Rolodex file stood beside his phone. She flipped through it until she found the number she was looking for.

Moments later, a sleepy voice said, *"¿Bueno?"*

"Emilio?"

"Sí."

"This is Sedonia."

Silence.

Sedonia wondered if he'd gone back to sleep. "Are you there?"

"Yes," he said. "What do you want?"

"I want to play some pool this afternoon."

"I thought you were . . . mad at me."

"I was. Do you want to play, or not?"

"Okay. What time?"

"Three o'clock, at Buster's."

"Okay. Three o'clock."

"And, Emilio . . ."

"Yes?"

"Bring some money."

A rumble of thunder drew Sedonia's attention. She turned and looked out the poolroom window. The first splatter of rain hit the cars of the few customers who were spending Sunday afternoon at Buster's.

Turning back she said, "Can you make a cue-ball jump?"

Emilio was screwing his cue stick together. "Sure."

"Show me how."

"You mean like you did at Chug's? You just gotta hit it hard and low."

"That was an accident. I want to be able to control the jump, so I can make an object ball. Friday night, I saw a guy do it, but I can't figure out what he did."

Emilio placed the tip of his stick between the bottom of the cue-ball and the felt tabletop. "At Chug's, you hit the ball here. That's why it went off the table." He raised the tip of his stick midway between the middle and top of the cue-ball. "For a good jump, you must hit it somewhere here." He shot and the ball jumped, but stayed on the table.

Sedonia noticed he'd also raised the butt of his stick to a 45-degree angle, so he'd actually driven the ball down against the slate. That's what she hadn't been doing! She'd practice it later. Now she said, "Race-to-9 for $20?"

"*You* want to gamble with *me*?"

She nodded.

"Okay," he said with a shrug.

She pulled a quarter from her jeans pocket. "Call it."

Sedonia and Emilio walked up to the bar. The pony-tailed bartender who'd been working the weekend day shift came over and said, "Who won?"

Emilio gave him a look of annoyance and said, "How much do we owe?"

"Let's see . . . y'all played about three hours . . . half price on Sundays . . . total of $12."

Emilio handed Sedonia two $20 bills to cover the two sets he'd lost to her. "You pay for the time."

"I'll pay my half."

"Winner is supposed to pay for *all* the time."

Sedonia suspected he was trying to pull one of his usual ploys, but she didn't call him on it. Instead she slid one of the $20 bills across the bar and told the bartender, "Give us a couple of Coors Lights too."

When he returned with their beers and her change, Sedonia tipped him two dollars, then pulled up a barstool. She noticed Emilio remained standing and was looking outside, as if anxious to be on his way. He'd been angry since dropping the second set, 9 to 2, after losing the first, 9 to 4. In addition to the $40, being beaten by a relatively inexperienced woman obviously had been hard on his *machismo*.

Sedonia took a sip from her beer and tried to figure out a tactful way to bring up what she wanted to discuss. Finally she said, "Is it possible . . . to gamble without . . . getting into arguments?"

He turned and frowned at her, as if to indicate he didn't know what she was talking about.

"I want to play competitive pool," she said, "but everywhere you and I have gone, there's been a confrontation."

"Con-fron-tation?" he drawled, as if unfamiliar with the word, then looked back toward the parking lot.

His reticence annoyed her, but she tried to not let it show. If she was going to develop her skills in actual matches, she needed him to accompany her to the bars where the competition was. She pressed on. "Wherever you and I have gone—Wayne's, Chug's, Juan's—you've gotten into arguments."

He turned back again. "I don't play in no country clubs . . . like you do."

Again she had to suppress her annoyance. "Why couldn't we just go in, challenge the table, and play without your starting an argument?"

"Why can't you play," he responded, "without gettin' all mad and runnin' off?"

Sedonia had to smile. At both Chug's and Juan's, she had, in fact, stormed out. And both times she'd been so angry, she'd temporarily vowed not to play again.

He waited, as if expecting her to dispute what he'd said. When she didn't, he finally pulled up a barstool and sat down. "You shot good this afternoon," he said in a grudging tone. "You been on a stall all this time?"

She chuckled and shook her head. "I haven't been on a stall. I've just learned a lot, both from you and from Buster."

"Buster don't like me," Emilio said.

Who does? Sedonia thought. Aloud she said, "What do you think? Could we just play pool, and skip the bullshit?"

Emilio studied her again, then said thoughtfully, "Where I play . . . most people have learned they can't beat me . . . but they ain't seen you play . . ."

Sedonia waited.

He smiled. "They wouldn't be expecting your game . . ."

Sedonia glanced at the speedometer as she drove south along Bayshore Drive, a two-lane blacktop highway that connected the coastal communities of Bacliff and San Leon. Although she lived only fifteen miles from here, she hadn't been on this particular stretch of road in a couple of years. She remembered, however, that the Galveston County Sheriff's Department monitored it closely, particularly where it entered San Leon and the speed limit changed abruptly from 50 to 30.

An eclectic mix of homes and small businesses flashed past on both sides. A fish farm stood off to the right, new since the last time she was here. A small motel had gone out of business, as had a convenience store. A couple hundred yards off to the left, between the residences, she caught glimpses of the bay, glistening in the fading, late evening light. Many of the roadside houses were aged, clapboard structures, but here and there stood new, bayside estates.

The ramshackle Do Drop Inn came into view. Behind it stood a small bait shop with a rickety wooden pier that extended into the bay. A faded, hand-painted sign near the roadside read: "Cold Beer. Live Mullet." Sedonia smiled. Locally, San Leon was known as "a small drinking community, with a large fishing problem."

As she entered the city limits, she spotted the "Speed Limit 30" sign, almost hidden by an untended oleander bush. And behind an abandoned filling station, she saw a parked green and white Sheriff's Department car. She quickly downshifted her Miata into fourth gear, then third. She looked in her rearview mirror. The patrol car didn't pull out.

Clapboard shacks, most built on pilings, now lined the highway and crammed the side streets that led to the bay. One house had been turned into an antique shop since Sedonia was last here. The front yard was covered with makeshift tables, fashioned from old sawhorses and sagging sheets of plywood. A sign hanging from the second floor balcony read: "Junk and Disorderly."

Sedonia chuckled. That could apply to this whole area.

A block ahead, the town's only traffic light blinked red for a four-way stop. And on the right stood Willy O's. Sedonia pulled into the potholed parking lot, amid a dozen or so dirty trucks and vans. No sign of Emilio's shiny pickup. She turned off her engine and sat for a moment. The two-story wooden building in front of her was painted a sickly pastel blue, muted further by years of accumulated grime. There was an empty café on the ground floor, apparently closed for the day. The lounge was upstairs.

She reached down and transferred three $20 bills and her driver's license from her purse to her jeans pocket. Then she slid the purse under the seat and climbed out of the car. When she'd driven by here in the past, she'd always been curious about what went on in a place like this. Now she was about to find out. As she crossed the parking lot, she heard the faint strains of music coming from the lounge above—Willie Nelson singing *Help Me Make It through the Night.*

Climbing the wooden stairway that led up the side of the building, she had second thoughts. She probably should have waited for Emilio. It was too late now, though. The door flew open just as she arrived at the upper landing, and a middle-aged drunk staggered out. Dressed in a filthy T-shirt and jeans, he looked and smelled as if he'd spent the day working on one of the local shrimp boats. He managed to focus his bleary eyes on her, then with a theatrical flair, he reached back held the door so she could enter.

"Thanks," she said with a smile.

The door closed behind her. She glanced at the two pool tables on the right, which were both occupied, and then started toward the U-shaped bar on the left. The room was so poorly lit that she had to look down to ensure she didn't stumble on the warped flooring. She located an empty stool at the crowded bar, and a thin brunette barmaid, perhaps thirty, came over.

"Hi," Sedonia said. "I'll have a Coors Light."

The door flew open again, and the drunk staggered back inside and headed toward her. Sedonia suspected she'd taken the stool where he'd been sitting.

"Ralph!" the barmaid yelled. "I told you, you're cut off."

"I wanna buy her a drink," he said, fumbling for his wallet.

"Ralph," the barmaid said in a stern tone, "go home."

The man responded with a hurt look, but then turned and shuffled back outside.

"Hope he's not driving," Sedonia said.

The barmaid shook her head. "Just lives over at the Do Drop, and he's walkin'."

Sedonia smiled. Not likely the Sheriff would stop him for speeding.

The barmaid set a beer in front of her. "A dollar fifty."

Sedonia paid, then looked around. She was the only woman customer. Several of the dozen or so men at the bar glanced in her direction, but then returned to their private conversations. Three seated across from her bantered with the barmaid. Judging by the noise level and the frequent bursts of laughter, everyone had been here for some time. Most of the clientele appeared to be laborers, probably shrimpers and oystermen who sailed out of nearby April Fools Point. Sedonia had worn jeans and a simple sleeveless top, but among this group, she felt overdressed. She wished Emilio would get here.

She turned her attention to the two faded and stained bar-boxes. Two Latinos were playing on the closest one. They apparently were between games; one was evenly distributing the balls against the rails. Sedonia hadn't seen this game before.

On the far table, two Anglos were playing Eight-Ball. One appeared to be a young laborer and was using with a house stick. The other was in his forties, with thinning red hair. He had a custom cue stick and shot with a practiced stroke. That was probably the game she'd need to get into. However, if Emilio didn't show up, she'd feel uncomfortable just walking up and challenging the table.

She watched the match for several more minutes, then finally the front door opened and in strolled Emilio. He gave Sedonia a quick nod of recognition and walked over to the far table, where the redheaded player was lining up on the 8-ball. He made it in the corner pocket, and then turned to Emilio. After they spoke for a moment, Emilio waved for Sedonia to join them.

As she approached, the younger player headed toward the bar. "Good luck," he said as they passed. "He's tough."

The other man greeted her with a smile. "They call me Red."

"I'm Sedonia," she replied as they shook hands.

"Your boyfriend says you like to gamble on pool," Red said.

Sedonia took a deep breath. That "boyfriend" crap again. However, this wasn't the time or the place to correct it. "I . . . play a little," she said.

"He wants a race-to-5 for $50. Okay with you?"

Sedonia nodded.

"I'll let you have first break," he said.

Sedonia suspected his giving her the break was a sign that he was taking her lightly. As he fed three quarters into the table, she whispered to Emilio, "Should I get my cue stick?"

"Play off the wall," he whispered back. "He's not that strong."

She responded with an uncertain nod. From what she'd seen of his last game, he'd looked pretty strong to her.

Emilio strolled up to the bar to get a beer, and the barmaid greeted him by name. Sedonia rummaged through a dozen sticks that hung from a rack on the wall. Most had flattened or missing tips, or warped shafts, but she finally found one that would do.

Emilio returned with his beer and whispered to Sedonia, "Red's a politician . . . councilman or something. Got plenty money and loves to gamble. Don't go on a stall, but let him win a few games each set. Don't scare him off."

Then he pulled up a chair close to the other table, and spoke in Spanish to the two Latino players. Sedonia understood pieces of the conversation. Emilio was telling them the stakes of her match and trying to talk them into placing side bets. They set aside their cue sticks and drew up chairs.

Red finished racking, and Sedonia walked over and picked up the cue-ball. She felt her pulse accelerate, and took a deep breath trying to quell it. A large, yellowish stain covered the break end of the table—a spilled beer, or worse. She hated to touch it, but had to in order to break. She took another deep breath. *Grip . . . stance . . . one, two, three . . . stroke.* A loud *crack!* and balls caromed about the table. Two solids and one stripe found pockets. The match was on.

She made three more solids, but then momentarily forgot about bar-box cue-balls being unusually heavy. It rolled too far and left her with an impossible next shot. She failed to hit a solid ball, giving Red ball-in-hand. He took full advantage, running his remaining stripes and then sinking the 8-ball. Sedonia was behind, 1 to 0.

As she racked the balls for the second game, she glanced over at Emilio. He was handing money to one of the Latinos. Apparently with them, he was betting by the game, not the set. Two men who had been sitting at the bar came over and perched on the unoccupied table to watch the action.

Red made a ball on the break, and then made three more before missing. Sedonia made a ball, but again allowed the cue-ball drift too far down the table. She shook her head in annoyance. *Concentrate!* She missed a thin cut shot, trying to recover. Red returned to the table and ran the rest of his balls, then the 8-ball. Sedonia was down, 2 to 0.

Emilio flashed an annoyed look in her direction as he paid off another bet. The recipient laughed and said something in Spanish. Sedonia only caught the phrase *su novia gringa.* He'd said something about "your Anglo girlfriend."

Red looked over with a patronizing smile, then broke and failed to make a ball. Sedonia returned to the table. The stripes looked like a possible run-out. She made her first six shots, then needed to shoot the blue-striped 12-ball the length of the table. The shot also required that she back up the cue-ball, so she'd have a shot on the 8-ball, which was resting against the end rail. *Heavy cue-ball,* she told herself. *Hit it low and hard. One, two, three . . . stroke.* The cue-ball backed up as she'd intended, but the 12-ball stuttered in the corner and failed to drop. She shook her head. Damn it! How could she miss a shot like that? And on such a small table!

"Too much green, sweetheart," Red said.

Sedonia didn't know if by "green" he was referring to the relatively long shot she'd just missed, or if he was insinuating she'd choked up because they were playing for money. With her stripes off the table, he had an easy run out. She watched as he made quick work of the solids, and then the 8-ball. She now trailed, 3 to 0 in the race-to-5 set.

Sedonia racked the balls again, and then walked over to the table where Emilio was sitting. As she took a sip from her beer, Emilio looked up as if he were about to speak, but then wisely kept his mouth shut. Instead, he stood up and shouted to the barmaid that he needed another beer.

Red broke poorly, and the balls stayed clustered at one end of the table. The game seesawed back and forth for nearly twenty minutes, as both players repeatedly had to shoot from poor position. Red's stripes were already off the table, when Sedonia finally made her last solid and lined up on the 8-ball. The shot had to go down the right rail, almost the length of the table. She positioned the tip of her cue stick to put right english on the cue-ball, so it would transfer left english to the 8-ball, and drift it by the side pocket on the way to the corner. *One, two, three . . . stroke.* The 8-ball touched the protruding point of the side pocket. *Damn it!* Instead of continuing down to the corner, the 8-ball drifted to the center of the table. The cue-ball stopped nearby, leaving Red an easy winning shot.

"Shit!" she heard Emilio explode.

"Tough luck," Red said, with obvious insincerity. "You caught the titty." Then barely pausing to aim, he slammed the 8-ball into the side pocket for the win.

Sedonia's hands shook as she racked for what could be the final game of the set. The barmaid and three more men from the bar came over to watch. Spectators now circled the table. Uncomfortable under the intense scrutiny, Sedonia walked over to where Emilio was sitting.

He shook his head and said, "You doggin' them balls!" Then he angrily turned and paid off the latest round of side bets he'd lost. The winners laughed and heckled him in Spanish. "Gimme another beer," Emilio told the barmaid. "And a shot of tequila."

The fifth game was similar to the fourth, seesawing back and forth. Finally, Red returned to the table, with two makeable stripes. He pocketed both, and then the 8-ball. Sedonia had lost the set, 5 to 0.

Emilio paid off the $50 bet, and then another round of side bets. He motioned for Sedonia to join him at the bar. "You shootin' like shit," he told her, loud enough that the customers sitting nearby could hear.

Sedonia gave an exasperated shake of her head. "I don't know what's wrong."

Emilio lowered his voice. "Sunday, you kick my ass on a nine-foot table, and now you can't make shit on a bar-box."

Sedonia could only respond with another shake of her head.

"I'm down almost $100," Emilio said. "Can you beat this guy, or not?"

"I ought to be able to," she replied without conviction.

The barmaid came over. "Do y'all want something to drink?"

Sedonia declined.

Emilio said, "Gimme a Coors Light and a double shot of tequila." Then he turned and shouted to Red, "We gotta have some weight this next set. You too strong, man."

"Just got lucky," Red replied; however, his tone indicated false modesty.

"Gotta give us two on the wire," Emilio said.

Red looked at Sedonia, and the trace of a smirk formed on his lips. "Fifty again?"

Emilio hesitated, then said, "A hundred."

Red pulled out a quarter. "Call it."

"Heads," Sedonia said, her voice breaking.

The coin came to rest on the table. "Tails," Red said. "Rack."

After she'd racked and he was preparing to break, it occurred to Sedonia that she should have gone out to her car between sets and got her custom cue stick. It seemed too late now, though.

There was a sharp *crack!* followed immediately by Red shouting, "On the break!" The black 8-ball rolled slowly toward the corner pocket, hung momentarily on the edge, then fell for an automatic win. With one stroke, he'd won back half of the two-game weight he'd given her.

Sedonia racked again, then said, "Time out."

A bemused look crossed Red's face. "Time out?"

"I'll be back in a minute," Sedonia said. She hurried from the bar, down the outside stairs, and across the parking lot. Her hands shook as she opened the car trunk and withdrew her cue case. As she slammed the lid shut, she looked over her shoulder and saw the green and white Sheriff's car roll up to the intersection and stop at the blinking red light. The occupant was only a silhouette, but she had the feeling he was watching her. She turned and headed back across the parking lot. As she climbed the stairs, she wondered again if gambling on pool was illegal.

"Uh-oh, Red," one of the spectators said in a loud voice as she reentered the room. "Little lady's done gone and got her own stick."

Red frowned as she screwed it together. Then he broke, and failed to make a ball.

Sedonia chalked her stick and eyed the layout. The stripes looked like the easier suit, beginning with a shot on the orange-striped 13-ball. *Grip . . . stance.* Her custom cue felt smooth and balanced. *One, two, three . . . stroke.* The 13-ball rolled toward the corner pocket, but then drifted to the left, missing badly.

"That fancy stick shoots just like the house cue, doesn't it?" Red said.

Sedonia grimaced, remembering too late that she needed to shoot harder than usual to offset the drift of a pool table in poor condition. *Concentrate!* she told herself.

Since she hadn't made a ball, the table was still open. Red also opted for the stripes and quickly pocketed all seven, and then sank the 8-ball, tying the score at 2 to 2 in the race-to-5.

On his next break, most of the balls stayed clustered near the far end of the table. The game went back and forth for a quarter of an hour. While Red was at the table, Sedonia occasionally glanced over at Emilio. He was slamming tequila shots and arguing in Spanish.

Red missed a makeable shot, giving her an unexpected chance to get back to the table. If she could make a tough cut on the maroon 7-ball, she'd have natural position on the 8-ball. *One, two, three . . . stroke.* The 7-ball rolled into the side pocket. And on the next shot, so did the 8-ball. She'd finally won a game, and with the two-game weight, was ahead, 3 to 2.

She waited while Red racked the balls.

"You may have to show me how to do this," he said as he dropped the balls into the wooden triangle. "It's been a while since I had to rack."

Sedonia ignored his sarcasm. For the break, she went back to the house stick she'd used earlier. She lined up on the right rail and took a deep breath. *One, two, three . . .*

An instant before she drove the stick forward, Red said, "You don't break with your own cue?"

The sound of his voice in mid stroke threw her off. She hit the cueball too low and to the right. It hit the side of the racked balls and flew off the table.

Emilio shouted, "You sharkin' motherfucker!"

Red retrieved the cue-ball off the floor. A self-satisfied smile formed on his lips as he decided where he wanted to place the ball to begin his next run.

Sedonia could only sit and watch as he methodically worked his way through the rack. She felt rattled by the press of people clustered around the table. Nothing on the golf course had prepared her for this constant clamor and unsportsmanlike behavior. Red finally sank the 8-ball, tying the score at 3 to 3. With a sigh, Sedonia returned to the table to rack the balls for the next game.

An instant before Red broke, something clattered to the floor. Sedonia turned. Emilio apparently had knocked over an empty beer bottle. The other Latino's were laughing at him. Sedonia turned back to the table. The clamor hadn't bothered Red; he was off on another methodical run out.

"Eight in the side," he said finally, then made the shot. The score was now 4 to 3. He needed one more game; she needed two.

"Time out," Sedonia said. Then she asked the barmaid, "Where's the restroom?"

The barmaid gestured toward the dimly-lit far corner. As Sedonia crossed the small dance floor, she felt as if everyone was watching her. Grime covered the restroom doorway, and undiluted antiseptic assailed her nostrils as she entered. One glance into the single stall was all she needed. *No way.* The sink looked almost as filthy, but she risked touching a faucet and dampened a paper towel. As she patted her face and the back of her neck, she stared at her reflection in the cracked mirror. What was she doing here!

A surge of angry male voices rose from the bar, Emilio's above the general din. Then they quieted again. She took a deep breath. She'd finish this set, and then get the hell out of this place.

As she returned to the pool table area, Red said, "Everything come out okay, sweetheart?" Several of the men who were clustered around the table laughed. Sedonia ignored him and racked the balls.

Before Red broke, he turned to Emilio. "How about givin' me some of that side action?"

Emilio sat slumped in his chair. He finally looked up and responded with a drunken shake of his head.

Red broke and made two stripes, but also made the cue-ball. As Sedonia returned to the table, he began talking in the background. He didn't speak directly *to* her, but loud enough for her to hear. "She's probably gonna kick my ass now."

Sedonia surveyed her options and tried unsuccessfully to block out the sound of his voice. The five remaining stripes looked makeable, and the 8-ball sat near the middle of the table. She simply needed to relax and shoot. The first three balls went easily, then she made a tough cut on the blue-striped 12-ball, sending it the length of the table and into the corner pocket.

Red was now talking directly to her. "Don't look so serious, sweetheart. It's just a game."

She made the yellow-striped 9-ball in the side, and got good position on the 8-ball. "Eight in the corner," she said, then quickly got into her stance, wanting to shoot before Red had a chance to say something. *Stroke. No!* She hadn't hit the cue-ball low enough. The heavy cue-ball followed the 8-ball into the corner pocket. *Damn it!* Scratching on the 8-ball was an automatic loss. She'd dropped the second set, 5 to 3.

"Pay up, *amigo!*" Red crowed to Emilio.

Emilio looked up at Sedonia through a tequila fog and shook his head in disgust.

She unscrewed her stick and returned it to its case. Then she walked over to Emilio and pulled $50 out of her jeans pocket. Having played so poorly, she felt obliged to cover at least half of his last bet. "Sorry," she said, handing him the money.

Emilio responded with an initial look of surprise, then with a grunt accepted it.

"Don't rush off, sweetheart," Red said with a grin.

Sedonia ignored him and headed for the door, cue case under one arm. As she stepped outside, her vision blurred. She hurried down the stairway and across the dark parking lot, wanting to get to her car before the tears of frustration broke loose. She blinked them back as she fumbled with her key, unable to fit it into the lock.

"Wait a minute!" she heard Emilio shout.

She turned in time to see him stumble and barely keep from falling face first into the parking lot.

"C'mon back," he said with a slur as he staggered up in front of her. "C'mon back an' have a drink."

Sedonia shook her head. "I'm sorry you lost all that money on me. That place . . . that table . . ."

"Shit," he responded with a sneer. "The table ain't the problem. You was just doggin' them balls."

His words stung. "I don't know what made me think I could play pool," she said. "I'm through with this shit!"

He slowly shook his head and said with contempt, "Just what I expected from a country club girl. No heart."

"The hell with you!" She turned her back on him, set her cue case on the convertible roof, and again fumbled with the key. Finally she managed to get it into the lock.

"C'mon, *chica*," she heard him say. "I buy you a drink." Then she felt his arms encircle her waist and his body press against her back. He pinned her against the car, his harsh breath blowing against her right cheek. She braced her hands on the roof and lunged back with all her strength. "Get away from me!"

He stumbled backward, gasping, then regained his balance. He looked as if he were about to attack. At that instant, a light blinded her and another man's voice rang out, "Got a problem here?"

Sedonia raised a hand to shield her eyes and could make out a green and white patrol car sitting in a dark corner of the parking lot. The silhouette of a deputy approached, one hand carrying a flashlight and the other hand resting on a holstered pistol.

"I said . . . do we have a problem here?"

The flashlight beam now was on Emilio, who raised his hands chest high, palms out. "No problem, sir," he said with a foolish grin.

The deputy looked at Sedonia.

"He's drunk," she said. "I just want to leave."

"Is he with you?"

"No. That's his truck over there."

The deputy studied her for a moment, possibly judging her sobriety. "Go ahead," he said finally. "Get going." Then he took Emilio by an arm and pulled him toward his truck. "Lemme see your driver's license and proof of insurance."

Moments later, Sedonia sped north on Bayshore Drive, ignoring the 50-mile-per-hour signs. She knew where the Sheriff's patrol car was. The pent-up tears of frustration finally released, and she slammed the steering wheel with both hands.

Chapter 6

Sedonia sat parked in front of Buster's Billiards with the air-conditioner on, watching her Miata temperature gauge creep toward "H". She checked her watch again: 11:10. Buster had told her he opened the poolroom at 11:00. With a sigh, she pushed in the clutch and placed her hand on the gearshift lever; however, at that moment an older model Ford sedan pulled in beside her, and Buster looked over with a surprised smile.

"Se-don-ia!" he said as they climbed out of their cars. "Been waiting long?"

She shook her head and tucked her cue case under one arm. The two of them headed toward the poolroom.

"Gonna get in some early practice this morning?" Buster said as he unlocked the door.

She followed him inside without replying.

"I'll get you some balls," he said, and walked around behind the bar.

"I'm . . . not here to play."

Buster walked over to the counter. "No?"

"I just came by to see if you wanted to buy back this stick."

"Something wrong with it?"

"Not with the stick," she said. "With the player. I've . . . decided to give up the game."

"But you just started playing," he protested.

"I'm not cut out for pool."

"Not cut out for it? What do you mean? You play good."

"It's the other stuff. The arguing and all the other . . . bullshit that goes along with it."

"Arguing? You mean like the other night, between Jimmy and Darrell?"

"Not just them. Last night I played for money in San Leon. It was the same thing there."

"Where'd you play in San Leon?"

"Willie O's."

"Willie O's is a dump. What the hell were you doing there?"

"You told me I needed actual competition. Remember?"

"Yeah, but I didn't have Willie O's in mind. What were you playing, and what were the stakes?"

"Eight-Ball. Race-to-5 for $100. Emilio was my ... stakehorse."

"E-mil-io," Buster said with obvious distaste. "Willie O's does sound like his kinda action."

"The problem's not just there; it's everywhere. Wayne's, Chug's, Juan's ..."

"You *have* been makin' the rounds," Buster said with a laugh. "So you lost last night. How bad?"

"The first set, 5 to 0. Then 5 to 3 the second set, even though I had two games on the wire."

"Who'd you play?

"Some guy named Red."

Buster rubbed his chin. "Red from San Leon ... politician or somethin'?"

"That's him."

"He came in here a few times last year, and robbed some kids playin' Eight-Ball. Then Darrell got hold of him in a Nine-Ball match. Cleaned him out, and I haven't seen Red since. Unless he's gotten a helluva lot better, you shouldn't have had any trouble with him."

"You're right."

"Then what was the problem?"

"Like I said. It was all the bullshit. The arguing, people standing around watching, side bets ..."

Buster shrugged. "All part of the game. You gotta get used to it."

"Players talking to you while you're shooting?" Sedonia said.

"Sharking."

"It's too ... cutthroat. I lose concentration, and I start missing easy shots."

"Dogging."

Sedonia shook her head. Buster's patent answers annoyed her.

Buster continued, "Women just don't have the ... what do you call it ... the temperament ... for competitive pool."

Sedonia didn't trust herself to reply. The last thing she wanted to hear this morning was Buster's view of the difference between men and women. She just wanted to get back the $225 she'd paid for the damned cue stick.

"I mean," Buster continued, "some of y'all—like you—play good and all. But basically, y'all are just too ... nice."

His male patronization reminded her of Emilio's "country club girl" accusation the night before. She glared at him and demanded, "Do you want to buy this stick, or not?"

He looked momentarily taken aback.

"I put a ding in it," she said. "I'll sell it to you for . . . $175."

Buster studied her for a moment, then shook his head. "There's no profit for me in buying back equipment. But I know a woman who might want to talk to you. Lemme have a phone number where she can reach you."

Sedonia felt like just telling him the hell with it, but she needed the money. "My office number is 281-555-1497."

Buster jotted it down on a drink napkin. "The woman's name's Hannah. I don't know her last name."

Sedonia forced herself to say, "Thanks," then picked up her cue case and headed for the door.

Moments later, as she pulled onto the NASA Parkway, she felt embarrassed at having gotten angry with Buster. He wasn't a bad guy. Matter of fact, he was a good guy. But he was a guy.

Shortly before noon, Sedonia drove through a new Friendswood subdivision, looking for Brad Landry's jobsite. She'd acquired a throbbing headache during the short drive over from Buster's, and squinting into the midday sun was making it worse.

She turned onto a recently-poured concrete street, and ahead lay several blocks of homes under construction, most still in the framing phase. The natural terrain was unattractive—former flat coastal farmland, punctuated by an occasional weed tree. However, for reasons she didn't understand, someone had decided this would be a good location for an upscale residential development. Most of the two-story structures looked as if they'd run 3,000 to 4,000 square feet.

Ahead she saw Raul's van, parked in front of what must be Brad's project. Raul was back at the office, but he sometimes allowed his workers to use his van if they had no other way to get to their jobsites. Brad's house was closer to completion than the others on the block. From Sedonia's experience, it looked as if it would be ready for occupancy within a month or so. As she pulled up to the curb and stopped, she glanced into her review mirror and saw a white Dodge Ram pickup pull in behind her.

"Darn," she muttered as Brad climbed out. She should have come here and familiarized herself with his project before he arrived, instead of first going to Buster's. She reached into the glove compartment and pulled out her cell phone, a small notepad, and a pen.

"Thought I recognized your car," Brad said when she got out.

"Good to see you," Sedonia said as they shook hands. His grip was firm and calloused—signs of a hands-on contractor.

They started toward the house. *Ranchera* music blared from the second floor, almost drowning out the sound of hammering.

"How far have you folks gotten this week?" Brad said.

"Uh . . . I think we're moving right along," Sedonia replied, trying to bluff through her unfamiliarity with his project. As they picked their way across the debris-strewn dirt that eventually would be turned into a manicured front lawn, she hoped Raul had again covered for her in her absence.

"¡Hola, Sedonia!" called out a young worker from an open upstairs window.

"¿Como estas, Luis?" she called back with a wave.

"Bien," he said with a smile, then he ducked back inside and the music abruptly quieted.

As Sedonia preceded Brad through the front door, she fervently hoped that all actually was "bien" inside.

A middle-aged Guatemalan woman was floating sheetrock in what was to be the living room. Her teenage grandson was assisting her.

"Hola, Marta," Sedonia said.

"Hola, señorita," the woman replied with a deferential bob of her head.

"How's it going, Alfonso?" Sedonia asked the grandson.

He responded with a noncommittal shrug.

Sedonia smiled. From their past exchanges, she knew he was American-ized and would have preferred being with his friends today. When she'd worked summers for her father on jobsites like this, she'd felt the same way.

Brad stood in a doorway and sighted down a living room wall. He gave a nod of approval, then walked alongside the wall and ran his hand over the tape that hid the cracks between the 4' x 8' pieces of sheetrock. "Good work," he told the woman, who responded with an uncertain nod. Then he asked Sedonia, "Has the crown molding arrived?"

"Uh . . . I'm not certain," she said, and jotted down a note to check.

"Sounded like we interrupted a fiesta that was going on upstairs," Brad said, then started up the freestanding stairway, which led to the loft that overlooked the living room.

Sedonia took a deep breath as she started up the stairs after him. General contractors usually hired her crew just to paint. As far as she knew, other than Raul, Luis was her only employee who knew how to hang sheetrock. She didn't know what to expect at the top of the stairs. Darn it! She should have come out here earlier.

The master bedroom overlooked the front yard. Luis and another young Latino stood on portable scaffolding, installing a piece of sheetrock on the ceiling. When they'd nailed it in place, Luis smiled down at Brad and said, "Look okay?"

"Damn good," Brad said.

Across the hall came the sound of more hammering. As Brad turned and started through the doorway, Sedonia motioned for Luis to come along too.

Marta's husband and their son-in-law were busy in the next room. Sedonia heaved a sigh of relief. This installation also seemed to be going well, though the sheetrock nails weren't lined up as precisely as Luis' had been in the other room.

Brad gave the two workers a nod of approval, then asked Sedonia, "Have you started in the other rooms yet?"

Sedonia had to turn to Luis, who fortunately picked up her signal.

"No," Luis said. "We start at the front, and work our way back. We do the bathrooms and closets last, so we can use the small pieces."

"Good," Brad said. "Don't let us slow you down."

"Thanks, Luis," Sedonia said, as he left the room.

Brad went into the bathroom and spent a few minutes checking the still-exposed pipes. From his annoyed frown, she gathered something about the plumbing disturbed him. He jotted some notes on a piece of paper, then looked out the bathroom window for a moment. When he turned back he said, "Have you had lunch?"

"Uh . . . no."

"The 'roach coach' just pulled up. Settle for a sandwich and a Coke?"

"Sounds good."

When they arrived outside, a young woman was opening the side of the canteen truck. She was dressed as if she'd just climbed off the back of a Harley Davidson, and she gave Brad a familiar smile as he walked up. "You get around, handsome."

Brad chuckled. "Hi, Mary. Got any roast beef and cheese today?"

"Of course. Always save at least one, just for you."

"I'll have the same," Sedonia said, "and a bag of potato chips and a Coke."

The young woman gave Sedonia an annoyed glance, as if she'd interrupted a private conversation.

"Chips and a Coke for me too," Brad said as he pulled out his wallet.

"Big spender," the woman said. "This y'all's first date?"

Brad glanced over at Sedonia with an amused smile. "So far."

Sedonia felt herself flush.

"Good," the woman said. "I still got a chance then."

Brad chuckled again as he received his change, then said, "See ya, Mary." He turned to Sedonia. "It's too hot to eat in the house. Let's use my truck."

A half-dozen rolled up blueprints and a tool belt occupied the passenger seat of his pickup. He moved them to the bench seat in the rear, and Sedonia climbed in. "Another hot one," he said as he started the engine and turned on the air-conditioner. He pulled a blue bandana from his jeans pocket and wiped his brow.

Something reminded Sedonia of her father, and it took her a moment to identify what it was: Old Spice. She suppressed a smile, wondering if her father had influenced Brad's choice of aftershave lotion. Most of the young men she knew would consider it old fashioned, but she found the scent reassuring.

"Sorry, I don't have candles," Brad said as they unwrapped their sandwiches and settled back.

"Pickup truck ambiance is fine," Sedonia said with a smile. "I'm starving. Only had a couple of pieces of toast for breakfast."

Construction workers from other projects formed a line at the canteen truck.

"Mary does a good business," Brad said, then bit into his sandwich. "She works most of the jobsites around here. Really gets out and hustles business. I respect that."

Sedonia took a bite from her sandwich without replying, again feeling uneasy at not having personally kept an eye on Brad's project.

"Good workers are hard to find nowadays," Brad continued, "particularly Anglos. And seems like the closer you get to the coast, the fewer there are."

"You've noticed that too?"

He nodded. "Casual lifestyle, I guess. Plus, we have to compete against the oyster and shrimp boats. A lot of the older laborers in coastal towns like San Leon and Bacliff prefer to be out dragging the bay at dawn, put in their eight to ten hours, and then spend their afternoons and evenings getting drunk, or stoned."

Sedonia smiled, remembering the clientele the night before at Willie O's in San Leon. "And the younger guys are just as bad," she said. "If surf's up in Galveston, don't expect them to show up at the jobsite."

Brad chuckled. "Once when surf was up, I no-showed on your dad. He reamed me good. I never missed another day."

The last person in line at the canteen truck walked away with his food. The operator quickly secured the side panels, turned the truck around in the driveway, and headed back in their direction. She blew the horn as she sped past, smiling at Brad and ignoring Sedonia.

Brad waved, and then turned to Sedonia. "I've got another house underway, two streets over. Ought to be ready for drywall, trim, and painting in a couple of weeks. You interested?"

"Sure."

"That would mean your crew will need to pick up the pace here."

"I'll see what we can do."

"When I was out here last week, I got the impression . . . Luis . . . is that his name?"

Sedonia nodded.

Brad continued, "I got the impression Luis was stretching this job out. I don't want sloppy work. But, on the other hand, I only make money when projects close."

"I understand," Sedonia said. She also understood why Luis was in no hurry to finish this project. As far as he knew, he might be out of work as soon as it was over.

"So," Brad said, "I'd like you or Raul to keep a close eye on things out here. Next week, we'll see how far you've gotten, and then talk about the other project."

Sedonia received his subtle message, loud and clear. Clearly, she hadn't bluffed him. He recognized her lack of familiarity with his project, and if she wanted the next one, she'd have to do better. She couldn't tell him she'd been preoccupied with pool. Anyway, it didn't matter, since she was done with that.

As they finished their lunches, Brad's cell phone rang. He spoke for a few minutes with someone who apparently worked for him. From what Sedonia overheard, there seemed to be a problem with construction reinforcement bars.

Finally Brad hung up. "I gotta get over to my shopping center remodel job. A load of rebar arrived early. I gotta figure out a place to offload and store it."

Sedonia reached for the door handle. "Thanks for lunch, Brad. And thanks for considering us for your other house. I'll get together with Raul this afternoon, and we'll see how quickly we can finish this one."

"Sorry I gotta rush off," he said as she climbed down from the truck. "Let's get together again and—"

"Sounds good," she said, but closed the door before he had a chance to suggest a specific date and time.

He waved as he pulled past, his dual rear tires churning up dirt and sawdust that covered the street.

A few moments later, Sedonia made a U-turn and headed back to her office. She'd sensed Brad had been about to ask her for a date again. Maybe they'd be able to get together in the future, but this wasn't the right time. For the past few months she'd been on an emotional yo-yo. Anything she initiated now would probably fail, like her foolish attempt to play competitive pool.

With that thought, she felt her energy drain. What in the hell was the matter with her? Why couldn't she be content simply running her business . . . hanging out at the Bullfrog Club . . . dating . . .

She knew the answer. For a fleeting period in her young life, she'd been heralded as world class. She tried to tell herself to forget about it, but the thought of resigning herself to a mundane work-and-play existence brought back an all-to-familiar sense of melancholy. And the headache from that morning returned with a vengeance.

Late that afternoon, Sedonia stepped outside her office. She returned Raul's wave, as he and several workers pulled out of the parking lot and headed for home. She'd thought this day would never end. Four aspirins had helped her headache, but now her stomach felt queasy. She locked the door, and as she started down the stairs, she glanced at her Miata. "Damn it!"

The front tire on the passenger side was flat. She'd probably picked up a nail at Brad's jobsite. She sprinted across the oyster shell parking lot, waving her arm and calling out, "Raul!"

His van turned the corner at Todville Road, and then disappeared from sight.

Sedonia shook her head. She'd never had to change a tire on the Miata before. She walked back to her car, opened the trunk, and discovered her spare tire was soft. "Damn it!" she swore again.

As she reentered the office to call her neighborhood service station, the phone rang. She grabbed it and angrily said, "Hello!"

There was a pause, then a woman's voice said, "Sounds like I caught you at a bad time."

"I'm sorry," Sedonia said. "I was just leaving work, and discovered I have a flat tire. This is Forbes Painting Company. May I help you?"

"Are you Sedonia?"

"Yes?"

"I'm Hannah Griswald. Buster tells me you're a pool player."

"Not any more," Sedonia said as she dropped into the chair behind her desk. "But I do have a cue stick I'd like to sell."

"Buster told me you were good. He suggested I call you and see if you'd like to play on my BCA team."

Sedonia shook her head in exasperation. "He was supposed to see if you wanted to buy my stick."

"I've got plenty of cue sticks," the woman said. "If I bring home another one, my husband will divorce me. And after thirty-five years of marriage, it's too late to break in a new husband."

"I don't see how Buster could have misunderstood what I told him," Sedonia said, then added, "What kind of team did you say you had?"

"BCA. Billiard Congress of America. It's a nationwide amateur organization. My team plays in a local league on Thursday nights."

"I've never heard of league pool."

"It's growing by leaps and bounds. There's BCA, and there's also the American Pool Players Association and the Valley National Eight-Ball Association. Between the three of them, they've got about 500,000 players."

"That's impressive," Sedonia said, "but I'm not interested in playing. Matter of fact, I'm quitting the game."

"Darn," the woman said. "We're starting a new session tonight, and one of my regulars just called me at the last minute. She's decided to play on her boyfriend's team. Could I talk you into substituting for her, at least for tonight?"

"I don't know anything about league pool."

"It's just Eight-Ball. All you gotta do is show up and play one game against each of the other team's five players. I'm the captain of our team, and I'll tell you who and when to play."

"I'm sorry . . . Hannah. I'd like to help you out, but I'm fed up with pool. Plus, I've got a splitting headache, a flat tire, and I just discovered my spare's flat too."

"We all get fed up with the game, honey," Hannah said with laugh. "Where you located right now?"

"Seabrook, on Waterfront Street."

"I'm in Kemah, starting up the bridge and heading in your direction. You close to Maybellene's Bar?"

"Right down the street."

"Forbes Painting Company you said?"

"Yeah."

"See you in a few minutes."

A beige, four-door Cadillac crunched into the oyster shell parking lot and pulled in beside Sedonia's Miata. A smiling, buxom woman in her fifties stepped out. Her silver hair was pulled up and neatly coiffed on top of her head. She wore blue jeans and a bright pink blouse with bold red lettering that read: "Cue-Ts."

Sedonia descended the stairs. "Hannah?"

"Pleased to meet you," the woman said. Then she looked over at Sedonia's car. "Glad we're not going anyplace in your buggy. I couldn't squeeze into that, any more than I could fit into a size 6."

Sedonia smiled. Hannah's accent didn't sound Texan—possibly Californian—but she had the amiable demeanor of a Gulf Coast resident. "My dad gave me the car when I graduated from U of H a couple of years ago," Sedonia said. "He assumed I was going to be playing golf professionally, not running his painting business. I really ought to trade it in on a pickup, but . . ."

"Naw, keep the sports car," Hannah said, "as long as you can climb into it. It's cute." Then she looked down at the flat tire. "You say your spare's flat too?"

"Yeah. I just called my neighborhood service station. They won't have anybody they can send over until tomorrow morning. I was about to call a cab when I saw you pull in."

"Where do you live?"

"Nassau Bay."

"C'mon. My team's playing at Carney's Billiards on El Camino Real. Your place is on the way. Plus, it'll give me a chance to talk you into substituting for us tonight."

The mention of pool reminded Sedonia that her cue stick was still in the trunk. She went around and got it, and then locked her car.

Moments later, as they headed up Waterfront Street, Hannah said, "I've got the only all-women team in the league."

Sedonia smiled. "That's where the name 'Cue-Ts' comes from, huh?"

Hannah gave a rueful nod. "My husband named us. At least that's better than his other suggestion: 'No Balls'."

Sedonia laughed. "How does your team do against the men's teams?"

"This last session, we finished in sixth place, in a twelve-team league. We needed one more strong player. From what Buster told me about your game, I was hoping I'd found her."

"I've been playing terrible."

"We all go through slumps."

"This isn't a slump. I . . . choke in the clutch."

"Where you been playing?"

"Practicing at Buster's, and playing in icehouses and beer gardens."

"Gambling on bar-boxes?"

Sedonia nodded. "Buster says . . ." she began, but then didn't feel like repeating his views on women and competition.

Hannah glanced over at her. "Did he give you his spiel about women being 'too nice'?"

"Yeah. You've heard it too?"

Hannah responded with a wry smile and nod.

"Do you buy it?" Sedonia said.

Hannah didn't respond for a moment. Finally she sighed and said, "I hate to admit it, but whatever level of competition you get into—BCA, local tournaments, or even the pros—the top players invariably are men."

"Why's that? Pool's not a game that requires strength, just coordination."

"I honestly don't know why," Hannah said, "but I'm not ready to accept Buster's explanation. We're playing an all-men's team tonight. Why don't you substitute for us, and then *you* tell *me* what the difference is."

Sedonia smiled at Hannah's tenacity. She obviously was a woman who pursued what she wanted. "What do you do for a living?"

"Real estate."

"Figured you must be in sales."

"Okay," Hannah said with a laugh, "I'll quit pressing you." She turned off Todville Road and started up the feeder road that led to Highway 146.

Sedonia liked this woman. She regretted not being able to accommodate her, but maybe they could get together for lunch some time. It would be nice to have a female friend, other than the young women who hung out at the Bullfrog Club. "How long have you been playing pool?" she said.

"About fifteen years," Hannah replied. "Wish I'd have started earlier, but I've tried to make up for lost time. I play league pool on Tuesday and Thursday nights, and in weekend tournaments whenever I can."

"Sounds like you enjoy it."

Hannah nodded. "I'm also a director of the Hunter Classics Women's Tour."

"What's that?"

"Hunter Classics is a semipro organization that operates here in the Southwest. There are several regional tours around the country, but we're the oldest and largest. We've got about 250 members, playing in Texas, Arizona, New Mexico, Nevada, and Colorado. We hold four tournaments each year. Women who do well in our events can qualify to play on the WPBA tour."

"WPBA?"

"Women's Professional Billiard Association," Hannah said. "The women pros who play on TV."

"Oh, yeah. I've seen some of their matches. Matter of fact, that's what got me interested in pool in the first place."

"Most of those women qualified to play in the WPBA by winning at a regional level."

They'd arrived at Highway 146, and Hannah had to concentrate on merging in with the bumper-to-bumper traffic that was streaming down the steep Kemah-Seabrook bridge. Finally, a pickup truck pulling a small bay boat slowed to let them in.

Sedonia said, "Is tonight's league connected with the Hunter Tour?"

"Completely separate. Thousands of women play in BCA leagues all over the country. The better ones go on to play on regional tours, like our Hunter Classics. And the best of those qualify to try their luck in the WPBA."

Sedonia frowned. She should have investigated the WPBA more thoroughly. According to Hannah, it sounded as if all the icehouse and beer garden bullshit she'd gone through hadn't been necessary.

Sedonia took a deep breath. "Tell me about tonight's match . . . and who I'd be playing . . ."

* * *

Carney's Billiards stood a hundred yards off a busy intersection, hidden behind a large drugstore. The parking lot was almost full, but Hannah found an empty spot at the side of the building.

"How long's this place been here?" Sedonia said as they headed toward the entrance, cue cases under their arms.

"Don't know," Hannah said. "Couple of years, at least."

"I drive down Bay Area Boulevard all the time," Sedonia said, "but I've never noticed it stuck back here."

Two men, also with cue cases, stood waiting for them at the front door. Both appeared to be in their thirties. They were casually dressed in safari shorts, T-shirts, and sandals. One said, "What's up, Hannah?"

"Hi, Mike," she replied. "I saw on the schedule that we're playing you guys tonight."

"Uh-huh," he said. Both men eyed Sedonia with interest.

"This is our new addition," Hannah said. "Sedonia, meet Mike and Ray. Their team, 'The Force,' won the league championship last session."

"Hi," Sedonia said, as a wave of uncertainty swept over her. She didn't fully understand the concept of team pool, but apparently her first match would be against the strongest players in the league. *Damn that flat tire!*

Ray held open the door, and Sedonia and Hannah entered the poolroom. A rectangular bar stood just inside the door. Customers were lined up elbow to elbow, most dressed as if they'd arrived straight from work. The pool area lay off to the left; the two dozen tables were all occupied. Conversations throughout the room, punctuated by occasional shouts, all but drowned out the jukebox.

"We're playin' on tables No. 15 and 16 tonight," Mike told Hannah. Then he smiled at Sedonia. "See ya over there."

She responded with an uncertain nod.

"C'mon," Hannah said. "We're running a little late. I need to pick up a score sheet and get you signed up."

Sedonia followed her over to a table in the corner, where Hannah introduced her to the man and wife who operated the league. As Sedonia paid her $10 BCA fee and received her membership card, she stole glances at the players nearby. Most were men; however, there also were a few women. The attire was casual—most of the players wore shorts and T-shirts—except for table No. 16, where Hannah's three teammates wore matching bright pink "Cue-Ts" blouses.

As Hannah spoke with the league operators, Sedonia studied the game at the next table. Both players shot well, and she sensed an undercurrent of male competitiveness, despite good-natured bantering between them. She slowly shook her head. Why had she allowed herself to get talked into this?

Hannah interrupted her musing. "We'd better get over there," she said. "We're about to start."

Sedonia felt uncomfortable as she followed Hannah through the maze of pool tables. Players and spectators were crowded around each, even worse than at Willie O's the previous night. She wondered how the players could concentrate in such close quarters and in the midst of all this confusion.

They arrived at a counter that served tables No. 15 and 16. A grinning Mike told his teammates, "Here's the new 'cutie' I told you about."

Hannah told her team, "This is Sedonia. She'll be taking Melissa's place."

"Just for tonight," Sedonia interjected.

"At *least* for tonight," Hannah said.

An announcement over the P.A. system told players to wrap up their current practice game. League play would start promptly at 7:00. Sedonia felt flustered. She wasn't sure what was expected of her, and she hadn't had a chance to warm up.

Hannah quickly introduced the other three members of the team. Flora was a heavyset Latina. She smiled and shook Sedonia's hand with a firm grip. Vicky was an attractive blond who, until Sedonia arrived, had been the center of male attention. She gave Sedonia a reserved nod. Cissy was slight, to the point of appearing anorexic. Her eyes darted with nervous intensity. It took Sedonia a moment to remember where she'd seen Cissy before. She'd been playing in the women's tournament at Champ's Billiards, that Sunday afternoon when Sedonia had first met Emilio.

As Cissy shook Sedonia's hand, she asked Hannah, "Do I play first?"

Hannah pulled up a stool and placed the score sheet on the counter. Then she looked at Sedonia. "You nervous?"

"Yeah," Sedonia admitted.

Hannah made an entry on the score sheet, then said, "I'm going to have you lead off on table No. 16. When you're nervous, it's good to get that first game out of the way."

"But I don't know the rules . . ."

"It's just 'call pocket' Eight-Ball. But you don't have to call a shot if it's obvious. There are a few other rules you need to know, but I'll explain them as you go."

Sedonia frowned. Before she could reply, however, Mike interrupted. "Looks like it's me and you in the first game. Y'all are the home team tonight, so I rack and you break."

Hannah pulled a small can of Johnson's Baby Powder from her cue case and set it on the counter. "Use some of this," she told Sedonia, "if your hands get sweaty."

As Sedonia screwed her cue stick together, she tried to figure out what Hannah had said about "call pocket." Call any shot that wasn't obvious? That must be it.

Mike finished racking the balls and said, "Good luck."

"Uh . . . you too," Sedonia said with an uncertain nod, not sure if he was being courteous or sarcastic. She looked about the room for a house cue to break with, but then decided the hell with it. She'd use her custom cue and get this damned game underway.

As she placed the cue-ball close to the right rail, her hand shook. Then as she leaned down to break, she felt a muscle in her right calf began to jump. Could the other players see it through her jeans? She remembered to bend her right knee slightly, and the muscle relaxed. Suddenly the unwanted recollection of having jumped the cue-ball off the table at Chug's Lounge flashed through her mind. She took a deep breath. *One, two, three . . . stroke.* She drove her stick forward with less force than she usually used on a break, to ensure she hit the cue-ball dead center. The balls scattered about the table, and the yellow 1-ball rolled slowly into the side pocket. The cue-ball stopped in the middle of the table, giving her a choice of either solids or stripes.

A sharp *crack!* from the next table momentarily drew her attention. Hannah had broken the rack on table No. 15. Sedonia turned to the work at hand, focusing on the options spread across dark green rectangle. The solid balls looked like a possible run-out. Her concentration partitioned out the confusion of the games going on around her, and her pre-match nervousness subsided.

"Seven in the side," she said. *One, two, three . . . stroke.* "Six down the rail." *One, two, three . . . stroke.* She called every shot, whether it was obvious or not. And finally, "Eight in the corner."

"Break-and-run!" her teammate, Flora, shrieked.

Sedonia looked up from the table. Her opponent, Mike, stared at her and slowly shook his head. "Nice run," he said in a grudging tone.

"Uh . . . thanks."

Hannah interrupted her game on the next table, and sidled over with a smile, "Pretty good start there, kiddo." Then she said to Cissy, "You're up next on No. 16. You break."

Flora and Vicky were seated at the counter. They gave Sedonia high-fives as she pulled up a stool and joined them. Seated nearby, Mike's teammates seemed now to look at her with newfound respect.

"When do I play again?" Sedonia said.

Flora laughed. "You're ready, huh?"

Sedonia flushed. But yes, she *was* ready. She wanted to get back out there, while she was in stroke.

"I'm goin' for beer," Vicky said. "What do you drink?"

Sedonia reached into her jeans pocket for some money. "Coors Light."

"It's on Hannah," Vicky said. "Our captain buys, whenever anyone has a B and R."

"B and R?"

"Break-and-run, baby," Flora said. "Break-and-run!"

Sedonia grinned, then turned her attention to the game on table No. 15. Hannah's stroke was slightly mechanical, and she played at a deliberate pace. Several times she played safeties, choosing to purposely miss a shot in order to leave her opponent in poor position. The game went back and forth, until her opponent finally made a difficult bank shot, and then went on to run the rest of the rack.

Hannah shook his hand and then joined her teammates at the counter. "At least I dragged it out long enough to score six points," she said.

"Points?" Sedonia said.

Hannah entered her game score, then explained, "The winning player gets ten points. The loser gets one point for each ball they make. The guy I just played got 10, and I got 6. Your break-and-run gave you 10 points, and you stuck Mike with a zero.

"So you add up everybody's score, and it's the team totals that count?"

"It's a little more complicated than that. Players have individual handicaps that get included—like in golf. But basically, it's like you say, team scores are what count."

Sedonia switched her attention to Cissy's game, just as the guy she was playing sank the 8-ball for the win. "Damn it," Cissy swore under her breath, but then walked over, shook his hand, and managed a terse, "Good game." She'd made only two balls, and Hannah entered the 10 to 2 loss on the score sheet.

While Flora and Vicky got ready for their games, Sedonia looked around at the matches in progress throughout the crowded poolroom. She smiled. Damn, this was fun!

However, a short while later, when Hannah told her she was up again, some of her pre-match nervousness returned. Maybe she'd just been lucky in that first game. Her hands again shook slightly as she racked the balls. Her next opponent was Ray, the other guy she'd met at the front door. He also wished her good luck, then made two solid balls on the break, and followed with four more before finally missing.

Sedonia's concentration and confidence returned as soon as she stepped back to the table. The stripes were evenly distributed, and her opponent had cleared most of the obstacles. Sedonia quickly pocketed three balls, then left herself in poor position. The blue 2-ball blocked her path to the maroon-striped 15-ball. As she chalked her cue stick, Hannah whispered, "Play a safety." Sedonia pretended she hadn't heard. She didn't believe in playing safeties. Raising the butt of her stick, she drove the cue-ball against the table slate. The cue-ball jumped the 2-ball and kissed the 15-ball into the side pocket.

"Damn!" Ray said. When Sedonia glanced over at him, he shook his head and added, "Helluva shot."

Sedonia smiled, thinking even "French Quarter" Jimmy would have been proud of that jump shot.

She ran the next three balls, and then the 8-ball. She'd won the game, 10 to 6. Ray congratulated her, and her teammates greeted her with high-fives and a second beer.

As Sedonia took a swallow, she realized she was feeling a slight buzz. It could have been the excitement, but more likely it was because she hadn't had anything to eat since the sandwich in Brad's truck, seven hours earlier. She asked Hannah, "Do they serve food here?"

Hannah shook her head. "Not even potato chips."

Sedonia took another swallow, and then chuckled.

"What's so funny?" Hannah said.

"I just . . . haven't had this much fun in a long time."

"Good," Hannah said with a smile. "You're up again, after Vicky. The guy you'll be playing next isn't as strong as the others."

Sedonia and her third opponent, a shy young man who looked as if he was barely out of his teens, wished each other good luck. As she leaned down to break, the beer buzz was more noticeable. She miscued slightly, and nothing went in. Most of the balls remained at the break end of the table.

The game took longer than the first two; however, she eventually won, 10 to 5. More high-fives and another beer awaited her. As Hannah entered her score, Sedonia looked over her shoulder. She didn't understand the handicapping system, but it appeared the two teams were playing evenly.

"I'm going for beer," Flora said.

"Do they have coffee?" Sedonia said.

Flora frowned. "I don't know."

"Make mine coffee if they do," Sedonia said. "I haven't had anything to eat since lunch."

Hannah overheard the exchange and gave Sedonia a nod of approval.

Before Sedonia's fourth game, Hannah called her aside and whispered, "This guy can be a jerk. Don't let him rattle you."

Her next opponent was bearded, burly, and probably in his mid thirties. As Sedonia racked the balls, he stood close by and watched. When she raised the wooden triangle and started to place it beneath the table, he leaned over, inspected the rack, and demanded, "Re-rack."

Sedonia looked at him with a frown.

"The seven's loose," he said. "Re-rack."

Sedonia looked down at the balls. All, including the 7-ball, were tightly racked. She remembered the first time she'd watched Emilio play, at Wayne's Icehouse. When he'd finally come off his stall, he'd also demanded a re-rack. Apparently it was gamesmanship, used by jerks to try to intimidate their opponents.

Sedonia carefully re-racked the balls, then said with an artificial smile. "How's that?"

Her opponent didn't reply. Instead he walked down to the break end of the table and made a production of placing the cue-ball precisely where he wanted it. He lunged forward on the break and there was a loud *crack!* The cue-ball had too much topspin; it hit the head ball, flew off to the side, and sent his teammates scattering. "Shit!" he shouted in disgust.

Sedonia retrieved the cue-ball and studied the layout, ignoring her opponent who was still fuming at the break end of the table. He'd made two solids and three stripes, but the solids looked to be the better choice. Sedonia politely asked him to step aside so she could shoot, then went to work. She called even the most obvious shots to ensure he'd have nothing to dispute. As she worked her way around the table, she could hear him in the background, griping to his teammates, but she managed to block him out. Finally, she looked over and said, "Eight in the corner."

He responded with a curt nod. Then after the 8-ball disappeared, he managed a grudging, "Good game."

Sedonia pulled up a stool beside Hannah. "How we doing?"

"Thanks to your four wins," Hannah said, "we're down by just two points. So stay on coffee. It'll be great if we can start this session by knocking off The Force."

"Who do I play next?"

Hannah studied the score sheet. "We've played a little out of sequence. Looks now like you'll play the last game of the match against their best player, Max. He's a BCA master."

"What's a 'BCA master'?"

"That means he's won at least one major tournament at the national level."

Sedonia stole a glance down the counter. Max sat relaxed on a stool, forearms resting on his protruding paunch, watching the games in progress. He appeared to be in his late forties or early fifties and was at least 100 pounds overweight. However, his thick, neatly-combed hair and his color-coordinated brown slacks and tan polo shirt gave him a dapper appearance, in comparison to the casually dressed players throughout the room. He reminded Sedonia of the "Minnesota Fats" character in the pool movie, *The Hustler*. She wondered if Max intentionally cultivated this resemblance.

While her teammates completed their final games of the match, Sedonia tried to stay relaxed. Flora and Cissy each won by 10 to 7 scores, giving the Cue-Ts a four-point lead, with one game left to play.

Hannah turned to Sedonia. "You're up, and you break."

Sedonia felt her pulse accelerate.

Max racked the balls with the fluid dexterity of a Las Vegas card dealer. As he returned to his stool, he said with a friendly smile, "Good luck."

Sedonia wished him the same, then walked over to where her teammates were sitting and sprinkled some talcum powder on her bridge hand.

"Sedonia," Hannah whispered, "we're up by four. All you need to do is make seven balls."

Sedonia returned to the break end of the table, frowning. Seven balls? Let's see . . . they were ahead by four. Seven would have them ahead by eleven. And ten was the most Max could score if he won. She understood. Seven balls.

She chalked her cue stick, took a deep breath, and then leaned over the table. *One, two, three . . . stroke.* As she had done in the first game, she again struck the cue-ball with less than full force, to ensure a solid hit. The balls scattered, but most stayed at the break end of the table, and none found a pocket.

Max heaved himself off his stool. He delicately chalked the tip of his inlaid custom cue, and then shot the maroon-striped 15-ball into the side pocket. The blue-striped 10-ball could be made in the corner; however, the other stripes were in a cluster. Sedonia watched with interest to see how he would try to break them out to get position for the following shot, after he made the 10-ball.

"Safety," Max said, then shot the 10-ball into the corner. He walked over and sat back down on his stool.

Sedonia frowned, then heard Hannah say, "It's your shot, honey."

Sedonia turned to her. "But he made a ball."

"He called a safety," Hannah said. "It's your shot next, even though he made it."

Sedonia shook her head. What a chicken-shit way to play! She walked around the table, looking for a makeable shot. Max had purposely left the cue-ball where she had no direct path to any of her solid balls. If she failed to hit one, he'd get ball-in-hand and be able to place the cue-ball anywhere on the table. This undoubtedly was what he'd intended when he'd chosen to play a safety.

Sedonia saw only one remote chance to hit one of her balls. The orange 5-ball was to her left, two feet away from the near corner pocket. To hit it, she'd have to send the cue-ball the length of the table, kick it off the end rail, and hope it hit the 5-ball on its return trip.

"Five in the corner," she told Max, though she had no real hope of making the shot. She just wanted to hit the 5-ball to avoid giving him ball-in-hand.

She took a deep breath and focused on an imaginary spot on the far rail. *One, two, three . . . stroke*. The cue-ball rolled down the table, kicked off the spot where she'd aimed, then started its return trip. Sedonia's eyes widened. *Don't tell me!*

The cue-ball kissed the 5-ball at precisely the correct angle, and knocked it into the corner pocket. Her teammates let out simultaneous shrieks. Sedonia suppressed her surprise at having made the shot. She didn't have time to celebrate; the cue-ball again had come to rest in the problem area. This time, however, she had a thin cut on the red 3-ball into the side pocket. She lined up and told herself to hit it softly. Her stroke felt good, but the 3-ball drifted slightly to the left, hit the far tit, and died directly in front of the pocket. *Damn it!*

Max returned to the table. He made three balls, but then he left himself with too straight a shot on the green-striped 14-ball. He didn't have the angle he wanted to break out his other two balls, which were frozen together. He turned to Sedonia and said, "Safety." Then he made the 14-ball, and left the cue-ball sitting against the rail.

Sedonia paced around the table. For her team to win the match, she needed to make all six of her remaining solids. Max had left the cue-ball where she only had two possibilities: she could play a safety on the yellow 1-ball, which she could hit but not make; or she could kick at the red 3-ball, which still sat on the edge of the side pocket.

She lined up for the kick shot and selected an imaginary spot on the far rail. *One, two, three . . . stroke*. The cue-ball hit where she'd aimed, kicked back, and rolled toward the 3-ball. As it crossed the middle of the table, Sedonia winced. She'd hit it too hard! The cue-ball tapped in the 3-ball, then followed it into the side pocket. Her teammates groaned. She'd given Max ball-in-hand.

He rose from his stool, and made quick work of the remaining two stripes. Then called and made the 8-ball in the side. He'd won the game, 10 to 2, and his team had won the match.

While his teammates celebrated, Max extended his hand. "Good game."

Sedonia quickly shook his hand, but was too irked at his having played safeties to risk a reply. Crestfallen, she walked over to her teammates. "Sorry," she said with a rueful shake of her head.

"Nothing to apologize for," Hannah said. "You played great tonight."

"Yeah," Flora said. "Without you, we wouldn't even have been close." Cissy and Vicky nodded their concurrence.

Sedonia unscrewed her stick.

"We're going to stay and play some," Cissy said. "Want to join us?"

"No thanks," Sedonia said as she slipped her stick into its case.

Hannah said, "Their captain and I have to write up the official score sheet. You can wait for me at the bar, if you like. Then I'll give you a ride home."

Sedonia nodded, and headed across the room. As she approached the bar, she was surprised to see Buster sitting there, grinning at her.

"What are you doing here?" she said.

"Checking out the competition." Then he added, "Naw, actually I came by to see how you did tonight."

Sedonia gave him an annoyed look. Had he intended all along for her to join Hannah's team?

The young brunette working behind the bar set a Coors Light in front of Sedonia. "It's on him," she said.

"Thanks," Sedonia said. "After that last game, I need a beer."

Buster chuckled. "I saw those two safeties Max put on you. He's tough."

"He's chicken-shit," she muttered.

"He wants to win," Buster said.

Sedonia shot him another annoyed look. She wasn't in the mood for another dose of Buster's pool wisdom. "You were supposed to help me sell my stick," she said. "Instead, you set it up where Hannah could talk me into playing tonight."

Buster looked down for a moment, as if embarrassed, then looked up and said, "Listen . . . when you left my place this morning . . . I felt bad. Like I'd . . . discouraged you, or something."

"You did discourage me," she said. "But you just told me the way it is."

He shook his head. "I also once told you not to pay too much attention to what anybody tells you. And that included me."

Hannah came over and interrupted them. "That's some player you got for me," she told Buster.

"I told you she was strong," Buster said.

Sedonia looked back and forth between them. They had her outnumbered. Someone tapped her on the shoulder. She turned; it was Max.

"You shot good tonight, kid," he said.

"You shot . . . safe tonight, Max," Sedonia said, an edge to her voice.

"All part of the game," he said with an unconcerned smile. "All part of the game." Then he told Hannah, "See y'all next week," and headed for the front door, cue case under his arm.

"If playing safeties like that is 'all part of the game'," Sedonia told Hannah and Buster, "then I don't want any part of it."

"Ever hear of Vivian Villarreal?" Hannah said.

Sedonia shook her head.

"The 'Texas Tor-nado'," Buster drawled. "Outta San An-ton-io."

Hannah nodded. "She's one of the top women pros on the WPBA tour. Hates defense. Insists on playing fast and loose, just like you do."

"And she's good?" Sedonia said.

"Purty damned good," Buster interjected, then added, "for a woman." He flinched when Hannah punched him in the shoulder.

Hannah told Sedonia, "You scored 42 out of a possible 50 points, against the best team in the league. I'd like you to be a permanent member of the Cue-Ts. Your game's fine, as is."

Sedonia hesitated.

Hannah pressed, "We'd just need to get you a shirt. What size are you?"

Sedonia looked down at Hannah's bright pink blouse and slowly shook her head. After growing up as a tomboy, maturing as a high school jock, and blossoming into a world-class golfer, she couldn't believe she was now considering becoming a "Cue-T."

"Size 10," she said.

Part II

Chapter 7

Sedonia smiled as she stepped through the doorway of Carney's Billiards, carrying her cue case. Crystal, the afternoon barmaid, already had a Coors Light and a tray of balls waiting on the counter for her. For several months, Sedonia had played league pool every Thursday night at Carney's, and the staff now considered her a regular customer. Sedonia enjoyed the notoriety she'd established here, as well as at Buster's Billiards, where she still practiced most afternoons.

"Saw you pull up," Crystal said.

Sedonia set her cue case on table No. 1 and looked around. The other tables were unoccupied, except for one in the corner, where two elderly men were playing. Sedonia recognized one of them; he was a regular at Buster's.

Sedonia walked over to the bar. "It's quiet in here this afternoon."

"Yeah, it's been slow all day," Crystal said.

Sedonia frowned. "Lemme see your tongue."

Crystal grinned, then opened her mouth and showed Sedonia two small metal balls, one on top and one underneath her tongue, connected by a thin rod. "I got it, Monday," Crystal said. The miniature barbell slid up and down as she spoke.

Sedonia responded with a mock shudder. "Can't believe you did that! Did it hurt?"

"A little bit, when they pierced it. But it doesn't bother me now."

"What does your boyfriend think?"

"Billy *likes* it."

Sedonia slowly shook her head. Crystal was a cute nineteen, and her boyfriend was a slovenly thirty. Sedonia decided not to press for details as to why Billy found oral jewelry pleasing. "Hannah and the rest of our team will be here in a little while," she said. "We need to practice. We've got a tournament here tomorrow."

"I know," Crystal said with a rueful expression. "Boss told me I gotta work. Billy's pissed. He wanted to go out of town tonight, but I gotta open here in the morning."

"Sorry about that," Sedonia said with a smile, then turned and carried her beer and the tray of balls over to table No. 1.

The elderly man she knew from Buster's waved to her.

"How's it going, Elmer?" she called over.

"Don't tell Buster you saw me," he said with a sheepish expression. "We come here for the free pool on Friday afternoons."

"I won't tell him," she said.

"Wanna play with us?" he said. "We'll work you into a ring game."

"Another time," Sedonia called back. She'd played against him before. He was a nice old guy, but at least half the time he played safeties. Defensive play not only took the fun out of the game, but continually having to shoot out of impossible positions eventually caused her to get out of stroke.

For the next half-hour she went through her practice routine, which after several months had become a ritual. First, she reviewed fundamentals by practicing long shots, both down the rails and diagonally across the table. When she was assured the mechanics of her stance, bridge, grip, and stroke were coordinated, she then worked on position—shooting one ball and trying to get perfect shape on whichever one she wanted to shoot next. Then she practiced specific shots that had given her trouble in recent games. Today, it was having an object ball frozen against one rail and the cue-ball frozen against another. Then she worked on thin cuts, where controlling cue-ball speed always was a challenge. And finally, she racked the balls for Eight-Ball, and shot as if it were an actual game. Her objective was to make one suit and then the other, without missing—a double run-out. More than half the time she was successful.

Sedonia was lining up on the 8-ball, when the front door opened and Hannah's voice rang out, "Damn, woman! Do you *live* here?"

Sedonia sank the 8-ball, then looked over and said, "Just getting in a little practice."

"Yeah, like you need it," Hannah said. She set her cue case on the next table, opened a zippered compartment, and pulled out a folded sheet of paper. "Final stats from the winter session."

Sedonia unfolded the sheet and checked the league standings. "So we finished in second place, two games out of first, huh?"

"Yeah, we almost caught 'em. First time in three years that The Force has had any real competition. Anyway, we had 'em looking over their shoulders."

"Would have been nice to have won that trip to Las Vegas for the BCA nationals," Sedonia said.

"At least we're top seeded for the runner-up tournament tomorrow," Hannah said. "All we gotta do is win that, and we're headin' for Vegas too."

Sedonia returned the sheet without replying. Winning an eleven-team tournament would be tough.

Hannah said, "Did you notice the individual standings?"

Sedonia took back the sheet and looked down at the bottom. "I beat Max?"

"You both averaged 47 out of 50. They had to carry the figures out three decimal places to see who won. You beat him by .003. This is the first time Max hasn't been the top shooter since the league was formed."

Sedonia suppressed a smile. Modesty aside, she was pleased at having won the individual scoring title, particularly having edged out a BCA master player.

Hannah said, "Flora and Vicky ought to be here in a few minutes."

"How about Cissy?"

Hannah gave a disgusted shake of her head. "Her doper boyfriend left a message on my recorder. Said she was sick. And she's the one who needs practice the most."

"She was really out of stroke last night," Sedonia said.

"You see the size of her pupils?" Hannah said. "They looked like 8-balls."

Sedonia nodded.

"I almost replaced her during the summer session," Hannah said. "But then she broke up with her boyfriend, and I thought she might get her act together. Instead, she moved back in with him. Also, about that time Melissa told me she was going to drop off the team, so I was already short one player." Hannah sighed. "Well, too late to do anything about it now. We'll just have to see how Cissy does tomorrow."

Their exchange was interrupted as Flora and Vicky burst through the door, boisterously demanding beer from Crystal. Hannah walked over to the bar and joined the banter.

Sedonia smiled as she pulled balls from the pockets and prepared to rack for the Cue-Ts' first practice game. A poolroom and friends: what a great way to spend an afternoon.

Saturday morning traffic moved slowly along El Camino Real. As Sedonia arrived at the intersection with Bay Area Boulevard, she saw the reason for the delay. Several Clear Lake High School girls, clad in cutoff blue jeans and tank tops, were flitting between the cars, holding up homemade placards that advertised a drill-team fund-raiser. A number of motorists, most of whom were male, were filing into the nearby bank parking lot to take advantage of the $3 carwash.

Sedonia finally made it through the intersection, and pulled into the Carney's Billiards parking lot. The tournament wasn't scheduled to start until 11:00 a.m.; however, she'd arrived an hour early, hoping to get in a few practice games. There were no other cars out front and the windows were dark. Apparently Crystal hadn't arrived yet.

As Sedonia reached over for the McDonald's sack on the passenger seat, she was surprised to see Cissy's battered Ford Pinto pull in beside her. Cissy got out, holding a large Styrofoam coffee cup, and came over to Sedonia's car.

"Have you had breakfast?" Sedonia said as Cissy climbed in.

"No. I don't eat in the morning."

Sedonia checked Cissy's eyes; the pupils were normal size. "You'd better eat something," Sedonia said. "They don't serve food here, remember? And once we start playing, we may not get a chance to go out for lunch. Have an Egg McMuffin. I've got two."

Cissy hesitated, then took one. As she looked down at the sandwich and peeled back the wrapper, her gaunt face reminded Sedonia of an orphan on a Save the Children poster.

"Sorry I didn't make the practice yesterday," Cissy said between nibbles.

Sedonia saw no reason to belabor the past. "Crystal's supposed to work today," she said. "Hopefully she'll get here early enough that we can get in a few games before the tournament starts."

As if on cue, a rusty pickup truck pulled into the parking lot. Crystal climbed out and barely had time to close the door behind her, before her boyfriend pulled away, without so much as a wave.

Crystal had a hurt look on her face as she watched him speed up El Camino Real. Then she gave Sedonia a quick wave of recognition, and unlocked the poolroom door.

Sedonia shook her head. Where did these women find these guys?

Cissy folded the wrapper around her half-eaten sandwich and opened the car door. "I'm gonna play good today," she said, seemingly as much to herself as to Sedonia.

Crystal was flipping on the interior lights when Sedonia and Cissy entered. An air-handler started with a loud clunk, and the jukebox lit and began to blare. Crystal handed Sedonia a tray of pool balls and said, "Y'all want some coffee? I'll put some on."

"I do," Cissy said.

Sedonia nodded that she'd like some too, and then walked over to table No. 1. As she racked for a practice game, she wondered if Cissy physically would be able to hold up all day and possibly well into the night. If the Cue-Ts were going to win the trip to the BCA national tournament, they'd all need to be at their best. And as tight as money was at Sedonia's company, she couldn't afford the trip to Las Vegas, unless all expenses were paid.

Activity in the parking lot drew her attention. Several cars and pickups had arrived, and others were filing in. For the first time in months, Sedonia felt pre-match butterflies.

It was almost 1:00 in the afternoon before the announcement finally came over the poolroom speakers: "Cue-Ts and Balls of Fire, you're up on tables No. 11 and 12." Sedonia and her teammates picked up their cue cases and moved from the bar where they'd waited for the past two hours. They'd received a bye in the first round, in recognition of their having finished second in the league standings during the regular session. The bye was an advantage, in that it gave them an uncontested win; however, it also meant that now they'd have to play a team who had already dealt with its early jitters and had won a match.

At tables No. 11 and 12, Hannah gathered her team around her. "Balls of Fire finished fifth this session, so we can't take 'em for granted." She turned to Sedonia. "I've got you playing first on table No. 11. Get us off to a good start."

Sedonia nodded, trying to show confidence to her teammates, which at this moment she didn't actually feel. Just another game, she tried to tell herself. But doubt remained in the back of her mind. This was for a trip to the Las Vegas nationals.

Her opponent, a portly bearded man in his forties, flipped a coin for the break, and Sedonia won. As she waited for him to rack the balls, she chalked the tip of a house cue and watched Cissy get ready for her game on the next table. Sedonia had to smile. As nervous as Sedonia felt, she was tranquil compared to the always-agitated Cissy, who now had been drinking coffee for the past two hours. Sedonia glanced over at her other teammates. Hannah was busy making entries on the score sheet. Flora and Vicky were ordering their third beers.

"Good luck," Sedonia's opponent said.

Sedonia turned back to the table and replied, "Good luck." As she placed the cue-ball close to the side rail, she noted her hand was steady. And as she leaned down to break, her body felt like a coiled spring. It reminded her of the pent-up emotions before playing in major golf championships. The thought of past successes restored her confidence. *One, two, three . . . stroke!* She drove the cue-ball forward with full force and heard a resounding *crack!* The red 3-ball and the maroon 7-ball found corner pockets, and the rest of the solids were spread for a possible run-out. Sedonia smiled. It was like hitting a 275-yard drive off the first tee, straight down the middle.

Six shots later, she called and made the 8-ball in the side pocket.

"Guess that's the reason you led the league," her opponent said. "Good game."

"Thanks," Sedonia said. Then she joined her teammates at the nearby counter, where they gave her high-fives.

"That's the kinda start we needed!" Hannah said.

Sedonia looked down at the score sheet as Hannah entered a "W" by her name and an "L" by her opponent's, instead of a "10" and a "0."

"No point system?" Sedonia said.

Hannah shook her head. "These tournaments are set up like it'll be in Las Vegas. No point system and no handicaps. Just a race-to-13."

"Good," Sedonia said. 'Scratch play' would be to the Cue-Ts' advantage. During the regular season, their opponents had received 20 to 40 handicap points, due to her high average. Now she felt her team had a good chance to win this tournament, if Cissy didn't fly apart, and if Flora and Vicky would slow down their beer consumption.

A little after six that evening, Sedonia and her teammates exchanged high-fives after winning their second match of the tournament. They'd won both easily, by scores of 13 to 5 and 13 to 2.

As Sedonia unscrewed her stick, Flora and Vicky headed toward the bar with two guys from the team they'd just beaten. Cissy still sat hunched on a stool, gnawing on a fingernail that was already bitten down to the quick. Of the total of seven games the Cue-Ts had lost during their two matches, Cissy had lost four.

Sedonia walked over and placed a hand on her shoulder. "C'mon."

Without replying, Cissy got up and followed Sedonia to the front of the room, her eyes fixed on the floor as she walked.

The league operator ran the tournament from a pool table that had been reserved near the bar. A large flowchart covered most of the table. On the chart, one set of brackets extended to the right, showing the teams who were undefeated. The other set of brackets extended to the left, showing the teams who were playing with one loss.

As he entered the Cue-Ts' latest win, Sedonia asked, "How long before we play again? I'd like to go get something to eat."

He studied the chart for a moment. "With your bye and your two wins, you ladies have won the winners' side. It'll probably take a couple of hours before the one-loss side is decided. Then you'll play them for the championship. So if you leave here, plan on being back no later than eight o'clock."

Sedonia turned to Hannah, "Want to get something to eat too?"

Hannah glanced over to the bar, where Flora and Vicky were about to order yet another beer. "Good idea," Hannah said, "for all of us." Then she called over to Flora and Vicky, "Hold up on those beers."

"I'll wait for y'all here," Cissy said.

"C'mon with us," Sedonia said. "You need to eat too."

Cissy avoided eye contact. "My boyfriend's supposed to come by. He'll bring me . . . something."

Sedonia and Hannah exchanged glances.

Flora and Vicky came over, and Hannah told them, "We're gonna go eat." Then she placed a hand on Cissy's shoulder and gently pushed her toward the door.

An hour and a half later, the Cue-Ts returned from the nearby Taco Bell. As Sedonia entered the poolroom, she noticed that the crowd had thinned out. Most of the players who had been eliminated from the competition had already left, and the regular Saturday night customers hadn't yet arrived.

As she and her teammates headed over to the league operator's table, a familiar voice called out from the bar, "Heard you gals are kickin' ass."

Sedonia was surprised to see Buster standing there. She walked over and said, "What brings you here?"

"I called to see how y'all were makin' out, and Crystal told me you were about to win this thing. Figured I could get away from my place, long enough to watch my star pupil play."

"Hey," Sedonia said with a smile, "there's enough pressure today. Don't add to it with that 'star pupil' stuff."

"Just go take care of business," he said.

Sedonia nodded, and then walked over to join her teammates at the league operator's table. As she arrived, Cissy looked past her and muttered, "Oh shit." A man sitting close to Buster was scowling in their direction. Cissy pushed past Sedonia and hurried over to talk to him.

Sedonia asked Hannah, "Is that her boyfriend?"

"Yeah. Eddy Lane. He's a piece of crap . . . really bad for her."

While Hannah checked in with the league operator and Flora and Vicky ordered beers, Sedonia watched the exchange between Cissy and her boyfriend. She couldn't hear what they were saying, but Cissy was standing stoop-shouldered, like a waif in front of an angry parent. Her boyfriend's dissipated appearance made his age difficult to estimate; however, he had to be at least 20 years older than Cissy.

The P.A. system clicked on. "Okay, folks," the league operator said, "we've got the final match of the evening. For the tournament championship and the all-expense-paid-trip to the Las Vegas nationals, we've got the top-seeded Cue-Ts, who won the winners' bracket, going against the second-seeded Randy's Cabaret, who won the one-loss bracket. The championship will be two race-to-7s."

Sedonia glanced over at the bar. Cissy's boyfriend dug something out of his pocket and handed it to her. Sedonia couldn't see what it was.

The league operator concluded over the P.A., "Players, report to table No. 1. We'll start the championship match in five minutes."

Sedonia glanced back at the bar. Cissy said something to her boyfriend, then turned and hurried toward the ladies room. Sedonia handed her cue case to Hannah and said, "Take this over there for me. I'm gonna see about Cissy."

Max, the BCA master player, was sitting at the far end of the bar. As Sedonia hurried past, he said, "Good luck in the finals. We'd like to see you ladies make it to Las Vegas too."

Sedonia paused long enough to thank him, then continued down a short hallway that led to ladies room. She pushed through the door, just as Cissy leaned over a sink so she could put her mouth underneath the faucet. Sedonia quickly looked around; they were the only people in the room.

"Cissy! What are you doing?"

Cissy straightened up. "Taking . . . an aspirin."

"Lemme see."

"Why?"

"Lemme see!"

Cissy reluctantly opened her fist. The pill was white, but larger than an aspirin and scored with an "X" so it could be divided into quarters.

"What is it?" Sedonia said.

Cissy didn't reply.

"Tell me what it is!" Sedonia demanded.

Cissy's expression turned sullen. "Crank."

"Amphetamine?"

"I need something! I'm not playing worth a shit."

"You don't need that. Get rid of it."

"It's none of your business!"

Sedonia sighed. "C'mon, Cissy . . ."

Cissy bent down, took a mouthful of water, and popped the pill into her mouth. As she swallowed, she looked at Sedonia with defiance. Then she blinked and her expression changed to one of chagrin.

Sedonia gave a disapproving shake of her head. There was nothing she could do. She turned and went back into the poolroom.

Hannah gave her an inquiring look as she approached. "Cissy okay?"

"I don't know. She . . . took something."

"Damn . . . on an empty stomach too. She only ate part of one taco at dinner."

"Nothing we can do about it now," Sedonia said. "Who's leading off for us?"

"You. Since it's race-to-7, we'll just be playing on one table. And I'll move Cissy to fifth. That'll reduce the number of games she plays."

Sedonia pulled her cue stick out of its case and began screwing it together. Flora and Vicky were laughing with a couple of the guys they were about to play. The Randy's Cabaret team was all men, in their twenties and thirties. They wore matching purple shirts, with black lettering and the silhouette of a reclining nude woman. Sedonia wondered what would inspire men to advertise that they frequented an infamous local topless club.

Cissy returned from the ladies room. She avoided eye contact with Sedonia and began screwing her stick together.

Hannah told her, "Sedonia's leading off. You're playing fifth."

"Why?" Cissy demanded.

"Because I said so," Hannah said.

Cissy gave Sedonia an accusing glare, then angrily plopped down on a stool to wait for her game.

"Flora! Vicky!" Hannah said. "We're about to start." They reluctantly disengaged themselves from their flirtations with the opposing team.

Sedonia lost the flip of the coin for the first break. As she racked the balls, she tried to collect her thoughts. She needed to quit worrying about the condition of her teammates, and simply concentrate on getting them off to a good start. Her first opponent would be Randy's Cabaret's best player, a muscular young man who had finished sixth in the individual player rankings.

Sedonia lifted the wooden triangle from the balls, and said, "Good luck."

"Good luck," he replied, then leaned down and hit the cue-ball with a sledgehammer-like break. Three balls found pockets, and the rest spread across the table. Sedonia grimaced; it looked like a run-out. But maybe she'd get lucky, and he'd miss.

He didn't. Sedonia walked over and shook his hand. "Nice break-and-run."

"Thanks," he replied, then went over and accepted the shouts and high-fives of his teammates.

Sedonia glanced over to the bar, where Buster was standing. He gave her a reassuring nod. His having come here to watch her play, however, added to the pressure she was feeling.

Flora was up next. She was always carefree and jovial, but now after an afternoon of beer drinking and socializing, she seemed downright giddy. She was matched against a guy she'd been flirting with, and he beat her easily.

Vicky tried to get serious when it was her turn to play, but she got careless with the cue-ball and accidentally knocked in the 8-ball prematurely, for an automatic loss. The Cue-Ts were behind, 3 to 0.

"C'mon, Hannah!" Sedonia called out. "It's up to you. Stop the bleeding!"

Hannah responded with her usual methodical game, resorting to frequent safeties in order to leave her opponent in poor position. The game went back and forth until she finally got ball-in-hand, and then made the 8-ball in the corner.

Cissy jumped to her feet. "I'm up!"

Her opponent, a meek looking guy wearing glasses, grinned as she hurried to the break end of the table. "Uh . . . it's my break," he said.

Cissy gave him an impatient look, then rushed to the other end. She threw the balls into the rack, made a haphazard effort at placing the head ball on the spot, and then threw the wooden triangle under the table.

Sedonia could see from where she and Hannah were sitting that the rack wasn't straight and the balls weren't tight. She looked over at Hannah and whispered, "Cissy's wired."

Cissy's opponent checked the balls. "Uh . . . re-rack, please," he said, sounding apologetic.

"What do you mean 're-rack'?" Cissy said, a pugnacious expression on her face.

Hannah stood up and walked over to the table. "Re-rack, Cissy," she said.

"This is my game! Not yours."

"I'm the team captain," Hannah said, obviously struggling to quell her annoyance. "Re-rack the balls."

Cissy placed her hands on her hips, then shook her head and reached down and retrieved the triangle. "Re-rack, they want. Re-rack they get." As she fumbled with the balls, she continued to chatter to herself. When she lifted the triangle, the maroon 7-ball moved at least a half-inch from the other balls. She seemed not to notice.

"Cissy—," Hannah began.

"That's okay," Cissy's opponent interjected. "Let's play."

Hannah gave him a nod of appreciation, and then returned to her seat.

He broke and failed to make a ball. Cissy hurried to the table. Without studying the layout, she lined up on a straight-in shot on the red 3-ball, and missed it. Her opponent returned to the table. He too decided to take the solids, and made three before missing. Cissy rushed back to the table and again didn't study the layout; she simply lined up on the 3-ball.

Sedonia instinctively started to warn her, but the words froze in her throat. Coaching while a teammate was shooting was against league rules.

Cissy's opponent called out, "You've got the—"

However, she fired the 3-ball into the side, and began looking around the table for her next shot.

"You've got the stripes," her opponent said. "I've got the solids."

"What?" Cissy said.

"Sorry," he said, walked over and then picked up the cue-ball. Cissy's having hit the wrong suit gave him ball-in-hand.

"You should have told me," Cissy said belligerently.

"He tried to," Hannah said. "Come over here and sit down."

Cissy finally moved away from the table, but stood nearby, continuing to mutter that someone should have told her. Her opponent made quick work of the remaining three solids, and then called and made the 8-ball. The Cue-Ts now trailed, 4 to 1, in the first race-to-7.

Sedonia shook her head in frustration as she prepared to break for her second game. She'd dedicated the past several months to practicing and playing pool, just so she could compete in Las Vegas. And now all the time and effort she'd expended were about to be wasted, because Cissy, Flora, and Vicky weren't in condition to play.

Her next opponent was the player who had just beaten Cissy. He made it a point to ensure he gave Sedonia a tight rack. She took out her frustration on the cue-ball, driving it as hard as she could into the rack. For the first time in several weeks, she felt a warning twinge from her right shoulder. Balls scattered about the table, and two stripes found pockets. Sedonia studied the table, determining the sequence in which she planned to shot the balls. The solids looked to be the better suit, a possible run-out.

She began to shoot, and suddenly felt as if she were in autopilot. Rather than studying each shot, she seemed to react to the entire table. As she worked her way through the balls, the thought repeatedly flashed into her mind that she was playing too quickly. However, her stroke was flawless and each shot left her in perfect position on the next. It seemed that only seconds had passed before her opponent and her teammates were congratulating her on a break-and-run.

Sedonia took a seat and tried to figure out what had come over her. Finally she gave up trying to understand it. She just hoped her decisive win would inspire better efforts from her teammates.

Flora and Vicky were serious when they returned to the table for their second games, but each lost. The Cue-Ts now trailed, 6 to 2. Hannah would have to win her game, and then Cissy somehow would need to pull herself together. Sedonia looked around. Cissy was at the bar, talking mile-a-minute to her sleazy boyfriend. Sedonia shook her head in exasperation, and then returned her attention to the next game.

Hannah called on all her pool-playing guile and repeatedly resorted to safeties, but her opponent was too strong. The Cue-Ts had lost the first set, 7 to 2.

"Okay folks," the league operator announced over the P.A. system. "There'll be a five-minute break, and then we'll begin the final race-to-7."

Flora and Vicky came over to where Sedonia and Hannah were standing. "I played like shit," Flora said.

"Me too," Vicky said.

"Table No. 2 is open," Hannah said. "You two hit some practice balls. And no more beer!"

As Flora and Vicky hurried over to table No. 2, Sedonia said, "What are we going to do about Cissy?"

"I'll talk to her," Hannah said.

At the bar, Hannah stopped for a moment to speak to Buster, and then moved over to where Cissy and her boyfriend were seated.

Sedonia turned her attention to table No. 2. She wanted to hit a few balls herself, but Flora and Vicky needed the practice more than she did.

Suddenly Cissy's shrill voice carried from the bar. "You can't do that!"

Sedonia turned in time to see Cissy jump to her feet and shove Hannah, who stumbled backward. Buster caught Hannah in time to keep her from falling to the floor.

Sedonia ran to the bar and positioned herself in front of Cissy. "What the hell are you doing!"

Cissy made a move toward Sedonia, but her boyfriend grabbed her by the shoulders. Cissy's face was livid. "She can't kick me off the team!"

Hannah regained her composure and stepped beside Sedonia. "She's in no condition to play."

"That's bullshit!" Cissy's boyfriend snarled.

"No!" Sedonia said. "*You're* the bullshit. You're the one responsible for the condition she's in!"

"Fuck you," he muttered, and then shoved Cissy toward the front door.

"No!" Cissy wailed. "I gotta play!" She was still protesting when he pushed her through the doorway. A moment later, tires screeched as they roared out of the parking lot.

Hannah looked at Sedonia with a pained expression. "I'm sorry."

"You're not responsible for that."

"Yes I am. I'm the captain."

The league operator, Flora and Vicky, and the entire Randy's Cabaret team gathered around. The league operator said to Hannah, "Looks like you lost a player."

"I'm afraid so."

"You forfeiting the match?"

When Hannah hesitated, Sedonia spoke up. "Just Cissy's games. We'll go with four players."

Hannah looked at Sedonia for a moment, and then turned to the league operator. "We'll play the same lineup as last time. But whenever Cissy's up, Randy's will automatically get a win.

The league operator turned to the other team captain. "That's within the rules."

"Okay," the Randy's captain said with an unconcerned shrug. "Let's play."

As the two teams headed back to table No. 1, Sedonia heard the player who had beaten Cissy ask his captain, "Why don't we make it fair, and just use four players ourselves?"

"The hell with that!" his captain replied. "We're playin' for Las fuckin' Vegas. If those women can't keep a team together, that's *their* problem, not ours."

His words stung, but Sedonia silently agreed with him. Her team had picked a hell of a time to fall apart.

As they arrived back at the table, Sedonia noticed the regular Saturday night crowd had begun to arrive during the previous set. A number of them now were taking vantage points nearby, so they could watch the tournament finale. She didn't like playing in such close quarters. The immediate area was almost as congested as that forgettable night at Willie O's.

Hannah came over and said, "You lead off again. Your break."

Randy's Cabaret again matched their strongest player against Sedonia in the first game. As she waited for him to rack the balls, she looked over at his teammates. Two were sharing a joke; they all looked relaxed and confident. Her opponent appeared almost smug as he lifted the wooden triangle and said, "Good luck."

"Good luck," she replied, then leaned down to break. She took a deep breath and thought, the hell with it! She drove the cue-ball into the rack as hard as she could. There was a stab of pain, but it was quickly forgotten when the orange 5-ball and the green 6-ball found corner pockets.

Sedonia studied possible sequences for shooting the remaining five solids. Three were makeable, but the other two were locked together and frozen against a rail. She didn't see any way to break them apart before she'd have to shoot them. The striped balls, however, offered a run-out possibility, even though there were two more of them. She determined the sequence in which she planned to shoot the stripes, and then went to work. As she methodically circled the table, pocketing them cleanly and leaving herself in perfect position for the next shot, she again experienced the unusual feeling that she was in autopilot, or watching someone else perform. Finally she said, "Eight in the side."

"That's good," her opponent said. He reached over and raked the 8-ball into the side pocket with his cue stick, not requiring her to shoot the game winning shot.

Sedonia walked around to the side pocket, put the 8-ball on the table where it had been, and fired it back into the side pocket. She'd had golf competitors concede putts early in a round, only to make her play them out when the match was on the line. She'd learned that conceding shots early, and then later requiring a person to make them, was a ploy intended to increase pressure.

Her opponent returned to where his teammates were sitting, without offering her the usual, "Good game."

As Flora stood up for her next game, her cue stick clattered to the floor. She dropped it again when she tried to pick it up. Sedonia had never seen Flora so nervous. "Relax," she told her. "Just do your best."

Flora never seemed to relax, but she did manage to grind out a win to give the Cue-Ts a 2 to 0 lead in games. Vicky also was serious when she took the table, but she lost after making only one ball. Then Hanna dropped a drawn-out game.

After the first round of the second set, including Cissy's forfeit, The Cue-Ts trailed 3 to 2 in the race-to-7.

Sedonia racked for her second game, and her opponent failed to make a ball on the break. Again she determined the sequence in which she intended to shoot her balls, and then methodically executed her plan without variation or second thoughts.

As the 8-ball disappeared in the corner pocket, her opponent said in a grudging tone, "Good shootin', lady."

"Thanks," she replied. She still didn't understand what was going on with her game, but she decided it was best not to risk analyzing it now. Whatever it was, she just hoped it wouldn't go away.

Flora's next opponent got careless and made the 8-ball prematurely, giving the Cue-Ts the lead, 4 to 3. Then Vicky followed by snapping out of her funk and grinding out a hard-fought win.

Hannah was up next, and she again controlled the tempo against a stronger player. The game lasted almost half an hour, and she managed to eke out the victory. Cissy's forfeit broke the Cue-Ts' four-game win streak, but still left them with a 6 to 4 lead in the race-to-7.

Sedonia returned to the table to break for her third game of the set. Her next opponent was a tall, pony-tailed guy in his thirties. This would be the first game between them, and his hands shook slightly as he racked the balls. Sedonia glanced down at the score sheet and saw he'd won only one of the four games he'd played. Although her team had a two-game lead in this set, she felt pressure to win now. Her teammates' play had been erratic; she needed to capitalize on this opportunity to tie the match at one set each.

"Good luck," he said.

"Good luck," she replied. As she leaned down to break, she remembered the shoulder twinge on her last break, and this time she hit the cue-ball with about three-quarter strength. The balls scattered, and for a moment it didn't look as if anything would fall, but then the yellow 1-ball rolled slowly toward the side pocket. It hesitated, then dropped.

Sedonia set aside the house stick she'd used on the break, and chalked the tip of her custom cue while she carefully planned her sequence of shots. Finally she took a deep breath and lined up on the purple 4-ball, down the rail. She told herself to concentrate on each shot this time, but the instant she bent over the table, she again seemed to go on autopilot. "Four in the side," she said. The 4-ball disappeared, and she had dead shape on the green 6-ball. "Six in the corner . . ." And finally, "Eight in corner."

The crowd broke into spontaneous applause. Sedonia looked up in surprise. She usually felt uncomfortable playing in front of a crowd, but this time she'd been unaware of their presence.

"Okay, folks!" the league operator shouted over the P.A. system. "It doesn't get any closer than this. Each team has won a race-to-7. For the tournament championship . . . and the trip to the Las Vegas nationals . . . there'll be a one game playoff. Race-to-1 . . . sudden death!"

A murmur went through the poolroom, and then there was shuffling of feet as more customers interrupted their own matches and came over to watch the dramatic final game. Spectators now circled table No. 1, four and five rows deep.

"Captains," the league operator continued, "chose the player you want to represent your teams.

Neither captain had to struggle with the decision. Sedonia had three break-and-runs and one rack-and-run in the five games she'd played. And Randy's strongest player had beaten her with a break-and-run of his own in the one game she'd lost. As well as both of them had played, the coin flip would be all-important.

The league operator placed a quarter on his thumbnail and smiled, obviously enjoying the drama of the moment. "Call it," he told Sedonia.

"Heads."

The coin flashed as it arched though the air, then landed on the green felt and rolled to a stop.

"Heads it is."

Sedonia walked down to the break end of the table and waited for her opponent to rack. He had a little difficulty removing the wooden triangle from the balls, as if his hands might be shaking. He gave her the perfunctory "Good luck."

"Good luck," Sedonia replied. But instead of breaking, on impulse she walked down to the other end of the table and inspected the balls. "Re-rack, please."

Her opponent returned to the table with a frown. "What's wrong with it?"

"Seven ball's loose," Sedonia said, although it wasn't. The first night she'd watched Emilio play at Wayne's Icehouse, he'd used this re-rack ploy to shark an opponent. And since then, she'd seen other players use it.

Her opponent gave her an exasperated glance, but then re-racked. When he lifted the triangle, the blue 2-ball moved. He slammed the triangle back down and re-racked a third time. Then he lifted the triangle again, and gave Sedonia an inquiring look.

Sedonia decided she'd pushed him enough, and returned to the break end of the table. *One, two, three . . . stroke!* A stab of shoulder pain, a loud *crack!* and the balls scattered about the table. Nothing fell.

Her opponent approached the table and studied the layout. From Sedonia's vantage point, the stripes appeared to be the better suit. Minutes passed before he finally called the yellow-striped 9-ball and began to shoot. Once underway, he continued to work slowly, analyzing each shot from several angles before taking it.

At five balls, Sedonia experienced the sinking feeling that he wasn't going to let her get back to the table. However, on his next shot, though he made the object ball, he left himself with an impossible angle on his one remaining stripe, the 12-ball, which was sitting close to the corner. Exasperated, he went over to where his teammates were sitting and took a swallow from his beer. Then he returned to the table and for several minutes studied the possibilities. Finally, he said, "Safety."

Sedonia moved forward on her stool, straining to see what kind of shot he was going to leave her. He shot the cue-ball softly and barely grazed his blue-striped 12-ball. The cue-ball rolled across the table, bounced off the side rail, then rolled back and came to rest behind the 12-ball. From where Sedonia was sitting, it didn't look good.

She reluctantly got to her feet and walked over for a closer look. Although she had seven solid balls on the table, he'd left her where she didn't have a direct path to any of them. And the cue-ball was so close to his 12-ball, that she couldn't attempt a jump shot without fouling and giving him ball-in-hand.

She desperately studied the table. One of her solids, the red 3-ball, was directly in front of the far corner pocket. She didn't have a direct path, or even a one-rail kick shot at it, but with hard left english, she thought she might be able to hit it with a two-rail kick. She shook her head. She'd not only have to take into account two angles, but also the spin and the speed she needed to put on the cue-ball. She didn't like the shot, but she couldn't find an alternative. It would be do or die.

"Three in the corner," she said, then focused on an imaginary point on the end rail and leaned down to shoot. *One, two, three—*

Her opponent shattered the silence. "What ball are you playing?"

Sedonia froze on her backstroke. Then she straightened up, and a murmur went through the spectators. She'd called the shot loudly enough that everyone watching the game had to have heard. He was trying to shark her. Without replying, she turned and walked over to where her team was sitting.

Hannah gave her a sympathetic smile and started to say something. Sedonia cut her off with a quick shake of her head. She didn't want her opponent to claim she'd received coaching, which was illegal. She picked up Hannah's can of talcum powder, sprinkled a small amount on her bridge hand, and ran her powdered fingers along the shaft of her cue stick.

Then she took a deep breath and returned to the table. "Three ball in the corner," she said firmly. And to be sure there would be no misunderstanding, she pointed with the tip of her cue stick to the 3-ball and then to the corner. Her opponent made no response.

Sedonia focused again on the imaginary point on the end rail and leaned down to shoot. *One, two, three . . . stroke.* The cue-ball hit the spot where she'd aimed, kicked off the end rail, and rolled toward the side rail. There it hit where she'd planned, and began its long trip down to the far corner. Sedonia's eyes widened. *Yes!*

She was scarcely aware of the spectator roar. She paced around the table, determining the sequence in which she planned to shoot the remaining balls. Then she chalked her cue stick and said, "One in the corner." The cue-ball came to rest precisely where she'd intended. "Seven in the side." As she worked her way around the table, she called even the most obvious shots. Finally she said, "Eight in the side."

As the 8-ball dropped, the spectators erupted. For an instant it didn't register on Sedonia what she'd done. As in her other games tonight, she'd reacted to the entire table and could scarcely recall individual shots.

Her opponent came over. "Good shootin'," he said in a grudging tone. "Thanks," she said. "Good match." Then her teammates swarmed her.

When she finally disengaged, Buster was standing there. They exchanged a quick hug, then Buster said, "Great shootin', kid."

"I don't know what came over me," Sedonia said. "It was like . . . I was watching somebody else play."

Buster laughed. "Like you were watchin' somebody who was pretty damn good."

"I was in a zone, or something," she said. "I don't know how to explain it."

"You don't have to," he said. "Been there myself, a time or two...back when I was younger. Don't remember ever seein' a woman shoot like that, though."

Sedonia frowned.

Buster smiled. "That 'zone' you were in? In pool, it's called 'dead stroke'."

* * *

The following morning, as Sedonia dried off from her shower, she caught a whiff of stale cigarette smoke coming from the wicker clothes hamper. She and her Cue-Ts teammates had celebrated their tournament victory at Carney's Billiards until 2:00 a.m. When she'd finally arrived home, she hadn't run a load of wash as she usually did to get rid of the poolroom odor. She'd been concerned the washing machine noise might disturb the elderly woman who lived in the condo next-door.

She pulled on her robe and moved over to the dressing table. As she blow-dried her hair, she studied her reflection in the mirror. Her eyes were still red, but not quite as bloodshot as when she'd first awakened. And the two aspirin she'd taken were finally kicking in. She didn't know which affected her worse: beer or secondhand smoke. Thank God it was Sunday. At least she didn't have to go into the office.

The telephone rang on the bedside table, causing her to jump. As she crossed the room to answer it, she glanced at the clock: 10:17.

"Hello?"

There was a pause. "Sedonia?"

"Yeah. Cissy?"

"How did we . . . y'all do?" Cissy's voice sounded subdued.

Sedonia hesitated. She wished Cissy had called Hannah; this was going to be awkward. "Uh . . . we won."

Cissy grew excited. "We're going to Vegas?"

"Uh . . . Cissy, you need to talk to Hannah," Sedonia said. Over beers the night before, Hannah had told Sedonia that BCA rules permitted teams to add as many as two players to their rosters for the national tournament. Hannah planned to replace Cissy.

"Is Hannah still mad at me?" Cissy said.

Sedonia took a deep breath. "You . . . let us down yesterday, Cissy."

"I know . . ."

Sedonia took another deep breath. Talking to Cissy was like talking to a 13-year-old.

Cissy said, "Hannah's gonna let me go to Las Vegas . . . isn't she?"

"I . . . don't think so."

"But I was sick," Cissy said in a whine.

Sedonia's patience ran out. "You were stoned."

Cissy hung up.

"Darn it!" Sedonia said as she put down the receiver. She hesitated a moment, then hurried out of the bedroom, down the hallway, and into the kitchen. She picked up her cell phone off the bar and entered Hannah's auto-dial number. After five rings, she got Hannah's recording and had to settle for leaving a message. "Hannah, this is Sedonia. Call me back. I need to talk to you right away." She hung up, and then dialed Cissy's number.

Cissy picked it up after the first ring. "Hello?" She sounded congested, as if she'd been crying.

"I'll talk to Hannah," Sedonia said.

"Will you?" Cissy said. "Please, Sedonia, I'll get straight. I promise."

"I don't know what she'll say, but I'll talk to her. I gotta go now."

"Thanks, I—"

Sedonia hung up before Cissy had a chance to finish. Sedonia shook her head. Why the hell had she gotten involved in this? It was Hannah's responsibility. Sedonia tried to push her concern from her mind. Right now, she needed some breakfast.

She opened the refrigerator. Cheerios? No, she'd forgotten to stop at the corner convenience store to pick up a carton of milk on her way home last night. Orange juice, two hardboiled eggs, and toast made from the last two slices of a loaf of bread would have to do. She was putting a cup of water into the microwave for instant coffee, when her cell phone rang.

"Hello?"

"Hi, Sedonia. It's Hannah. Just got back from church. What's up?"

"Cissy."

"What about her?"

"I know it's your decision, but I feel bad about her not going to Las Vegas with us."

"You're kidding," Hannah said.

"She called here a few minutes ago. Asked me point blank if you were going to let her go. I had to tell her, I didn't think so."

"Damn right!" Hannah said, and then began to vent, recounting how Cissy had let them down the night before.

Sedonia interjected, "I know. But . . . she's really broken up about not going."

"I've already replaced her," Hannah said. "I called Melissa just before I left for church. What am I supposed to do? Call Melissa back, and tell her I've changed my mind?"

Sedonia didn't reply.

"Plus," Hannah continued, "if we took Cissy to Vegas, we couldn't count on her. She proved that last night."

"Damn," Sedonia said softly.

"Sedonia, why is this so important to you? You hardly know Cissy."

That was the same question Sedonia had asked herself just a few minutes ago. There was no ignoring it now. "Last year . . . I had a problem with a prescription drug. I started taking pain medication for my shoulder, and then I . . . began abusing it."

"Really?" Hannah said, sounding surprised. "You're so . . . together. It's hard for me to imagine you could ever have a problem like that."

Sedonia started to continue, but decided against it. Even though she and Hannah had become close friends, Sedonia couldn't bring herself to confide the circumstances that had led to her drug overdose. However, something she'd heard in Cissy's voice kept the incident in her mind.

After a long pause, Hannah said, "Sedonia, I just don't see how I can withdraw my invitation to Melissa."

Sedonia thought for a moment. "Can we take more than five players?"

"You mean, take Cissy along too? We could. BCA allows for two substitutes. But the Bay Area league only picks up the expenses for five players."

"I'll pay my own way."

"No way!" Hannah protested. "If anyone on our team has earned an expense-paid trip to Vegas, it's you."

"Please, Hannah. This is important to me. Call Cissy, and tell her she's going. I'll make my own plane reservations."

"Hmmm," Hannah said. "We'll already have three hotel rooms. So, with two people per room, the price of a plane ticket would be the only extra expense. Probably run about $200."

"Okay with you?"

"Yeah," Hannah said finally. "Personally, I don't think Cissy deserves the consideration, but if it's that important to you . . ."

"It is."

"Okay," Hannah said, resignation in her tone. "She'll be the substitute, though. Melissa will take her spot in the regular rotation."

"That's reasonable."

"Go ahead and call Cissy," Hannah said, "and tell her she's going."

"It would be better if she heard it from you. Tell her she screwed up last night, but you're counting on her in Las Vegas."

Hannah chuckled. "You act like . . . 'the Bay Area Bomber' or somebody, when you're playing pool, but inside you're a softy. Okay, I'll call her. And, I'll split the cost of the extra plane ticket with you."

"Who's the softy now?"

"You're pushing your luck, Forbes."

Sedonia laughed. "Thanks, Hannah."

"Good-bye."

Sedonia heaved a sigh of relief, and then collected her breakfast and padded into the living room to eat. She sat down on the floor beside the coffee table, and looked around as she peeled her hardboiled eggs. The living room was a mess. She needed to do some long-overdue housecleaning today, but she'd found it difficult to get enthused about her surroundings, ever since she'd "redecorated." She'd sold her dinette set and desk, and replaced them with a used, 8-foot Brunswick. Buster had found it for her at a cost of only $500, plus $150 to replace the felt. The table had stretched her limited finances, but it had proven to be a good investment. Her performance last night had been the result of practice. For the past several months, she'd studied pool books and videos, and spent countless hours applying the lessons and honing her stroke.

She smiled. "Dead stroke" Buster had called it. Would it still be there the next time she played? More importantly, would it still be there in two weeks, when she played in the BCA nationals? A surge of excitement stirred within her. She'd been playing competitive pool for barely a year now, but she'd already qualified to compete in Las Vegas.

She cast a critical glance around the cluttered room, but decided to put off house cleaning to another day. After breakfast, she'd practice here for a couple of hours, and then go see if she could match up at Buster's.

Chapter 8

Sedonia clicked on "Print," and the laser printer on the other side of the office sprang to life. Late afternoon sun streamed through the front mini-blinds. Other than the rhythmic spewing of report pages, the Forbes Painting Company was quiet. Sedonia leaned back in her chair and interlaced her fingers behind her head. For the first time this year, she felt as if there might be a light at the end of the financial tunnel. Three of Brad Landry's houses had closed in May, and cash flow for the current fiscal year had finally swung positive.

A passing van drew her attention, but it continued down Waterfront Street. Raul should be returning from the job site shortly. When he arrived, she needed to see if he had any last-minute questions, since tomorrow morning she would leave for Las Vegas.

Sedonia felt a pang of anxiety. Neither she nor her teammates had taken advantage of the past two weeks to prepare for the national tournament. Hannah and the others had begged off practice sessions, saying they had business and personal commitments they needed to attend to, since they'd be gone for a week. And Sedonia's own practice time had been limited to an hour or two at home each evening.

This past Saturday night was the only time she'd managed to get over to Buster's. There, she'd played well enough to win a couple of low stakes matches, but she hadn't played as well as she knew she could, and she hadn't come close to again experiencing "dead stroke."

The telephone on her desk rang. She hoped it was Raul saying he was on his way.

"Forbes Painting Company."

"Sedonia?" said a woman's voice.

Sedonia winced, immediately recognizing her former golf coach at the University of Houston. "Hi, Coach."

"We missed you at the Cougar alumni dinner Saturday night." There was an edge to her tone.

"Sorry, Coach. I've was . . . tied up. I've been real busy the past couple of weeks."

"I'm sorry too. We had a couple of recruits down from Pflugerville. One of them in particular was looking forward to seeing you again. She told me she'd met you in Austin, when you won the championship."

Sedonia frowned. She'd met so many people that exciting week.

Her coach continued, "You apparently made quite an impression on her. She said one afternoon on the driving range, you took time from your own practice session to give her some tips and encouragement."

"Oh, yeah," Sedonia said. "Kathy . . . something?"

"Kathy Watson. Led Pflugerville High to the state championship this year."

Sedonia winced again. She could have attended the alumni dinner—should have attended it—but at the last minute she'd decided preparing for Las Vegas was more important. That was the night she'd managed to make it to Buster's. "Do you have her phone number, Coach? I'll give her a call and apologize."

"I'd appreciate that," her former coach said, still with a slight edge to her tone. She gave her the number.

Sedonia jotted it down on a slip of paper and dropped it into her "In" basket.

"Sedonia," the coach said, "you were the top golfer ever to come out of our women's program. We'd really appreciate your supporting it."

"I'm sorry, Coach. My business . . ."

"Over on the men's side, guys like Marty Fleckman, Homero Blancas, Freddie Couples, and Steve Elkington all showed up. We need women like you, who've made names for yourselves, to support *our* program the same way."

A wave of melancholy swept over Sedonia. The names the coach had rattled off were, or had been, top players on the men's Professional Golf Association tour. Just a couple of years ago, her coach had told her that someday she'd be as well known as these men were. With an annoyed shake of her head, Sedonia pushed the onset of self-pity from her mind. "I'll be there next time for you, Coach. I promise."

"Okay, honey," she said. "I know it's been tough on you, not being able to play and all. But we still think a lot of you here."

"Thanks, Coach. I'll see you next time."

They hung up, and Sedonia leaned back in her chair again. Tears unexpectedly filled her eyes. She blinked them back. Then, as she'd done countless times during the past two years, she replayed the final hole of the U. S. Women's Amateur Tournament.

In the match-play championship round, she'd led her opponent by one stroke, with one hole to go. Her college coach was caddying for her, and she advised Sedonia to play it safe and to tee off with a 3-wood. Instead, Sedonia decided to "grip it and rip it." She pulled her 1-wood from the bag, and sent a towering drive 275 yards down the center of the fairway. When the ball came to rest, she still had 240 yards to negotiate, with pin placement on the bunkered left side of the green. Caution called for a 5-iron, followed by a pitching wedge. Instead, she pulled out her 3-wood and went for the flag. Her swing was so effortless that for an instant, she thought she might have missed the ball altogether; however, she'd hit it "dead-solid-perfect." The ball soared high into the air, faded slightly to the left, dropped onto the green, bounced three times, and then rolled to within 8 inches of the pin! As she strode up the fairway for the tap-in eagle putt that would give her the U. S. Women's Amateur Golf Championship by three strokes, the crowd around the 18th green welcomed her with a thunderous ovation.

Now, sitting in her office, she could still visualize and feel those two towering shots, and she whispered, "Grip it and rip it." Tears welled again, and this time she let them flow. Once to be able to do something so well, and now not to be able to do it at all. She'd been cheated!

Again, she gave an annoyed shake of her head, trying to force self-pity from her thoughts. She took a deep breath. She'd run over to Buster's for a practice session, as soon as she got things wrapped up here. Damn! That reminded her: she'd intended to call Brad and tell him she'd be out of town for a week. She checked her watch: 5:55. Hopefully, he was still working.

She managed to reach him on his cell phone. "Wish you'd have told me earlier that you were leaving town," he said. "I've got those three new projects starting this week, and I plan to change the way you and I handle interim financing from now on. My new procedures will be outside of Raul's experience. I need to go over them with you."

"If you're available right now, I could meet you at your office," Sedonia said. Las Vegas or not, she needed to keep her primary customer happy.

"Hmmm . . . it's almost 6:00," he said. "Do you already have plans for this evening?"

"Nothing I can't change. What time would you like to get together?"

"How about 30 minutes from now. Do you like Mexican food?"

"Sure," Sedonia said. She was about to suggest her favorite place.

"Okay, then how about the Cadillac Bar on the Kemah boardwalk? It's close to where you are. We can go over the changes I want to make, and then grab a bite to eat."

"Sounds good," Sedonia said, though disappointed. Dinner with Brad would cut into her limited practice time.

As they hung up, she heard Raul's van pull into the parking lot. Good. She had enough time make sure he was ready to take over for a week, before leaving to meet Brad. She'd get through their dinner as quickly as possible, and then get over to Buster's.

The Cadillac Bar in Kemah was less than a hundred yards from Sedonia's office in Seabrook. However, the two communities were separated by the narrow channel that linked Galveston Bay and Clear Lake. It took Sedonia almost a half-hour to negotiate the late afternoon traffic that clogged both the bridge that spanned the channel and the narrow streets that wound through Kemah's curio and antique shops.

Early arrivals already filled the parking lot in front of the Cadillac Bar, and Sedonia had to settle for a spot a block away. She glanced at her watch and grimaced as she hurried up the sidewalk toward the restaurant row. Brad was already irked that she was going to be out of town for a week, and now she was almost 20 minutes late for their meeting.

As she approached the restaurant, she saw him standing out front, arms folded across his chest. When he spotted her, however, his welcoming smile seemed genuine, and he didn't seem annoyed. Maybe he too had just arrived.

"Sorry I'm late," she said. "I should have swum the channel, instead of fighting the bridge traffic."

"No problem," he said with a laugh. "It's good to see you."

As they headed toward the entrance, Sedonia noted that Brad's jeans and western shirt were clean and pressed. And instead of his customary engineering boots, this evening he was wearing polished cowboy boots. He'd apparently gone home and changed clothes after getting off work. He looked as if he were going out on a date. For an instant, Sedonia regretted not having had a chance to change also, but then reassured herself that this was just to be a quick business dinner.

Although all of the half-dozen restaurants along the boardwalk were owned by the same company, each had a unique décor. The Cadillac Bar's was faux *cantina*. It was intended to look like its namesake in the infamous border town, Nuevo Laredo, Mexico.

A young hostess met them at the door and asked if they preferred to sit inside or outside. Outside they agreed, and she led them past the long, crowded bar. The border-town motif had been carried into the restaurant's interior. Stark wood and brick walls, covered with graffiti, rose from the bare concrete floor, and *ranchero* music blared from the sound system.

As they followed the hostess through the dining area, Brad got Sedonia's attention and pointed toward the ceiling, where rough-hewn beams had been installed in an irregular pattern to add to the restaurant's ramshackle atmosphere. Brad said, "Looks like my crew framed this place."

Sedonia laughed, since one thing she'd learned over the past year was that Brad was a stickler for quality. Anything out of spec on his projects was ripped out and redone correctly.

The hostess seated them at a table overlooking the channel. Over on the Seabrook side, neglected oyster and shrimp boats rode at anchor behind the row of dilapidated seafood markets. Here on the Kemah side, a dozen sleek pleasure crafts bobbed at their moorings behind the row of trendy restaurants. A Swan-55 luxury sailboat passed the restaurant, under the power of its auxiliary engine. As it entered Galveston Bay, the crew raised the sails, and moments later they tacked toward the open water.

A Latino waiter came over and took their drink order. Brad ordered a Corona Beer with lime, and Sedonia said she'd have the same, departing from her usual Coors Light. When the waiter returned with their drinks, Brad told him they'd order their food later.

Sedonia said, "Do you eat here often?"

"Sometimes, when I'm down this way. Mexican food's my favorite. Usually, though, I go to *Restaurante Merida*, over on the NASA Parkway."

"Me too!" she said. "I even eat breakfast there sometimes."

Brad chuckled. "I'm not surprised. It was one of your dad's favorite hangouts. Matter of fact, he's the one who took me there for the first time. Man, I remember one night, he and I . . ."

When he didn't finish his thought, Sedonia said, "You and he what?"

"No," Brad said with a quick laugh, "I'd better skip that story."

"Why?"

"Just . . . because."

"Tell me."

"If you insist. Well, late one night, he and I were still in the bar, and these two women came in—"

"You're right," Sedonia interrupted. "I don't think his daughter needs to know this story."

Brad chuckled. Then he turned serious. "Your dad was a good man, Sedonia."

She nodded, and raised her Corona. *"Salud."*

"Salud," Brad replied as he clinked his bottle against hers, and they drank a toast to her father. They both looked out at the bay for a moment, then Brad turned and said, "Okay, let's get the business out of the way."

For the next half-hour, they discussed Brad's new plan for interim finances. The primary change was that he had set up a special bank account for the projects involving Sedonia's company. He'd put $25,000 into this account and planned to replenish it as needed. Sedonia was authorized to draw upon this account for supplies, without having to get his approval for each individual requisition.

Sedonia was pleased. Aside from the convenience of this new account, it also indicated that her company had earned the position as one of Brad's preferred service providers. Sedonia recognized that Raul deserved most of the credit; he'd overseen Brad's projects. Sedonia and Brad agreed, however, that she wouldn't delegate Raul access to this new account, at least until the procedures had been in practice for a few months.

Brad pulled a small Post-it note out of his wallet and handed it to her. "Here's the password to the account."

She glanced at the note, and then put it into her purse. "Acropolis" meant nothing to her. It was a good thing he'd jotted it down.

"Okay," Brad said, "we're all set then." He signaled the waiter that they were ready to order. Brad obviously was hungry; he ordered the enchilada dinner with a side order of tacos. He frowned when Sedonia ordered *sopa del tortilla*. "Is soup all you're having? I thought you liked Mexican food."

"I'd better eat light," she said. "I've got a morning flight, and plan to get to bed early tonight."

"You mentioned you'd be out of town this week. Where are you going?"

"Uh . . . Las Vegas." Sedonia felt uneasy naming her destination, concerned that with Brad about to start three important projects this week, a pool-playing junket would sound trivial.

"If you go to Las Vegas for a week at a time," he said, "maybe I'd better reconsider giving you access to that account."

Sedonia knew he was joking, but still felt the need to offer some sort of explanation. "I'm not really a gambler . . . like black jack, craps, and roulette. I play pool in a local league, and my team qualified for the national tournament." She saw no reason to volunteer the gambling aspects of pool.

"That's great," Brad said. "I play a little pool myself. Maybe we could get together sometime."

Sedonia hesitated. Balancing the time demands of playing pool and running her business had been a constant struggle. She sensed that for some reason, despite her having been unavailable for so long, this attractive man was still interested in her and was trying to carve out some time for himself. She momentarily considered inviting him to join her at Buster's after dinner, but then decided against it. She needed to practice without distractions.

When she didn't reply, Brad continued, "Of course, I'm just an amateur."

"I am too," she said quickly.

"Are you still seeing someone?" he said.

She remembered the last time when he'd asked her to dinner, she'd allowed him to think that Emilio was her boyfriend. "We're . . . not seeing each other now." Sedonia felt her cheeks begin to tingle. She was no good at being evasive. "I'll call you when I get back," she said. "Maybe we can get together."

By the skeptical expression that crossed Brad's face, Sedonia sensed that her "I'll call you" had sounded like a standard put-off line, though as handsome as Brad was, she doubted he'd heard it often. To Sedonia's relief, the waiter arrived with their orders, and they dropped the topic.

They engaged in polite small talk during the meal. When they were finished, the waiter came over and asked what they'd like for dessert. Sedonia was about to order flan, when Brad said, "Nothing, thanks. You can bring us the bill." Then turning to Sedonia he said, "You mentioned you wanted to get home early."

Sedonia offered to pay, but Brad insisted, saying he could use the meal as business tax write-off. His demeanor had, in fact, become quite business-like. Sedonia regretted the evening was concluding on strained terms. She knew that she was the problem, but she couldn't deal with it right now. Her thoughts were too jumbled. She had too much going on. Plus, he was her customer. Her *primary* customer.

As they emerged from the restaurant, Brad insisted on walking her to her car. The boardwalk had become a hive of activity while they'd been inside. To their left, the brightly-lit Ferris wheel was in operation, and the cheerful sound of calliope music drifted from the nearby merry-go-round. A shrill blast from a steam whistle brought them to a halt, and a small red train, filled with smiling tourists, clattered past. Several couples waited beside them. Under ordinary circumstances, it would have been an ideal night for a stroll. But not tonight. Again, Sedonia felt responsible for the awkward end to the evening. After the train passed, and they resumed walking in silence, she decided she'd head straight for home, rather than stopping off at Buster's. She just wanted this day to end.

When they arrived at her car, he stood nearby while she fumbled through her purse for her keys. As she turned to thank Brad for dinner, the keys slipped through her fingers. She and Brad bent down simultaneously to pick them up, and her forehead struck him sharply across his nose. He straightened in surprise, tears of pain welling in his eyes. She instinctively stepped closer and gently placed her finger tips against the bridge of his nose. He took her hand and kissed the inside of her wrist, and then pressed his lips against hers. She responded, and their long kiss was followed by a longer embrace.

Finally they separated, and he stepped back. "Let me do it this time." He bent down and picked up the keys. As he handed them back to her, he said, "Call me if you'd like to get together sometime." Then he turned, and headed toward the boardwalk.

* * *

Sedonia sped down the NASA Parkway, still preoccupied with the jumble of conflicting thoughts and emotions. Nighttime traffic had begun to thin out along the usually busy thoroughfare, and a brisk breeze blew off Clear Lake, which lay off to the left. As she rounded a bend, the sight of the twelve-story Nassau Bay Hilton brought her back to her immediate surroundings. She was almost home. She flipped on her left blinker and prepared to turn onto Lakeside Lane, which ran alongside the hotel grounds. At the last moment, however, she changed her mind and continued south. There was no use going to bed now. She'd never get to sleep. Maybe driving around a while would help relax her.

A few blocks farther, she had to stop for a traffic light. The Johnson Space Center sprawled off to the right. Despite the late hour, a half-dozen cars were parked near the main gate in front of the space capsule and booster display. A retired Saturn-V dominated the scene, lying on its side, yet still towering over the tourists clustered around it.

A battered pickup truck stopped beside her, towing a large horse trailer. The lake breeze blew the pungent smell of hay and horse dung through Sedonia's open side windows. The light changed, and she hurried to put distance between her car and the trailer. A wry smile tugged at the corners of her mouth. She'd lived her entire life in this area; nevertheless, she still could recognize and appreciate its eclectic quality. The renowned Johnson Space Center had once been part of an enormous cattle ranch, owned by "Diamond" Jim West, and working farms were still commonplace in the area. And nearby, the state's highest concentration of recreational boats shared Galveston Bay with shrimp and oyster trawlers. And just few miles to the west, within view of Houston's futuristic skyline, mile after mile of oil refineries and chemical plants served the southwest United States. Sedonia smiled again. Somehow, the environmental jumble around her seemed to parallel her own life: golf, the university, business, pool. And now she ran the risk of adding Brad Landry.

Ahead, a traffic light switched to yellow. Sedonia sped up and made it through, and a few moments later saw the familiar red neon sign that read: "Buster's Billiards." Three cars were lined up in front, a small turnout, even for a Monday night. On impulse, she turned into the parking lot. One beer, and then she'd to head for home. The other Cue-Ts were flying out at 7:30 the next morning. Her flight was four hours later, but she still needed to pack.

A familiar cry of "Se-don-ia!" rang out as she stepped through the doorway. She walked over to the bar. "Hi, Buster. You working a double shift today?"

"Yeah," he said as he opened a bottle of Coors Light for her. "We wasn't doin' no business, so I told Jenna to take the night off."

Sedonia took a sip of her beer and glanced around the room. Only two tables were in use. A young couple near the jukebox was playing a friendly game. In the far corner, Elmer and another elderly man were engrossed in a more serious match. From the tight cluster of balls, she surmised they must be playing One-Pocket. She wondered where they found the patience, since most shots in One-Pocket were defensive. She couldn't imagine a more boring and frustrating game.

Buster continued, "It's gonna be slow all week, with so many of y'all in Vegas."

"I'm surprised nobody's in here tonight, getting in some last-minute practice."

"Most of 'em been practicin' over at Chug's."

"Chug's?" Sedonia said, surprised. "They've only got bar-boxes there. Why are they practicing at Chug's?"

Buster frowned. "Because y'all are gonna be playin' on bar-boxes in Vegas."

Sedonia looked at him in disbelief. "You're kidding."

"No, I'm not kidding. You didn't know that? Most local leagues don't play in poolrooms. They play in neighborhood joints, like Chug's. So the BCA uses bar-boxes for the national tournament."

Sedonia slowly shook her head. "Hannah never mentioned it."

Buster said, "Since I ain't seen you all week, I figured you were practicin' at Chug's too."

Sedonia heaved a sigh. This Las Vegas trip was turning into a disaster. "Buster," she said, "I don't play worth a damn on bar-boxes."

"You'll do fine."

"Don't you remember? I was about to quit pool altogether, before you and Hannah conned me into playing on 8-foot tables."

"'Conned' you?" Buster said, but then smiled. "Well, maybe we did. But you're glad we did, aren't you?"

Sedonia forced a return smile; however, she felt dejected. After months of working hard to earn the right to play in Las Vegas, here the last few days she'd blown the opportunity. She should have let her damned painting business slide the past two weeks, and concentrated instead on getting ready for the tournament. She glanced at her watch. "I'm gonna go over to Chug's and hit some balls."

"Bad idea," he said.

"Why?"

"I can see you're worked up over the bar-box thing. Goin' over there tonight will just make it worse. The tables at Chug's are different than you'll be playing on in Vegas."

"Different?"

"Like most beer joints, Chug's tables ain't level, the felt's worn, and the cue-balls are hard to stop and back up. In Vegas, you'll be playing on *new* tables. They'll be in perfect shape. Those people who've been practicing at Chug's have been wasting their time."

Sedonia took a deep breath. Those other players may have wasted their time, but that didn't make her any better prepared.

Buster seemed to recognize her continuing concern. "Don't worry about Vegas. I match up players all the time, and I'm here to tell you, you shoot better than ninety percent of the people you'll be going up against."

"But bar-boxes . . ."

"When bar-boxes are in good shape, like they'll be in Vegas, there's only two things you gotta remember. One is to concentrate on position, and the other is to play safe unless you're positive you've got a run-out."

Sedonia turned away and gazed out at the passing cars.

Buster said, "Are you payin' attention to what I'm sayin'?"

Sedonia turned back. "Yeah, but—"

"'Yeah, but' nothing. I don't need to be talkin' to myself. I know this shit."

"Sorry."

"Position. Most players, who play on regulation tables, get too confident when they play on bar-boxes, since the tables are so much smaller. Actually, though, it ought to be just the opposite. Because the tables are smaller, there's less open space to work with and more chance of balls gettin' tied up. So, you gotta concentrate even *harder* than if you were playin' on an eight- or nine-foot table."

"That's it!" Sedonia interjected. "That's what I wasn't doing. Like at Willie O's. I kept telling myself, there was no way I could miss, since the tables were so small."

Buster nodded. "Another thing about position on a bar-box is to hit the cue-ball as low as possible. On a regulation table, it's important to avoid leaving a long shot, so we take chances and run the cue-ball all over the table. Since a bar-box is so much smaller, there *are* no long shots. So the trick is to use as much 'stop' on the cue-ball as you can get away with. That way, you're less likely to lose control of it and leave yourself with poor position."

"Makes sense."

"The other thing to remember," Buster said, "is don't try for a run-out, unless you're absolutely positive that you have one."

"Explain that."

"The reason behind it is the same. Because the table's smaller, there's more chance the balls are gonna be tied up. If they are, don't put 'follow' on the cue-ball and try to break 'em out. Instead, play safe. Use 'stop' and leave the other guy with a tough shot. Make *him* break 'em out."

Sedonia nodded, a smile forming. "Wish you'd have told me all this a long time ago."

Buster snorted. "Hell, if I had of, you'd still be hustling pool with E-mil-io." Then he added with a chuckle, "And I'd never have got you as regular customer."

"And I wouldn't be headed for Las Vegas in the morning," Sedonia said in a rueful tone.

Buster smiled. "You'll do fine out there, kid."

She heaved a sigh. "It's just that . . . I always like to be prepared. All the years I played golf, I *never* went into a tournament unprepared like I am for Las Vegas. And once I get there, there'll be no place to practice, will there?"

"In addition to the 300 tables set up for the tournament—"

"Three hundred!"

"They'll have at least that many. They're expecting almost 10,000 players this year."

"Good grief. Ten thousand?"

"As I was sayin', in addition to the 300 tournament tables, there'll be additional ones set off in a side room, supposedly for practice. But usually, they'll be tied up with people gamblin'. I can give you the names of a couple of poolrooms there in Vegas, in case you get out of stroke and wanna go somewhere else to practice."

"Yeah. Please."

Buster walked down to the end of the bar and entered his small cluttered office. Sedonia could see him rummaging through the top drawer of a scarred wooden desk. He returned with a couple of worn business cards. "These are the two best poolrooms in Vegas, and they're both located pretty close to the Riviera Hotel."

Sedonia took the first card from him. It read "Cue-Nique."

"If you need to get off by yourself to practice," Buster said, "go there. Last time I was in Vegas, they had a couple of bar-boxes. Owner's name is Sal. Used to be a road player, out of New York. He'll remember me."

Sedonia nodded.

Buster handed her the second card. "Go to the Billiard Club to watch strong players, and if you want to gamble. Beside your BCA Eight-Ball tournament, there's also gonna be a couple of pro Nine-Ball tournaments goin' on at the Riviera this week. One tournament for the men and one for the women. The pro tournaments will be upstairs in the penthouse. Between matches, though, a lot of 'em will be over at the Billiard Club, lookin' for action."

"During their tournament?"

"Yeah. First place in the tournament pays out $15,000, but some of the side action at the Billiard Club could make fifteen grand look like chump change."

"Wow," Sedonia said. "Will the pros be gambling with other pros?"

"They'll play whoever's got the money and the gamble. Don't matter if it's pros, road players, or Las Vegas locals." He smiled. "Or even one of you BCA hotshots."

Sedonia smiled. "I don't think I'm quite ready to take on the pros."

Buster studied her for a moment, and then said, "Wait here."

He went back to his office again, and this time returned with a copy of *Billiards Digest* magazine. He flipped to a back page and showed Sedonia a ranking of the current top twenty Women's Professional Billiard Association players. "Almost all of 'em will be in Vegas for the women's tournament. The WPBA has designated it as one of their official tour stops. See these gals, from about . . . numbers 16 to 20?"

Sedonia nodded.

"When you're in stroke," Buster said, "you could beat 'em. But, you don't have the experience—or the gamble—to play the top fifteen."

"I think you're wrong."

He frowned. "You think you're good enough to beat the top women pros?"

"No," Sedonia said with a laugh. "I meant I don't think I have a chance against the five women at the *bottom* of this list."

Buster pulled two $100 bills from his wallet. "If one of those five shows up at the Billiard Club, walk right up and challenge her. Ya gotta do it before the stakes get high. Tell her you want to play, Eight-Ball, race-to-7 for $200. Don't let her talk you into Nine-Ball, One-Pocket, or anything else. Eight-Ball only. Race-to-7 for $200."

"Buster, I'm already nervous about the BCA tournament. And now you're telling me to challenge the pros while I'm out there? Get serious."

"I *am* serious," he said, and his expression indicated that he was. "Try to match up with at least one of these five women. If they won't play you, then use the money to gamble with men, but not the men pros. You're not ready for them. Look for a local guy, or even a road player. Speakin' of road players, that coonass, Jimmy Dupre, told me he was gonna be out there."

Sedonia had no intention of having anything to do with "French Quarter" Jimmy, on or off a pool table. "I can't believe we're talking about this, Buster," she said. "I'd be scared stiff, walking into a strange poolroom and challenging some professional to gamble with me."

"That's the way you learn, kid. Don't sweat the money. Just don't come back here and tell me you couldn't get a match, because I'll know you're lyin'. That town ain't nuthin' but gamble."

Sedonia didn't respond.

"I'm your stakehorse," Buster continued. "I get half if you win, and I take *all* the loss."

"That doesn't seem fair."

As he carefully ripped out the magazine page, he slowly shook his head, as if he were talking to a not-so-bright child. "Pool ain't about bein' fair. Pool's about who wins the money."

He handed her the $200 and the magazine page, and Sedonia reluctantly accepted them. Then he reached over, took her half-full bottle of beer and poured the remainder into the sink. "If you try to practice tonight, you'll just get more uptight than you already are. Go home and get a good night's rest."

Sedonia doubted she'd be able to sleep, but she responded with a grudging nod. "Okay, Coach. Thanks for the tips. And for the encouragement." She stood up and headed toward the door.

"Hey!" he called out.

She paused and turned, hand on the door.

"Remember," he said, "it's just a game . . . Se-don-ia."

Chapter 9

Sedonia waited at an intersection near McCarran Airport; the traffic light seemed stuck on red. The Nevada desert sun radiated through the metal roof and ricocheted off the concrete street. The rental car's air-conditioner roared, blowing an icy stream across her arms and chest. She drummed her fingers on the steering wheel and gazed at the row of hotel-casinos one block to her left. Although this was her first trip to Las Vegas, she'd seen the famed "Strip" so often in movies that it now seemed familiar, as did the names atop the buildings: Excalibur, New York New York, MGM Grand, Aladdin, Caesar's Palace . . . The Luxor's glass replica of the Great Pyramid of Cheops dominated the garish architectural mishmash.

The signal finally changed to green, and Sedonia pulled onto Paradise Road. She glanced down at the odometer: 63,387. Rent-a-Heap-Cheap, indeed. The four-door sedan reeked of recently-sprayed air freshener. Despite the intense heat outside, she lowered the driver-side window a couple of inches to dilute the sickeningly sweet odor.

She crossed Tropicana Avenue, and a sign on the right indicated she was passing the University of Nevada, Las Vegas. Thermal waves radiated off its stark buildings and concreted expanses. No sign of students, just dust-covered construction workers, pouring more concrete.

The next major intersection was Flamingo Road. Sedonia squinted. She ought to be getting close . . . there! She turned right onto Twain Avenue. Moments later, nestled in a neighborhood strip center, she saw the sign she was looking for: Cue-Nique Billiards. The parking lot in front of the poolroom was empty. She checked her watch: 2:45. Apparently it was too early for the locals. She decided she'd check into her hotel, and come back later.

Continuing north on Paradise Road, she stole glances to her left and again caught glimpses of the Strip: Treasure Island, the Stardust, and Circus Circus. Ahead, the futuristic Stratosphere Tower loomed high above the other hotel-casinos.

She spotted the Riviera as she crossed Desert Inn Road, and moments later she turned up an asphalt driveway that led to a five-story parking garage. The Riviera probably once had been a grand hotel, but now it seemed outdated compared to the gaudy theme complexes that had sprung up around it.

She found a parking spot on the first floor. A few minutes later, cue case slung over one shoulder and rolling her suitcase behind her, she headed up the sidewalk toward the hotel entrance. A bank of glass doors led to the hotel on the left and the convention center on the right. The marquee above the stairs read:

Welcome to the
BCA National 8-Ball Championships
$1,000,000 in Total Prize Money

A few minutes later, Sedonia knocked on a hotel room door. When Hannah opened it, she had her cell phone pressed to her ear. She gave Sedonia a quick hug, and then stepped back and resumed her phone conversation while Sedonia pulled her luggage inside.

Sedonia set her cue case on the credenza, and pointed to the bed closest to the window. Hannah nodded. Sedonia threw her suitcase onto the bed, and looked about the room, slightly disappointed. The accommodations were functional, but she'd expected more from Las Vegas.

She stepped over to the window and drew back the curtains. Colorful, downtown Las Vegas apparently was on the other side of the building. This vantage point overlooked a golf course, eight stories below. Vivid green fairways contrasted to the surrounding drab terrain, but trees were scarce, as were water hazards. Beyond the golf course, terracotta-roofed neighborhoods stretched for miles, and then in the distance, barren brown hills rose toward the cloudless desert sky.

"I love you," Hannah said.

Sedonia turned and saw Hannah smile as she apparently got the desired reply from her cell phone. She switched it off, and said, "I was talking to my husband."

"Better be," Sedonia said with a laugh.

"He's arriving Saturday. All the rooms here are booked, so we'll be staying across the street at Circus Circus."

"Second honeymoon, huh?"

"You bet," Hannah said with a wicked smile.

"Where are the others?" Sedonia said.

"Probably in the casino. We had lunch when we arrived, and that's the last I've seen of them." A look of concern crossed her face. "We've got a problem . . . with Cissy."

"Don't tell me," Sedonia said in a resigned tone. "Drugs again?"

"Worse."

"Worse?"

Hannah nodded. "She's supposed to go to jail on Saturday."

"Jail! Go to jail here?"

"No," Hannah said with a quick laugh. "In Houston. She didn't tell me about it until we were on the plane. A few weeks ago, she and that piece-of-crap boyfriend of hers were both stoned, and he had a car wreck. He's on parole, and she was afraid he'd get thrown back in prison. So, they told the cop she'd been the one driving. It went down as her third DUI. Her court case came up on Friday, and she was sentenced to 30 days in the Harris County jail, to be served on the next 15 weekends."

"But we're not going back until Sunday."

"She knows that. She also knows when she does get back, they're going to lock her up, and it won't just be on weekends. It'll probably be for a lot longer than 30 days. She doesn't care. This tournament's that important to her."

"Doesn't make any sense," Sedonia said. "Two weeks ago, she got stoned and almost cost us the trip. Now she's risking jail to play here."

Hannah smiled. "I think it's called 'redemption'."

"Redemption? Going to jail?"

"No. Not letting us down this time."

"Oh, hell, Hannah. You're telling me we're responsible?"

"No, we're not responsible. But if possible, we need to see if we can help her deal with it." Hannah checked her watch. "There's a captains' meeting downstairs in five minutes. They're going to give us the lowdown on how the tournament's going to be run. Want to come along?"

Sedonia thought for a moment, then said, "If you don't need me, I'm going to get in some practice. Last night, Buster told me about a couple of poolrooms close to here."

Hannah smiled and started toward the door. "You and your practicing. It's good, though. We're gonna need you at top form this week."

Sedonia stepped inside Cue-Nique Billiards, and then hesitated, letting her eyes adjust from desert sunlight to poolroom gloom. Dozens of unoccupied tables lay off to her right; the lights above each were turned off. At first glance, it looked as if the place were closed; however, two young men were sitting at the raised bar, which occupied the center of the room. Judging by their clothes, they were construction workers. A swarthy, middle-aged man was working behind the bar.

All three stared at Sedonia as she approached. She set her cue case on the counter and checked the other side of the room. Two bar-boxes stood off to one side, but they looked in as poor condition as those at Chug's. She decided she'd be better off with her usual practice routine, and asked the bartender, "Got any nine-foot tables?"

"Brunswick Gold Crown, over in the corner," he said, in what had to be a New York City accent.

"I'll take it," Sedonia said.

The bartender stepped over to a row of toggle switches and flipped one. The light above the nine-foot table came on. Then he reached beneath the counter and pulled out a tray of chipped, mismatched balls. He shoved it toward Sedonia and said, "Four dollars, per hour."

Sedonia shoved the balls back. "Got anything newer."

He studied her for a moment, then brought up a tray of shiny balls.

Sedonia picked up the beige cue-ball and handed it back.

He gave an annoyed shake of his head, then reached below the counter again and replaced the soft break ball with a white game ball. "Want something to drink?"

"No thanks."

The two customers had watched the exchange. Their eyes were still on Sedonia as she walked past them and headed toward the light in the far corner.

Throughout the room, black-framed 8" x 10" photos were mounted on the wall. As Sedonia screwed her stick together, she studied those nearby. The meticulously aligned pictures were of pool celebrities, most signed with personal notes to "Sal." She remembered Buster had told her that was the owner's name.

The room reeked from decades of cigarette smoke and spilled beer. The dark green carpet didn't hide the stains. The Brunswick Gold Crown had seen better days. Its felt was worn and faded; a small piece of gray duct tape covered a rip near the left break position. Sedonia glanced at the nearby eight-foot tables. They were in better condition, but this was what she needed. If she could find her stroke on this old nine-foot table, she ought to be able to handle the new six-foot bar-boxes at the Riviera.

A half-hour later, she shook her head in frustration. Where the hell had her stroke gone! She wiped a film of perspiration from her upper lip with the back of her hand, took a deep breath, and again bent over the table, lining up a long shot down the side rail. She consciously tried to relax her arm and shoulder muscles. *One, two, three . . . stroke.* The cue-ball struck the blue 2-ball, which veered slightly from the rail, stuttered in the jaws of the corner pocket, but didn't drop. *Damn it!*

"What kind of stick is that?" asked a male voice.

Sedonia straightened up. The two young men from the bar had walked up, unnoticed. One, thin and pock-marked, apparently had spoken and awaited her reply. His heavy-set companion dropped onto a nearby stool.

Sedonia showed them her cue stick. "It's a Jerry Olivier."

The thin youth sneered. "Never heard of it. I got a McDermott I'll let you have for . . . $400."

Sedonia turned back to the table. "No thanks."

"Okay, then let's me and you play some cheap Nine-Ball."

"Not today," Sedonia said.

"C'mon," the youth pressed. "Cheap. Ten dollars a game."

Sedonia shook her head and leaned over the table for her next shot.

The young man said, "You're one of those girls who likes to play with herself, huh?"

Sedonia straightened up. "Get lost."

He took a step forward. "Who you think you're talkin' to?" His heavyset companion looked on with a blank expression.

Sedonia's pulse accelerated. They literally had her cornered.

The bartender's voice rang out, "Randy! James!"

The two men hesitated, as if to establish they weren't to be bossed around, but then sauntered back to the bar. Moments later, the front door opened, and Sedonia caught a glimpse of their leaving.

She heaved a sigh, and then bent over the table and tried to concentrate on her next shot, the red 3-ball down the rail. She missed it badly, and angrily slammed the orange 5-ball into the side pocket. She took another deep breath, unscrewed her cue stick, and returned it to the case.

A few moments later, she returned the tray of balls to the bartender. "Leavin' already?" he said.

Sedonia nodded and handed him a ten-dollar bill.

"There's a one-hour minimum," he said, his defensive tone indicating he expected an argument, since she'd only played for 30 minutes.

Sedonia didn't reply. She was concerned whether the two men were waiting in the parking lot, not the price of pool. "Are you Sal?"

He frowned. "Yeah."

"I'm in town for the BCA tournament. A friend of mine, Buster Harris, told me to look you up."

"Buster? In Texas?"

Sedonia nodded.

A trace of a smile formed on the man's hard face. "Good old Buster. Still bald as a cue-ball?"

Sedonia nodded again.

"Your time's on me," he said, returning her ten dollars. "You lookin' to match up while you're in town?"

"Maybe. Buster told me the action was going to be at a place called the Billiard Club."

"Yeah, up on Sahara Avenue. Most of the strong players are gonna be there all week. Buster stakin' you?"

"Uh-huh," Sedonia said. She saw no reason to mention her stake was only $200. "Well, I need to get back to the hotel," she said, and turned to leave.

"Wait a minute," he said. "I'll walk you out."

They stepped outside and both surveyed the scene. No sign of the two customers. "Sorry about those guys givin' you a bad time," Sal said.

Sedonia responded with a quick nod, and then climbed into her car and quickly rolled down the windows to let out the stifling heat.

"Hey!" Sal called out from the sidewalk. "I'll probably see you over at the Billiard Club this week. Let me know if you run short. Might stake you myself."

Moments later, Sedonia headed west on Twain Avenue, trying to collect her thoughts. She was out of stroke and unprepared for the tournament, yet men who supposedly knew pool wanted to gamble on her. She felt like an imposter. This was turning into a week in hell, despite the street sign that indicated she was approaching Paradise Road.

When Sedonia arrived back at the Riviera, she found the parking garage almost full. Apparently a number of players had checked in during the afternoon. She had to settle for an uncovered spot on the top floor. As the garage elevator made its descent, it stopped on the fourth floor, and three young men got in. Like Sedonia, each had a cue case slung over one shoulder. The door closed, but there was a pause before the elevator moved again. The men stole glances at her as they waited.

Finally their boldest member said, "Have you played here before?"

"Nope," Sedonia replied. "This'll be my first time."

"Ours too," one of the others said. Her friendliness seemed to put them more at ease. "We're from Rhinelander, Wisconsin."

"I'm from Nassau Bay, Texas," Sedonia said as the elevator finally shuddered and resumed its descent.

"A cowgirl, huh?" the third said, and then looked slightly embarrassed, as if he knew he'd said something dumb.

Before Sedonia had to attempt a reply, they arrived at the first floor. "Good luck in the tournament," she said.

"Good luck," they chorused.

She crossed the service road, and then started up the sidewalk to the hotel entrance. Clusters of players congregated around the bank of glass doors, and others streamed in and out, most carrying cue cases. I'm definitely in my element, Sedonia thought.

Inside, an expansive foyer connected the hotel and the convention center, and a sea of pool-playing humanity surged in both directions. On the other side of the room, above a set of open double doors, Sedonia caught a glimpse of a sign that read "Grande Ballroom." This apparently was where the tournament would be played. She threaded her way across the foyer, her cue case frequently banging against others.

Inside the ballroom, the press of people wasn't as dense. A row of vendor stalls lined the walls, featuring everything from pool tables to wearing apparel. Directly in front of her, a dozen 6' x 8' freestanding bulletin boards were aligned end to end. They held large flowcharts that would allow the tournament directors to track the progress of the hundreds of teams and individuals who would be competing during the week. Players crowded around the boards, studying the brackets and seeing who and when they'd be playing. Sedonia had no idea how to locate the Cue-Ts' place in this maze. Hopefully, Hannah had it figured out.

Sedonia stepped around the bulletin boards and stifled a gasp as she got her first look at the cavernous ballroom. A football field would fit into this room. An acre of bar-boxes lay before her, neatly aligned in rows and columns. Over each table hung a placard with a number. The one in the far corner read "324." Sedonia shook her head. Bar-boxes. Her nemesis. Three-hundred and twenty-four of them.

Looking out at the following day's venue only increased her anxiety. She turned and walked back toward the vendor stalls. One had drawn a crowd. A large banner read:

The Frog Jump Cue
Robin Dodson
WPBA World 9-Ball Champion

As Sedonia approached, she saw a regulation pool table, and a woman lining up on the gold-striped 9-ball. She struck the cue-ball with a smooth, firm stroke, and the 9-ball disappeared into the side pocket. The spectators responded with a round of applause. The player acknowledged the crowd with a wave and a smile, and Sedonia immediately recognized her: WPBA star Jeanette Lee. Sedonia had seen the attractive Korean-American professional play on ESPN. In person, Jeanette was even more striking than she was on TV. Tall and slim, with jet black hair down to her waist, she was clad in a skin-tight black leather outfit, including high-heeled boots. She looked as exotic as her nickname: The Black Widow.

Jeanette's opponent in the exhibition game had been a portly, middle-aged man. He was wearing a red-and-white striped BCA league shirt that read: Main Street Billiards, Mesa, Arizona. An attractive brunette—Sedonia surmised this must be WPBA professional Robin Dodson—took a Polaroid photo of the man with Jeanette. Then Jeanette presented him with the picture and a signed poster, and encouraged the spectators to give him a round of applause. The man beamed and waved. This obviously would be the highlight of his trip to Las Vegas.

While Robin racked the balls, Jeanette chatted amiably with the people clustered around her. Sedonia recalled her own brief period of celebrity during her run for the Women's Amateur Golf Championship, and she was impressed by how accessible and comfortable Jeanette was with her fans.

Robin picked up a cordless microphone and said, "Okay, folks, who's next? One game of 9-Ball with Jeanette Lee. Just $20!"

Sedonia heard a familiar voice behind her cry out, "Got a player right here!" She turned and saw Hannah working her way through the crowd. Hannah smiled and patted Sedonia on the shoulder as she moved past with her $20.

Sedonia chuckled. Hannah was going to challenge Jeanette Lee? This ought to be fun.

Hannah spoke briefly with Robin and Jeanette. Then Robin looked over at Sedonia and said, "You're up, honey."

"Not me," Sedonia said in surprise.

The crowd laughed at her reluctance. Someone behind her touched her shoulder and gently pushed forward.

Hannah walked back, grinning. "This is on me. Kick her ass."

"Hannah!" Sedonia protested.

"C'mon, honey," Robin called out. "Let's go. We got other people here who want to play."

Sedonia stumbled slightly as she walked over to where Robin and Jeanette were waiting. Robin put a microphone in front of Sedonia's face and said, "What's your name?"

"Sedonia . . ."

"Sedona? Like in Arizona?"

"Sedon*ia*."

"Oh, Sedon-ya. Okay, where you from, Sedon-ya?"

"Nassau Bay, Texas."

"And what team do you play for?"

Sedonia felt herself reddening. "The . . . uh . . . Cue-Ts."

Robin turned to the crowd. "Okay, folks, we got a 'cutie' here, going against Jeanette. One game of Nine-Ball. Challenger breaks."

Sedonia hastily screwed her cue stick together. Then as she moved to the break end of the table, she instinctively checked the playing surface. The table wasn't top-of-the-line, but the felt was new and it was an 8-footer. Hopefully, having just practiced on a 9-footer, she wouldn't embarrass herself too badly. She took a deep breath. *One, two, three . . . stroke!*

The balls scattered, and she kept her eye on the yellow 1-ball, which was rolling slowly toward the side pocket. Suddenly a man's voice rang out, "On the snap!" Sedonia shifted her attention to the break end of the table, in time to see the gold-striped 9-ball disappear into the corner pocket. The spectators burst into spontaneous applause. Sedonia had won the game on the break.

Jeanette laid her cue stick on the table and joined the crowd in applause. Then she held up a hand for quiet and said, "Okay, folks, she beat me fair and square. But, let's let her play again. She didn't get her $20 worth. She only got *one* shot." Jeanette theatrically narrowed her eyes in mock anger. "And I didn't get *any* . . ."

The crowd clapped their approval. Someone on one side said, "Uh-oh," which drew a laugh from the crowd. And someone standing near Sedonia told her, "You're in for it now."

"Your break," Jeanette said.

Sedonia chalked her cue. Jeanette had challenged her with teasing good humor, but it had, in fact, been a challenge. Sedonia glanced at the balls. The rack looked tight. She assumed her break stance, checked her grip, and leaned over the table. *One, two, three . . . stroke!*

The orange 5-ball darted into the side pocket, and rest of the balls scattered about the table. Sedonia took a moment to study the layout. For the past seven months, she'd played Eight-Ball exclusively. This, however, was Nine-Ball. The objective of this game was to shoot the balls in numerical order, and whoever made the 9-ball was the winner. It was essential to determine the sequence of shots in advance, and to always get good position when moving from one shot to the next.

Shot sequence in mind, Sedonia focused on her first ball. She didn't know if they were playing "call shot," so she took no chances. "One in the side." The yellow 1-ball disappeared into the side pocket. "Two in the side." The presence of WPBA professionals and the press of the crowd now were partitioned from her thoughts as she methodically worked her way through the balls. "Three in the corner . . ."

Finally, she was down to the last two balls. She studied the critical second-to-last shot, then said, "Eight in the corner." She hit it perfectly, but put too much top spin on the cue-ball. The 8-ball dropped, but she left herself in poor position on the potential game winning shot on the 9-ball. Her only offensive shot would be to drive the 9-ball into the opposite rail, and bank it back across the table and into the near side pocket. Had she wanted to play defensively, she could just tap the 9-ball against the end rail, and leave Jeanette in poor position down at the other end of the table, but Sedonia never played defensively.

"Nine-ball, cross side," she said, and struck the cue-ball with a firm, smooth stroke. The 9-ball banked off the side rail and rolled back across the table and into the side pocket, dead center. She heard Hannah cry out, "Break-and-run!"

Jeanette stared at Sedonia for a moment, then walked over and extended her hand. "Good shooting."

"I don't know . . . what happened," Sedonia stammered. "I just . . . got lucky . . . I guess."

Robin handed Jeanette the microphone. Playing to the crowd, Jeanette asked Sedonia, "Are you sure you'll be in the BCA Eight-Ball tournament, not the pro Nine-Ball?"

Sedonia smiled and nodded.

"Whew!" Jeanette said, pantomiming wiping sweat from her brow. The crowd gave an appreciative laugh. Then she posed for the Polaroid photo with Sedonia and signed a poster for her. After another handshake, Robin resumed her pitch for someone else to pay $20 to play a game of Nine-Ball against The Black Widow.

Sedonia walked over to where Hannah waited, smiling. She unrolled the poster and read Jeanette's inscription:

> To Sedonia.
> "Break and run!"
> Hope to play you again.
> Jeanette "The Black Widow" Lee

Sedonia looked over where the next exhibition game was already underway. Jeanette leaned gracefully over the table, her forearm moved in a smooth pendulum motion, and the blue 2-ball rolled the length of the table and fell into the corner pocket.

For reasons Sedonia didn't understand, tears welled in her eyes. She turned away from the table and found Hannah looking at her with a quizzical expression.

"What's the matter?" Hannah said.

"I don't know," Sedonia said with a shake of her head. "It's just . . . those pros have got so much . . . class."

"Yeah, but you beat her."

"In an exhibition game," Sedonia said. "In a real match, it would be different."

"I don't know about that. If I didn't think you were good enough to beat her, I wouldn't have put up my $20."

Sedonia opened one eye and checked the hotel clock-radio: 4:47. Hannah snored from a deep sleep in the next bed. "Damn it," Sedonia muttered, then rolled over onto her side and pulled the extra pillow over her head. She'd gone to bed early, wanting to be well rested for their first match at 9:00 a.m. However, so far she'd managed only three or fours hours of broken sleep.

Hannah had awakened her about midnight, when she came up from the casino. And then sometime after 2:00 a.m., Sedonia had been asleep again, only to be awakened by laughing and talking in the hallway. She'd recognized Flora, Vicky, and Melissa's voices, but hadn't heard Cissy's. God only knew where Cissy had wound up last night. Then, since Sedonia's headboard was next to the wall that separated her room from Flora and Vicky's, for another hour she'd had to listen to the muffled sounds of their inebriated exuberance.

Now, she pulled the pillow off her head and rolled onto her back. She'd experienced pre-match jitters before important golf matches, but never this severe. Her teammates were counting on her again this week, and she'd lost confidence in her game. She tried to psyche herself up by recalling her two exhibition wins over Jeanette Lee. If only this tournament were being played on regulation tables. Or if only she'd practiced on bar-boxes.

She turned her head and checked the clock again: 4:53. That was 6:53 Nassau Bay time. That would have to do. She threw back the covers. She'd try to shower and dress without disturbing Hannah, and then go downstairs and see if she could find a place to have breakfast. And then, find a bar-box to practice on.

Sedonia frowned as she wandered through the Riviera's first-floor maze. Hannah had awakened just long enough to tell her that the coffee shop was located near the main entrance. The layout of slot machines, video poker machines, and gaming tables seemed designed to keep patrons from escaping the casino. At this hour of the morning, most of the gambling stations were idle; however, a few hardy customers still manned their posts. They sat stoop-shouldered, usually one person per aisle, mechanically inserting bills and pushing buttons. Apparently they thought sleep was for the faint of heart, and it was the early bird who got the jackpot.

Sedonia finally spotted the casino's main entrance, and moments later arrived at the coffee shop, only to find it was closed. Through the front plate-glass window, however, she saw a McDonald's on the other side of Las Vegas Boulevard. Three cars were parked out front, so apparently it was open.

As Sedonia stepped outside, she glanced up and down the street. The Strip was nearly deserted; however, its gaudy neon signs still blazed and flashed, though the desert sky had already begun to glow with a predawn, yellowish haze. She waited at the curb while a garbage truck rumbled past, and then she crossed to the other side.

The contrast of a standard neighborhood McDonald's sitting next to the sprawling Circus Circus complex drew a wry smile. She stepped inside and headed over to the food-order station. The only person in line was an exhausted looking woman in black slacks and a white blouse—probably a casino dealer grabbing a bite to eat on her way home. As Sedonia waited to place her order, she glanced back and to her surprise saw Cissy, sitting in a corner booth, staring at her.

Sedonia hesitated, then called over, "Do you want something while I'm up here?"

Cissy gave a curt shake of her head. Then she turned away and directed her gaze down Las Vegas Boulevard.

A few minutes later, Sedonia joined Cissy in the booth. She checked Cissy's pupils; they looked normal. Then she glanced down at an empty Styrofoam plate on the table.

"Yes," Cissy said, pique in her tone, "I've eaten."

Sedonia unwrapped her Egg McMuffin. Before she took her first bite she said, "Are you out late, or up early?"

Cissy shrugged.

Sedonia said, "Hannah told me you had some . . . uh . . . legal problems."

Cissy gave a grudging nod, but didn't reply.

"You shouldn't have come to Las Vegas with us," Sedonia said. "Not if they're going to put you in jail when you get back."

"I told you and Hannah that you could count on me this time."

"We didn't want you going to jail, though," Sedonia said.

Cissy didn't reply.

"How can we help you?" Sedonia pressed.

"By butting out," Cissy snapped.

"Cissy—"

"Just stay out of it," Cissy interrupted. "Sedonia, I know you think you're perfect . . . but some of us aren't!"

Sedonia took a deep breath. She sure as hell didn't consider herself perfect. Plus, she had her own damned problems this morning. She finished her breakfast sandwich in silence, and then took the lid off her coffee. Then on second thought, she replaced the lid, and stood up. "I'm gonna see if I can find a place to practice."

"The tournament room's open," Cissy said. "Tables in there cost a dollar a game, but they only take tokens. The token machines are over by the bulletin boards."

Sedonia nodded. At least Cissy had started responding. "Do you want to come along, and hit some balls?"

Cissy shook her head. Then as Sedonia turned to leave, Cissy said, "I just left there. I've been practicing since three o'clock."

Sedonia turned back and studied her again. A faint smile tugged at the corners of her mouth. "Sounds like you've . . . come to play."

Cissy hesitated, then said, "I've been here before, so I know what it's like. Eddy brought me a couple of years ago . . . to watch *him* play. This time, *I'm* playing." Then she turned away, and redirected her gaze down Las Vegas Boulevard.

Sedonia checked her watch as she entered the Grande Ballroom: 6:40. She had more than two hours before her first match. The overhead lights were still dim and the only person in sight was a janitor wielding a push broom. The row of vendor stalls had been secured overnight. Near the long bulletin board row, she found the token machine and fed it a $20 bill. Then she continued over to the playing area.

She paused at the head of the main aisle, again momentarily awed by the 324-table matrix spread out before her. Only a half-dozen players were scattered throughout the room. The phrase "calm before the storm" came to mind. The scene reminded her of the Bay Oaks Country Club golf course at first light, and the countless mornings she'd teed off alone. She'd loved the solitude of those morning practice rounds. Her putts throwing up rooster tails and marking their paths as they rolled across the greens . . .

Sedonia shook her head, annoyed with herself. This wasn't the time for nostalgia. She wasn't here to play golf, and there sure as hell wasn't any dew on *these* greens, not in this desert casino.

She started down the main aisle toward the center of the room. Hannah had told her their first match would be on tables No. 151 and 152. As Sedonia approached, she saw a man practicing on No. 151. He appeared to be in his forties and was dressed in black, including a league shirt that read "Corner Pocket Poolroom, Modesto, California." His unkempt ponytail was streaked with gray and pulled behind his head with a rubber band.

Sedonia walked over and said, "You playing here at 9:00?"

He responded with a smile that displayed an expanse of bad teeth. "Yeah. We playing you?"

"Must be," Sedonia said. "Okay if I practice on the other table?"

"Sure."

Sedonia felt self-conscious as she screwed her stick together, and then fed a token into the table and retrieved the balls. A few minutes later, however, she fell into her practice routine and gave little thought to the man at the next table. At one point, though, she glanced over and noticed he used a small, rolled-up towel to block the pockets he was shooting for. Sedonia pulled a towel out of her cue case and began doing the same. It saved her from paying a dollar to retrieve the balls after every 15 shots.

Buster had coached her to hit the cue-ball low when she was playing on bar-boxes, so now while practicing, she made it a point to put "stop" on each shot. For a while it affected her accuracy, but soon she grew accustomed to it and the object balls began hitting the pockets dead center.

From time to time, Sedonia would look up and notice that additional players on the opposing team were arriving, also dressed in black. And other players were reporting throughout the room. An undertone of predominantly male voices rose, punctuated by the staccato of pool balls colliding.

Sedonia was concentrating on a shot, when Hannah's voice rang out, "Have you seen the others?"

Sedonia looked up. "Just Cissy. We had breakfast together."

"I don't care about Cissy. It's the ones who are going to play that I'm worried about."

"Aren't they in their rooms?"

"Somebody knocked on our door, just as I was getting out of the shower. I think it was Flora and Vicky. When I called their room, though, I didn't get an answer. Same thing with Melissa and Cissy's room."

Sedonia checked her watch: 8:35. "There's still plenty of time."

"I told them I wanted them here an hour before the match," Hannah said, exasperation in her tone. Then she glanced over at the next table. "The other team's already here."

"Speaking of Cissy," Sedonia said, "she was in here practicing before I was. I think you ought to play her."

Hannah shot Sedonia an annoyed look. "I told you, and Cissy, she's just going to be a substitute. Melissa's in the regular rotation."

"Yeah, but there's something about Cissy's attitude this morning."

"Melissa's taking her place."

"I'm telling you—"

"Sedonia!"

Sedonia held up her hands. "Okay. You're the captain. It's up to you." Then she nodded toward the main aisle. "Here come Flora and Vicky."

"About time," Hannah snapped as they walked up. "Where's Melissa?"

Flora shrugged; Vicky was already starting a conversation with a younger member of the opposing team.

"Vicky!" Hannah said. "Do you know where Melissa is?"

Vicky pulled herself away from the man in black. "When I called to see if she wanted to go to breakfast with us, she said she was sick. She really got wasted last night."

"Damn it!" Hannah exploded. She dialed a number on her cell phone, waited, and then shook her head. "No answer. I'll go knock on her door."

"Wait a minute," Sedonia said. "Here comes Cissy. We've got five players now."

Hanna gave a grudging nod. When Cissy arrived, Hannah said, "If Melissa doesn't show up, you'll be playing in her place."

Cissy responded with a barely perceptible nod, then asked Sedonia, "Want to play a practice game?"

"Sure."

Sedonia broke and ran five balls, and then intentionally missed her next shot, rather than run the rack without giving Cissy a shot. One of the things she'd learned during league play was not to discourage her team-mates, when they were warming up before a match. Cissy made four balls before she missed, and then Sedonia finished the game.

Hannah told them to let Flora and Vicky shoot a game to get warmed up. Sedonia and Cissy took seats behind the scorekeeping table, and Hannah made another attempt to phone Melissa's room.

Sedonia checked her watch: 8:51. She felt butterflies take wing in her stomach, and she looked around the cavernous room, trying to take her mind off the upcoming match. "They must be making a fortune, just off the pool tables," she told Cissy.

Cissy frowned.

Sedonia continued, "At a dollar a game, 324 tables going all day and into the night . . . for a week . . ."

Cissy seemed lost in thought and didn't reply.

The opposing player with the ponytail came over, handed Hannah his copy of the score sheet, and told her, "It's almost 9:00. I need your lineup."

Hannah looked around one last time, and then entered Cissy's name as their fifth player.

"Hannah doesn't like me," Cissy said in an aside to Sedonia.

Sedonia heaved a sigh. She couldn't imagine the team being more ill prepared to play: one player missing, one not warmed up, two barely warmed up, one pouting, and she herself suffering from a severe case of pre-match nerves.

Hannah spoke briefly with the opposing captain, and then turned and said, "Sedonia, you're up on table No. 151. Your break."

Matches were getting underway throughout the room. Sedonia's first opponent, the younger player Vicky had been talking to, fed a token into the table and began racking the balls. Since he was leading off, Sedonia assumed he must be their strongest player. She felt her pulse accelerate and took a deep breath trying to calm her jitters. Despite being in the midst of hundreds of players, somehow she still felt on-stage, alone.

She glanced to her right. Hannah was up on table No. 152. Sedonia had never seen her so intense. The pressure of the national tournament was getting to her too.

When Sedonia's opponent finished racking the balls, she offered him the perfunctory "Good luck." Her hand shook as she placed the cue-ball close to the right rail, and when she leaned down to break, a muscle in her right calf began to jump. Not that again! she thought. The people seated behind her must surely be able to see it through her jeans. Anxious to get the game underway, she skipped her usual pre-shot routine, and simply drove the cue-ball forward as hard as she could. She miscued. The cue-ball hit the side of the rack, ricocheted over to the side rail, jumped an inch or two into the air, and flew back into the knot of balls still clustered in the center of the table. It was a terrible break. She'd failed to make an object ball, but at least the cue-ball had stayed on the table.

A sharp *crack!* came from the next table, and Sedonia caught a glimpse of a cue-ball streaking by, landing on the floor between the next row of tables, and then rolling out of sight. Her eyes met those of a horrified Hannah. "Well," Sedonia said, trying to lighten the tension, "at least we didn't rip the felt." With a distracted shake of her head, Hannah hurried off to retrieve her cue-ball.

Sedonia's opponent twice made two balls, and then resorted to playing safeties. After each, Sedonia managed to hit her object ball, but couldn't come close to pocketing it. Her annoyance at his forcing her to shoot unmakeable shots affected her concentration, and on her third trip to the table she missed a makeable shot. Her opponent hurried back to the table, made the rest of his balls, and then sank the 8-ball for the win.

"Good safeties," Sedonia told him through clenched teeth, rather than the usual, "Good game." As she walked away, she glanced over at Hannah's table and saw her opponent make the 8-ball. Hannah still had five balls on the table. The Cue-Ts were down 2 to 0 in the race-to-13.

Flora and Vicky were next up, and they obviously weren't prepared to play. Their games lasted longer, because their opponents also were struggling, but the men hung on and eked out wins. The Cue-Ts now trailed 4 to 0.

"It's up to you, Cissy," Sedonia encouraged. "Stop the bleeding." Cissy looked tense as she prepared to break, but then, Cissy always looked tense.

Hannah called over to Sedonia, "You're up on 152."

Sedonia racked for her second game, then took a seat while her opponent broke. She looked over at the other table and saw Cissy play a brutal safety. Her opponent was unable to hit his object ball, giving Cissy ball-in-hand, and she ran the rest of her suit for the Cue-Ts' first win. Sedonia jumped up and joined her teammates, including Hannah, in giving Cissy high-fives.

Sedonia returned to her seat and saw that, while she'd been celebrating, her opponent had been busy running the rack. Moments later, he sank the 8-ball. Sedonia had lost her first two games in Las Vegas, and the Cue-Ts now trailed, 5 to 1.

Hannah, Flora, and Vicky followed suit, and each dropped another game. However, Cissy won again, this time against the other team's best player. She was playing as well as Sedonia had ever seen her play. After two rounds, however, the Cute-Ts trailed 8 to 2. Their opponents only needed to win 5 more games.

Hannah called a timeout and gathered her team around her. As she started to speak, Melissa walked up and said, "Am I playing?"

Hannah looked as if she might explode. Finally she said in a measured tone, "Cissy has taken your place." Then she turned back to the others. "Cissy, you just keep doing whatever it is you've been doing. You're playing great. The rest of us, we gotta try and relax. Let's just play like we're back at Carney's. We've beaten better teams than this."

Sedonia and the others nodded in uncertain assent.

"Okay, Sedonia," Hannah said, "get the rest of us started."

As Sedonia stood at the break end of the table, for the first time in the match she felt as if her team was ready to play. "Good luck," she told her opponent, then assumed her break stance. *One, two, three . . . stroke!* Three solids fought their way into pockets, and the rest spread out across the table. Concentrating on putting low spin on the cue-ball with each shot, Sedonia methodically worked her way around the table. Finally she said, "Eight in the corner." The Cue-Ts now trailed, 8 to 3.

Hannah lost a hard-fought game, but Flora and Vicky rallied with their first wins of the match. Cissy won her third game handily. The Cue-Ts had closed the score, 9 to 6.

Sedonia started the fourth round with a rack-and-run. Hannah won, but Flora and Vicky both lost. Cissy and her opponent played a cat-and-mouse defensive contest, before Cissy finally sank the 8-ball for the win. The Cue-Ts now trailed, 12 to 8. They'd need to win all five games in the final round to win the match.

While Sedonia waited to break for her fifth and final game, she glanced down at the score sheet. Her next opponent had lost to both Flora and Hannah, so he must not be too strong. Sedonia's teammates were seated together nearby. She leaned over and said, "Okay, guys. Cissy's carried us this far. She's got the last game of the match, so it's up to the rest of us to win our games, to give her a chance to bring it home."

Her teammates, except Melissa, chorused their assent.

"Good luck," Sedonia's opponent said.

"Good luck," she replied as she walked to the break end of the table. *One, two, three . . . stroke!* The green-striped 14-ball darted into the near corner. The stripes were spread out; the solids were knotted together in three clusters. "Eleven in the side. Nine in the corner . . ." Sedonia methodically worked her way around the table until she was down to the 8-ball. She'd left herself an easy shot: down the side rail to where the 8-ball sat in front of the corner pocket.

"Eight in the corner," she said. Smooth stroke, then a sharp intake of air. She'd put top spin on the cue-ball! It kissed the 8-ball into the pocket, but then hit the end rail too hard, clipped a cluster of solid balls near the center of the table, and veered toward the side pocket. *Scratch!* The match was over.

Her opponent came over and said, "Tough luck."

Sedonia stared at the side pocket in disbelief. Finally she acknowledged her opponent with a perfunctory, "Good game," though he hadn't made a single ball.

Hannah came up and placed a hand on Sedonia's shoulder. "Shake it off. That's just our first loss, and this is a double-elimination tournament."

Then the other women, except Melissa, came over and offered their condolences. Cissy was the last. "Playin' in Vegas is different," she said. "Don't worry. You'll get used to it."

Sedonia pulled up a chair beside Hannah, who was completing her score sheet. Sedonia stared down at the table, fighting back tears. She'd never felt so crushed by a defeat, either in pool or in golf. The opposing captain was seated nearby, completing his sheet. One of his players, who apparently had been in the restroom, walked up and was surprised to discover the match was over. He asked how they'd won. Without looking up, his captain replied, "The good-lookin' chick dogged the 8-ball." Sedonia gritted her teeth, but knew she had, in fact, dogged the 8-ball. Hannah also heard comment, and reached over and gave Sedonia a reassuring pat on the knee.

Finally, both teams headed up the main aisle to turn in the score sheets. Sedonia brought up the rear of the procession, still stunned at having lost the critical game of the match. Most of the nine o'clock matches hadn't yet completed. More than 600 teams were on the floor, and players were struggling under the pressure that had proven too much for her. Intermittent, spontaneous cheers erupted from the winners, and disappointment, anger, and disgust showed on the faces of the losers.

The tournament organizers operated from a raised platform that gave them a view of the entire Grande Ballroom. One of the men in charge took Hannah's score sheet, checked a computer printout, and then told her, "Your team plays again at 3:00. Tables No. 97 and 98."

Hannah gathered her team around her. "Everybody hear that? I want you gals here an hour early. Two o'clock. Got it?"

Flora and Vicky nodded, then hurried off to join two members of the team that had just beaten them.

Melissa came over and said, "Am I gonna get to play this afternoon?"

"You're the sub now," Hannah said. "Cissy not only was on time and ready to play this morning, she won all four of her games."

Melissa turned on her heel and walked away, without replying.

Cissy had been standing off to the side during the exchange. A faint smile formed on her gaunt face.

"Two o'clock, Cissy," Hannah said.

Cissy nodded. "Tables No. 97 and 98." Then she turned and headed back toward the playing area.

"You told me she was ready to play," Hannah said to Sedonia. "She sure as hell surprised me, though."

They both watched Cissy strolling though the playing area. She looked like an emaciated waif, wandering through a field of green.

Sedonia said. "She really came through in the clutch, didn't she?"

Hannah nodded. "Get her away from that piece-of-crap boyfriend, and she shows a lot of heart."

Sedonia slowly shook her head. "I sure didn't show any. That guy back there was right. I dogged my brains out on that last 8-ball."

"Don't be so hard on yourself."

"Maybe you ought to let Melissa play in my place."

Hannah gave her an annoyed look. "Don't be ridiculous. And stop whining."

Sedonia had to chuckle. Her friend and captain didn't mince words. "You're right. I feel like shit for letting the team down, and I'm . . . whining."

"Well stop it," Hannah said. "It's out of character for you."

Sedonia sighed. "I don't know what to do. Find a place to practice, or go upstairs and take a nap? I didn't get much sleep last night."

Hannah arched one eye brow. "My snoring keep you awake?"

"It didn't help, but I probably couldn't have slept anyway. For the past couple of days, I've been uptight about playing here."

"You're shooting good, kid. I don't think you need any more practice. Go on up to the room and take a nap. I'll call you at 1:30."

Sedonia looked around the bustling room. It was hard to pull herself away from all the activity, but maybe getting some rest would help. As poorly as she'd played this morning, a nap sure as hell couldn't hurt.

Chapter 10

Sedonia wove through the crowded foyer that linked the hotel and the convention center, and then entered the Grande Ballroom. The vendor stalls were doing a bustling business, and off to the right, Robin Dodson again was challenging BCA players to test their skills against WPBA star Jeanette "The Black Widow" Lee.

In the tournament area, about half of the 324 tables were in use. A few matches were running late, and the rest of the tables were occupied by players who were getting in some practice. Sedonia spotted Hannah shooting alone on table No. 97.

As Sedonia approached, Hannah said, "Were you able to sleep?"

"Yeah. I must have been more tired than I thought. I was out as soon as my head hit the pillow, until you phoned." She looked around. "Nobody else here?"

"Cissy left a few minutes ago to get something to eat. She's been practicing since this morning's match." They exchanged smiles and Hannah added, "She's eating too. And something other than little white pills."

Sedonia racked the balls, and she and Hannah played a practice game. Hannah was racking for a second game, when Flora and Vicky arrived. Hannah made no mention of their being late; apparently she'd decided nagging these young women didn't do any good. They began practicing on table No. 98.

Then Cissy returned with a sub sandwich and nibbled it at the scorer's table, while she watched the others play. For the first time since arriving in Las Vegas, Sedonia relaxed. The Cue-Ts' camaraderie had returned, and the tournament surroundings were becoming more familiar—not as comfortable as Buster's or Carney's, but not as intimidating as they'd been that morning.

Ten minutes before the scheduled match time, the five members of the opposing team arrived together. Sedonia was pleasantly surprised to see that two young women were included on the five-person team. The logo on their shirts read "Fat Freddie's Billiards."

As they got settled and ready to play, one of the women asked Sedonia, "Where y'all from?"

"Nassau Bay, Texas. It's—"

"You're kidding!" the woman interrupted. "We're from Baytown!"

"Did you hear that, Hannah?" Sedonia said. "We've come all the way to Las Vegas to play a Baytown team."

"Hell," the woman chimed in, "y'all could have just driven 15 miles up Highway 146 and played us at Fat Freddie's."

The players from the two teams visited for a quarter-hour, discovering mutual acquaintances among pool players in their area. Cissy, in particular, seemed to know everyone. Sedonia surmised it was from accompanying her pool-playing, dope-pushing boyfriend up and down that particular stretch of the Gulf Coast. When Hannah announced it was after 3:00, and they'd better start playing, it seemed like an annoying interruption to a social gathering.

As the match got underway, Sedonia discovered their opponents weren't very good. One mentioned they'd dropped their morning session, 13 to 2. Another said they'd finished last in the Baytown league and had paid their own way to this tournament. For them, this trip was a lark, an opportunity to get away from the tedium of their daily lives.

The games moved quickly, and the Fat Freddie's players accepted their eventual defeat with good humor. The final score was 13 to 3, with Sedonia and Cissy going undefeated and Hannah, Vicky, and Flora losing just one game each. After handshakes and promises to get together sometime later for drinks, the two teams went their separate ways.

Hannah turned in her score sheet at the tournament organizers' platform, and then gathered her team around her. "We don't play again until noon, tomorrow. We'll be on tables No. 7 and 8. So, you're on your own 'til then. If one of y'all runs into Melissa, be sure and tell her what our schedule is."

"Is she still on the team?" Vicky said.

"I assume since she didn't show up this afternoon, she's quit. But, I'm not going to worry about it. As far as I'm concerned, *we're* the team. If she shows up tomorrow . . . well, we'll just have to see how it goes."

The others nodded their assent.

"Which brings up something else," Hannah said. "Now that it looks like we'll be in the tournament for at least another day, we need more than one set of shirts. We can't rinse and dry these as fast as we may be playing. Okay with you if I buy another set from one of these vendors?"

They all agreed to reimburse her for the expense, and then they discussed where they were going from here. Flora and Vicky had made plans to meet two of the players from the morning match. Cissy was going to see if she could match up in the practice room, and Hannah said somewhere in the casino there was a blackjack table with her name on it.

Sedonia checked her watch: 5:25. "I'm just gonna look around for a while," she said. "Maybe catch up with y'all later."

Sedonia descended the escalator from the Riviera's second-floor cafeteria. She'd planned to eat sensibly and exercise daily on this trip. However, she'd just given in to the temptations that had been spread across the hotel's hundred-foot buffet. For her entrée alone, she'd sampled pecan-crusted chicken, crab-stuffed flounder, and rare prime rib. As the escalator arrived at the ground floor, she decided she'd eaten too much to work out tonight. Instead, she'd get up early in the morning, do her stretching routine, and go for a jog.

At the foot of the elevator, a stream of pool players passed in both directions. Most, like herself, had cue cases slung over their shoulders. Sedonia worked her way over to a bank of elevators marked "Monte Carlo Towers." An easel held a poster that read:

Professional 9-Ball Championships
Penthouse Floor

An elevator arrived and a full load of BCA players got off. Sedonia entered and pushed the "Penthouse" button. Before the doors closed, Jeanette Lee entered, followed by another well-known WPBA professional, Ewa Laurance. Jeanette acknowledged Sedonia with a hesitant nod and smile, as if trying to remember where she'd seen her before. Ewa continued a conversation the two women were having, and Sedonia noted the hint of a pleasant Swedish accent. The topic, surprisingly, was golf. Jeanette complained that spinal problems were preventing her from playing. Ewa said when she got back home she'd send Jeanette a copy of a pamphlet on stretching exercises. Sedonia wanted to join the conversation, but a number of other BCA players now piled into the elevator. The men, in particular, did double-takes at their unexpected good fortune in being in such close proximity to the two renowned professionals. One of the bolder men asked how they were doing, and was rewarded with polite, friendly replies.

The doors closed and the elevator began its ascent. Both Jeanette and Ewa stood tall, slim, and attractive, yet it was their contrasting features that Sedonia found most interesting. Jeanette was a classic Asian beauty, while Ewa looked like a latter-day Ingrid Bergman. Sedonia suppressed a smile. She was accustomed to drawing male attention. Here, however, sharing an elevator with The Black Widow and The Striking Viking, men completely ignored her. She might as well have been the elevator operator.

They arrived at the penthouse floor, and everyone allowed the two professionals to precede them. As they started toward the doorway that led to the playing area, Jeanette abruptly turned and pointed back at Sedonia. "Hey!" she said with a mock frown, apparently having remembered where she'd met Sedonia. "I thought I told you to stay away from the professional tournament. You're too good!"

Sedonia smiled, pleased at the recognition. "I've come to watch y'all play. See if I can learn something. Good luck!"

Both professionals acknowledged her with smiles and thanks, then continued into the tournament room. As Sedonia took her place in line to buy a ticket, she sensed that the male interest had switched to her.

A wall-mounted bulletin board displayed the tournament brackets and listed the prize money. The men and women's tournaments each had 64 entrants. First place paid $15,000, second place paid half of that, and so on. Sedonia scanned the names on the women's bracket and saw that all the best known WPBA players were competing. She was pleased to see she'd have the opportunity to see Jeanette and Ewa play against each other tonight.

A heavyset hotel employee sat behind the ticket sales table. She glanced at Sedonia's cue case and said, "You playing in the BCA tournament downstairs?"

"Yeah."

"That'll be $5 then. Gets you in all three sessions tonight. The first row is reserved seats. They're sold out. But you can take any of the general admission seats, and feel free to move around." Sedonia paid, and the woman clipped a green Mylar band around her wrist, and nodded she could enter.

The doorway opened into the middle of the long, rectangular room. The Monte Carlo Penthouse lived up to its name. Plate glass walls on three sides presented a panoramic view of the Las Vegas Strip. The sun was setting behind the mountains in the distance. Plush burgundy carpeting covered the floor, and angled mirrors reflected from the ceiling. A tuxedoed bartender dispensed mixed drinks and wine.

This week, gaming tables had given way to pool tables. Four 9-foot Connellys stood off to the left, and four more to the right. Each group of four was surrounded by a single row of cushioned Queen Anne chairs, and then a raised platform with four rows of metal folding chairs. Players were warming up throughout the room. Sedonia noted that although men and women were playing in separate tournaments, table assignments had their games interspersed. She spotted Jeanette and Ewa preparing to play on table No. 8, far down on the right.

As she made her way down the aisle between the reserved and the general admission seats, she recognized the owner of Cue-Nique Billiards, sitting in a reserved seat near the second-to-last table. She stopped and said, "How's it going, Sal?"

He looked up with a frown, which promptly turned into a smile. "Hey, kid! Pull up a chair."

Sedonia glanced down at his wrist. His pink Mylar band indicated reserved seat status. She showed him her green general admission band.

"Don't sweat it. They don't check."

Feeling like a trespasser, Sedonia pulled up a cushioned chair beside him. She'd talk to him for a few minutes, then find a seat in the general admission section. Two men were warming up less than ten feet away. One was a clean-cut kid, who looked barely out of his teens; the other was fortyish, with swarthy features and the demeanor of a mobster. Sedonia would have preferred to be one table over, where she could watch the Jeanette-Ewa match, but this would do for now. She asked Sal, "Are these guys good?"

He dismissed her question with a brusque wave, and called over to the kid, "Hey! You got gamble?"

The kid gave Sal a glance, then continued working his way around the table, shooting bank shots. Some fell; some didn't.

As he leaned over for his next shot, Sal said, "Betcha a dime."

The kid banked the red 3-ball into the side pocket, then straightened up and strolled over to where Sal was sitting. "What's the bet?"

"Straight up. I'll take Mike."

The kid looked at Sedonia and smiled. Then he walked back to the table and banked the purple-striped 12-ball the length of the table and into the corner pocket. He turned back to Sal, gave a quick nod, and said, "A thousand dollars, straight up. You got it."

Sedonia was surprised to discover that professional players gambled during their tournament matches. She didn't know of any other competitive endeavor where it was allowed. She told Sal, "You must know these players pretty well."

"Mike's a Snooker champion in Canada. Doesn't play a lot of Nine-Ball, but Canadians are tough when they come down here. Do you play Snooker?"

Sedonia shook her head. "None of the poolrooms where I play have Snooker tables. Don't know much about it, except it's a European game and the tables are bigger."

"European *and* Canadian. The tables are 12 feet long, so even our 9-footers look small to them. Plus, they play a lot of defensive shots. Guess that's where the expression 'getting snookered' comes from."

"How about the younger guy?" Sedonia said.

"Chris is a road player, with local backers. For the match to be even, Mike would have to give him the eight."

From watching gamblers at Buster's, Sedonia knew that "give him eight" was a handicap device in Nine-Ball, used to match up players of different skill levels. The lesser player only had to get to the 8-ball to win, while the better player had to get to the 9-ball. If Sal's handicapping was correct, getting the Canadian straight up was a good bet.

"What about Jeanette and Ewa?" Sedonia said. "How do they match up?"

Sal shrugged. "They don't gamble. WPBA won't let 'em."

"But are they as good as the men?"

"Naw. They play good . . . better than me. But the top women players can't compete with the top men."

The conversation reminded Sedonia of one she'd had with Buster not too long ago. "Why do you say that?"

Sal studied Jeanette and Ewa for a moment. Finally he said, "Men are just . . . better."

Sedonia bristled at his offhand dismissal of women players. "But *why* do you think that's so?"

"Well," Sal said, "take these matches for example. In both the men's and the women's tournaments, these matches have to be completed within two hours, so the next ones can get started. Because of that, the men's tournament is a race-to-11, but the women's is only a race-to-9. If the women played race-to-11 too, their matches would run longer than two hours. Eleven versus nine. That's a good ratio of men's skills versus women's skills."

Sedonia frowned. She didn't see any reason that woman shouldn't be playing the same number of games as the men. Pool wasn't like golf and tennis, where relative physical strength was a factor. In golf, since women typically couldn't hit the ball as far as men, they were allowed to play from tees closer to the green. And in tennis, since women didn't hit the ball as hard, their rallies lasted longer. So it made sense that they played best two out of three sets, where the men played best three out of five. But she didn't see any justification for there being a difference in pool.

"Do women miss more shots than the men do?" Sedonia said. "Is that the reason their matches last longer?"

Sal looked over at the two women professionals again, then at the two men, and finally back at Sedonia. "I guess they shoot as good. But for one thing, like I said, they don't gamble as much. So, they don't have the same amount of experience playing under pressure. They're more likely to dog key shots. They know that, so they play a lot more safeties than men do."

Sedonia gave a grudging nod. Women she'd played against did seem more inclined to play safeties than did men. Her game, though, was more like the men's. If there was any possibility of making a ball, she'd go for it.

"For another thing," Sal continued, "women are just naturally . . . nicer. You're not as . . . aggressive as men are."

"I don't know about that . . ." Sedonia began.

"Keep an eye on these two tables," Sal said. "The women walked up buddy-buddy, and they'll leave buddy-buddy. The men hardly talk to each other."

At that moment, the Canadian gestured for the younger player to relinquish the table; now it was his turn to practice.

"See?" Sal said. "Intimidation, each guy trying to get the other guy to fear him. That's the difference between men and women players."

"Some people might say it's a matter of sportsmanship," Sedonia said.

"Pool's not about sportsmanship," Sal said. "Pool's about getting paid."

Sedonia chuckled. There was no doubt that Sal and Buster had graduated from the same school of thought, which held that men were better players than women, and pool was all about getting paid. Still, she felt it important to explore the perceived differences between men and women players, and she tried a different approach. "Who do you think is the best male player today?

"Victor Morella."

"Best female?"

"Margaret Faulkson."

"How would you match them up?"

"Victor would have to give her the eight and the breaks."

Sedonia looked back over to where Jeanette and Ewa were completing their warm-ups. "Eight and the breaks" was a significant amount of weight for a better player to offer a lesser player. She wondered if Sal was right.

"Excuse me," said a voice behind her. "This is reserved seating."

A middle-aged man with a hotel name tag on his shirt was looking down at her.

Sedonia stood up. "I was just leaving." Sal looked as if he were about to argue with the man, but Sedonia told him, "I'll see you later. I want to watch the women play."

Sedonia stood up and stretched, trying to restore circulation to her lower extremities after sitting on a metal chair for an hour and a half. The match between the two men had finished, and Sal was collecting his $1,000 bet from the young loser. Jeanette and Ewa were both on-the-hill, tied 8 to 8 in their race-to-9.

As matches concluded throughout the room, Sal's charge that women took longer to play seemed to have merit. One hour into the session, an announcement had been made that two women on table No. 5 had been put on the clock for playing too slowly. A tournament official now stood over their game and allowed them only 30 seconds between shots, or be penalized and lose their turn at the table. Sedonia took satisfaction in knowing she played as quickly as the men she'd been watching.

Sal walked back to where Sedonia was standing and flashed the $1,000. "Action ought to be picking up at the Billiard Club about now," he said. "Wanna ride over with me?"

"You don't want to see how this turns out?" Sedonia said, indicating the Jeanette-Ewa match. "It's hill-hill."

Sal responded with a derisive snort and shake of his head. "Buddy-buddy. C'mon, let's go find some real action."

Sedonia had the $200 Buster had given her, and she needed to gamble with it, or he'd never let her hear the last of it. However, first she wanted to see how this match played out. "I'll see you over there later," she said.

Sal nodded and left, and Sedonia sat back down. Jeanette broke and made a ball on the break. She had a reasonably makeable bank shot, but instead opted to play a safety. Sedonia sighed. Conservative play notwithstanding, however, these women impressed her. While the men looked and behaved like the players she'd encountered in neighborhood poolrooms, the women were more professional in terms of their appearance, behavior, and interaction with the spectators. From what Sedonia had seen so far, WPBA members made it a point to promote their game—not only their personal image, but the image of women's pool in general.

At the table, Jeanette and Ewa exchanged safeties until Jeanette found herself with a wide-open shot. She took advantage of it and ran the rest of the rack for the win. Ewa congratulated her, and they chatted amiably as they unscrewed their custom cue sticks—their entrée to celebrity—and returned them to their inlaid leather cases. Then shoulder to shoulder, they strolled from the playing area, pausing frequently to acknowledge their fans and to sign programs thrust before them.

Sedonia shook her head. Sal underestimated these women. They were consummate professionals, with dreams and aspirations. They were women cueists.

Although it was after 10:00 when Sedonia turned off Paradise Road and onto Sahara Avenue, the temperature was still in the nineties. Hot as it was, however, she had the car windows open to dilute the sickening smell of the artificial air freshener. She missed her Miata, now sitting in a Houston airport parking garage.

She'd watched the first few games of the next round of professional matches, but then decided that if she was going to gamble with Buster's money, she'd better do it tonight. The Eight-Ball tournament might have her tied up the rest of the week.

A mix of small motels and businesses lined the thoroughfare, and she strained, looking for a street number. A car behind her gave a blast on its horn, and a teenage boy glared at her as he roared past in a Pontiac Firebird. Locals here apparently had little patience with lost visitors.

Another block, and still no indication of a street number. Then ahead on the right she saw a small green neon sign that read: "Las Vegas Billiard Club." The building stood on the corner, pushed up against both sidewalks. There was a doorway in front, but no place to park, not even parking meters. She drove slowly past the building, made a U-turn on Sahara, and then turned left up the side street. Passing the rear of a row of small businesses, she felt as if she were looking for the entrance to a desert fort. Finally she came to a driveway between buildings, and turned left.

Once inside, the "fort" feeling persisted. A dozen dingy eateries and other small businesses surrounded a potholed asphalt parking lot. Many of the signs were written in Spanish and Vietnamese. Down at the far end, she saw the rear entrance of the Billiard Club.

She pulled into a parking spot and transferred Buster's $200, plus $200 of her own, from her purse to her rear jeans pocket. Then she secured her purse under the car seat, grabbed her cue case, and climbed out. Her Rent-a-Heap-Cheap, four-door sedan looked at home among the unwashed cars, pickups, and vans clustered behind the poolroom. Sometime in the past, the tall plate-glass windows and rear entrance had been painted an ominous flat black, which now was peeling. The storefronts on either side appeared have been abandoned long ago. From inside the Billiard Club, however, she heard the familiar, reassuring sounds of a juke box playing and pool balls colliding.

She pushed open the glass door and stepped inside. The usual poolroom smells of cigarette smoke and stale beer saturated the air. Video games lined the wall on the left, and a row of 8-foot pool tables stood off to the right. The only lighting in the room came from the fixtures that hung above the pool tables.

Sedonia started up a long ramp that led to the raised lounge area. A dozen spectators, including Sal, crowded the wooden railing and peered down at two pool tables, where games were in progress. These must be the money tables.

As Sedonia arrived at the top of the ramp, a thin, pockmarked young man intercepted her. "Are you meeting someone? Do you want to play a game?"

Sedonia drew back from his rapid-fire delivery, not knowing if he was trying to pick her up, or if he was an over-eager gambler. "Uh . . . what game, and how much?"

"Oh," he said. "You're a pro? I just wanted to play for fun."

"No, thanks." She stepped by him and continued over to where Sal was sitting.

He smiled as she approached, and then moved over to give her a place at the rail. "Who's your boyfriend back there?"

Sedonia simply shook her head. The lounge area was four feet higher than the main floor and offered a good view of the two tables below. "Any action?" she said.

"Table on the left is a race-to-9," Sal whispered. "They're just starting. I got Jelly, even, for $500 a set."

"Which one's 'Jelly'?"

"Jelly Belly. The fat white guy. The black guy's in town for the BCA tournament. I'm robbin' him. Jelly's down from Reno. He's strong."

Sedonia suppressed a smile. "Jelly Belly" appeared to be only in his early thirties, but he certainly lived up to his name.

"On the right," Sal continued, "the match is a race-to-5, and they're hill-hill. The older guy is the house pro here. To get a $100 bet out of the kid he's playing, I had to give him the 8-ball wild."

"That's a lot of weight." Sedonia said. The "8-ball wild" meant that while the one player had a single money ball, the other had two. The house pro had to sink the 9-ball to win; however, the kid could win by sinking either the 8-ball or the 9-ball.

"Watch these four guys," Sal said, "and then give me an idea what your speed is."

Sedonia felt uneasy. Buster had been confident she could compete here, but he'd also told her she needed to stick to her game, Eight-Ball. The players below, like most gamblers, were playing Nine-Ball. On the other hand, she knew the rules of Nine-Ball . . . and she'd impressed Jeanette Lee yesterday . . .

A young brunette waitress tapped her on the shoulder. "Want something to drink?"

Sedonia turned, leaned back, and said, "Ginger ale." The road players who passed through Buster's often drank ginger ale, letting its amber color mislead locals that they were drinking cocktails, which might impair their ability.

Sal glanced over with a half-smile, then turned his attention back to the games below.

Sedonia continued to vacillate. One instant she felt intimidated by the surroundings—as if she were an imposter—and she wished she was back at the Riviera. But the next instant she was confident she could beat at least three of the players below—only Jelly looked strong—and she wanted to compete.

The race-to-5 set came to an end, with the player Sal had bet against sinking the 8-ball on a combination shot. Sal handed down the $100 and said, "You robbed me, kid. I knew I was giving you too much weight." He turned to Sedonia. "You wanna play him?"

Sedonia hesitated. Buster had wanted her to gamble with one of the WPBA pros, but there weren't any women on the money tables. She took a deep breath and told the young player below, "I'll play you some Eight-Ball."

"Eight-Ball?" he said with a sneer.

His reaction didn't surprise her. Most gamblers considered Eight-Ball too easy, since the shooter usually had a choice of object balls to shoot at, while in Nine-Ball it had to be the next ball in numerical sequence. She was about to go against Buster's advice and agree to play Nine-Ball, when a strident voice behind her said, "Eight-Ball's the lady's game."

Sedonia turned and found herself looking into the sardonic face of "French Quarter" Jimmy Dupre.

Jimmy called down to the player below, "If you don't want to match up with her playin' Eight-Ball, I'll shoot you some Nine-Ball. Give ya the 8-ball and the breaks."

The young man shook his head.

"Give ya the 7, 8, and the breaks," Jimmy said.

Another shake of the head. "I saw you play last night."

"Give ya the 6, 7, 8, and the breaks," Jimmy pressed.

Sedonia looked on with annoyance. Jimmy had been a jerk when she'd seen him play at Buster's, and he was holding true to form here. Public intimidation obviously was an integral part of his game.

Sal stepped in and called down, "The girl here wants to play Eight-Ball." He turned to Sedonia. "How much you wanna play for?"

Sedonia hesitated. "A hundred dollars."

Sal turned back. "She's in town for the BCA tournament and wants to match up for $100. Give her one game on the wire in a race-to-5, and I'll put up a $100 with hers."

"I ain't givin' her no weight. I ain't seen her shoot."

"Hell," Sal said, "I've never seen her shoot either."

Jimmy jumped back in. "Play me some Nine-Ball, and I'll let you have the 'Orange Crush'. Down to the 5-ball and the breaks!"

The young player took a half-step back, then turned to Sedonia and Sal. "Eight-Ball, race-to-5, $100 from each of you. No weight."

Sal asked Sedonia, "No weight okay with you?"

She nodded and headed for the stairs that led down to the playing area. The railbirds eyed her as she passed. As she descended the stairs she heard one tell another, "I'll take the girl for fifty."

Her opponent was waiting with a coin. Sedonia called heads and won the first break. She introduced herself, and he responded with a sullen mumble that his name was Robert. Sedonia wondered if his attitude was due to the pre-match haggling, or having to play a woman.

While he racked the balls, she found a 21-ounce house cue to break with. Her fingers shook slightly as she chalked the tip. She glanced up at the railbirds. Playing with spectators standing around was tough enough, but here they were literally on top of her. She was glad she'd worn a blouse with a high-cut neck.

"Good luck," she said automatically as she prepared to break.

He gave her an annoyed glance and took a seat on a stool without replying. His display of antagonism annoyed her, which somehow calmed her pre-game jitters. *One, two, three . . . stroke!* The balls scattered, and two stripes dropped. It looked like a run-out. It was.

Her opponent slammed the balls into the triangle as he racked for the second game. Then he returned to his stool. Sedonia broke again, and ran again. She led 2 to 0 in the race-to-5.

While she waited for the third rack, she glanced up at the lounge area. Sal was scowling down at her, obviously annoyed at something. Maybe Jimmy was bugging him. The rest of the railbirds seemed to have lost interest in the higher stakes match at the next table, and now were watching her.

On her third break, she made a solid and a stripe, but scratched on the cue-ball. Her opponent came to the table for the first time in the match. As soon as he began to shoot, Sedonia sensed what had been bothering him. She'd assumed anyone gambling here at the Las Vegas Billiard Club would be formidable, but half the players in the BCA league back home played as well as this guy, and she beat them on a regular basis. He must have realized that he was overmatched, and now she knew it too.

After making three sloppy shots, he miscued, giving her ball-in-hand. He slunk back to his stool and signaled the waitress he needed a drink. Sedonia felt sorry for him, but she also felt an unusual thrill of being in complete control. She was onstage, playing for high stakes, yet she was confident she could steer this match in any direction she chose. Neither the games going on around her nor the spectators overhead were distractions. There was just the lit table in front of her, balls that responded to her will, and a score that could be anything she wished it to be.

In each of the remaining games, she purposely missed once, to give her opponent a chance to get to the table. Only in the second-to-last game did he take advantage of it and manage to get out. Sedonia won the match, 5 to 1. Her opponent handed up $100 to Sal and threw Sedonia's $100 on the table. Then he quickly unscrewed his cue stick, slammed it into its case, and stalked out of the poolroom.

Sedonia looked around. "Would someone else like to play?" When no one responded, she returned her cue stick to its case, and went back upstairs to the lounge area.

Sal met her with an annoyed shake of his head. Sitting shoulder to shoulder at the rail and looking out across the poolroom, he said in a hoarse whisper, so the men nearby couldn't hear, "What was that shit you pulled in the first two games? You shoulda gone 'on the lemon' from the start."

"I didn't know how good he was."

"Well, you shoulda asked me. Now everyone in here knows your speed. Goin' on a stall after the first two games didn't fool anybody."

"Damn," Sedonia muttered. Her adrenaline was up, and she wanted to play. She couldn't remember ever having such a strong desire to play pool, or even golf.

"Just sit back," Sal said. "Maybe somebody else will come in, and we can get you matched up later." Then he turned his attention to the other table, where he had $500 riding on the outcome.

Jimmy took over the table that Sedonia had vacated and began warming up by slamming balls as if he were practicing his break shot. Half his shots missed their intended pockets, and once the cue-ball jumped off the table and crashed into the wall. In between shots, he challenged other players and harangued the railbirds in his strident, grating voice.

Sedonia checked her watch: almost midnight. She wondered how late they played here. She couldn't hang around too long; her next BCA match was in twelve hours.

Sedonia yawned and checked her watch again: 2:12. That would be 4:12 Nassau Bay time. She could barely keep her eyes open. Sal was below, collecting his latest bet. He pocketed $250 and gave $250 to Jelly. The black BCA player, who had just lost, packed up his cue stick and left the poolroom.

Sedonia yawned again, and decided as soon as Sal came back up to the lounge area, she'd tell him she was leaving too. She jumped when the railbird sitting next to her suddenly called out, "Baby girl!"

Sedonia turned and saw a smiling Latina stride into the playing area. She was slight and not much more than five feet in height, yet she had a confident swagger that indicated she was on familiar turf. She wore a starched white shirt that set off her tan complexion, and black tailored slacks and polished zippered boots. A fancy leather cue case hung from her shoulder.

"Who's that?" Sedonia asked the railbird sitting next to her.

He frowned. "You don't know her? That's Vivian Villarreal. She's from San Antonio, Texas. They call her the 'Texas Tornado'."

Sedonia smiled. Buster once had mentioned that name. She reached into her rear jeans pocket and pulled out the folded magazine page he'd given her, which showed the current top twenty WBPA players. Vivian was No. 6, putting her in the group he had said were too strong for Sedonia to challenge. Like Jeanette and Ewa, the Texas Tornado was a professional cueist.

Jimmy unleashed his grating verbiage on Vivian, but Sedonia sensed it didn't have its usual edge, as if he weren't actually interested in matching up with her. Vivian acknowledged him at the onset, and then ignored him and solicited a match with Jelly.

Sal rejoined Sedonia at the rail, but closely monitored the negotiations.

"How do you think I'd match-up against Vivian?" Sedonia said.

"Haven't seen you play enough to tell," Sal said. "You might do all right, though. You two shoot similar: fast and loose."

Sedonia looked back at Vivian, tempted to challenge, but she hesitated. If Vivian had walked in two hours ago, right after Sedonia had won her first match, she might have taken a chance. But now she'd been sitting idle and wasn't warmed up. Maybe she was no longer in stroke. Plus, there would be the Eight-Ball versus Nine-Ball awkwardness . . . unless she asked to play Nine-Ball. On the other hand, she had Buster's $200 she needed to gamble with . . . and she'd run a rack on Jeanette Lee . . . and she really wanted to play . . .

While Sedonia struggled with indecision, Jelly turned to Sal and said, "Nine-Ball, three race-to-9s for $500 each, no weight."

With a quick nod, Sal agreed to back Jelly in the match.

Sedonia was glad she hadn't embarrassed herself proposing Eight-Ball for $200. She pulled out her $200, plus the $100 she'd won earlier that evening, held it up, and announced to the other railbirds, "I'll put $100 a set on Vivian."

"I'll cover that," Sal said.

Sedonia perched on a stool, resting her elbows on the lounge railing and her chin in the palm of one hand. She yawned; it was 4:40. The desert sun would be rising soon. Vivian had taken only an hour and a half to win the first set, 9 to 3. It had been a fun set to watch; the Texas Tornado played with reckless abandon. She invariably took two quick practice strokes, followed immediately by the shot stroke—no pause. And between shots as she circled the table, she whistled, sang along with the jukebox, and bantered with the railbirds. Jimmy was playing a $300 set against the house pro at the next table, and even he seemed sedate compared to the animated Vivian.

After Jelly had dropped the first set, however, he'd begun stalling between shots, apparently trying to upset her rhythm. He'd also begun playing frequent safeties. His slowdown tactics seemed to be working; Vivian's impatience showed, and she trailed, 4 to 1.

Sedonia sighed. This set probably would last at least another hour, and they were scheduled to play a third set when this one was over.

Sedonia checked her watch yet again, and turned to Sal, who was intently following the matches he was staking on both tables. "I've got to get out of here," she said.

He responded with a frown. "You're leaving?"

"Yeah. I've got a BCA match in a few hours. How do you want to handle our bet on this set, and the next one?"

Sal reached into his front pocket and pulled out a fat roll of bills. He peeled off $100 to cover his loss on the first set and handed it to her. "Call over to Cue-Nique tomorrow. I probably won't be there, but I'll tell the English broad who works for me how the sets went. If I owe you, I'll leave it with her. If you owe me, drop it off with her."

"You trust me?"

"Kid, you're the only person in this poolroom tonight I *would* trust."

Chapter 11

Sedonia glanced down at her watch as she fought her way through the pool players who jammed the foyer between the hotel and the convention center. She'd overslept, something she seldom did. The Cue-Ts' match was scheduled to start in less than five minutes.

Two women stood chatting in the Grande Ballroom doorway. "Excuse me," Sedonia said, pushing her way between them. She ignored the activities around the vendor stalls and bulletin boards, and broke into a jog as she headed toward the main aisle. Tables No. 7 and 8 should be near the front of the room . . . there! She stopped, confused. Two men's teams, not the Cue-Ts, were at the tables, preparing to begin their match. Sedonia was positive Hannah had said tables No. 7 and 8. And the match was supposed to start at noon, wasn't it?

She interrupted two players who were talking. "Do you know where the Cue-Ts are?"

Both frowned, then the younger one smiled and quipped, "Looks like one just arrived."

"No," she said, pointing to the logo on her pink shirt. "I mean my team, the Cue-Ts. We're supposed to be on tables No. 7 and 8 this morning."

"There was some kind of screw-up on table assignments," the older man said. "A lot of us got changed. You might want to check the bulletin boards over there."

Sedonia looked back at the hundred-foot display. She'd never locate her team in time.

"Or," the younger man said, "stay here and play with us. Hell, I'll kick this guy off the team to make room for *you*."

Sedonia scanned the nearby pool tables. No sign of her team. The room was enormous: more than 300 tables and 600 teams. *Damn it!* She was going to miss the match! If so, they were out of the tournament.

In near panic, she took off down the main aisle again. As she wove through milling players, she frantically looked for her teammates' bright pink shirts. Where the hell were they?

"Sedonia!" a familiar voice cried out. "Sedonia!"

She turned and to her relief saw Hannah, outfitted in a new, navy-blue shirt. Sedonia hurried over.

"So nice of you to join us, Sleeping Beauty," Hannah said.

"Oh, God, Hannah, I'm sorry. I—"

"Tell me about it later. Cissy won the first game. Flora and Vicky are playing now, but they're both gettin' their asses kicked. I've got you playin' fifth. If you hadn't showed up, we'd have had to forfeit."

"Hannah, I'm sorry about—"

"Hannah! Sedonia!" Cissy shouted. "Y'all are up!"

Hannah handed Sedonia a blue shirt. "Quick, put this on, or the other team can call a penalty."

Sedonia automatically checked the size: "XXL."

Hannah gave her an annoyed look. "It's Melissa's. Your shirt's hanging in the closet, right where I told you it was this morning."

"Oh, hell, Hannah. I don't even remember talking to you."

"Melissa came by and officially dropped off the team. I told you that, and you agreed it was okay for me to swap your plane reservations. Now you're traveling with us, and she's traveling alone."

"That's fine," Sedonia said. "I'm sorry, I—"

Before she could finish, Hannah hurried off to begin her game.

Cissy walked up, a pugnacious expression on her face. "Where the hell have you been?"

"Where can I change shirts?" Sedonia said.

"You don't have time to go get all pretty . . . Miss Astor. We're in the middle of a fuckin' pool match! You're up!"

Sedonia quickly pulled the blue shirt over her pink one. She screwed her stick together as she hurried over to the open table.

Her opponent was a young man with a two-day beard. He smiled as she approached and said, "Looks like you had a rough night, too."

"I'm sorry," Sedonia mumbled. "Am I racking or breaking?"

He pointed to the already-racked balls and said, "Your break." Then he took his seat.

Sedonia walked up to the break end of the table. She took a deep breath and tried to regain her composure. Instead, frustration and embarrassment welled within her, and her vision began to blur.

"C'mon, Miss Astor!" Cissy shouted.

Without going through her usual pre-shot routine, Sedonia drove the cue-ball as hard as she could. A resounding *crack!* and balls flew about the table, two solids and a stripe finding pockets. And for the first time in months, Sedonia felt a stab of pain from her right shoulder. She clenched her teeth. The hell with Cissy! And the hell with this God-damned shoulder! She moved around the table at a pace that rivaled Vivian Villarreal's, putting low spin on the cue-ball and slamming the object balls harder than necessary. Finally she drilled the 8-ball into the side pocket for the win.

Her opponent, who hadn't had a chance to shoot, walked up to the table with a bemused expression. "Damn, lady. Did I say somethin' to piss you off?"

Sedonia managed a smile. "You were right," she said. "I had a rough night."

"Good shootin', though," he said.

Cissy approached the table to rack for her next game, and Sedonia pointed a forefinger at her. "I don't want to hear anything else out of you."

"I told you what you needed to hear," Cissy said, "when you needed to hear it."

Sedonia gazed at Cissy for a moment, then gave a quick nod. Cissy's taunt had, in fact, produced the rage that had gotten Sedonia through a moment when she'd wanted to quit.

Flora and Vicky let out a cheer, and Sedonia turned in time to see Hannah being congratulated by her opponent. The Cue-Ts had pulled into a 3 to 2 lead in the race-to-13.

As Cissy racked the balls for her game, she looked at Sedonia with a half-smile and said, "You've got time to go change your shirt now."

"Are you kidding?" Sedonia retorted. "In the middle of a pool match?"

Sedonia sat in front of a video poker machine at the edge of the casino. She dropped in four more quarters, killing time while waiting for Hannah to join her for a late lunch. Hannah was turning in the score sheet from the Cue-Ts' 13 to 8 victory and finding out when they were scheduled to play next.

Behind Sedonia, slot machines generated a constant din—the bong-bong of scores being tallied, punctuated by occasional shouts from winners. Sedonia's vantage point gave her a view of the Mardi Gras food court and the row of mini fast-food outlets. A man and a woman, perhaps in their forties, waited in line in front of the Riksson Pastry Shop. Sedonia had seen them competing in the pool tournaments being held in the penthouse. The two professionals seemed at home in the Riviera, and Sedonia felt a tinge of envy.

Hannah walked up and placed a hand on Sedonia's shoulder. "You ready?"

"Yeah," Sedonia said, then drew one last card on the poker machine. Three of clubs. No help. "When do we play next?" she said, standing up.

"Nine tonight."

They walked over to the fast-food counters. Hannah chose a burger and fries from Burger King, and Sedonia a turkey sandwich from Quizno's Subs. Then they found a table next to a plate glass window that overlooked Las Vegas Boulevard. A steady stream of pedestrians and traffic clogged the sidewalk and the street.

Sedonia said, "Do you recognize that couple, on your left, two tables over?" The man and woman she'd noticed earlier now were signing autographs for members of a BCA team.

"Allen and Dawn Hopkins. Married, and both pros. Good ones."

Sedonia nodded. "I couldn't remember their names. Since I arrived here, I've been impressed how accommodating professional players are. Like those two. I can't think of another sport where pros have such close contact with their public, even playing against them."

Hannah smiled. "You thinking about turning pro?"

Sedonia rolled her eyes, as if dismissing the idea. However, despite not wanting to admit it, turning pro was exactly what she wished she could do.

"You shoot good enough," Hannah said. "You'd just need more . . . experience."

"A lot of WPBA members are my age, or even younger."

"I'm not talking about age," Hannah said. "Most of these women grew up in poolrooms. And almost all of them have pool player boyfriends. They've paid their dues."

"Like Cissy?"

"Yeah, like Cissy. I'll be the first to tell you, her boyfriend's a jerk. Remember, though, that young woman's gone 11 and 0 here in Las Vegas."

"Better than I've done," Sedonia said with a rueful shake of her head. "And she's got a jail sentence hanging over her head when we get back."

"Your 9 and 3 isn't that bad."

"Except all three losses came in the match we lost."

"Cissy's like most women players," Hannah said. "She's learned the hard way. You on the other hand . . ."

"What about me?" Sedonia pressed, when Hannah didn't finish. "I'm Miss Astor?"

Hannah chuckled. "I heard Cissy call you that."

Sedonia waited, but her friend didn't dispute Cissy's allegation. "I can't figure it out, Hannah. Sometimes I play great, and other times I'm totally helpless. It wasn't that way in golf. I was consistent. Consistently good."

Hannah nodded. "In pool, you play good too. Good enough that most of the time you keep your opponent in his chair. And as long as he can't shoot, he can't win. But there's more to winning in pool than making balls. That's the 'experience' factor I'm talking about. It's how you handle your opponent."

"You mean like trying to psyche him out with the woofing and all the other bullshit that goes on in high-stakes matches?"

Hannah nodded. "Ever notice how many road players come across like jerks?"

Sedonia glanced over at the fast-food outlets. "Hannah, the poster boy for what you just said, just walked up to the Pizza Hut counter."

Hannah turned in her chair. "Who's he?"

"A road player from New Orleans. They call him 'French Quarter' Jimmy Dupre. I saw him gamble for high stakes at Buster's last year, and then again last night at the Billiard Club. He's a complete jerk."

"Hmmm," Hannah said, "handsome one, though."

"I guess," Sedonia said noncommittally. Jimmy *was* good looking, and this afternoon he didn't seem quite as intimidating as when she'd encountered him in the past. Then she realized that this was the first time she'd seen him without his cue stick. Maybe that had something to do with it.

They were finishing their sandwiches when he approached their table. "Can I join you ladies?"

"Sure," Hannah said.

Sedonia made the introductions, and then asked Jimmy, "How'd you come out last night?"

"Made a couple of thousand. You?" He took a bite of pizza.

"I'm not sure," Sedonia said. "I had to leave about 5:00 this morning. Depends how Vivian did against Jelly in their second and third sets."

"She tortured him," he said, mouth full. "Took all three sets off him."

"Then I won $400. Three hundred on that session, plus a hundred on mine."

Hannah smiled. "I may need to rethink what I said earlier about your not paying your dues."

Jimmy frowned. "What's that about 'paying dues'?"

"Nothing," Sedonia and Hannah said simultaneously.

Hannah asked him, "Are you here for the BCA tournament?"

He responded with a quick chortle, which seemed out of place, given his usual intimidating manner. "No, not the tournament. I'm here for the side action."

"You staying at the Riviera?" Hannah said.

"Yeah. When these tournaments are in town, there's always a lot of amateurs with gamble and money. I match up with 'em here in the practice room, and then take 'em over to the Billiard Club."

"Sedonia tells me you're a road player," Hannah said. "Where do you go after Vegas?"

"Back to Naw'lins. I've haven't been home for over a month."

"That's a long time," Hannah said. "How far from home do you travel?"

Jimmy thought for a moment. "California's as far as I've gone. There's a little town outside L.A., called Bellflower, and a poolroom known as Tough Times. Mainly Filipinos and Mexicans hang out there, but lots of gamble. I've taken a bunch of money out of that place."

"I've heard of Tough Times," Hannah said. "I grew up in Redondo Beach, about 20 miles from Bellflower."

"Do you work," Sedonia asked Jimmy, "or play pool fulltime?"

He smiled. "I work fulltime at playing pool."

Both women laughed, and Hannah said, "Do you ever play in tournaments?"

"Not too often," Jimmy said. "Problem with tournaments is, I gotta shoot my best shot, or I get knocked out of 'em. But if I show my speed, then the word gets out and I can't get anybody to gamble with me."

Sedonia turned and looked out the window. She wondered how strong Jimmy actually was. The hierarchy of pool, from the top down, seemed to be: professionals, hustlers, tournament players, amateurs. Yet players blurred these distinctions by moving up and down the hierarchy. Throw in the gamesmanship of players "going on a stall," or otherwise manipulating the outcome of games, and Sedonia wondered how even experts like Buster were able to judge relative strength.

She turned back to Jimmy, who was saying, "Sometimes, though, tournament money's too good to turn down. Next month's 'Eight-Ball Showdown' on South Padre Island, for example. First place will pay $25,000. I'll drive over to Texas for that. I'm playin' good, and ought to win it."

Sedonia suppressed a sigh. Jimmy's road-player bravado was beginning to wear on her again. Too bad; when he'd first sat down, she'd started to warm to him. She turned to Hannah and said, "I'm going up to the room and rest for tonight."

Hannah nodded, and she also prepared to leave. "Well," she told Jimmy, "when you get to Texas next month, stop by and see us in Nassau Bay."

"I *always* stop by Buster's," he said. Then he asked Sedonia, "You gonna be at the Billiard Club tonight?"

"We've got a BCA match at 9:00."

"How 'bout later?"

Sedonia hesitated. "Probably."

At 7:20 that night, Sedonia strolled through the foyer that connected the hotel and convention center. She'd had a two-hour nap, a long shower, an early dinner, and now wanted to get in some practice before the Cue-Ts' nine o'clock match.

The passageway in front of the Grande Ballroom wasn't as crowded as usual; most players probably were still having dinner. For the first time, Sedonia noticed a doorway opposite the tournament room. A poster on an easel read "Practice Room." She decided to check it out. This might be a better place to warm up.

A dozen bar-boxes, arranged side by side, filled the rectangular room. However, all the tables were occupied. She was about to turn and leave, when she saw Max, the BCA masters player from Nassau Bay. He was shooting on a table at the far end of the room. As usual, despite his bulk, he looked dapper for a pool player, in his color-coordinated tan slacks and light green shirt. It was the first time Sedonia had seen him since arriving in Las Vegas. As she walked over to say hello, Max executed one of his notorious safety shots, then took a seat on a stool and rested his forearms across his protruding paunch.

Sedonia walked up beside him. "Hi, Max," she whispered, so as not to disturb his opponent, who was studying the table and trying to improvise a shot from the poor position Max had left him.

Max turned with a frown, and then smiled in recognition. "Hi, Sedonia. Your team still in the tournament?"

"Yeah. We lost the first match, but we've won the last two."

"Better than we did. We lost our first two and were out of it. I'm still in the Masters Singles Tournament, though. I play again at 9:00."

"We play at 9:00, too."

"Been doing any gambling?"

"A little. Last night, over at the Billiard Club."

Max smiled. "You learned your way around Las Vegas pretty quick."

"Do you play over there?"

"Not me. I'm just a 'shortstop'."

Sedonia frowned.

Max said, "That's what they call a player with my speed. I can beat most locals, but road players and professionals are out of my league."

Max's opponent shot and missed. He gave Max an annoyed look, and held up the cue-ball.

"Excuse me," Max told Sedonia. He heaved himself off the stool, took ball-in-hand, and quickly ran the table.

His opponent came over and handed Max a $10 bill. "Go again? Same way?"

Max nodded. As he waited for the man to rack, he asked Sedonia, "How'd you do at the Billiard Club?"

"Won $400."

Max smiled. "*You* ought to be playing in the Masters, not me."

"You're up," Max's opponent told him.

"I'll let you get back to your game," Sedonia said. "I'm gonna go hit some practice balls in the tournament room."

"Good luck tonight," Max said. "The teams you play from now on are probably gonna be tougher than the ones you've seen so far. The easier teams get knocked out in the first two or three rounds."

Sedonia nodded. "That's what Hannah told me. She said we'd need to play well tonight. We're going up against a Canadian team."

Max had started toward the table for his next game, but now stopped and turned back. "A Canadian team?"

"Yeah."

Max responded with a wry smile. "You . . . might have a problem."

"Why's that?"

Max hesitated, then said, "They play a lot of Snooker in Canada."

Sedonia frowned. Sal had made a similar comment the night before, talking about Canadian professionals.

"You shoot good pool," Max continued, "and I don't want to psyche you out. So I'll just say this: you'd better play *smart* tonight."

Sedonia had been practicing for nearly an hour before her first teammate, Cissy, arrived at tables No. 271 and 272.

Cissy acknowledged her with a nod. "No one from the Calgary Stampeders here yet?" she said as she screwed her cue stick together.

Sedonia shook her head.

"They're good," Cissy said. "I watched 'em play this afternoon. They finished fourth here last year."

"Fourth is great," Sedonia said, "out of 700 teams." For the first time this evening, she felt a pang of apprehension over the upcoming match. She was confident she was back in stroke, even on these bar-boxes, but one more loss and the Cue-Ts were out of the tournament.

Cissy put a token into the other table. "They take it serious. One of 'em told me they even have a pool table in their room."

"In their room?"

"Yeah. They rented one of the penthouse suites for the week, and they had a vendor install a bar-box up there to practice on."

"They *are* taking it seriously," Sedonia said. "Of course, with $15,000 for first place, and finishing fourth last year, I can see why they would." She resumed hitting balls. The more she heard about these Canadians, the more apprehensive she was becoming.

One by one, the rest of the Cue-Ts arrived, and they began playing practice games against each other. As she usually did, Sedonia made sure that when her teammates played her, they got at least one chance to get to the table. She only lost one game, that to Cissy, who still was in stroke, as she had been throughout the past two days.

At 8:45, the Stampeders arrived as a group, and the Cue-Ts relinquished both tables so their opponents could get warmed up. As the women watched the men play, it appeared they'd *arrived* "warmed up."

Hannah called her team together, and then turned to Cissy. "I'm gonna move Sedonia back into the leadoff spot, and have you play second. These guys are strong, so we need to jump on 'em quick."

Cissy flashed an expression of annoyance that she wouldn't be leading off, but she quickly replaced it with one of indifference. Sedonia would have been glad to relinquish her position; Cissy had earned it with her play so far in the tournament. Now, however, wasn't the time to second-guess Hannah's decisions.

"We're ready," the Canadian captain said.

Sedonia headed for table No. 271, and Cissy to No. 272.

Sedonia's first opponent was tall, perhaps 6' 4", and in his thirties. He flashed a smile and extended his hand. "I'm Paul. We break first."

Sedonia introduced herself, and then walked down to the far end of the table. Her hand shook slightly as she inserted the token into the slot and retrieved the balls. She took a deep breath, and tried to reassure herself that she'd relax as soon as the match got underway. It took her several tries to produce a tight rack, but finally she pulled the triangle away and stepped back from the table.

"Good luck," her opponent said, and then before she could reply, he drove the cue-ball into the rack. Balls scattered and the maroon 7-ball found its way into the side pocket. The solids appeared to be the better suit: three were in the open, but the other three were clustered together. He shot the yellow 1-ball into the corner pocket, then said, "Safety."

Sedonia frowned. Why was he playing safe? He had two makeable balls on the table. He carefully lined up his shot and executed it. When the cue-ball and object ball came to rest, he'd left a tortuous shot that Max would have been proud of. Sedonia remembered what both Max and Sal had said of Canadian Snooker players: they played defensively. And this must have been what Max was referring to, when he told her she'd have to play "smart."

Sedonia gave her opponent a questioning look.

He smiled and said, "A couple of us saw you play that exhibition game against 'The Black Widow'. You shoot like God."

Sedonia turned back to the table and drew a deep breath as she surveyed the shot he'd left. So that would be their strategy. Knowing she was likely to run her remaining balls anytime she got to the table, they planned to deal her a steady dose of safeties.

The cue-ball was penned behind his three clustered solids, and she couldn't devise a way to get a legal hit on any of her stripes. She finally made a halfhearted attempt at kicking the cue-ball off the near rail, but instead it broke out the cluster. Now, all five of his remaining solids were makeable. He returned to the table and methodically ran out. The Cue-Ts trailed 1 to 0 in the race-to-13.

Sedonia gave him the perfunctory "Good game," but didn't mean it. Purposely missing, so as to intentionally leave your opponent an impossible shot, not only took the joy out of the game, it seemed downright unsportsmanlike. She pulled up a chair and tried to not let her resentment show. Hannah was next up on table No. 271, and she patted Sedonia on the shoulder as she walked past.

Sedonia turned her attention to table No. 272. Cissy and her opponent were exchanging safeties, and Cissy was holding her own. The game dragged on until finally Cissy got the opening she was looking for. She won the game, making the team score 1 to 1.

Moments later, however, Hannah lost. And then Flora and Vicky clearly were overmatched, their games lasting only a few minutes. After the first round, the Cue-Ts trailed, 4 to 1.

Cissy led off the second round playing the man who had beaten Sedonia. Again, she matched her opponent safety for safety, and again she ground out a hard-fought win. Hannah, whose game depended on guile, including safeties, also won, making the score 4 to 3. But then Flora and Vicky again dropped one-sided games.

As Sedonia returned to the table for her second game, the Cue-Ts trailed, 6 to 3. But this time, it was her turn to break. Her next opponent was a heavyset young man; they exchanged nods before he racked the balls. Sedonia chalked her cue and tried to get into a positive frame of mind, reminding herself how well she'd played against Jeanette Lee, and later at the Billiard Club. She'd played Nine-Ball on 9-foot tables. Eight-Ball on this 6-foot table was nothing. Low spin on every shot. She just needed to make a ball on the break.

"Good luck," her opponent said as he put away the triangle.

"Good luck," she replied automatically. *One, two, three . . . stroke!* No resounding *crack!* Instead, she heard the flat *clunk!* and saw little ball action. Only four balls made it to a rail, and nothing went in. Her opponent's blasé reaction seemed affected as he approached the table. Sedonia suspected he'd given her a "house-rack," intentionally leaving a space between the second and third row of balls, to ensure she didn't break-and-run. *Damn it! She should have checked the rack!*

He made an easy stripe, and then said, "Safety." When he shot, he intentionally left the cue-ball lodged behind the purple 4-ball. Sedonia gave him a hard stare as he walked past and took a seat. He avoided eye contact.

Sedonia studied the table and tried to quell her anger. On the break, the yellow 1-ball had rolled in front of the side pocket. She had an outside chance of making it on a combination shot, but she'd have to hit the 4-ball hard, since she'd be cutting it almost 90-degrees. And if she used top spin, she'd also be able to break out the balls that were clustered nearby. It was either that, or devise a safety of her own. She shook her head. Defense wasn't her game; she'd play aggressively.

She drove the cue-ball hard—too hard. It slammed into the clustered balls and then flew off the table. The 4-ball did its job, tapping in the 1-ball; however, Sedonia had given her opponent ball-in-hand.

He retrieved the ball off the floor, and seven shots later, he called and made the 8-ball. Sedonia couldn't muster the hypocrisy necessary to tell him "Good game." His teammates, however, greeted him with congratulations and high-fives. The Cue-Ts now trailed, 7 to 3 in the race-to-13.

Hannah led off the third round with a loss, and Flora and Vicky each dropped their third games of the match. The score was 10 to 3 in favor of the Canadians.

Still angry over the house-rack she'd received, Sedonia slammed the balls on the table as she racked for her third game. When she pulled the triangle away, she glared at her next opponent. He was a slight, friendly looking guy. He didn't check the rack, and seemed almost apologetic as he said, "Good luck."

"Good luck," Sedonia muttered.

He broke and made a stripe and a solid. Then to Sedonia's surprise, he didn't call a safety. Instead, he called and made a stripe, and then continued on the offensive. His run stopped at five, when the orange-striped 13-ball stuttered in the jaws of the corner pocket.

Sedonia approached the table with her first real opportunity. She forced herself to take her time, study the layout, and focus her thoughts. When she began to shoot, her strokes were smooth. She applied low spin on each shot as she carefully worked her way around the table. Finally she said, "Eight in the side." It dropped, and she heaved a sigh of relief.

"Good game," her opponent said. Before she could reply, he turned and started toward his four teammates. They were scowling and shaking their heads. Obviously, he hadn't followed the team's game plan. For a moment, Sedonia felt sorry for him.

Cissy won yet again, and after three rounds, the Cue-Ts now trailed 10 to 5 in the race-to-13.

Flora and Vicky opened the fourth round of play, and each dropped their fourth games of the match. Sedonia's next opponent was short, bald, and probably in his forties. From the disapproval he and his teammates had shown her last opponent, Sedonia was sure this guy was going to stick with the nothing-but-safeties game plan. As she waited for him to rack, she looked down at the score sheet. So far, Cissy was the only one to have beaten him. If Sedonia won, Cissy would play next. If not, the match was over and the Cue-Ts were eliminated from the tournament.

When he lifted the triangle, Sedonia walked down to inspect the rack. It looked fine, but she called for a re-rack anyway. He frowned, but re-racked without comment.

Sedonia inspected the balls again, and again they looked fine. "Re-rack," she said.

"There's nothing wrong with that rack," he protested.

"Re-rack," Sedonia repeated. In part, she hoped making him angry would throw off his game, and in part she was punishing him for the house-rack his teammate had given her in the second round. She turned her back on him and chalked her cue stick. Behind her, she heard balls slamming on the table.

"How about now?" he said angrily.

"Fine," she said, without even glancing at the balls. She returned to the break end of the table. *One, two, three . . . stroke!* Two stripes found pockets. Four others were makeable, but the 12-ball was frozen against a side rail and partially hidden by the 6-ball. Of the two, the 12-ball would be the more difficult to break out. The solid balls presented problems, and there were two more of them, but at least they offered the possibility of a run-out.

Sedonia mapped out the shot sequence in her mind. If she played good position throughout the run, she thought she'd be able to break out the 6-ball. She started with the orange 5-ball. It dropped into the side. As she worked her way through her planned sequence, position on the each successive shot grew increasingly difficult. And when she reached her last solid, the green 6-ball, the cue-ball was completely out of position.

Sedonia heaved a sigh of exasperation, and then studied her options. She had no problem simply hitting the 6-ball, as required by the rules, but her only chance of pocketing it was to shoot hard and attempt a two-rail bank shot into the far corner. Or, she could play a safety—shoot softly, barely graze the 6-ball, and hide the cue-ball behind her opponent's purple-striped 12-ball.

She walked over to where Hannah was sitting and picked up her can of talcum powder. As she sprinkled some on her bridge hand, she looked around at her four teammates. Coaching was not permitted, but from their pleading expressions, she knew they were imploring her to play a safety. Hannah managed a chuckle, then shook her head and covered her eyes.

Sedonia returned to the table, still undecided. She hated defensive play. She glanced back at her teammates. Cissy was waiting to see who won this game, before starting her next one. If Sedonia lost, the match was over.

Cissy, undefeated so far in tournament play, chalked her cue and locked her gaze on Sedonia, communicating her desire to play again.

Sedonia took her stance and lined up on the 6-ball. She hesitated, then looked up at her opponent. "Safety."

She lowered her head again, aimed, and told herself to hit it easy. *One, two, three . . . stroke . . .* the shaft of her cue stick wavered slightly as it slid through her bridge hand, and at that instant she realized she'd failed to put low spin on the cue-ball. It kissed the 6-ball as planned, but then instead of hiding behind his 12-ball, broke it out. The 12-ball had been his only problem ball; now it was playable.

Sedonia dropped into her chair and watched her opponent pace around the table, planning his shot sequence. When he lined up his first shot, she looked away. Two other teams were playing on tables No. 269 and 270. One team wore wide yellow and red vertical stripes, and the other narrow blue and white horizontal stripes. She hadn't even been aware they'd been playing. She heard balls begin to drop on table No. 271, but continued to stare at the match on the adjacent tables.

Finally she heard her opponent say, "Eight in the corner."

"Good shot," she said without turning, but acknowledging his calling of the 8-ball.

She heard the final ball of the match drop into the pocket, and the exuberant shouts of his teammates. Sedonia took a deep breath, stood up, and walked over and extended her hand. "Good game."

"Good game," he said quickly, then turned and joined the victory clamor.

Hannah hurried over and embraced Sedonia. They didn't speak; the two friends didn't have to. Sedonia already was on the verge of tears. Flora and Vicky came over next and tried console her, but since they hadn't won a single game between them, there wasn't much they could say.

Cissy closed her cue case, slung it over her shoulder, and walked up. She still wore her combative game face. "You're not used to playin' safeties," she said. For a moment, Sedonia took her comment as criticism, until Cissy forced a grudging smile and added, "Good try, though."

Sedonia heaved a sigh. "I'm sorry, Cissy. I know you wanted to get back to the table, at least one more time. I tried, but I let you down. I let everybody down . . ."

Cissy looked down at the floor for a moment, obviously uncomfortable. Then she looked up again and made eye contact. "Don't be so damned hard on yourself. If it wasn't for you, I wouldn't have got to come to Vegas in the first place."

"You were the one who proved you belonged here," Sedonia said.

Cissy smiled. "Thanks," she said, and started to turn away. But then she turned back. "Would you do one more thing for me?"

Sedonia waited.

"When we get back home," Cissy said, "if anyone ever asks you how I play, be sure and tell 'em, I went 14 and 0 in Vegas."

Sedonia smiled and nodded, then watched her frail, pugnacious teammate walk away.

Sedonia stood in the dark hotel room, staring out the eighth-floor window. Below, although it was almost midnight, lights from the surrounding hotel-casinos illuminated the fairways of the Las Vegas Country Club. The membership there often hosted tournaments for women golf professionals. Sedonia's musing turned to the women pool professionals who were competing at this moment up in the penthouse. Their skill and dedication equaled or surpassed those of their golfing counterparts, yet the recognition and financial rewards of the two sports were so different. How ironic that before her shoulder injury, she could have competed on the lucrative professional golf tour and one day probably would have played at the Las Vegas Country Club. Instead, playing pool this week at the Las Vegas Riviera, she'd learned she couldn't compete in a semipro tournament on the first floor, much less with the professionals in the penthouse.

Lost in melancholy, she jumped at the thud of the magnetic card reader and the rattle of the room door handle. A shaft of light from the hallway split the darkness, then the room was fully lit. Sedonia blinked.

"Sedonia!" Hannah said, alarm in her voice. "What are you doing in the dark? Are you all right?"

"Yeah, I'm okay. The windows don't open."

A look of concern flashed across Hannah's face.

"I'm just kidding, Hannah. I wasn't thinking about jumping."

Hannah looked relieved. "Listen," she said, urgency in her tone, "I should have checked with you first, but I had to make a quick decision. A Houston league operator caught me right after you left. One of his teams is scheduled to fly back tonight on the three o'clock redeye, but they're winning and need to stay on until Saturday. Since Las Vegas to Houston flights are already fully booked, he asked if we'd consider exchanging plane reservations with them. I took him up on it, and we made the arrangements. The airline charged a penalty for making the change, but the Houston league paid it."

Sedonia frowned. "You mean we leave in three hours?"

"Yeah. Like I say, I had to make a quick decision, before the others got lost in the casino. Flora and Vicky said they'd go along with it. This way, we'll get Cissy back in time for her to report to jail tomorrow night, and she won't get in more trouble for being AWOL."

"That's great," Sedonia said, relieved for Cissy. "But what about you and your husband's plans?"

"I just called him, and told him not to fly out."

"Hard-hearted Hannah," Sedonia said with a wry smile, "cancelled her second honeymoon, so Cissy could go to jail."

Hannah chuckled, then said, "I know you probably wanted to stay and play some more at the Billiard Club, but—"

"Hannah," Sedonia interrupted, "if I'm not good enough to play BCA pool on a bar-box, I sure don't belong at the Billiard Club." She walked over, grabbed her suitcase, and threw it on the bed. "Let's get the hell out of here."

Chapter 12

Sedonia arrived at Buster's Billiards just before 11:00 on Monday morning. Usually, Buster was five to ten minutes late in opening, but today his old Ford was parked out front. The lights were on in the poolroom, but when Sedonia stepped inside, no one was in sight.

"Buster?" she called out.

She heard a muffled voice from the rear of the room. "Back here."

Sedonia walked past the bar and the row of video machines, and came to the restroom hallway. The door to the men's room was open. "Buster?"

"In here."

Sedonia ventured a look inside. Buster was wielding a damp mop across the black and white checkered tile.

"The glamour side of being a poolroom owner," Buster said with a rueful grin and shake of his head.

"Tell me about it," Sedonia said with a laugh. "The owner of Forbes Painting Company has the same responsibility. But I thought Monk did the cleaning around here."

"A social worker called me at home, bright and early this morning. Somebody dropped him off at a mental health agency in Houston yesterday. Now they're investigatin', what they call, 'his situation'. He raised hell with 'em, sayin' he had to be at work. They finally agreed to call in for him. Woman who phoned me was pissed. Monk has mentioned being involved in gamblin' here. She said she's gonna investigate that too."

Sedonia responded with a sympathetic shake of her head. "I think there's a saying: 'Leave no good turn unpunished'."

Buster nodded, and gave the far corner a final swipe. "I'm done here." Then as he wrung out the mop he said, "Think I'll fix some coffee. Want some?"

"If you wash your hands first."

Buster chuckled. "You're kinda smart-alecky for someone who got her ass kicked in Vegas a couple of days ago."

"Word gets around fast, doesn't it?"

Buster stored the mop and bucket in a utility closet, and they headed toward the bar area. "Cissy and her boyfriend came by last night, after she got out of jail. She told me how y'all did."

Sedonia took a seat at the bar. "Cissy did great. She went 14 and 0."

Buster walked around behind the counter. "So she told me. At least five times." He washed his hands, then prepared a pot of coffee. As he flipped on the switch he said, "What the hell happened to you in Vegas?"

"Like you said, I got my ass kicked."

"How'd that happen?"

"I dogged a few shots, but mainly they 'safed me' to death."

"People are gonna do that, since you refuse to play safeties yourself. Pool's all about—"

"Getting paid," Sedonia interrupted. She'd grown tired of that line.

"That's right," Buster said, "gettin' paid. And speaking of gettin' paid, Sal Butera called me yesterday."

"Sal in Las Vegas?"

"Uh-huh. Said you blew town and left *him* owing *you* money. Said he'd never had that happen before."

"Hannah swapped plane reservations with another team. It was the middle of the night, and I didn't think about the $200 Sal owed me until we were at the airport. By that time, it was too late."

"He said you robbed some local kid, but you showed everybody how strong you were before he could get any *real* money down on you."

Sedonia responded with a wry smile and shake of her head. "Make a mistake in Las Vegas, and the next week everybody in Texas knows about it. I'm just not used to 'going on the lemon' and all that other gamesmanship."

"I told him I was backin' you, and he said he'd mail me a check."

"Good. Keep it. That'll pay you back the $200 you staked me. Plus, I owe you $50 of the $100 I won off that local kid."

"We'll call it even with the $200."

"Sal must think I'm an idiot," Sedonia said.

"What he thinks is, you got as good a stroke as anybody he's ever seen. Like most women, though, you don't know how to use what you got."

Sedonia stifled her reply. There it was again, that backhanded compliment: you're good, Sedonia, but you're a woman.

"So what now?" Buster said. "Are you here to try and sell me back that cue stick again?"

"No, I'm not here to quit this time. I want to enroll in one of your 'pool schools'. I want you to show me Nine-Ball strategy and ... how to play safeties."

"You? Playin' safeties?"

"Will you teach me or not?"

"First of all, if you want to learn to play safeties, you need to start playin' One-Pocket, not Nine-Ball."

Sedonia slowly shook her head. In One-Pocket, the object was to be the first player to make eight balls in a predetermined, single corner pocket. Ninety percent of shots were safeties. "One-Pocket's too boring," she said.

"You got a college degree, right?"

"Yeah?"

"To get that degree, did the college tell you what course you *had* to take, or did you tell them what course you *would* take?"

Sedonia didn't reply. She was unconvinced about playing One-Pocket, but knew it was pointless to argue. When it came to pool, Buster had fixed ideas.

He continued, "You know Elmer and those other old-timers, who are always playin' One-Pocket over there in the corner?"

"Yeah?"

"They don't have stroke anymore, but they wanna compete. So they play *smart*."

Sedonia responded with a smile. There was that word again: smart.

"None of 'em can shoot nowhere near as good as you," Buster said. "But in One-Pocket, you'd have to get 'three on the wire' to have a chance of beatin' *any* of 'em."

Sedonia wanted to protest, but she knew handicapping pool players was Buster's specialty. "Okay, professor," she said. "One-Pocket it is. When can you teach me?"

"I don't have time."

"I'll pay you."

"You don't have enough money." He walked out from behind the bar and said, "Pour us some coffee. I'll be back in a minute."

Sedonia heard him place a telephone call from his office, but couldn't hear what he said. A couple of minutes later he returned.

"I just called Elmer. He's on his way."

Sedonia climbed out of her Miata and looked around. Predawn darkness still encased Waterfront Street. The only signs of activity were the lights from her office windows and those from the Vietnamese seafood market across the street. She turned, ascended the short flight of concrete steps, and pushed open her office door.

Raul was standing at the coffee bar. *"Hola, Sedonia,"* he said with a smile.

"Hola, Raul," she said as she tossed her purse onto her desk.

Raul poured her a cup of coffee. "I thought you would be back yesterday."

"I had some personal stuff to take care of." She reflexively rubbed her shoulder, sore from the previous day's twelve-hour, One-Pocket marathon.

"How was Las Vegas?" Raul said. "Did you win?"

"No, I got my butt kicked. But I learned a lot. How'd things go here?"

Raul launched into a detailed account of what had taken place on Brad Landry's projects during the past week, plus he filled her in on follow-up work he'd done on another job. Sedonia paid only partial attention, confident that her foreman had been on top of things, as he always was.

Suddenly she was aware Raul was waiting for her to respond to something he'd said. "Uh . . . what was that last, Raul?"

"Money to pay Hawkins Paint Supply."

"For Brad's project?"

"Uh-huh."

"Funds are supposed to come from the new account he set up just before I left."

"I don't know . . . how to do it."

"I'll have to figure it out myself first," Sedonia said. "Brad wants me to do all the transactions . . . for a while. We want to get the bugs worked out of the system." She felt uncomfortable at being evasive with Raul. Over the years, first her father, and now she, had trusted Raul with all aspects of their business. But Brad had specified that only he and Sedonia were to have access to this new account.

Raul nodded, and didn't seem concerned. "Oh," he said, "yesterday a girl called three times for you."

"Did she leave her name?"

He frowned. "I think she said . . . 'sister'?"

"Cissy?"

"Yes, 'Cissy'. She said she was looking for a job."

"Here?"

"Uh-huh. Said she would do anything."

Sedonia thought for a moment. She hadn't spoken with Cissy since they'd returned from Las Vegas. Maybe she was trying to take charge of her life, the way she'd taken charge at BCA nationals. If so, this could be an opportune time to help her. "I doubt Cissy's got any painting experience," Sedonia said, "but maybe she could help Marta, now that Alfonso's back in school. What do you think?"

"This Cissy . . . she sounded white."

Sedonia smiled. "She is, and she's not very big. But little white girls need jobs too, you know."

"I know," Raul said with mock seriousness. "The last one who worked for me is now my boss."

Sedonia laughed. "Okay with you if we give Cissy a try?"

"No problem," he said.

"I'll call her later, and tell her to report tomorrow morning at 5:30."

Raul nodded, and then turned and headed into the warehouse.

Sedonia switched on her PC, and rummaged through her purse for the Post-it note Brad had given her at the Cadillac Bar and Grill. She found it stuck to the back of a credit card. "Acropolis" was the password he'd chosen. She slid the note under her mouse pad for safekeeping, and logged into the account.

Sedonia switched off her PC shortly before noon. As promised, Brad had opened the account with $25,000, and during the morning she had printed checks to suppliers totaling almost $7,000. Brad's system worked well, and before logging off, she'd sent him an email saying so.

She stood up and stretched. While she'd been working, a dull ache had spread through her right shoulder and into the base of her neck. She massaged the sore area as she gazed out the window. The One-Pocket session the previous night had gone well. She'd resisted the game for the first hour or so, but then finally had stopped complaining about defensive play being boring and had begun applying herself to learning the strategy. Early in the session, she'd dropped sets, 8 to 2 and 8 to 3. Elmer was a competitive old coot, and he'd enjoyed her frustration at being unable to rely on her superior shooting skill. But his enjoyment had tailed off when she'd begun picking up his defensive tactics and turning them against him.

At the end of the session, Elmer dropped three consecutive 8 to 1 sets, and said he had to go. His wife was expecting him. Buster remarked this was the earliest he'd ever seen Elmer leave. And, he'd never known Elmer had a wife. Another elderly One-Pocket player had challenged Sedonia to play for $10 a set. He was a stronger player than Elmer, and he too picked up early wins. However, after three hours he was down $40, and he too decided he'd had enough.

Sedonia sat back down behind her desk. A faint smile formed. She had to admit, toward the end last night, she'd begun to enjoy the defensive chess game that One-Pocket presented. Too bad she hadn't learned to play safeties before Las Vegas, instead of after.

She picked up the phone and called Hannah.

"I can't believe it!" Hannah said, when Sedonia told her she'd spent the previous day learning to play defensive pool.

"If you can't beat 'em, join 'em," Sedonia said.

"What prompted this sudden change in attitude?"

"Las Vegas. Not just getting my ass kicked by those Canadians, but also watching the women professionals."

"Starting to think you could beat 'em?"

"I don't know if I could ever play that well, but I want to find out. They impressed me, not only with their skill, but also with how they handle themselves."

"Kid, I don't know if you could ever be as good as they are, but I do know, if you add defense to your game, you're *really* gonna be strong. Listen, I've got a couple of openings for next month's Hunter's Classics semipro tournament at Big Ernie's in Alvin. Why don't you enter?"

"Nine-Ball isn't it?"

"Yeah. I know you're used to Eight-Ball, but you'd have four weeks to get ready."

"You're on," Sedonia said. "What do I need to do?"

"Membership is $15 a year, and the entry fee is $30. First place in the tournament will pay $1,000. Plus, you can put up another $50 if you want to compete in the WPBA qualifier. If you do, and you're the high finisher among all the women who put up the extra $50, the WPBA will let you play in one of their tournaments."

"You mean compete against the pros I saw play last week?"

"Uh-huh," Hannah said, then added with a chuckle, "Hell, you've already got Jeanette Lee intimidated."

"Sure I do," Sedonia replied with heavy sarcasm. Her mind was racing, though: play against top semipros, with a chance to earn a spot in a professional tournament. "Hannah," she said, "I want to enter that qualifier thing too."

"I'll get you signed up. You can pay me back the $95 when you see me next."

After they'd hung up, Sedonia stood up and stepped back to the window. A smile played at the corners of her mouth. She was aware that for the first time since last year, she was genuinely enthusiastic about something. This would be no halfhearted effort. She had a month to get ready, which was more than enough. She'd play One-Pocket in the afternoons and Nine-Ball at night. Raul would be able to cover for her here.

Lost in her plans, she rubbed her shoulder and felt a warning twinge. She made a mental note to stop by Walgreen's this afternoon and get some Advil.

Late that afternoon, Sedonia was sitting at her desk and considering locking up a half-hour early, when the phone rang.

Brad's pleasant, deep voice said, "When did you get back?"

Sedonia grimaced, knowing she should have contacted Brad on Friday evening. "Uh . . . over the weekend," she said, stretching the truth. The Cue-Ts actually had arrived late Friday morning.

"How'd it go?"

Sedonia felt Brad was far too businesslike to understand her dedication to pool, so she gave him a lighthearted account of her general impressions of Las Vegas, and then simply added that she'd won some games and lost some games.

"Well, sounds like you had a good time," he said when she was finished.

Sedonia responded with a wry smile. Whatever Las Vegas had been, it hadn't been a good time. "I tried the new account this morning," she said. "It works great."

"Yeah, I saw your note." Then he launched into an update on the status of his projects.

Sedonia leaned back in her chair as she listened. Raul, as usual, had taken care of things in her absence. She checked her watch: 5:42. The One-Pocket players should be arriving at Buster's Billiards about now.

"Have you made any plans for this weekend?" Brad said.

Sedonia sat up in her chair. This was going to be awkward. "Uh . . . I'll be practicing."

"Practicing? You mean pool?"

"Yeah, there's a tournament coming up next month, and I'm getting ready for it."

"In Las Vegas again?"

"No," she said with a quick laugh. "I'll just be driving over to Alvin this time. It's a semipro event, but if I get lucky and win, it would qualify me to compete in a pro tournament later."

"Interesting," Brad said, though not sounding interested at all.

There was a pause, and Sedonia felt she ought to say something. She liked Brad. The recollection of his kiss in the restaurant parking lot flashed into her mind. "Uh—"

But before she could speak, he interrupted. "Okay then, sounds like you're gonna be busy. But I'd like one of y'all, either you or Raul, to start giving me a status report every Friday afternoon. A phone call will be fine. I have all my subcontractors check in at the end of the week."

Sedonia hesitated, realizing Brad had just relegated her to the status of his other subcontractors. She should be relieved that she'd sidestepped the pressure of his personal interest in her, but she wasn't.

"One of us will contact you every Friday afternoon," was all she could muster.

"Talk to you later," he said, and hung up.

Sedonia pulled into a parking spot in front of Buster's Billiards. She transferred $100, her driver's license, and a small envelope containing six

Advil tablets into her jeans pocket. Then she leaned back for a minute to collect her thoughts.

The two weeks since returning from Las Vegas had flown past. She found it hard to believe it was already Friday night again. She'd averaged seven hours a day on the tables, usually playing with the elderly One-Pocket group. But at least once a night, Buster would challenge her to a Nine-Ball, race-to-5 set for $20. The closest he'd come to beating her was a 5 to 4 loss on Wednesday night. Her other wins had been one-sided.

Tonight he'd matched her up with a road player from Austin. With the Hunter Classics tournament only two weeks away, this Nine-Ball match should let her know if her game was improving. For some reason, though, she was having trouble getting psyched up. She ought to be feeling nervous about this match, but she wasn't. Probably too tired, she thought, from having put in hours equivalent to working two jobs during the past two weeks. Plus, the nagging ache in her shoulder made sleeping difficult.

She heaved a sigh. Tonight's match might run into the morning hours. Sometime over the weekend, she needed to go into the office and get her accounts straightened out. *Damn it!* She'd forgotten to make the Friday call to Brad this afternoon. She gave an angry jerk on the door handle and climbed out. She'd have to call tomorrow and apologize.

Sedonia, Buster, and three railbirds slouched on chairs in the back room. A moth circled the light over the unoccupied pool table. It was after 10:00, but there was no sign of the Austin road player.

"Wanna shoot a practice game?" Buster said.

Sedonia shook her head. She'd started warming up earlier, but then sat down when she felt a warning twinge from her shoulder.

The door to the main room opened and Monk shuffled in. Sedonia smiled. It was the first time she'd seen him since returning from Las Vegas. Shyly avoiding eye contact, he took a seat beside her and fixed his attention on the moth.

"Hi, Monk," Sedonia said.

"Hi."

"I haven't seen you in a while."

He turned to her, eyes wide. "They made me stay in Houston."

"They did?"

"The lady was looking into my situation." Monk's expression turned solemn as he said 'looking into my situation,' as if it were an ominous phrase he'd heard repeated during his stay at the mental health facility.

"What did she decide?" Sedonia said.

Monk frowned, and turned to Buster.

"The social worker's name is Mickelson," Buster said. "She let me pick him up this morning. But, she's coming down here tomorrow to do what they call a 'home and work visit'. I could use your help."

"Sure," Sedonia said, frowning. "What can I do?"

"You're one of my more . . . 'respectable' customers. You know, college gal, own your own business, and the like."

Sedonia waited.

"This Miss Mickelson's coming by Monk's boarding house at 9:00 in the morning. I'm supposed to meet her there, since I've kinda become his guardian or somethin'. After she checks where he lives, we're supposed to come over here so she can see where he works. It might help if you were with me."

"Here?"

"Both places." When Sedonia hesitated, Buster said, "If it's too much trouble—"

"Of course not," Sedonia said quickly. "There's a business call I have to make in the morning. I'll just have to remember to call early, or when we're done."

"Good," Buster said. "Then meet me here about 8:30, and we'll go over to Monk's together."

Monk had listened to their exchange without expression. Sedonia wondered how much he understood, and if he knew his independence was in jeopardy. She decided to steer the conversation back into familiar territory. "Monk, do you know the guy I'm supposed to play tonight?"

"'Austin' Danny."

"How do he and I match up in Nine-Ball?"

"You don't play Nine-Ball."

"I do now. Buster's been teaching me while you've been gone."

Monk frowned, and turned to Buster, who confirmed Sedonia now played Nine-Ball. Monk began to nod and rock. Finally he said, "You need to give 'Austin' Danny the eight."

"Give him the eight?" Sedonia said. She doubted she was that much better than an established road player.

"You need to give 'Austin' Danny the eight," Monk repeated

"I've never seen Monk do that," Buster said, "handicap a Nine-Ball player based on Eight-Ball. I think he's got the weight about right, though."

Sedonia smiled at Monk. "Don't tell 'Austin' Danny he needs to get the eight from me."

Monk placed the tip of his index finger against his lips. "I only tell weight to Buster. And to you."

The door to the main room opened again, and Buster muttered, "About time."

A wiry young man with an arrogant demeanor strolled into the room, followed by an older man in drugstore-cowboy garb, probably the player's stakehorse. Buster got up and met them. Since Buster was fronting the money, Sedonia was more than willing to let him handle the haggling.

A few minutes later, Buster returned. Speaking softly, so only Sedonia and Monk could hear, he said, "We're set. Race-to-9, $500, no weight."

Sedonia swallowed. Five hundred dollars. For the first time all evening, her fatigue lifted and she felt alert. She looked past Buster and could see 'Austin' Danny screwing his stick together. He looked back at her with what he probably thought was an intimidating scowl. He reminded Sedonia of an imitation "French Quarter" Jimmy Dupre, but he wasn't nearly as good looking. She smiled, and it seemed to throw Danny off. His scowl faded into a bewildered frown.

Buster regained her attention. "We're after more than $500," he said. "We need this first set, but we don't want to scare Danny off too early, like you did that guy in Vegas. Understand?"

Sedonia nodded, but wasn't sure how she was supposed to ensure a win, if she wasn't permitted to play her best.

"I've seen Danny and his backer go for $1,000 a set," Buster said. "That's what we're shootin' for. But we need to win the first one. I've got less than a grand on hand."

Sedonia nodded again. On the other side of the room, the three railbirds were placing bets, between themselves and with Danny's backer.

"Call it!" Danny shouted. He stood at the rack end of the table, poised to flip a coin.

Sedonia walked over and shooed the moth away. "Heads."

Danny flipped the coin and it came up tails. Sedonia racked the nine balls into the required diamond configuration, and went to extra pains to ensure they were pressed tightly together. Danny stood over her, watching, then gave a nod of approval and walked up to the break end of the table. He broke with a sledgehammer-like stroke—a full lunge forward, with the tip of his cue stick winding up extended over the far end of the table. Two balls scurried into pockets, and the rest of the table looked like a run-out. It was.

As Sedonia racked for the second game, Danny watched from the break end of the table. When Sedonia sat down, Buster leaned over and whispered, "Don't worry about goin' on a stall. He's in stroke. When you get to the table, just shoot your best shot."

"*If* I get to the table," Sedonia muttered.

The second game was a repeat of the first. Danny broke and ran again. Now Sedonia was down 2 to 0 in the race-to-9, and had yet to get to the table. Danny had appeared confident when he'd arrived; now he acted downright cocky. He turned his back on Sedonia while she racked, and started chiding his stakehorse, something about a bet they'd had on a baseball game. Sedonia lifted the wooden triangle and noticed she'd unintentionally left a slight gap between the second and third rows of balls. Normally, she would have re-racked, but this time she didn't. When Danny lunged into another powerful break, there was noticeably less action. The maroon 7-ball made it into the side pocket. Running eight more balls, however, would present a challenge. Danny ran the first four, and then missed a long cut shot in the corner.

Sedonia approached the table for her first shot in the match. Again, she was aware of how emotionless she felt, despite the stakes and the need to win this first set. It had to be fatigue overriding nerves. Somehow, she needed to maintain this relaxed feeling, but play *smart*. She took a moment to figure out how she wanted to negotiate this rack. The 5-ball and the 6-ball were out in the open, but the 8-ball was frozen between the rail and the 9-ball.

The 5-ball went cleanly, as did the 6-ball. Then she switched from offense to defense. The cue-ball kissed the 8-ball away from the 9-ball and sent it to the far end of the table, where it came to rest against the rail. She'd left Danny with a table-length bank shot. He made a futile attempt, but instead scratched in the corner. Sedonia took ball-in-hand, and made quick work of the 8-ball and the game-winning 9-ball.

Sedonia chalked her cue while Danny racked for the fourth game. She looked back at Monk, whose gaze was fixed on the pool table. He rocked and nodded, his strange savant computer seemingly processing the recent shot data. Was there a special code for safeties? She smiled at the thought.

Danny lifted the triangle, and Sedonia walked down and inspected the rack. "Re-rack."

Danny scowled at her.

"Space between the 3-ball and the 7-ball," she said.

Danny re-racked and Sedonia returned to the break end of the table. *One, two, three . . . stroke!* The stab of pain from her shoulder almost made her cry out. She walked over and dropped onto a chair next to Buster.

"What's the matter?" he said.

"Shoulder," was all she could muster. She put her head in her hands and took deep breaths to quell rising nausea.

'Austin' Danny came over. "What's goin' on?"

Sedonia got to her feet. "Time out."

"Time out?" he said belligerently.

Sedonia pushed past him, and then hurried through the doorway into the main poolroom and down the hallway to the ladies room. No one was inside. Sedonia ran cool water over the inside of her wrists, then doused her face. The nausea subsided, but her shoulder and lower neck still ached. She took a mouthful of water, and pulled the Advil envelope from her jeans pocket. She popped two pills into her mouth, swallowed, and then decided to take two more.

The door opened and a high-school-age girl entered, wearing too much makeup and exposing too much bare, adolescent paunch over grimy jeans. "Watcha got?" she said.

"Advil," Sedonia said, and washed down the second two.

"Right," the girl said with heavy sarcasm.

Sedonia remembered having caught Cissy leaning over a sink like this, swallowing amphetamines, a few weeks earlier. Now this juvenile delinquent suspected her of the same. Sedonia didn't care. Somehow, she just needed to make it through this evening's match.

A few minutes later as she reentered the back room, Danny called out, "What's the matter, sweetheart? Wrong time of the month?"

Laughter rippled through the railbirds. One shouted, "Hey, Danny! Give her a break. Don't you like women?"

"I *love* women," Danny said. "They make my dick get hard."

More laughter.

Sedonia ignored their drivel. Discomfort and fatigue made it difficult to think, but it also helped partition out distractions. She focused all of her available thought process on the table. Resuming play, she shot softly and executed flawless position. A few minutes later, she dropped the 9-ball, tying the set, 2 to 2. The ache in her shoulder continued to subside. The trick would be to continue running racks, without shooting hard.

The next four games passed quickly. Sedonia only allowed Danny back to the table twice, and each time it was after she'd played a safety, from which he was unable to recover. Danny now trailed 6 to 2 in the race-to-9. As he racked for the ninth game, his banter was gone and his face was set in a sullen mask.

Waiting at the break end of the table, Sedonia glanced over at Buster, who responded with a barely perceptible shake of his head. She looked back at Danny. From his body language, she realized it was doubtful he'd want to play another set after this one. Sedonia experienced the same revelation she'd had in Las Vegas at the Billiard Club. Although she was only one of the two players in this match, she felt she could make the score whatever she chose it to be.

She took a deep breath. It was time to see if she could go on a believable stall. She placed the cue-ball six inches to the left of her usual break spot. When she broke, balls scattered, but as she'd planned, nothing went in. Danny leaped to his feet and quickly executed a rack-and-run. Some of his cocky demeanor returned as he chalked his cue and waited for her to rack for the next game.

Over the next four games, Sedonia orchestrated a split—winning one, losing two, winning one. With score now 8 to 5 and her break, she decided she'd better not take any more chances; Danny had demonstrated he could run racks. She returned to her regular routine, placing the cue-ball close to the side rail and breaking with full force. Again, her shoulder responded with a blinding stab of pain, and a surge of nausea brought perspiration to her forehead.

She tried to block the pain from her mind and focus on the table. The 3-ball and the 4-ball had gone on the break, and the rest were spread out. Sensing a possible run, she began to shoot quickly, paying only limited attention to cue-ball position. She simply wanted to get this set over with. The shots grew increasing difficult, and finally she had to slow when she reached the 8-ball. She took a deep breath. There was no alternative except to attempt a cross-table bank. She made it, but left herself with another difficult shot. The gold-striped 9-ball—the money ball—lay close to the side rail, seven feet from the far corner pocket. She took another deep breath. *One, two, three . . . stroke.* The 9-ball rolled slowly down the table, slipped past the side pocket, hesitated in the corner, then dropped. She'd won the set.

Ignoring Danny, she unscrewed her stick as she walked over to Buster. "I gotta go. My shoulder's killing me."

"We got him where we want him," he whispered, urgency in his tone. Then he apparently realized how much pain she was in. "It's that bad?"

"Yeah."

Danny walked over. "Hey! Where the fuck you goin'?"

Buster pushed Danny back. "She's sick." Then he asked Sedonia, "Do you need someone to take you home?"

"I can make it. I just need to leave *now.*"

As Sedonia walked out, she heard Danny grousing in the background that she'd quit on him, just because he was getting in stroke, and Buster offering to match him up with Darrell from Champ's Billiards.

Sedonia awoke with a start, and glanced at the luminescent dial of her clock-radio: 2:57. She'd dozed for a quarter-hour this time. She tried to raise her head from the pillow, and gasped. She worked her feet to the edge of the mattress, and then gingerly lowered her legs over the side. Another stab of pain, but she fought through it and pulled herself into a sitting position. She sat still for a few moments, letting the pain and nausea subside. Another glance at the clock. In five and a half hours, she needed to meet Buster to go over to Monk's. How could she possibly make it?

She reached over and turned on the bedside lamp, and then cautiously stood up. As long as she kept her shoulder and neck immobile, the ache was bearable. She padded over to the medicine cabinet and pulled out the large Advil bottle she'd bought just two weeks ago. It already was half empty. Her stomach turned, still queasy from the four pills she'd swallowed at Buster's. She returned the bottle to the cabinet and looked down at the tier of four drawers beneath the vanity counter.

Slowly, she lowered herself into a kneeling position and pulled out the bottom drawer. Her shoulder ached as she reached into the back, fumbling through the cache of Band-Aids, Ace bandages, adhesive tape, and gauze from her golfing days. Finally she felt the small plastic container she was looking for and withdrew it. The pharmacy label read:

"HYDROCO/APAP 5/500 MG.
One tablet every 6 to 8 hours
as needed for pain."

Sedonia took two.

Chapter 13

Buster pulled away from the poolroom and onto the NASA Parkway, and Sedonia put on her sunglasses to shield her sensitive eyes from the morning sun. She hoped they didn't have far to drive; the pain medication she'd taken five hours earlier had left her with a fuzzy head and a queasy stomach. Compounding her discomfort, Buster's old Ford smelled as bad as her Las Vegas rental car.

Buster glanced over and said, "You doin' okay?"

She shook her head. "Feeling pretty bad."

"Too bad about that shoulder of yours."

"Did you match up 'Austin' Danny with somebody else last night?"

"Darrell came over from Champ's. Danny robbed us."

Sedonia didn't respond. Conversation took more mental energy than she could muster. They bounced over the railroad tracks, crossed Highway 3, and then turned into an old neighborhood Sedonia was unfamiliar with. Modest wood-frame houses, probably 50 years old, lined both sides of the narrow street. A small one-story apartment complex stood on the next corner. Its dozen or so units were laid out in an "L."

"That's where Monk lives," Buster said as he turned into the potholed parking area. He pulled in beside an inexpensive, but spotless, white Plymouth sedan. It looked out of place among the rusty pickups and vans that apparently belonged to the apartment residents. "Damn," he muttered, "that's probably Miss Mickelson's car. I wanted to get here before she did, to be sure Monk was ready."

Sedonia felt a pang of apprehension, concerned she might not be alert enough deal with this situation. She reached for the door handle, anxious to get some fresh air, but Buster placed a hand on her arm.

"You gonna be able to get through this?" he said.

"I'm . . . really . . . not in very good shape," she admitted. "If this woman asks me anything complicated, bail me out."

"This is important, Sedonia," Buster said. "That mental health place in Houston ain't bad. It's kinda like a dormitory. But Monk's miserable there, and he's countin' on us to keep him . . . independent."

"C'mon," Sedonia said in a moment of clarity, and threw open the car door. But as they started up the uneven sidewalk, she stumbled slightly, as if she'd been drinking.

Buster took her by the elbow. "Monk lives down at the end."

They cut across the neatly-trimmed lawn. Sedonia frowned as they approached the end unit; the front door stood open. They stopped in the doorway, and Sedonia took off her sunglasses and looked inside. What apparently at one time had been the living room and dining area, now held two clothes washers, a dryer, and a small sorting table. The former kitchen area was now a storeroom, which held brooms, mops, and an old lawnmower.

"Used to be an apartment," Buster said. "They let Monk use the bedroom and bathroom area, rent free, and he's responsible for maintaining this room and the outside. Owner used to catch hell from the neighbors about the condition of the complex, but not since Monk took over."

They entered the makeshift washateria, and Buster knocked on a door that had been installed across the entrance to the bedroom hallway. A moment later, Monk opened the door. Sedonia had never seen him in this state. Eyes wide with fright, he looked as if he might bolt past them and run out into the street.

"Morning, Monk," Buster said. He placed a reassuring hand on Monk's shoulder and guided him down the short hallway.

Sedonia followed them into what once had been the apartment bedroom, and now served as Monk's living quarters. The room was austere, but clean. A made-up futon stood against one wall; an old Formica and chrome table, with two chairs, stood against another. A two-burner electric hotplate and an Igloo ice chest sat on the table. There was no television set, not even a radio.

A woman was sitting at the table. Now she stood up as they approached. She reminded Sedonia of a stern nun she'd had for a teacher in the third grade—fortyish, stocky, hair cropped in a mannish pageboy. Monk looked back and forth between his three visitors, futilely trying to discern who controlled his fate.

"Good morning, Miss Mickelson," Buster said.

The woman responded with a curt nod and turned her attention to Sedonia.

"This is Sedonia . . ." Buster began, then struggled, apparently realizing he didn't know Sedonia's last name.

"Sedonia Forbes," she finished for him, and extended her hand. Miss Mickelson frowned as she squeezed it in her own meaty grip.

"Sedonia is my friend," Monk said. His sudden entrance into the exchange momentarily silenced the others.

Then Buster said, "Has he showed you around here?"

"Yes," Miss Mickelson said, "but I'd expected to meet the owner of the complex."

"He lives in Florida now," Buster said.

Miss Mickelson raised an eyebrow. "He's an absentee landlord?"

"I've known him for a long time," Buster said hastily. "I've got his phone number back at my office, if you need to contact him."

"So Charles is unsupervised here?"

"Uh . . . 'Charles' really doesn't require much supervision. He's a good worker. Just take a look at that yard out there. The hardest thing is keeping him from mowing and edging it every day."

"He thinks he's supposed to mow and edge every day?" Miss Mickelson said, sounding concerned.

Sedonia tried to fight through her mental fatigue and help Buster deal with this inquisitor. "Buster's just kidding about that. What he means is—"

"And what is *your* relationship with Charles?" Miss Mickelson interrupted.

Sedonia felt her pulse accelerate. Monk's independence depended on her not making a mistake. "Like Monk says, I'm his friend."

"'Monk'?" Miss Mickelson said. "Who decided to call Charles, 'Monk'?"

Sedonia and Buster both turned to Monk, who responded with a frown. He apparently had no knowledge, or perhaps recollection, where his nickname had come from, and he seemed perplexed as to why these people were discussing it.

Finally Buster said, "I've known Monk for three or four years. Never knew his name was Charles, until you called him that a couple of weeks ago."

Miss Mickelson returned her attention to Sedonia. "Are you involved in looking after Charles also?"

Sedonia took a deep breath, wanting to help Monk, but unable to assume responsibility for him.

"Well, Ms. Forbes?" Miss Mickelson pressed.

Sedonia chose her words carefully. "Monk is my friend, and so is Buster. Anything I can do to help Buster look after Monk, I will."

For the first time, Miss Mickelson seemed to accept a response. She studied Sedonia for a moment, then the hint of a smile tugged at one corner of her mouth. "Are you by any chance a golfer, Ms. Forbes?"

Sedonia frowned. "I used to be."

"So did I. U of H, class of '79."

Sedonia felt a surge of hope. "You played for Coach Bolton?"

"Yes, and I'm currently a member of the alumni association. I've heard about you. An injury of some sort kept you from turning professional?"

Sedonia nodded.

"What happened?" Miss Mickelson said.

"I tore my rotator cuff in a golf tournament, and did further damage by continuing to play through the pain. Later, I had surgery, but there were complications when they tried to reattach a muscle. Now I can't raise my right arm above shoulder height."

"No further surgery possible?"

Sedonia shook her head.

"That's too bad," Miss Mickelson said. "I understand you were quite good. By the way, weren't you supposed to be at the annual Cougar alumni dinner last month?"

"I . . . had a schedule conflict," Sedonia said. "I don't intend to miss another one."

Miss Mickelson nodded. "And are you a pool player now?"

"I'm trying to become one."

"Are you any good?"

"Damn good," Buster volunteered.

"My former companion is a pool player," Miss Mickelson said. "She plays at a place called the Silver Bullet Saloon."

"In the Montrose District?" Buster interjected with a grin.

Miss Mickelson turned to him, again raising an eyebrow. "Yes?"

"Uh . . . nice little place," he said, dropping the grin. "So I hear."

Miss Mickelson turned back to Sedonia. "Are you familiar with it?"

"I don't think so," Sedonia said, and felt herself blush. Miss Mickelson had indicated her sexual preference by using the word "companion," and Buster's emphasis of "the Montrose District" seemed to validate Sedonia's recollection that the Silver Bullet Saloon was a gay bar.

"They have a women's tournament every Saturday night at 8:00," Miss Mickelson said. "You might like to enter."

"Sure," Sedonia said. For Monk's sake, she was willing to do anything within reason to build upon this unexpected rapport.

"Good," Miss Mickelson said. "I'll look for you there next Saturday night." Then she turned to Monk. "Well, Charles, everything's in order here. Now let's go see where you work."

Sedonia pulled into her office parking lot, and glanced down at her dashboard clock: 7:30. Most mornings she was at work by 6:00, but the previous evening the pain in her shoulder had finally subsided, and she'd enjoyed her first good rest in three nights. She was confident that today she'd be able to discontinue the pain pills.

As she climbed out of her car, Raul's van pulled out of the warehouse. He was behind the wheel and Cissy was seated on the passenger side.

Raul stopped and leaned out the side window. *"Hola, jefe."*

Sedonia smiled and walked over. *"Hola."*

"What does *'jefe'* mean," Cissy asked Raul.

"'Boss'," Raul and Sedonia said simultaneously.

"Hola, jefe," Cissy said.

"Hola, Hermanita," Sedonia replied.

"¿Hermanita?" Cissy said.

Raul laughed. "Means 'little sister'." Then he told Sedonia, "She's learnin' Spanish fast. Turnin' brown too."

Sedonia chuckled. Raul was right. Although still frail, after two weeks on the job, Cissy's poolroom pallor had turned to brown. "You two heading out to Brad's site?" she said.

"Yeah," Raul said. "We was just waitin' for you to get here."

"Okay, I got it covered," Sedonia said. "And there's no need for you to come back at 1:00."

"No practice today?"

"No, my shoulder's been bothering me, so I'm going to take the day off."

Cissy said, "You're still playin' in the Hunter Classics tournament in two weeks, aren't you?"

"Yeah, and I think you ought to sign up too."

"They're too good for me. I may come out and watch you play, though . . . *jefe.*"

Sedonia chuckled. "Watch what you teach her, Raul. A little knowledge can be a dangerous thing." She smiled as they waved and pulled away. She was pleased with how well Cissy was getting along with Raul and the rest of the Latino paint crew.

Sedonia entered the office and discovered Raul had left a fresh pot of coffee. She poured a cup, and continued over to her desk. As she sat down, she noticed what looked like a large aspirin bottle, almost hidden behind her telephone. A torn scrap of paper lay beneath it. The printed label on the bottle indicated the content was Hydrocodone, Quantity 200, distributed by *Farmacia del los Americas* in Matamoras, Mexico. The childish scrawl on the note read:

> *I heard your shoulder was hurting again.*
> C.

Sedonia sighed. Hannah had told her that Cissy's boyfriend made frequent trips to Matamoras, where prescription drugs were available for the asking. Undoubtedly, Cissy was trying to be helpful, but Sedonia didn't want any medication that had been brought up from Mexico. She thought for a moment, then dropped the bottle into her desk drawer. She planned to return it, but decided to wait until after the Hunter Classics tournament, just in case.

She switched on her PC, and while she waited for the operating system to come up, she glanced down at her watch. It was almost 8:00. Hannah was an early riser; she'd give her a call.

Hannah's husband answered. He sounded reserved, as he usually did when Sedonia phoned, but he called Hannah to the phone.

"What's up?" Hannah said.

"I need a date for Saturday night."

"I think you got the wrong number," Hannah said.

Sedonia laughed. "You may be closer than you think." She recapped her encounter with Miss Mickelson two days earlier, Monk's tenuous situation, and her commitment to meet Miss Mickelson and play in a Montrose District pool tournament.

"Lemme get this straight," Hannah said. "You're inviting me to go to a lesbian bar with you?"

"C'mon, Hannah. I don't wanna go there by myself."

"I gotta turn you down, kid," Hannah said. "I'm already jeopardizing my marriage by hanging out in poolrooms a couple of nights a week. I'm not about to ask my husband if I can go cruising gay bars with you on Saturday night."

Sedonia chuckled. She was disappointed, but appreciated Hannah's position. "Okay, I'll go by myself. If I cross over, can we still be friends?"

"Depends. I'll have to see what you look like with a crew cut."

Sedonia exited Interstate 59 South, and moments later turned onto Montrose Boulevard. The Montrose District was considered Houston's bohemian community. The shaded neighborhood was an eclectic collection of old homes, apartment buildings, bistros, and art shops. Sedonia was familiar with the surroundings; one of her University of Houston boyfriends had been an artist and had lived here for a while.

Approaching the Westheimer intersection, she pulled into the left-turn lane and stopped for a red light. Two young men stepped into the crosswalk, holding hands. One made eye contact with her and said something, but the whir of Sedonia's air-conditioner drowned out his words. He and his companion laughed, so Sedonia just smiled. The couple waved and continued across the street.

Sedonia sighed, uncomfortable at being here alone. After Hannah had turned her down, she'd asked Buster to accompany her, but he needed to manage his poolroom on Saturday nights. Plus, he'd matched up two road players who were scheduled to arrive sometime later that evening. Sedonia hadn't had any other close friends she could ask.

The green arrow lit, and Sedonia turned left onto Westheimer. At the next intersection, she turned right onto Waugh Drive and began looking for the 2200 block. Then ahead on the corner, she spotted a neon sign that read: SILVER BULLET SALOON. Beneath the bold purple letters was a depiction of a leggy female, sitting astride a large silver bullet and gaily waving a cowgirl hat.

Sedonia glanced down at the digital clock on her dashboard: 8:05. The pool tournament was supposed to have started five minutes ago. For Monk's sake, she'd felt obliged to meet Miss Mickelson here tonight, but she hoped by arriving late she'd be able to avoid playing and could get away early.

The parking lot was almost full, but she found a spot wide enough for her Miata. She made the usual transfer of cash and driver's license from her purse to her jeans, and then climbed out and got her cue stick out of the trunk. As she crossed the parking lot, she checked her surroundings. Pre World War II houses, most featuring red brick veneer and large front porches, lined the narrow side street. The neighborhood had the appearance of an unkempt southern town. This was one section of the Montrose District that had yet to succumb to gentrification.

Sedonia arrived at the entrance, took a deep breath, and stepped inside. The poolroom was smaller than she'd anticipated, perhaps half the size of Buster's, and it had the feel of a neighborhood tavern. The half-dozen people standing at the bar were all women, and most turned and watched her approach. None of them, however, was Miss Mickelson.

Sedonia found an unoccupied place at the bar, and nodded to the young women on either side. They both returned her nod, neither friendly nor hostile, simply interested. Sedonia noticed the young woman on her right had a cue case lying on the counter. The bartender, a stocky woman in her forties, was busy loading the cash register from a money tray. Apparently, she'd just come on duty.

Sedonia looked around the room. A row of five tables ran down each side—a bar-box, followed by four 8-foot Brunswicks. Women were playing on all but the last table on the left, which was unoccupied. There were no men in the room, and no sign of Miss Mickelson.

A k.d. lang CD came up on the jukebox. The artist and the moderate volume level weren't what Sedonia was used to at Buster's and Carney's. She looked around again, regretting there wasn't a poolroom in Nassau Bay that had this quiet atmosphere. If there were, it would make a great place to practice.

The bartender closed the cash register, then turned and said, "What can I get you?"

"Uh . . . Coors Light," Sedonia said.

"Silver Bullet," the bartender replied with a grin. "Always a good choice. When in doubt, ride a Silver Bullet."

Sedonia responded with an uncertain smile.

The bartender returned with her beer and said, "You gonna play in the tournament tonight? I'm running late getting started. We still got an opening."

"I'm not sure," Sedonia said. "I'm supposed to meet a woman named Mickelson here. Do you know her?"

"Mick?" the bartender said. "Sure, she's a regular. Ought to be in any minute now." Then she looked over at the woman standing to Sedonia's right, and grinned. The woman scowled, picked up her cue case, and walked back to the pool table area. The bartender grinned again. "That's Mick's former girlfriend."

Sedonia responded with a nod, and watched the woman take the last unoccupied table. Most of the players appeared to be in their twenties or thirties. A few wore leather, and looked butch, but most were dressed in jeans and T-shirts, and simply looked trim and athletic. They reminded Sedonia of girls she'd grown up with, playing soccer, volleyball, and golf. Typically, those girls had been the better athletes on the teams. She suspected these young women had been too.

"Glad you could make it," said a voice behind her.

Sedonia turned and saw Miss Mickelson. She expected a handshake, but instead found herself pulled into a forceful hug. She extracted herself and said, "Uh . . . your directions were good. I didn't have any trouble finding the place."

"Did Maggie sign you up?"

The bartender interjected, "She wasn't sure she wanted to play."

"Of course she does," Miss Mickelson said. She pulled a wallet from her back pocket and gave the bartender a $10 bill. "Her name's Sedonia. Sign her up."

"You don't need to do that," Sedonia protested.

"You're wasting your time arguing with Mick," the bartender said.

Sedonia gave a resigned shake of her head. "Okay, 'Mick'. Thanks."

The bartender wrote Sedonia's name on a tournament bracket sheet, then brought Mick a Coors Light. "We've already had the drawing," the bartender told Sedonia. "With you, now we've got a full bracket of 16 players. You're up right now on table No. 5, playing Shelly, the woman who was sitting next to you a minute ago."

Sedonia sensed both the bartender and Mick found the first-round pairing amusing.

"I'll watch from here," Mick said. "Kick her ass."

Sedonia slung her cue stick over her shoulder, picked up her beer, and headed toward the back of the room. The other players watched as she passed. Sedonia hoped it was just because she was new to the poolroom, but doubted it. Shelly was practicing and pointedly ignored her as she approached.

Sedonia shook her head, annoyed at somehow having been thrust between two former lovers. She set her beer on a nearby table, pulled up a stool, and screwed her cue stick together. Shelly continued to practice without acknowledging Sedonia's presence. Sedonia noted her technique was good, but she was missing half her shots, maybe because she was upset about Mick, or maybe because she was self-conscious.

Shelly finally pocketed the black 8-ball, then looked up with a sullen expression. "You want to practice?"

Sedonia stood up. "No, let's play. What's the race?"

"Race-to-2."

They flipped for the break and Sedonia won. She'd only practiced once during the past week, and her shoulder felt good. But now to protect it, she broke with only half her usual force. The yellow 1-ball went in, and the rest of the balls spread across the table. Either suit looked like a run-out. Sedonia chose the stripes, and ran them with no problem, and then made the 8-ball for the win.

Shelly remained seated on a stool. "Where'd Mick find *you*?" she said.

Her tone struck Sedonia as neither bitter nor hostile, simply sad. Sedonia sensed what was troubling her and said, "It's not like that."

"Oh, no?" Shelly replied, obviously disbelieving.

"One of Mick's clients is a friend of mine. Mick and I met last weekend while she was checking up on him."

Shelly brightened. "Then you're not . . ."

Sedonia shook her head. "I'm straight," she said. "And it's your rack."

"I appreciate your clearing that up," Shelly said, smiling. She was noticeably more relaxed as she racked for the second game.

Sedonia made a solid ball on the break and ran four more, before intentionally missing to give Shelly a chance to get to the table. Shelly made four balls before missing. Sedonia ran the rest of the rack.

"You're good," Shelly said as she shook Sedonia's hand.

"Thanks. I . . . play a lot."

When Sedonia returned to the bar, Mick said, "You made that look easy. I knew you'd been a helluva golfer. Are you as good a pool player?"

Sedonia looked out over the poolroom where the other matches were in progress. "I don't know . . . it's hard to measure." However, at that moment, she again experienced the unusual sensation that she had complete control over the outcome of matches.

Mick was frowning.

Sedonia continued, "In golf, I just competed against whatever course I was playing. I'd shoot the lowest score I could, and what the other person shot was beyond my control. In pool, though, the opponent presents another variable. How *they* play impacts how *you* play, since you've got to play the cue-ball, wherever they leave it."

Mick nodded. "Interesting proposition."

Sedonia didn't mention, however, that at that particular moment, she felt she could win this tournament, no matter what the other players had to offer. This unusual confidence seemed to be occurring with increasing frequency. She wondered if she was passing some sort of pool plateau.

Maggie interrupted them, saying, "You're up on table No. 3."

A little after 10:00, Sedonia sat at the bar sipping a beer while she waited for the winner of the one-loss bracket to be decided. Shelly had won three matches since losing to Sedonia. If she won this one, she'd have a chance to play Sedonia again, this time for the championship.

Sedonia was pleased with her own game. The competition had been stronger than she'd expected, yet despite not being able to practice most of the past week, she'd won all three of her matches in the winners' bracket without losing a game. She felt comfortable in her surroundings now. Even watching two young women slow dancing nearby to a Melissa Ethridge CD didn't seem unusual. And the other players had accepted her. Earlier, Sedonia had been in the ladies room, when two players came in and didn't realize she was there.

"Is she lipstick?" one had said.

"No, I think she's straight. Nice, though."

"Is she a professional player?"

"I don't know. Good as she is, she sure as hell oughta be."

Now Sedonia smiled at the recollection.

"What's so funny?" Mick said. She was now on her fifth or sixth beer, and her usual brusque demeanor was growing belligerent.

"Nothing," Sedonia said. "Just enjoying myself."

"When we get done here," Mick said, "how'd you like to come by my place?"

"No thanks. It's an hour drive home, and I don't like to be out on Houston freeways at night."

"You could drive home in the morning," Mick said.

"I don't think my boyfriend would approve," Sedonia said with a smile, hoping she wouldn't have to invent a name and details for this fictitious boyfriend.

Mick responded with a peeved expression and ordered another beer. Then she turned her attention back to Sedonia. "What do you think about Charles' situation?"

Sedonia sensed the sudden shift in topic was a subtle attempt at coercion, but she kept her tone friendly and responded as if unaware. "I think it's wonderful that Buster's given him a chance to care for himself and live independently. With Monk's . . . Charles' handicap, opportunities like that must be limited."

"His involvement in gambling troubles me," Mick said.

"He doesn't actually gamble," Sedonia countered. "He's got an uncanny knack for judging relative strengths of pool players, but he just offers his opinions to Buster. He's not involved in the gambling itself. He's more like a . . . financial consultant."

Mick looked at Sedonia for a moment, then slowly nodded in apparent resignation. Finally she said, "Well, if he ever learns to handicap the dog races, let me know. I go down to Gulf Greyhound Park almost every Sunday."

Sedonia was pleased to note that Mick wouldn't actually compromise a client's well being to promote her love life. She turned her attention back to the table, where Shelly was being congratulated.

Maggie told Sedonia, "You're up. Since it's double-elimination, you just have to win one match; Shelly has to win two."

Shelly was smiling when Sedonia walked over. "I might as well forfeit," Shelly said. However, after winning the flip of the coin, she then proceeded to run the rack.

"Way to go, Shelly!" Mick called out from the bar.

While Sedonia racked, Shelly walked over and spoke briefly with Mick. When she returned to the table she was smiling. However, she failed to make a ball on the next break.

Sedonia called on the defensive guile she'd acquired over the past three weeks. She won the final two games, but kept them close, by intentionally missing shots from time to time, without being obvious. Shelly was the first to congratulate her when the last 8-ball fell.

Back at the bar, Maggie counted out Sedonia's $80 first place money.

Sedonia handed it back to her and said, "Beer's on me 'til the money's gone."

Maggie announced that Sedonia was buying, and a cheer went up. Then everyone crowded around the bar. Shelly added her $40 second place money to the pot, and another cheer went up.

Maggie held up her hands. "Wait a minute! We've still got the trophy ceremony!"

The regular customers frowned and looked at each other. Sedonia sensed this wasn't part of their usual Saturday night ritual. Maggie presented her with a small rectangular box, perhaps six inches long, wrapped in aluminum foil. Something told Sedonia what to expect, and when she peeled back the foil, her suspicions were confirmed. This Silver Bullet was not a Coors Light.

A roar of laughter went up from the women around her. "Straight girls use 'em too, don't they?" one shouted, and another roar went up.

Sedonia laughed, but felt herself turning red and quickly slipped the vibrator into an unused pocket at the bottom of her cue case.

After everyone had a full beer, one of the women complimented Sedonia on her pool game and asked where she'd learned to play. Before she could reply, Mick interrupted. "Sedonia's a natural athlete. She was one of the best golfers ever to come out of Texas. Second to Babe Didrikson Zaharias, of course."

Another cheer went up. Sedonia didn't know if the enthusiasm was for her, the legendary Babe, or maybe just the free beer.

Mick and Shelly moved to a side table and entered into in a quiet conversation. They'd apparently set aside their differences, at least for tonight. Sedonia hung around for one more beer, then said her goodbyes, explaining she had a long drive down the Gulf Freeway ahead of her.

A few moments later, a smile formed as she crossed the parking lot. She'd thoroughly enjoyed herself tonight. As she climbed into her car, however, her smile faded. The following weekend's Hunter Classics tournament would present more of a challenge. She'd be playing against semipros for $1,000 and a chance to qualify to compete against the pros. She hoped tonight had been an omen, or at least had provided a good tune-up.

Chapter 14

Sedonia sped south on FM-528, a six-lane thoroughfare designed to handle Friendswood's future commuter traffic. On this Saturday morning, however, she only had to share the road with a few other early risers. The passing scenery was a work in progress. New subdivisions were gobbling up the coastal plain farms, and utilitarian shopping centers were popping up like mushrooms, featuring the obligatory grocery store, drugstore, liquor store, and fast-food outlets.

"ALVIN 5 MILES" read a green sign. Hannah had told Sedonia that drawings for the tournament pairings would begin at 9:30, but that she and the other organizers would start arriving around 8:00. Sedonia planned to be there shortly after that, so she'd have time to get acclimated to the unfamiliar surroundings.

As she approached the intersection of Sunset Drive, the traffic light turned red. She stopped, and glanced to her right. Brad Landry's current housing projects were less than a mile from here. She suspected he'd be over there sometime this morning, inspecting things. A wry smile formed. This intersection seemed symbolic: Brad in one direction, a poolroom in the other.

Her smile faded as self-doubt resurfaced, as it often did. She had a business to run and an attractive man who was interested in her. And she definitely was interested in him. Why, then, was she pursuing this dubious dream of playing professional pool? She reflexively reached back and massaged her right shoulder. Then her two brief encounters with Jeanette Lee in Las Vegas flashed into her mind. Jeanette's banter had been in fun, but it also had indicated acceptance. During those moments, Sedonia felt that she too, had been a woman cueist.

The light changed to green, and she continued south on FM-528.

A short while later, Sedonia exited FM-528 where Hannah had instructed, and headed down a side street. Alvin was a lackluster community. Even the billboards on the outskirts, which heralded it as the home of Baseball Hall of Fame pitcher Nolan Ryan, were fading and peeling. Muddy fields, rundown homes, and small service businesses lined both sides of the two-lane blacktop road. Sedonia came to an intersection and turned to the left. Ahead on the right, she saw a drab gray building with bold black letters painted on the front: Big Ernie's Billiards. One section of the front wall was a wide garage door; apparently the structure hadn't always been a poolroom. Sedonia had expected something more upscale for an important semipro tournament.

A dozen cars were already parked out front, including Hannah's beige Cadillac. Sedonia pulled in, and a few moments later entered the well-lit poolroom. A long bar ran down the left side, and video games and four bar-boxes stood off to the right. The sole customer at the bar sat with his back to her. Hannah and several other women were gathered around one of the dozen 8-foot tables that lined the rear of the room. As Sedonia started toward them, the man at the bar turned and smiled.

"Buster told me you were gonna be here," he said.

Sedonia responded with a wry smile and shake of her head. "'French Quarter' Jimmy," she said as she approached. "What are you doing here? Playing in women's tournaments now?"

He chuckled. "Been down on South Padre Island this past week. Played in the 'Eight-Ball Showdown'."

"How'd you do?"

"Finished third. It paid $5,000."

"Heading back to New Orleans now?"

He smiled. "No, I'll be around a while."

Sedonia looked toward the rear of the room, and Hannah waved. "Well, I'll see you later," Sedonia told Jimmy.

He smiled again, and nodded.

As Sedonia walked up, Hannah said, "You saw what the cat drug in?"

"Uh-huh."

"He's interested in you, kid. I saw the way he looked at you in Las Vegas. And when we started talking this morning, first thing he asked was if you were going to be here."

Sedonia glanced back at Jimmy, made eye contact, then turned back to Hannah, who was grinning.

"He's awfully good looking," Hannah said.

Sedonia responded with a dismissive shake of her head. However, she had to agree, Jimmy was handsome, and he seemed pleasant enough, when he didn't have a cue stick in his hand. But now she was ready to change the subject. "How do these tournaments work?"

"In about an hour, we'll get everybody together and go over the rules and announce the pairings. Then we'll do the Calcutta."

"What's that?"

"Spectators bid on the players they think are going to win. For the better players, I've seen bids as high as $300. The players have the option to buy back up to fifty percent of whatever they go for. The bids all go into a pot, and at the end of the tournament, it's divided up like the prize money. Sometimes the Calcutta purse is more than the prize money."

Sedonia glanced back at Jimmy, who was now talking to the barmaid. She turned back to Hannah, "I'm surprised so many people are here this early."

"Out-of-towners, mainly. There's nothing to do in the motels around this neighborhood. We've got women coming in from all over Texas, and even a few from out of state."

"How many women will be in the tournament?"

"So far, we've got 61. Three more and we'll have a full bracket."

Sedonia responded with a noncommittal nod, but actually she regretted the large turnout. Winning would be all the more difficult. These women were semipros, and many were confident enough in their skills that they'd made long trips to compete here. Then, annoyed with herself, she vowed to stop the defeatist thinking. Just shoot your best shot, she told herself.

A little before 10:00, Sedonia leaned against a pool table. She estimated about 200 players and spectators now crammed the room. Hannah, microphone in hand, had already recapped the rules and announced the pairings. Sedonia had drawn position four on the chart, meaning she'd play in the first round of matches. Now Hannah was conducting the Calcutta auction.

"In position four," Hannah said, "we have Sedonia Forbes. She recently completed her first session of BCA play, and had the top average in the Bay Area League. What's the opening bid for . . . 'The Bay Area Bomber'?"

"Hannah!" Sedonia protested at the nickname.

"One hundred dollars!" came a shout from the bar area. Sedonia couldn't see past the players and spectators who had crowded into the playing area for the auction, but she recognized the voice.

"One twenty-five," said a wiry young man standing nearby on Sedonia's right.

"Two hundred!" countered the voice from the bar.

"Two ten," bid an overweight man on Sedonia's left.

"Three hundred!" came the bid from the bar.

The two men nearby, who'd been bidding against each other, now got together and conferred. They reached agreement, and the wiry man offered their combined bid. "Three fifty."

"Five hundred dollars!" countered the voice at the bar.

The other two bidders standing nearby looked at each other, and each shook his head. Silence filled the room. Finally Hannah said, "Folks, I think we've had a close-out bid. Five hundred dollars going once . . . going twice . . . going three times. Sold! Sedonia Forbes, sold to 'French Quarter' Jimmy Dupre, for $500."

Jimmy had worked his way through the crowd. He smiled at Sedonia and said, "How much do you want to buy back?"

"Buy back?"

"You can bet on yourself, by buying back up to $250 of my $500. Then whatever you win in the Calcutta, we split proportionally."

"Okay, I'll buy back $100."

"Just $100? You must not be too sure of yourself."

"It's all I've got on me."

"Okay," he said with a quick laugh.

They gave Hannah their combined $500, and then Jimmy returned to the bar.

"'Bay Area Bomber'?" Sedonia said to Hannah with a shake of her head.

Hannah chuckled. "Hey, kid, that's part of my job as a tournament director, driving up the Calcutta pot. That's the first $500 bid I've ever seen." Then she raised the microphone again. "Okay, folks. Now in position No. 5 . . ."

The spectators had withdrawn from the playing area. Some now sat on folding chairs on a long, raised platform that ran across the middle of the room; others had moved into the bar area. Sedonia and her first opponent shook hands at table No. 2.

"I heard you're good," the short, attractive Latina said.

Sedonia wasn't sure how to reply. Her opponent seemed more nervous than she was, so she simply said, "Thanks. Good luck."

Matches were to be race-to-7s, and Sedonia won the flip for the first break. As she waited while her opponent racked the balls, she took several deep breaths to quell her jitters. The young woman lifted the wooden triangle and gave her an inquiring look. Sedonia didn't bother inspecting the rack; she simply nodded, anxious to get the match underway. She decided on a half-speed break, to protect her shoulder. *One, two, three . . . stroke.* A slight warning twinge, but no severe pain. Two balls dropped. The match was on. Seven shots later, she made the gold-striped 9-ball in the side. She'd run the first rack.

As Hannah had explained in her pre-tournament instructions, Hunter Classics rules called for alternating breaks on Saturdays and winners to break on Sundays. This was to give lesser players a chance to win some games in the early rounds. Now as Sedonia racked for her second game, she was aware that her nervousness had passed. She felt as relaxed as she'd been the previous weekend at the Silver Bullet Saloon—more so, in fact.

Her opponent miscued badly on her break attempt, showing she still was nervous. Sedonia empathized with her, but stayed focused on her objective, which was to make balls disappear. She ran the second rack.

The next three games were similarly one-sided, and Sedonia led 5 to 0 in the race-to-7. Her opponent clearly was embarrassed and now simply wanted to get the humiliation over with. Sedonia had to miss twice intentionally to dump the sixth game. The young woman looked so relieved at not having been shut out, that Sedonia considered letting her have another game, but then thought better of it.

A few minutes later, the young woman shook Sedonia's hand. "Good shooting," she said. The final score had been 7 to 1.

"Good luck the rest of the way," Sedonia replied.

The young woman shook her head. "I shouldn't have signed up. You people are too good. I think you'll win the tournament, though."

Sedonia walked over to the unused pool table, where Hannah served as official scorer and charted tournament results. Hannah congratulated Sedonia on her first win, recorded her score, and then recommended she find a place to relax between matches. "It's gonna be a long afternoon and evening."

Sedonia was uncertain how to pass the time. The seats down the center of the poolroom were all filled, so she headed over to the bar. Jimmy moved over to make a place for her. She saw he was drinking coffee, and when the barmaid came over, she ordered a cup.

"Good shootin'," Jimmy said.

"Thanks."

"Keep it up. Looks like the Calcutta's gonna pay about $1,500 for first place. I'll get $1,200 for putting up $400. You'll get $300 for putting up $100, in addition to the $1,000 prize money."

"I gotta win first," Sedonia protested.

Jimmy frowned, as if surprised by her uncertainty. "I've seen you play," he said, "and I've seen most of these women. There's only one you gotta sweat."

"Who's that?"

He studied her for a moment, then said, "I'll let you know, after the tournament. Just play 'em all strong, and don't go on any more stalls, like I saw you do in that first match. Competition gets tougher the deeper you get into the winners' bracket."

Hannah's voice over the speaker system interrupted them. "Sedonia Forbes and Rossi Martinez, you're up on table No. 16."

* * *

Sedonia stood beside the scorer's table and waited for Hannah to announce her final pairing of the day. Despite Jimmy's warning, her two afternoon victories had been as uneventful as her morning match, and she'd won by scores of 7 to 3 and 7 to 2. After the third match, however, she'd experienced the all-too-familiar shoulder ache, which now was spreading to her lower neck.

Hannah turned to her. "You'll be up in a few minutes, soon as they finish on table No. 9. You'll be playing Lynn Black. She's strong. Won the overall Hunter Classics' tour championship last year, and she's the defending champion here at Big Ernie's."

Sedonia nodded, and even that slight movement of her head aggravated the inflammation. She surmised Lynn Black must be the strong player Jimmy had mentioned. Sedonia placed her cue case on the table next to Hannah and said, "Keep an eye on this for me. I'll be back in a minute."

A woman left the restroom as Sedonia entered. Sedonia looked to confirm she was alone, then pulled a folded envelope from her jeans pocket. She withdrew a pain pill, and washed it down with a gulp of water from the sink faucet. Then she wet a paper towel, and as she wiped her face, she studied her reflection in the mirror. Disappointment showed, and she shook her head. She'd held off all day, but to get through this next match, she felt she needed something to mask the pain. If somehow she could beat this Lynn Black, she'd be in good position when play resumed tomorrow.

The door opened and another woman entered the restroom, just as Hannah's voice came over the speaker system: "Sedonia Forbes and Lynn Black, you're up on table No. 9."

Lynn was already at the table when Sedonia arrived. Trim and in her late twenties, her neat attire and businesslike demeanor reminded Sedonia of the women professionals she'd seen in Las Vegas.

After perfunctory introductions, Sedonia won the coin flip for the first break. While she waited for Lynn to rack, she tried to collect her thoughts. She needed to get off to a good start, beginning with a strong break. She placed the cue-ball near the right rail, and leaned down. A sense of vertigo swept over her. Recognizing the side effect of the hydrocodone, she straightened to let the momentary dizziness pass.

Lynn frowned. "Something wrong with the rack?"

"No, I just got something in my eye," Sedonia lied. She leaned over again and quickly went through her routine. *One, two, three . . . stroke!* She felt the expected stab of pain, but kept her attention on the balls that were ricocheting about the table. The maroon 7-ball and the blue 2-ball found the same side pocket. Sedonia chalked her cue stick and waited for the pain to subside. It didn't take long; the pill was working. Now she just needed to stay focused, despite the medication's dulling side effect. She determined her position sequence, and then went to work.

The first six games went quickly, and despite the alternating-break rule, Sedonia won five. She just needed two games to take the race-to-7. As she waited for Lynn to rack, she had to fight off increasing drowsiness. Although it was only 8:30, she felt as if she'd been awake all night. She wasn't sure if coffee would help or hinder.

Her break was weak, but the red 3-ball dropped into a corner pocket. Sedonia didn't bother figuring out her shot sequence; she simply began rapidly pocketing balls. Despite her lassitude, her stroke was smooth and true. Then just as the orange 5-ball dropped into a corner pocket, Lynn abruptly jumped to her feet. "Foul!"

"What?" Sedonia said.

Lynn pointed to the purple 4-ball, and Sedonia realized she'd shot the 5-ball out of sequence. She shook her head. She'd *never* done that before in a match. Damn those pain pills!

Lynn took ball-in-hand, and ran the rest of the table. The score was now 5 to 2. Then she broke and ran the next rack, making the score 5 to 3. Sedonia broke for the ninth game, and the cue-ball ricocheted into the side pocket, again giving Lynn ball-in-hand. And again Lynn took advantage of it, making the score 5 to 4. The tenth game of the match, Lynn broke and ran. In 15 minutes, she'd come from being down, 5 to 1, to tying the match, 5 to 5.

"Time out," Sedonia said. She stumbled slightly as she left the playing area, then was surprised to find Jimmy in step with her as she headed for the restroom. He draped his right arm across her shoulder and pulled her closer to him as they walked. "What are you taking?"

"What?" Sedonia said.

"You're on something," he hissed. "I can tell by the way you're playing."

"Pain medication," she admitted, then felt his left hand touch her upper pelvic area. He'd pushed something into her front jeans pocket. She broke stride, but his arm across her shoulder pushed her forward.

They were approaching the restroom door. "Black molly," he whispered. "It'll pick you up." Then he removed his arm, and headed toward the bar.

Sedonia entered the restroom and found it unoccupied. She went over to a sink, ran cold water, and splashed it in her face. She was repeating the process, when she heard the door open.

"Eye bothering you again?" Lynn said.

"Uh . . . yeah."

Lynn entered one of the stalls and closed the door. Sedonia reached over and pulled a couple of paper towels from the dispenser. As she wiped her face, she checked to see what Jimmy had put in her pocket. She found a small red plastic vial. She didn't bother opening it. She didn't know Jimmy and wasn't sure what a "black molly" was, though she suspected it probably was an amphetamine. Just two more games, she told herself. Three at the most.

The balls were already racked when she returned to the table. Lynn came back a few moments later. Lynn smiled and said, "Now it's a race-to-2. Good luck."

"Good luck," Sedonia replied. She broke and made two balls on the break. The timeout had helped; her thoughts were more focused as she worked her way around the table. Twice she employed stifling safeties. Each time, Lynn managed to hit her object ball, but had no chance of making it. After the second safety, Sedonia returned to the table and ran the remaining three balls. She'd broken Lynn's run of four games. Now she was on-the-hill, leading 6 to 5 and needing only one more game to win the match.

As Sedonia racked for Lynn, the feeling of drowsiness swept over her again. Hang on, she told herself. She'd have two opportunities to win one more game. A few minutes later, however, Lynn made the 9-ball. She'd run the rack and tied the match, "hill-hill."

Lynn racked the balls for the final game, then looked up and smiled. "Race-to-1." She seemed to be enjoying the pressure. Sedonia wasn't.

Sedonia placed the cue-ball near the right rail, and carefully positioned her feet as she assumed her stance. She took a slow, deep breath, then leaned over. Shoulder or no shoulder, she needed a killer break this time. *One, two, three . . . stroke!* A stab of pain, but she kept her eyes riveted on the gold-striped 9-ball as it rolled slowly toward the side pocket. The blue 2-ball kicked off the end rail and headed back, looking as if it was going to intercept the 9-ball . . . It missed! The 9-ball dropped! Sedonia had won the game and the match on the break.

She dropped her cue stick and was only vaguely aware of its hitting the edge of the table, then clattering to the floor. She covered her eyes with both hands and struggled to fight back tears of relief and fatigue. A reassuring hand touched her shoulder, and Lynn's voice said, "Are you okay?"

Sedonia wiped her eyes with the palms of her hands. "Yeah, I'm okay. Good match."

"Good shooting," Lynn replied. "Maybe we'll match up again tomorrow."

"I hope not," Sedonia said, then realizing she'd sounded rude, she smiled and added, "You're too strong."

Sedonia picked up her cue stick and automatically checked for dings. She found a large one, three inches from the tip. But, she'd worry about that later—sand it when she got home. Right now, she just wanted to enjoy having escaped with a win.

At the scorer's table, Hannah looked up with a frown. "Good match. Are you feeling okay?"

"No, I'm not. Can I leave my car here, and ride home with you tonight?"

"Sure, kid. What's wrong?"

"I'll tell you later," Sedonia said. Jimmy was approaching.

"Had me worried there for a while," he said. "C'mon, lemme buy you a beer."

"No thanks."

"Good shootin'. Looked like 'Miss Molly' took care of you."

Sedonia shook her head. "I don't use stuff like that." There were too many people standing around for her to return the vial.

Jimmy shrugged.

Sedonia said, "Was Lynn Black the player you thought would be my strongest competition?"

Jimmy shook his head. Sedonia looked over at Hannah.

"Probably, Audri Krump," Hannah said.

Jimmy nodded, and Sedonia felt a pang of disappointment. She thought she'd defeated her primary threat.

"Sure you don't want that beer?" Jimmy said.

Sedonia shook her head. "I'm going home."

"See ya tomorrow, then," Jimmy said, then turned and walked away. He stopped at an unoccupied table and screwed together his cue stick. A short, heavyset black man joined him. Apparently Jimmy had matched up and would be gambling tonight.

Sedonia yawned, and Hannah said, "Only got two matches still going on. We'll be out of here in half an hour."

Sedonia nodded. She wanted to go home, stand under a hot shower, then get some sleep.

The following morning, Sedonia sat on her balcony, sipping her third cup of coffee. The caffeine, however, seemed to be having little effect in clearing her hydrocodone-induced fog. She rotated her shoulder; either the inflammation finally had subsided or the pain pill was masking it. Good. She was down to her last prescribed pill. The ones Cissy had given her were still locked in her desk drawer at the office.

Across Egret Bay, the usual weekend armada of pleasure boats filed out of the South Shore Harbor marina. A jet-ski roared by, driven by a man with two young women seated behind him. Sedonia directed her attention to a small catamaran, and a couple out for a leisurely sail. Sedonia wished her day was going to be as carefree. Why was she driving herself this way?

Her cell phone lay on the patio table beside her, and began to buzz. She answered it and heard Hannah's cheery voice. "Ya awake, kid?"

"Barely. I had to take another pain pill in the middle of the night."

"You gonna be able to make it?"

"Gotta try."

"Good," Hannah said. "You're in the semifinals. Hate to see you have to quit now. Pick you up in about 15 minutes.

"I'm as ready as I'll ever be," Sedonia said, and hung up. Then for the first time that morning, she remembered the ding she'd put in her cue stick the night before. She got up and went inside to get the sandpaper. In the kitchen, she decided she had enough time to make another cup of instant coffee. Her stomach growled, so she also decided to fix a couple of pieces of toast.

Sedonia sat at the bar, sipping a Coke and waiting for her first match of the day. Big Ernie's Billiards was as crowded this morning as it had been the day before, although many of the original 64 entrants had lost two matches and had been eliminated. For those players, Hannah now announced pairings for a "second chance" tournament, which would be held concurrent with the main one.

Jimmy walked up behind Sedonia and said, "Good morning."

"Good morning," she said. Her voice sounded thick, as if she'd just awakened. "I saw you matching up with a guy, just before I left last night."

"The black guy? That was 'Cannonball'. Remember I told you Audri Krump would be your main competition? Cannonball is her boyfriend."

"How'd you do against him?"

Jimmy shook his head. "He's a road player too, and last night he wanted too much weight. I took a couple of cheap sets off him, but he probably was on a stall. He got pissed when I quit him at midnight." Jimmy sighed. "Wasted evening. There's not much gamble at these women's tournaments."

"Then why do you bother going to them?"

"Usually I don't," he said with a smile. "But when Buster mentioned you were gonna be here, I made an exception."

Sedonia smiled, momentarily responding to his flirtation. She sensed he could be a charming son of a bitch, when he wanted to be. But then she reached into her jeans pocket and withdrew the small red vial he'd forced on her the night before. "I don't use this kind of stuff."

"You said you were on pain pills?"

"Prescribed," Sedonia said, stretching the truth, since the pain medication had been prescribed at the time of her surgery, more than a year ago. "I've got a shoulder injury that acts up sometimes."

Jimmy shrugged and took back the vial.

Hannah's voice came over the sound system, "Sedonia Forbes and Edith Burton, you're up on table No. 6."

"Gotta go," Sedonia told Jimmy.

"Make us some money," he replied, reminding her of his eighty percent of their $1,500 Calcutta side bet.

When Sedonia arrived at table No. 6, her opponent was waiting. She appeared to be in her forties, with a pale complexion and reddish hair that had been teased to the point that it looked as if she'd been caught in a wind storm.

"I'm Edith," she said, "from Austin."

From the way she had introduced herself, first name only, Sedonia wondered if she was a well-known player, whose name she should recognize. "I'm Sedonia," she replied, "from Nassau Bay."

"Yeah, the 'Bay Area Bomber'. I heard Hannah introduce you at the Calcutta bidding."

"Hannah was just . . ." Sedonia began, but didn't finish. She didn't have the mental energy for modesty or for chit-chat.

They flipped for the break, and Sedonia lost. She'd have to rack for the first game. After that, it would be losers rack. She didn't feel anxious about this match, but as she raised the wooden triangle, her hands felt jittery—probably from too much caffeine that morning.

Edith made a ball on the break, then missed a relatively easy second shot. Sedonia rose from her chair, sensing her opponent was somehow intimidated by her. As bad as she felt this morning, she couldn't imagine how she possibly could intimidate anyone.

The balls were spread out across the table. As Sedonia leaned over for her first shot, she felt the ding she'd put in her stick the previous night. She straightened up, annoyed with herself. That morning, she'd gone into the kitchen for sandpaper, but had forgotten about her cue stick and had made coffee and toast instead. Damn those pain pills!

She leaned over the table again and rotated the shaft until the ding was least noticeable. *One, two, three . . . stroke.* The yellow 1-ball disappeared into the corner pocket. *One, two, three . . . stroke.*

The first five games progressed slowly. Sedonia protected her shoulder with half-speed breaks and employed safeties whenever she didn't have a sure shot. She realized she was playing what Buster and Sal thought of as being a typical, slow woman's game, but with it she'd forged to a 5 to 0 lead.

Now, her opponent stared at the table, seemingly discouraged. The few shots Sedonia had allowed her had been unmakeable. Sedonia's instinct was to ease up, but she forced herself to remember how close she'd come to blowing a similar lead in her previous match.

With that near failure in mind, as she leaned over the table to begin the sixth game, she decided to close out the match as quickly as possible, and went to her full-speed break. Her shoulder responded with a sharp stab of pain, but then subsided to a dull ache, and she managed to run the rack.

For the seventh game, she went back to her half-speed break, and failed to make a ball. By this time, though, her opponent was obviously demoralized. She made a halfhearted attempt at banking the yellow 1-ball, and scratched. Sedonia took ball-in-hand and ran the rack. She'd blanked her semi-final opponent, 7 to 0.

Edith extended her hand. "Good luck in the finals."

"Thanks," Sedonia said, barely able to mask the pain the handshake produced.

Jimmy fell in step with her as she headed over to the scorer's table. "Just one more match, babe."

Hannah looked up and smiled. "Seven to nothing? That's pretty strong."

"Thanks. Who do I play next?"

"You've won the winner's bracket. That was Edith's first loss, but after that butt kicking you just put on her, my guess is either Lynn Black and Audri Krump will win the one-loss bracket. Then one of them will play you for the championship."

"Any idea what time that'll be?" Jimmy said.

Hannah checked her watch, then turned to Sedonia. "You've got at least two hours to kill. Probably be a good idea for you to get out of here for a while."

"Want to get something to eat?" Jimmy said. "There's a barbecue place down the street."

"I need to find some sandpaper. I put a ding in my stick."

"Bring it along. I'll fix it for you."

Sedonia hesitated. She did want to get away from the poolroom for a while, and food might help settle her system. But, she really didn't feel like driving. "Okay," she said finally.

"Be back by 5:00," Hannah said as they turned to leave.

As Jimmy wheeled his black Camaro Z-28 into the restaurant parking lot, Sedonia noticed a sign near the entrance that advertised the Sunday brunch buffet for $8.95. Judging by the number of cars, vans, and pickups that encircled the building, apparently many of Alvin's faithful had come here directly from church. A pickup pulled out, and Jimmy was able to get a spot close to the front door.

He shut off the engine and said, "Lemme see that shaft." She pulled it from her cue case and handed it to him.

Jimmy studied it for a moment, then said, "Yeah, I can smooth that out." He took her cue case from her and opened the car door.

"You're taking it with you?" Sedonia said as they climbed out.

"Just the shaft. I'll work on it in there." He went around to the rear of the car, opened the trunk lid, and placed her case beside his. Before closing the trunk, he unzipped a pocket on his case and withdrew a smoothing device—two inches long, curved like a miniature gutter, and lined with a fine grade of sandpaper.

They headed up the short walkway. The exterior of the restaurant looked like a rustic ranch house, as did the interior. The tables were rough hewn, and several had been pulled together to accommodate large family gatherings. A hostess in a cowgirl outfit met them at the door and led them to a table for two. A young waitress, also in a cowgirl outfit, came over to take their order. Jimmy chose the buffet, but Sedonia just wanted a barbecue beef sandwich and a glass of iced tea. Before the waitress left with their orders, Jimmy asked for a piece of ice.

"A piece of ice?" the waitress said.

"Yeah, about this big." He held his thumb and forefinger about an inch apart.

Jimmy was in the buffet line, creating a salad, when the waitress returned with a small glass and a single ice cube. "What's he want this for?" she asked Sedonia.

"I have no idea."

Jimmy returned. He nodded his thanks to the waitress, then withdrew the ice cube and began rubbing it against the dinged spot on Sedonia's shaft.

"What are you doing?" Sedonia said, alarmed.

Jimmy grinned.

"I'm serious," Sedonia said. "I gotta play with that in a couple of hours."

"The ice helps take the ding out," Jimmy said. "It works better, though, if you do it right away."

"Are you sure you're not confused with treating sprains?"

He grinned again, and dried the shaft with his napkin. Then he began to lightly sand, stopping frequently to test with his finger tips.

The waitress said, "Are y'all playin' at Big Ernie's? We had some other players in here yesterday and today."

Jimmy nodded toward Sedonia. "She's in the finals. Gonna be playing for the championship at 5:00."

"I like to play pool," the waitress said, "but I'm not that good."

"If you get off in time, come over and watch," Jimmy said, still concentrating on his refinishing job. "She'll show you how it's done. She's strong."

"I'll do that," the waitress promised, then went off to check on another table.

"I'm nervous enough," Sedonia said, "without you inviting people to come watch me."

"Don't sweat it," Jimmy replied. "You're good. Damn good." He wiped the shaft with his napkin again, tested it one final time, then handed it to her. "And, now you got a good stick again."

Sedonia ran her fingers over where the ding had been. It felt smooth. Then she slid the shaft through her bridge hand, as if shooting. She smiled. "You're a magician," she said. "Thanks."

Jimmy looked at her for a moment, then gave a quick bob of his head and turned his attention to the salad in front of him. Sedonia looked away, but her thoughts were still on the man across the table. Get him away from the competitive pool environment, and he actually seemed quite nice. He'd come to Alvin just to see her, and he'd been nothing but supportive. She'd noticed most other women players had pool-playing boyfriends. It must be nice having someone who appreciated what they did, someone who understood both the attraction and the demands of the sport, someone *pulling* for them. Too bad this guy was just passing through.

The waitress returned with Sedonia's barbecue sandwich.

Sedonia and Jimmy got back to the poolroom shortly before 5:00. At the restaurant, they'd enjoyed a relaxing conversation, mostly about pool, and the long break had done Sedonia a world of good. Now, to her relief, her shoulder had stopped throbbing and the pain-pill fog had lifted.

Hannah waited for them at the scorer's table. "You're playing Audri," she told Sedonia. "She beat Lynn, 7 to 1."

Sedonia winced at the one-sided score. She'd barely eked out her win over Lynn, 7 to 6. "Which one's Audri?" she said.

"I am," said a gruff voice behind her.

Sedonia turned and looked into the pallid, unsmiling face of a woman in her forties. Her features seemed distended, giving the impression of an unusually large head. She had a squat physique, reminding Sedonia of a football lineman.

"You ready to play?" Audri said in a demanding voice. When she spoke, two gaps showed where once teeth had been.

Hannah interjected, "Sedonia, you can warm up, if you want to."

"No, that's okay." Sedonia was anxious to get the match underway. She followed Audri over to table No 1. Audri's gait was more than a swagger; it was a roll, as if she'd spent years at sea.

Hannah switched on her microphone. "Okay, folks, gather 'round. We're about to start the championship match." There was a shuffling of feet as the hundred or more people in the room stopped what they'd been doing and congregated around table No. 1. "Our two finalists are Audri Krump and Sedonia Forbes. Audri had three high finishes in WPBA tournaments and was ranked No. 27 before . . . her career was interrupted. Welcome back, Audri!"

The crowd responded with a subdued round of applause, and Audri raised both hands, like a heavyweight boxer.

Sedonia turned to Jimmy. "Hannah said 'welcome back'. Where's Audri been?"

"Prison."

"Prison!" Sedonia said. "What for?"

"Assault and battery."

"Didn't beat up an opponent, I hope," Sedonia said, only partially kidding.

"Ex-husband. Almost killed him."

Hannah continued, "And our other finalist is playing in her first Hunter Classics tournament. From Nassau Bay . . . the Bay Area Bomber . . . Sedonia!"

Applause for Sedonia was enthusiastic, and someone in the crowd let loose a loud wolf whistle. Sedonia felt herself redden. She noticed a scowl form on Audri's face, apparently resentment of Sedonia's instant popularity, or perhaps it was the silly nickname Hannah insisted on using.

Hannah concluded, "This year's championship match will be one set, race-to-11. They'll be playing for $1,000. Good luck ladies!"

Audri stood at the table, poised to flip a coin.

"Heads," Sedonia said.

It came up heads. Audri scowled again, and began racking the balls.

Sedonia screwed her stick together and glanced at the crowd. Jimmy and Cannonball were standing together and seemed to be arguing. Then abruptly, both nodded. Apparently they'd agreed on a side bet.

Sedonia turned her attention back to the table and collected her thoughts. Despite the high stakes—$1,000 and qualifying to play in a WPBA event—she felt unusually relaxed. When she'd felt this way in the past, she'd played well. She didn't try to analyze it; she just hoped it would work again.

Audri lifted the wooden triangle, and Sedonia walked down to the other end of the table. "The 2-ball and the 5-ball aren't touching," she said.

Audri scowled again, but re-racked the balls. Sedonia again checked the rack. Now the 6-ball and the 7-ball weren't touching, but since they were at the tail end of the diamond formation, she let it go. Her intimidating opponent already looked as if she were about to explode.

Half-speed break, she told herself. *One, two, three . . . stroke*. The blue 2-ball rolled slowly into the corner pocket, and the rest looked easy.

The match progressed quickly. In her earlier 7 to 0 victory over Edith, Sedonia had won through concentration and discipline. From the opening games of this match, however, she again experienced the exhilarating feeling of being in stroke and in complete control. She made all the possible shots, and when presented with impossible shots, she responded with safeties that stymied Audri.

Now, as Audri racked again and Sedonia waited to break, Hannah announced the score. "Sedonia 7 and Audri 1, in this race-to-11."

Audri raised the wooden triangle, and then shambled over to her stool and slumped onto it. Her movements, on and off the table were awkward, like those of a much older person. Life obviously had been hard on her, and from her body language, she appeared resigned to defeat.

As Sedonia prepared to break, she felt confident of victory, and didn't bother checking the rack. Sometime during the fifth game her shoulder had begun to ache, but she was in stroke and needed to win only four more games. Audri needed to win ten.

Protecting her shoulder, Sedonia broke too easily, and nothing fell.

"Go now!" shouted a resonant male voice, probably Cannonball.

"Close it out!" countered another male voice, which Sedonia recognized as Jimmy's.

Audri lumbered to her feet, and went to work. There was nothing smooth about her technique as she moved about the table with her odd rolling gait. And between shots she grimaced, muttered, and beseeched a pool god, who apparently resided in the dark recesses high above the poolroom rafters. But despite her ongoing display of despair, she was pocketing balls and keeping Sedonia anchored on her stool.

Sedonia watched in disbelief as Audri ran off five straight wins. Sedonia's seemingly insurmountable lead had dwindled to 7 to 6. Finally, Audri missed a difficult cut shot on the gold-striped 9-ball, and left it in front of the side pocket.

Sedonia stood up. Her confidence had forsaken her. She leaned over for the relatively simple shot, but then had to straighten, take a deep breath, and lean over again. *One, two, three . . . stroke.* The 9-ball fell, giving her an 8 to 6 lead. Rather than feeling exhilaration over breaking Audri's streak, Sedonia simply felt relieved.

"Close it out!" Jimmy again exhorted from the sideline.

Sedonia just needed three more games. It was time to return to the hard break. *One, two, three . . . stroke!* A blinding stab of pain, and the sight of the cue-ball flying off the end of the table. Her shoulder throbbed as she sat down on her stool and watched Audri take ball-in-hand, and begin to methodically work her way around the table. Finally Audri made the 9-ball in the corner. The match now stood 8 to 7.

Sedonia's shoulder inflammation raged to the point that it was debilitating. Sedonia turned to Hannah. "Time out."

"Time out charged to Sedonia," Hannah announced to the crowd. "Each player is allowed one five-minute time-out."

Three women stood chatting just inside the restroom doorway. Sedonia ignored them and went over to a sink.

The door flew open and the waitress from the restaurant burst in. "Y'all are good!"

Sedonia nodded in recognition, then leaned over the sink, gulped in a mouth full of water, and took her last pain pill. When she straightened up, the waitress was frowning. "Aspirin," Sedonia lied.

She wanted to stall in the restroom as long as she could, to allow the medication to kick in, but now the waitress came over and looked as if she was about to start a conversation. Sedonia forced a smile and said, "Gotta get back in there."

Audri was talking to her boyfriend when Sedonia returned. The balls were already in place within the wooden triangle. Sedonia pushed them into a tight rack, then stood back as Audri broke. The 9-ball went into the side pocket on the break. The match was tied, 8 to 8.

As Sedonia racked for the seventeenth game of the set, her shoulder discomfort lessened. Hopefully the pain pill was kicking in. Now if she could just get back to the table.

Audri failed to make a ball on the ensuing break. Sedonia had her chance. She studied the layout, then leaned over for her first shot, the yellow 1-ball. *One, two, three . . . stroke.* The long rail shot dropped into the corner pocket, and Sedonia straightened and heaved a sigh of relief. She was on the blue 2-ball and confident she was back in stroke. She finished the run without incident. Then she also ran the next rack. She was on-the-hill, 10 to 8.

Audri's expression was impassive as she racked for what could be the final game. Sedonia heard Jimmy again shout, "Close it out!" and that's exactly what she planned to do. She gritted her teeth and drove the cue-ball into the rack as hard as she could. Her shoulder felt as if it had been doused with scalding water. And nothing fell. The balls stayed clustered at the far end of the table. Sedonia felt sure that Audri had given her a "house rack." Sedonia pulled up her stool and rubbed her shoulder. The pain was so intense now, she just wanted the match to be over and to be allowed to go home.

Audri ran the balls, pulling to within one, 10 to 9. Then in the twentieth game of the match, she made two balls on the break and then made five more, before having to resort to a safety. Sedonia stood up slowly, surprised at the chance to get back to the table in this game. Audri had left the black 8-ball frozen against the end rail, about two feet from the corner pocket. The cue-ball was in the middle of the table and only four feet away, but the shot would require a ninety-degree cut. At first glance it looked impossible, but Sedonia knew how to attempt it. Apply hard english, miss the 8-ball by the thinnest of margins, and hit the rail first. Then the english would spin the cue-ball off the rail and into the object ball, and drive it down the rail into the pocket. If she made the 8-ball, the 9-ball shouldn't be a problem; it too was in the middle of the table.

Sedonia double-checked the 8-ball to be sure it actually touched the rail. It did. Then she took a deep breath, released it, took another, released half of it, and leaned over the table and aimed the tip of her stick at the left side of the cue-ball to apply the necessary english. *One, two, three . . . stroke.* The cue-ball hit the rail precisely where she'd aimed, and the left english caught and spun it off the rail and into the 8-ball. Sedonia held her breath as the 8-ball rolled slowly toward the corner pocket. It fell! The spectators broke into spontaneous applause.

Sedonia heaved a sigh of relief. All she had left was a simple cut shot on the gold-striped 9-ball. She leaned over the table. *Stroke.* She missed!

Audri jumped to her feet and hurried over to the table. Sedonia stood rooted to the spot, unable to believe she'd missed such an easy shot. Audri pushed her aside, and then drilled the 9-ball into the corner pocket.

Moments later, in a daze, Sedonia racked the balls for the twenty-first and final game.

"Okay, folks," Hannah said over the sound system, "it doesn't get any better than this! It's hill-hill in the championship match. We've got a race-to-1 for $1,000!"

Sedonia dropped onto her stool, dejected. Audri stood motionless at the break end of the table, her hard features now frozen in a rigid mask. She gazed intently at the waiting rack of balls, without blinking. Sedonia had seen that countenance before. It was the one her father had called "the look of eagles."

Audri's break sounded like a thunderclap. Three balls found pockets and the rest scattered across the table. Never changing expression, she fired balls into pockets. Finally she lined up on the gold-striped 9-ball. "Yes!" Cannonball shouted an instant before it disappeared.

The match was over.

A short while later, Sedonia and Jimmy sat at the bar, while Hannah and the other Hunter Classics directors concluded the tournament activities, including distributing the prize money and the Calcutta pot.

"Sure you don't want a beer or something?" Jimmy said.

"No thanks," Sedonia said, taking another sip from her Coke. Actually, scotch was what she wanted at that moment, but she knew better than to throw alcohol on top of hydrocodone. But as soon as she got home . . .

"Cheer up, babe," Jimmy said.

She gave him an annoyed look, but before she could reply, Hannah came over and handed each of them a white envelope. "Your runner-up prize money, $500," she told Sedonia. "And, your runner-up Calcutta money, $750," she told Jimmy. "Since Sedonia put up $100 of the $500, then $150 of that is hers."

Jimmy nodded, and counted out Sedonia's share and handed it to her. He gave a disgusted shake of his head as he pocketed his $600. "Doesn't start to cover what I lost to Cannonball."

"How much?" Sedonia said as she pushed the envelope with her earnings into her jeans pocket.

"We had a 'dime' on the match. I should have known not to bet against Audri."

Sedonia gave an apologetic shake of her head. Her dogging the 9-ball had cost Jimmy $1,000.

"Hell, kid," Hannah told her, "Don't look so glum. You finished a strong second in your first semipro tournament, you won $650, and you qualified for a WPBA stop. Next time, you just need to—"

"What did you say?" Sedonia interrupted.

"I said, you finished a strong—"

"No. I mean about the WPBA. How could I qualify for a WPBA stop if I finished second?"

Hannah smiled. "If that's what's bothering you, forget it. The 'top qualifier' is the highest place finisher of the players who put up the extra $50."

"Audri didn't try to qualify?"

"She didn't have to. She's got an exemption, since she's already played on the WPBA tour and was a ranked player before she went to prison."

"She's may be done with the WPBA, anyway," Jimmy interjected. "She doesn't have the speed to compete with the top pros. But she's got heart . . . heart like a man. That's how she came back and beat you tonight. If she just had your stroke to go along with her heart, she'd rule the WPBA."

Sedonia stood up, stung by Jimmy's "if she just had your stroke to go along with her heart" comment. Another way of saying it could have been, "if you just had Audri's heart to go along with your stroke."

Hannah said, "I'll be back in a minute. I need to thank Ernie for hosting us again this year."

Hannah walked away and Sedonia turned to Jimmy. "Ever since I've been playing, people have told me how good my stroke is. Then they told me I had to learn to play 'smart,' and I learned to play safeties. But where does the rest of it come from?"

Jimmy shrugged, as if wanting to dismiss the topic.

"Tell me," Sedonia insisted. "Where does this thing you call 'heart' come from?"

Jimmy frowned. "I've never really thought about it. Audri's played pool all her life . . . but she could never hit balls as good as you do."

"But she knows how to win."

Jimmy nodded. "She spent at least ten years on the road with her ex-husband. Now she's back on the road with Cannonball."

"They showed her how to win."

"Them, and just being on the road. When you're on the road . . . you're playing all the time . . . all the time and for big stakes. You're in a motel room, waiting for a phone call—any time, night or day. And when somebody like Buster matches you up, you gotta get your ass in gear. You gotta walk into that poolroom, ready to gamble, and to win. Sometimes you make bets, and you don't even have the money to cover them. You *gotta* win, or you might wind up dead."

Hannah returned and said to Sedonia. "You ready to go?"

Sedonia nodded, then told Jimmy, "Sorry I didn't come through for you tonight."

Jimmy studied her for a moment. "I'll be in town the next few weeks," he said. "I'll be playing in Buster's some, but mostly I'll be working the poolrooms and bars around Houston. Wanna come along? Maybe I could teach you a little bit of what Audri's learned."

"I'd get to play?"

"Oh yeah," he said with a smile. "You most definitely would get to play."

Chapter 15

Late Monday morning, Sedonia entered her office, carrying a small drugstore bag. Raul was talking on the phone, and acknowledged her with a nod. "Yes, Mr. Landry," he said, and then pointed to the receiver and raised his eyebrows, inquiring if Sedonia wanted to talk to Brad. She shook her head and continued over to her desk.

"Yes, sir," Raul said into the phone. "When she gets back from the doctor, I will tell her you called."

Raul hung up, and Sedonia said, "Problem?"

"He expected you to call him on Friday. He needs to talk to you about the supplies account."

"Darn," she said. "I forgot again." She'd been at Buster's Billiards on Friday afternoon, practicing for the Hunter Classics tournament. Now she switched on her PC, and said, "Before I call him back, I'll check the account and see what might be bothering him."

Raul nodded, then asked, "What did your doctor say?"

"She gave me a cortisone shot, and told me to lay off pool." Sedonia opened the drugstore sack and pulled out a small plastic container and a bottle of Aquafina water. "She also prescribed Daypro, which is supposed to reduce inflammation." Sedonia didn't mention that Dr. Robinson had declined to prescribe any more hydrocodone, citing Sedonia's having over-dosed on the pain medication the year before.

Sedonia washed down two Daypro tablets. Then she opened her desk drawer and took a long look at the hydrocodone bottle that Cissy's boyfriend had brought back from Mexico. She sighed, and then put both pill containers into her purse.

Raul said, "Cissy called in this morning."

Sedonia looked up. "I was just thinking about her. Is she sick again?"

Raul shrugged. "She said she was."

Raul didn't sound convinced, and neither was Sedonia. After not missing a day her first three weeks on the job, Cissy had missed two days last week. And over the weekend, she hadn't come by the Hunter Classics tournament to watch Sedonia play, as she'd indicated she would. Sedonia hoped Cissy hadn't gone back to that damned boyfriend. She also felt a tinge of guilt, since she had Cissy's gift of bootleg medication in her purse.

Sedonia told Raul, "I'll talk with her tomorrow."

She turned to her PC and brought up the supplies account. The balance was almost $33,000. Brad must have made a deposit, assuming a large invoice would clear last week, which hadn't. Sedonia thumbed through the neat pile of bills that Raul had left for her on Friday. She found the likely problem: $9,780 owed for sheetrock and miscellaneous installation supplies. No problem. She'd get that payment transmitted; then she'd call Brad.

Her telephone rang. It was "French Quarter" Jimmy. "How's it goin'?" he said.

Sedonia smiled, wondering if New Orleanians had any idea how unusual their accents were—unlike any others in the South. "It's going fine," she said.

"Buster gave me your number," Jimmy said, "and I—"

"Hang on a minute," Sedonia interrupted, and covered the receiver with her hand. Raul had stood up, as if he were about to leave.

"If you're going to be here this afternoon," Raul said," I should go help on the job site. We're running a day behind schedule, since Cissy's been out."

"Okay, Raul. Thanks. I'll cover things here. I think I see what's troubling Brad about the account. I'll take care of it and call him."

Raul responded with a worried nod, and then left through the front door. A moment later, Sedonia heard his van start, and crunch across the oyster-shell parking lot.

"I'm back," she said into the phone. "What's up?"

"I'm goin' to Duke's Billiards tonight," Jimmy said. "Ever been there?"

"Never heard of it."

"It's up by Houston Intercontinental Airport. Open 24 hours, and lots of action. Wanna come along?"

"What time would we leave and get back?"

"Leave here about 8:30, and won't come back 'til somebody's busted—them or us."

Sedonia's mind raced. The morning cortisone shot had relieved most of her shoulder discomfort, and her doctor said the Daypro should take care of the rest. And, she had Cissy's hydrocodone to fall back on. She didn't plan to use it . . . but it was there . . . if worst came to worst. "How much money would I need to bring?"

"None," he said. "When you play, I'll stake you. We'll split anything you win, fifty-fifty. Anything I win, of course, is mine."

Sedonia hesitated. She'd have the rest of the day to get caught up here. Then, if the pool session ran late, Raul could cover for her again tomorrow morning, and she could take care of the accounts later that evening.

"So," Jimmy pressed, "are you coming?"

"Yeah."

"Good. I'll pick you up at 8:30."

She gave him her address, then said, "Where are you going to be coming from?"

"I'm staying at the Microtel on the NASA Parkway."

Sedonia frowned. The small hotel was less than a mile from where she lived. Was his close proximity just a coincidence?

Jimmy's black Camaro Z-28 sped north on the I-45 Freeway. Night had fallen, and after passing through downtown Houston, traffic had lightened. Sedonia looked out the window at the seemingly endless string of office buildings, shopping centers, car dealerships, and other commercial enterprises. A forest of gaudy signs lined the freeway, advertising everything from "Low-Priced Furniture!" to "Totally-Nude Girls!"

Sedonia sighed. I-45 North looked even tackier than the Gulf Freeway. She turned to Jimmy. "Have you been to Duke's before?"

"Nope."

"How'd you hear about it?"

"From a guy last week on South Padre Island, at the Eight-Ball Showdown. He said there was a lot of gamble at Duke's . . ." Jimmy's voice trailed off as he studied the approaching green signs suspended over the freeway. "There it is. FM-1960."

They exited the freeway, drove up the feeder road, and then turned right onto an exceptionally wide, well-lit thoroughfare. Low-rise office buildings, strip malls, and other small businesses lined both sides.

Sedonia smiled. "That 'FM', in 'FM-1960', stands for 'farm-to-market road'."

Jimmy responded with a wry smile and shake of his head. "A farm-to-market road, eight lanes wide. Only in Texas."

They stopped for a red light, and Sedonia said, "When you're playing on the road, do you generally travel alone?"

"Depends on the stakes, and how much I can cover. Sometimes I gotta bring a stakehorse with me, but I don't like to split what I win."

The light changed and they continued east. Jimmy said, "See that little poolroom up ahead on the right?"

"Ocho Loco?"

"Uh-huh. Buster told me there was a tournament there this past weekend. I'd have been in it, except I was watching you instead. Some of the people who played there might still be in the neighborhood. If there's no action at Duke's, we'll come back."

A few blocks later, Sedonia spotted a neon sign at the far end of a long strip mall. "There it is. Duke's."

From the outside, she could tell the poolroom was larger than most. And the parking lot was almost full, which seemed unusual for a Monday night. They found a spot and climbed out of the car. Jimmy opened the trunk and withdrew a large leather cue case. He flipped open the top, and Sedonia noticed it held not one, but three cue sticks.

"What weight do you use?" Jimmy said.

"Nineteen ounce."

"Good." He took her cue case from her, and put it in the trunk. Then he pulled a stick out of his case. "I want you to use this one tonight. Ever seen one like it?"

Sedonia frowned. It was a plain stick, without a wrap or fancy inlays. It looked like a house cue, except it was in two pieces.

"It's a nineteen-ounce Sneaky Pete," Jimmy said. "A lot of amateurs look at it and think I'm playing off the wall. Even if they notice the joint, a lot of 'em think it's just a cheap stick. This one cost $500."

Sedonia responded with a nod. "So they won't know you're a professional."

"Right. Here's the deal for tonight. We're on a date. You and I will shoot a few games, then I'll try to get matched up. I'll take 'em for whatever I can, then I'll turn 'em over to you."

"How?"

"You're a smart girl. You'll pick up on it. Main thing is, at the beginning, when we're playin' against each other, you go 'on the lemon'. Don't make it obvious, but I need to win without showin' my best game. That means you gotta miss about one out of every three shots you take. Later, when we get you matched up, you can come off your stall. But—and this is important— don't rob 'em too early, like you did at the Billiard Club in Vegas."

Jimmy left his cue case in the trunk, and carried the two-piece Sneaky Pete loose in his hand as they started across the parking lot.

Sedonia said, "I don't have much experience with going on and off a stall."

"Okay, we'll keep it simple. If the player's weak, just stay one to two games ahead. If the player's strong, give yourself a bigger cushion, like maybe three games. Before the match starts, I'll tip you off if the player's weak or strong."

Sedonia still was uncertain, but they'd arrived at the entrance. Jimmy pushed open the door and she stepped inside. The atmosphere surprised her. Unlike poolrooms where she'd played in the past, Duke's reminded her of a plush lounge. On the left, blue neon lights backlit a long mirrored bar. A half-dozen 9-foot Brunswicks stood off to the right, separated from the lounge area by a wooden counter, where a dozen railbirds perched on cushioned stools. And beyond the 9-foot tables, lay thirty or more 8-foot tables.

Sedonia and Jimmy made their way over to the bar. One of the two young men working there came over. "What'll you have?"

"Ginger ale," Sedonia said.

"The same," Jimmy said. "And we want table No. 7." Jimmy had selected an unoccupied 8-foot table, next to the 9-foot tables and close to the railbirds.

While they waited for the bartender to return with their drinks, Jimmy screwed the Sneaky Pete together. He handed it to her, and then strolled over to a cue stick rack mounted on the wall. He rummaged through the house cues, looking for something suitable.

While Jimmy was gone, the bartender returned with their drinks. "If you want to start a tab for your drinks and the pool time, I'll need a driver's license," he said.

Sedonia pulled hers out of her back pocket and handed it to him. He nodded and left, just as Jimmy returned with a house cue.

"This'll do," he said.

Sedonia took a sip of ginger ale and looked around the poolroom again. "Tables look like they're in good shape," she said. "Felt looks new."

"Yeah, nice and green," Jimmy said with a grin. "Like money."

Sedonia turned to him. "Is that where the movie title, *The Color of Money*, came from?"

"Guess so," he said. "Let's go find out."

An hour later, Sedonia racked for their fifth game of Eight-Ball. As instructed, she'd gone on the lemon and let Jimmy win the four games they'd played. A number of railbirds had positioned themselves to watch. Sedonia sensed her looks were attracting the audience, not the stroke she'd shown to that point.

As Jimmy waited at the break end of the table, he chided one of the railbirds, a swarthy young man with a cue case resting across his lap. "C'mon, buddy," Jimmy said. "My girlfriend's gettin' tired of racking." He turned to Sedonia. "Ain't that right, honey."

Sedonia responded with a resigned nod. She understood Jimmy's ploy, but that hardly diminished his abrasiveness.

"How about some cheap Nine-Ball?" Jimmy continued with the railbird. "Race-to-5 for $100.

The young man seemed to be considering the bet, when a player on the 9-foot table next to them spoke up. "You talk like a pool player," he told Jimmy, "but so far, all we've seen you do is whip up on a girl." The challenger appeared to be in his thirties and, like Jimmy, he wore jeans, a polo shirt, and athletic shoes. The man he'd been playing against was heavyset and wore overalls. His shoulder length hair merged into a shaggy full beard.

Jimmy smiled. "What would you like to play for?"

"That $100 sounds good," the challenger said.

"Make that $200," his bearded friend chimed in.

Jimmy pulled out a quarter. "Call it."

Shortly before midnight, Sedonia leaned against a pool table, watching Jimmy collect his second $200 bet. He'd won by scores of 5 to 2 and 5 to 3, and he'd had to dump two games in each set to keep it that close. Now, his opponent was unscrewing his stick.

"I'll give you two on the wire for—," Jimmy began, but halted in mid sentence, and then walked over to where Sedonia was standing. "Recognize the two blonds and the guy beside them?" he said, nodding toward the rail.

Three new arrivals, holding cue cases, now stood among the railbirds. The two young women were attractive, despite closely cropped hair. One looked familiar. She made brief eye contact with Sedonia, then turned and leaned toward the other woman and whispered in her ear. They both laughed, and their intimate manner suggested something more than friendship.

Sedonia asked Jimmy, "Was the woman on the right in Las Vegas last month?"

"They all were. The women play on the WPBA tour. The one you recognize is Inger Ruud. The other is her girlfriend, Kari Amundsen."

Sedonia nodded, now remembering where she'd seen Inger. During the professional tournament, Inger had been put on the clock for playing too slowly. Now, several other young women, apparently locals, approached the two professionals for autographs.

"The guy with them," Jimmy continued, "is Gunnar Tellefsen. He's a player too. They're originally from Norway or Sweden or someplace, and played on the European circuit before coming over here." Jimmy took Sedonia by the arm. "C'mon, I'll introduce you."

As they approached the trio, Gunnar made a cross with his index fingers, as if warding off a vampire.

Jimmy laughed. The two men shook hands and Jimmy said, "Race-to-9 for $1,000?"

"First you rob me in Las Vegas," Gunnar said with a heavy Scandinavian accent, "and now you follow me to Houston to rob me more?" His half-smile suggested he was only half-joking. He turned to Sedonia. "And who is this beautiful woman?" His two female companions also looked at Sedonia with interest.

Jimmy introduced everyone, then said, "Were you here for Jerry Johnston's Nine-Ball tournament at *Ocho Loco*?"

"Yeah," Gunnar said. "Kari and I got knocked out on Saturday, but Inger made it until last night and finished fifth." He looked around the room. "We hope to make a little money here."

Sedonia listened to the exchange, again trying to grasp the pool hierarchy. Last month, Inger had been in Las Vegas, playing in the Monte Carlo Penthouse against the world's best women professionals. Now, she was in Houston, playing in local tournaments on FM-1960 and hustling amateurs.

"How about it, Gunnar?" Jimmy said. "Race-to-9 for $1,000?"

"If I thought I could beat you, Jimmy, instead of $1,000, I would play you for your girlfriend. I would even give you some weight. I would put up these two girls." Inger punched Gunnar in the shoulder, and Kari swatted him behind the head.

"I'll give you the 8-ball," Jimmy said.

Gunnar declined.

"Eight and the breaks," Jimmy said.

As Sedonia listened to the exchange, Jimmy's banter reminded her of the night at the Las Vegas Billiard Club. She also remembered losing her nerve when she'd had an opportunity to play Vivian Villarreal, the WPBA's "Texas Tornado." Now, she abruptly turned to Inger. "Would you like to play?"

"What?" Inger said.

"I said, would you like to play?"

"For what?"

Sedonia looked over at Jimmy. He responded with a curt nod. Sedonia turned back to Inger. "Same way. Race-to-9 for $1,000. But I need some weight. You're a pro."

Jimmy appeared uneasy. "Yeah," he said, "you at least gotta give her the wild eight."

"No weight," Inger said. "I have never seen her play."

"Yeah," Gunnar chimed in good-naturedly, "for all we know, she's your sister. Maybe she plays as good as you."

"No weight, no bet," Jimmy said.

From Jimmy's tone, Sedonia sensed his comment wasn't simply a ploy to negotiate a handicap. She suspected he actually felt she needed weight to have a chance of winning. "Can I see you over here for a minute?" she said.

They walked back to the table where they'd played earlier. Out of earshot of the others, Sedonia said, "I really want to play her."

Jimmy frowned. "She's a pro . . . stronger than Audri Krump."

"I should have beaten Audri."

Jimmy shook his head.

Sedonia said, "Where is she in the WPBA rankings?"

"I don't know. I don't think she's won any WPBA tournaments, but she must have won some on the European tour. Otherwise, she wouldn't have come to the States."

Sedonia felt self-doubt beginning to form. Quickly, before it could take root, she said, "I want to play her. Either stake me and match us up, or take me home."

Jimmy studied her for a moment. "If she won't give you the eight, she's at least gotta give you all the breaks."

"The breaks aren't important to me, because of my shoulder. Match me up even, for whatever you're willing to cover."

Jimmy studied her again, then turned to the three professionals. "Nine-Ball . . . race-to-9 . . . no weight . . . $1,000."

Gunnar conferred briefly with the two women, then called back "You've got a bet, Jimmy."

A murmur went up among the railbirds, and they began jockeying for better vantage points to view the match. Sedonia heard the player who'd lost $400 to Jimmy say to his bearded friend, "What the fuck's goin' on here? *She's* gonna play for $1,000?"

"I want to use my own stick," Sedonia told Jimmy.

He handed her the Sneaky Pete. "Use this one. It's the same weight as yours."

"I need *my* stick."

Jimmy shook his head. "Change sticks now, and you'll blow our cover."

"My stick. And I shoot as good as I can. No stalls."

"Do what I say," he hissed.

Sedonia unscrewed the Sneaky Pete.

Jimmy looked as if he were about to argue some more, but finally grabbed the stick from her and said, "I'll be right back." He hurried through the front door and out to the parking lot.

Inger came over, laid her embossed leather case on the table, and pulled out her custom cue. From the fancy inlays, Sedonia could tell it was a top of the line. She wondered if Inger had a cue stick manufacturer for a sponsor.

Moments later, Jimmy returned with Sedonia's Naugahide case. As she withdrew her faithful, green $225 stick, she knew it looked cheap compared to Inger's. Simple elegance, she reminded herself as she screwed her stick together. Simple elegance.

Sedonia won the coin flip, and then watched closely as Inger racked for their first game. Assured the balls were tight, Sedonia returned to the break end of the table and assumed her stance. She hesitated, as she had so often on the first tee of a golf tournament. *Total commitment,* she told herself. *Total commitment. One, two, three . . . stroke!* She broke at three-quarter speed to protect her shoulder. The yellow 1-ball dropped into the side pocket, and the match was underway.

As Sedonia circled the table, flawlessly executing her planned sequence of shots, she again experienced the elation of being in complete control. Object balls hit the centers of the pockets, and the cue-ball repeatedly came to rest in perfect position for her next shot. Sedonia ran the first rack without giving her opponent an opportunity to get to the table.

Inger racked for the second game, then returned to her stool. Despite being a touring WPBA professional, concern already showed on her gamin-like features. Sedonia looked around the plush poolroom. It offered a marvelous venue in which to play, almost as good as the Las Vegas penthouse. Spectators standing nearby no longer disturbed her. As a matter of fact, she realized she now enjoyed being on stage. The myriad aspects of pool finally had come together. She'd developed an under-standing of the nuances of the game, and she knew how to play "smart." And, she was in stroke.

One, two, three . . . stroke! The maroon 7-ball dropped and the other eight balls were hers for the taking. She smiled. No, she wasn't in stroke. She was in dead stroke.

Sedonia and Jimmy walked over to the rail. Gunnar collected money from his two companions, added some of his own, and then handed it to Jimmy. "Your 'sister' shoots better than you do," he said.

"Go again?" Sedonia asked Inger.

Inger shook her head.

"I'll give you the breaks," Sedonia said.

Inger shook her head again.

"I'll give you the 8-ball," Sedonia said.

Inger unscrewed her cue stick.

"I'll give you the 8-ball, wild," Sedonia said, again increasing the handicap.

Inger ignored her and left the playing area.

Sedonia looked over at Kari, the other WPBA pro, and at Gunnar. "Either of you two wanna play?" Both shook their heads, and for the first time since arriving, Gunnar wasn't smiling.

Jimmy came over. "Let's go. We're done here."

Sedonia didn't move. "See if somebody else wants to play me."

"C'mon, Sedonia," he said, taking her by the arm. "You just robbed a touring pro, 9 to 0. You're not gonna get another game here . . . ever."

As they left the playing area, the man Jimmy had beaten earlier in the evening stepped in front of them. "You two are pretty cute, aren't you? Coupla hustlers." His bearded friend sidled up beside him.

"Get out of my way," Jimmy said, then pushed between the two men, and Sedonia followed. As they headed toward the bar, she realized the jeopardy she'd placed them in. The two men had seen her "real" game, and now they realized she'd set them up earlier in the evening by purposely losing to Jimmy.

At the bar, Jimmy asked for their tab. While they waited for the bartender to return, the two men remained in the playing area, watching them. The situation reminded Sedonia of the time, more than a year ago, when she and Emilio had fled Wayne's Icehouse. Now, she quickly unscrewed her cue stick and put it into its case. If she somehow got out of this, she had to ensure there wouldn't be another recurrence.

The bartender returned with their bill and Sedonia's driver's license. Jimmy paid, then glanced over his shoulder. The two men were still watching. Jimmy gazed back at them with the cocky expression he wore when he was intimidating an opponent on the pool table. His bravado did nothing to ease Sedonia's anxiety or generate confidence that he'd be able to handle the situation, but when he turned and started toward the door, she again followed.

They were half-way across the parking lot, when the door flew opened and the two men charged out. Jimmy and Sedonia broke into a trot toward Jimmy's car. Sedonia glanced over her shoulder. Their pursuers were slowed by the heavyset man's lumbering gait. She ran up to the passenger-side door, but Jimmy stopped to open the trunk. "Jimmy!" she shouted. "Hurry up!"

Jimmy seemed in no hurry as he closed the trunk lid, then turned toward the oncoming men, arms at his sides and lips parted in a sardonic smile.

"Jimmy!" Sedonia cried. "Unlock the car!" *What was he doing?*

"We got you, motherfucker!" the bearded man snarled as he and his companion slid to a stop just a few feet away.

"You ain't got shit, lard-ass," Jimmy said, and raised a small, chrome-plated revolver that had been hidden behind his leg.

"Don't . . ." Sedonia gasped.

Jimmy's eyes darted back and forth between the two men. "You see the Louisiana plate on this car? I'm about to blow your bullshit, Texas asses all over this parking lot. Then I'm gonna head for home, and never look back."

"Hold on!" the bearded man said, raising his open hands in front of his chest. The other man looked too terrified to move, or even to speak.

"Get out of here," Jimmy snarled. The two men bumped into each other as they turned, and both stumbled as they lurched toward the poolroom. Jimmy still had the pistol in the firing position. "Move!" he shouted. The two men broke into a dead run.

Jimmy reopened the trunk, slid the pistol into a clip-on holster, and secured it under a corner of the carpeting. Then he closed the trunk and, unhurried, walked around and unlocked the car.

Sedonia had no choice but to stay with him. The alternative was to rejoin the people they'd angered in the poolroom. She opened her door and climbed inside.

Moments later, they headed west on FM-1960. Jimmy still wore a cocky expression, but Sedonia noticed he frequently checked the rearview mirror. As they approached the smaller poolroom, *Ocho Loco*, he slowed and said, "Let's see if there's any action in here."

"Take me home!" Sedonia snapped.

Jimmy glanced over with a frown, then accelerated. Neither spoke again until they entered the nearly-deserted I-45 Freeway, and headed south toward the coast.

"Exciting, huh?" Jimmy said, smiling.

Sedonia responded with an angry glance, then riveted her attention to the freeway ahead. She wanted no part of this "exciting" life. Or of this man.

Jimmy pulled into a visitor parking spot in front of Sedonia's condominium complex. Her hand was already on the door handle.

"I'm sorry about what happened," he said.

Sedonia opened the car door, lighting the interior.

Jimmy said, "Just give me a minute."

Sedonia shook her head. "You're dangerous. You were about to shoot those men back there."

"Not if I didn't have to."

"Right," she said sarcastically.

"Look," he said, "I forgot this is all new to you."

"New?" she exclaimed. "You think I might get used to people waving pistols?"

He smiled. "No, I mean hustling pool. And, I didn't realize how good you were. I knew you had stroke, but doubted your . . . heart."

Sedonia allowed the door to close. The interior light went out, but Jimmy's features were still distinguishable by the illumination from the condominium grounds. "You didn't think I had heart?"

"I saw you play that one time in Vegas, then at that Hunter Classics tournament. I thought you were one of those broads . . . women, who shoot good when the stakes are low, but dog it when something's really on the line."

Sedonia leaned back in her seat and stared through the windshield, not replying. The lawn sprinklers suddenly sputtered to life, and she and Jimmy both jumped.

"Timer," Sedonia said. "Must be two o'clock."

Jimmy smiled. "Scared me."

Sedonia doubted anything really scared him. She took a deep breath, then released it. "I'm tired of hearing this stuff about my 'heart'. I'm just not . . . experienced." She started to mention her shoulder injury, but changed her mind. It would sound like a lame excuse. Instead she said, "I've played for bigger stakes than you can imagine, and won. But that was in golf."

"Golf?"

"Yes, golf. Ever hear of it."

"Pasture pool."

She had to smile. "Yeah, pasture pool."

"I play some golf myself," he said. "A couple of years ago, I heard there was a bunch of old-timers with gamble who hung out at City Park in Naw'lins, so I learned to play. Most of the time, we just gamble on the practice putting green, but I play enough that I carry an eight handicap. How about you?"

"I was the U. S. Women's Amateur Golf Champion two years ago."

"You serious?"

"Yes, I'm serious. And about my 'heart'? On the final day, I shot a 65, seven under par. Eagled the final hole for the win."

"Pretty strong," he said.

She smiled. "I was in 'dead stroke'. Just didn't know the name for it."

Jimmy lapsed into silence, seeming to reevaluate her. Finally he said, "About the pistol . . . I'm sorry if I scared you."

"This may come as a surprise," Sedonia replied, "but I don't hang out with people who carry guns."

"Didn't think you did," he said. "But sometimes it comes in handy. Like tonight. I usually leave it in the trunk—that's the law—but it's nice to have it nearby."

"Suppose you can't get to it?"

"If there's *two* guys, like tonight, I'd be in deep shit."

Sedonia wondered if his emphasis that it would take two guys was fact, or bravado. "Have you ever shot anybody?"

Jimmy shook his head. "I've had to pull it a couple of times, like tonight, but never . . . well . . . once, when I was a kid."

"You shot somebody when you were a kid?" Was he serious, or was this more of his hustler bullshit?

Jimmy responded with a slow nod, then looked out the driver side window. "You wouldn't understand."

"Try me."

He drew a deep breath. "I grew up in the Vieux Carré—the French Quarter. When I was a kid, my old lady was a stripper. We lived in a room over the club where she worked."

He paused and turned back, as if to see how Sedonia was reacting. She nodded for him to continue.

"When I was ten years old," he said, "she left. I guess she was into drugs and shit. She never came back."

"How'd you get by?"

"Colleen, the lady who ran the joint, kept me on. A couple of the girls who worked at the club also . . . worked for her up on the third floor. They looked after me too. When I was fifteen, Colleen figured it was time for me to start earnin' my keep, and she put me to work as a bouncer. I was just average size, so she gave me the pistol."

"And you shot somebody?"

Jimmy chuckled. "A drunk. Right after she gave it to me. I was waving it around, and it went off."

"Did you kill him?"

"Naw. Hit him in the leg. Like they say in the movies, 'just a flesh wound'. Colleen and the girls took care of him. He didn't even file charges."

They lapsed into silence. A mist from the sprinkler system began to cloud the windshield. Sedonia heaved a sigh. Events and revelations had come in rapid succession all night, not allowing time to reflect. Now, it abruptly came into focus that she was sitting in a car at 2:00 a.m., with a pool hustler who'd grown up sandwiched between a strip club and a whorehouse. She knew she should separate herself from this person, but curiosity persisted. "Is that when you learned to shoot pool?"

"Yeah. Little poolroom on Rampart Street. The old dago who owned the place took me under his wing. Taught me how to play, gamble pool, and work my way around the room. Soon as I turned 16, I dropped out of school, quit the bouncer job, and started making my living playin' pool. Colleen let me stay on, but made me start payin' rent."

Jimmy paused, apparently lost in private recollections. Finally he said, "The old dago's dead now, and the poolroom's torn down. Colleen's still there, though. Eight or nine years ago, I moved over to Algiers, on the other side of the river, but they still call me 'French Quarter' Jimmy."

The sprinklers shut off, and Sedonia said, "I need to go in." She opened the car door.

Jimmy opened his door too.

"That's okay," Sedonia said. "You don't need walk me to my condo. The Nassau Bay Police Department keeps this area well patrolled."

Jimmy responded with a wry smile, and closed his door. "Only dangerous guy in the neighborhood is me, right?"

She nodded.

"Listen," he said, "I admit it. I underestimated you—how good you play, and your heart."

Sedonia waited, suspecting he was trying to set her up for something.

"I plan to be in town for about a month," he said with a smile. "Let's forget about tonight, and make some money."

"No, I don't want to forget about tonight. If we ever play pool again, I want us to remember it, so there'll be no repeat."

His smile faded, his eyes narrowed, and he said in a measured tone, "I'm gonna be makin' the rounds of poolrooms all over Houston. I'll be drawing the top players. Do you want in on it? Yes or no?"

Common sense told her to say no and to simply get out of the car. But the residual excitement over having played so well hadn't worn off. "I wouldn't be interested in that 'going on the lemon' stuff, like we did tonight. Any time I'd play, I'd want to be able to shoot my best shot."

He slowly shook his head. "Scams are part of pool."

"Don't you ever feel guilty about ... scamming people out of their money."

"Never, because the people I rob, probably robbed somebody else the night before. This ain't country club golf, ya know."

Sedonia bristled. His comment sounded too much like the one Emilio had made about her being a "country club girl." Like most men players she'd encountered, and had seen accompanying other women players, Jimmy expected to treat her as a naive appendage, not as an equal.

She opened the car door and climbed out. Then she leaned down and said, "You owe me $500."

Jimmy smiled. He reached into his pocket, pulled out a fold of bills, and peeled off her winnings.

Sedonia counted it, then said, "About playing again? I'll let you know."

It was almost 3:00 a.m. by the time she'd showered. She'd thought she'd heard the phone ring, but it was hard to tell over the sound of the cascading water. The only person she knew who was up at this hour was Jimmy, and she'd had more than enough of him for one night. She pulled on an oversized T-shirt and turned down the covers. But then instead of climbing into bed, she headed for the kitchen. She still felt too keyed up to sleep.

She fixed herself a Dewar's and water, and then rummaged through her junk drawer until she found what she was looking for: the page from *Billiards Digest Magazine* that Buster had given her the night before she left for Las Vegas. She took a sip from her drink as she scanned the Top-20 ranking of players in the Women's Professional Billiard Association. There it was: 19) *Inger Ruud.*

Sedonia smiled. She'd beaten one of the top women professionals in the world, 9 to 0. Inger's girlfriend, Kari Amundsen, wasn't listed among the top 20. No wonder she'd declined to play. Sedonia wondered if the man who'd accompanied the two women was ranked among men players. He'd also not wanted to risk playing her. It was as if they . . . feared her. "Fear." She remembered that had been Buster's word for it. At the time, she'd disputed it and tried to make a case for "respect." Now she realized, Buster had been right.

She padded into the den, and saw her red voicemail light blinking. She pushed the "Messages" button, and Jimmy said in a contrite tone, "Okay, you can play matches your way. Straight up, no stalls. Call me tomorrow afternoon. After 2:00, though. I sleep late."

Sedonia erased the message, then went out onto the balcony and stood at the railing. A humid breeze blew low, fast-moving clouds across the night sky. For an instant she caught a glimpse of three aligned stars: Orion's Belt. Then they were hidden again. Orion was the only constellation she knew by name. Her father had first pointed it out to her when she was a little girl, and after that it had become a tradition for them to locate it whenever they were out at night.

The thought of her father brought a faint smile. For more than a year, spontaneous recollections of him had triggered emotions almost as painful as the night that the cardiologist had told her that he had died on the operating table. But now, while she still missed him, recollections were no longer so painful.

She moved away from the railing, sat down in one of the patio chairs, and took a sip from her drink. Her father wouldn't have approved of Jimmy, and certainly not the confrontations in poolroom parking lots. Nevertheless, he'd have been delighted at the way she'd dispatched the No. 19 player in the world.

After tonight, she couldn't simply go back to BCA amateur league play, or even to Hunter Classics semipro tournaments. Now, she wanted to compete against the best—the women of the WPBA. But she knew she needed more experience, more seasoning. Her U. S. Women's Amateur Golf

Championship had come only after she'd experienced—and overcome—the pressures of winning club and collegiate titles.

Jimmy held the key to the local poolrooms. Through him, she'd be able to gain access to the top players in the Greater Houston area. The downside was, he was aggressive and potentially dangerous. Also, she knew full well, his interest in her was personal, as well as professional. As Emilio's had been.

Chapter 16

Sedonia poured her first cup of coffee of the morning. Raul had brewed the pot five hours earlier, and it tasted as if it would dye her teeth brown. She dropped into the chair behind her desk and switched on her PC. While she waited for the system to come up, she glanced at the clock on the far wall: 10:07. Eight more hours. She took another sip, hoping the distilled caffeine would sharpen her wits. The night at Duke's Billiards, followed by the late-night conversation with Jimmy, had left her sleep deprived. As soon as she could close things down here, she planned to head for home and to bed.

In the storeroom she heard Raul loading his van. Was it just her imagination, or was he banging around more loudly than usual? He would never show disrespect, but she sensed his concern over her pool dedication. Instead of coming in at 5:30, as she had in the past, now she often arrived after 10:00. Some days she stayed late to get caught up; some days she didn't. Perhaps Raul felt responsible, thinking his nephew had sparked her interest in pool. She needed to reassure him, but they'd have to discuss it some other time. Today, it would be a struggle just to get through the next eight hours.

More clatter. Raul obviously was anxious to get out to the job site. They were still behind schedule on Brad's project, and Cissy had called in sick again. However, she had told Raul that she'd stop by later and pick up last week's check for the three days she'd worked. Sedonia sighed. She didn't feel up to dealing with Cissy's situation either, but knew she had to. Raul was covering Cissy's absences by working in her place, and he was too old to be climbing up and down ladders and scrambling across scaffolding.

Now, he stuck his head in the door and said, "I'm going."

"Okay, Raul. Don't try to do too much yourself." Her words rang hollow. She knew how conscientious he was.

He started to leave, then turned back. "I forgot to tell you. Mr. Huff called."

"George Huff?"

Raul nodded.

"Did he say what he wanted?"

"No, just that he will call back."

"Okay," Sedonia said. Huff Remodeling and Painting was a company much larger than hers. A couple of times, when Huff's workload had exceeded capacity, they'd farmed out the excess to her. But now, the last thing Sedonia wanted was more work.

Raul disappeared into the storeroom. Moments later Sedonia heard the loading door close, and then the sound of his van crunching out of the parking lot.

The phone rang. Probably Huff, she thought. Before picking up the receiver, she took a gulp of rancid coffee.

"Hey, kiddo!" came a cheery voice on the other end.

"Oh. Hi, Hannah."

"Well you certainly sound glad to hear from me."

"I'm sorry. I'm dragging this morning. Jimmy and I were out late last night."

"Hmmm . . . you and Jimmy, huh?"

"Just playing pool, Hannah."

"Right," Hannah drawled. "So, how are you and the handsome Cajun getting along?"

Sedonia smiled, then briefly recounted her win over Inger Ruud and the confrontation in the parking lot. She concluded, "Jimmy's interesting, but he's not the kind of guy you take home to mama."

"If I was your mama and you brought him home, you'd have some competition on your hands."

"Hannah!" Sedonia protested with a laugh. "Okay, I gotta admit, he's kinda growing on me. After he told me what a tough time he had growing up in the French Quarter, I can see why he comes across so . . . abrasive. He seemed okay, though, once we started talking."

"So you're gonna see him again?"

Sedonia hesitated. "I guess so . . . well . . . yeah. He can get me matched up with some top players."

"Right," Hannah said again in her teasing manner, "it's all about pool. And speaking of that, did you see the WPBA match on ESPN last night?"

"No. Who played?"

"Ewa Laurance and Margaret Faulkson. It was a delayed telecast of a match they played in Miami two months ago."

"Who won?"

"Margaret. She's won just about everything this year. This month's *Billiards Digest* ranks her as the top woman player in the world. Next stop on the tour is the Los Angeles Open next week. When are you going to use that exemption you won in Alvin, so you can see how you do against the pros?"

"I'm not ready for that level of competition."

"My other phone's ringing, kid," Hannah said. "Talk to you later. In the meantime, watch out for that Cajun."

After they hung up, Sedonia leaned back in her chair and smiled. She had to admit, she did find Jimmy attractive. She got up and walked over to the front window. On the other side of the channel, a few early-arriving tourists strolled up and down the Kemah Boardwalk. A flock of seagulls circled low over the far end of Restaurant Row, attracted by someone ignoring the "Don't Feed the Birds" sign. Sedonia sighed. She too was ignoring signs, running around with "French Quarter" Jimmy.

The phone interrupted her musing, and she returned to her desk. This time it was George Huff.

"I'd like to get together with you this week and talk some business," he said. "When would you be free for lunch?"

"I'm awfully busy this week, George."

"Yeah, I heard you were busy," he said. "Maybe too busy." There was a noticeable pause, before he said, "How about if I come by there?"

"George, we're booked up solid here. If you've got overflow work, we really can't take it on at this time."

There was another noticeable pause before Huff responded, "I want to talk about buying you out."

"Buying me out?"

"Yeah. Buying your business."

Sedonia was flabbergasted. "But why? And what makes you think I'd want to sell?"

"This is too involved to discuss over the phone," Huff said.

Sedonia's mind raced. He must be after Brad's account. That was her primary "asset," other than a hardworking staff and the goodwill that she and her father had fostered over the years. And, oh yes, the land on which the company stood, but that was mortgaged to the hilt. "George, if I ever consider selling, I'll let you know."

"Little lady, I think we ought to sit down, and see what we can work out. If we compete for business . . . well . . . I have a distinct advantage."

His "little lady" irked Sedonia, as did his veiled threat about competing. Huff had all but acknowledged he was after Brad's account. Not only was Brad's current business significant, but he would be expanding in the future.

"Well, whatcha say?" Huff pressed. "When can we get together."

The image of her mother seated in the family attorney's office flashed through Sedonia's mind. Motivated by greed, her mother had liquidated her share of the family estate, settling for perhaps seventy percent of its actual value. Sedonia's father had started the corporation with the painting company, and if Sedonia were to sell it, everything he had worked for and accomplished would no longer exist. And, she had her employees to consider, particularly Raul.

"I'm not interested, George," she said, with forced professional politeness.

"Well, I think you're makin' a mistake, little lady," he said. The edge to his voice made his comment sound like a threat.

They hung up, and Sedonia quickly dialed Brad's cell phone number. She needed to do some immediate customer relations. "Hi," she said when he answered. "It's Sedonia. I just wondered if you were free for lunch sometime this week."

Sedonia was making a fresh pot of coffee when she heard oyster shells crunch in the parking lot. She looked outside and saw Cissy climb out of a rusty sedan. Her doper boyfriend, Eddy, sat behind the wheel. Cissy started toward the front door, her shoulders slumped in a defeated posture that Sedonia hadn't seen since before the Las Vegas tournament. She heard Cissy clump up the outer stairs, then open the door.

"Oh," Cissy said. "I was looking for . . . I mean I told Raul I'd . . ."

"Come by and pick up your check," Sedonia finished for her. "I've got it made out." She handed the check to Cissy.

Cissy took it and said, "Thanks," and then quickly turned to leave.

"Cissy," Sedonia said, "wait a minute. I want to talk to you."

"Eddy's outside."

"I know. Sit down."

Cissy dropped into a chair on the other side of the desk and looked down at her feet. Sedonia felt as if she were a grade school principal, about to counsel a wayward student. "Are you okay?" she said.

Cissy fidgeted with the check, and avoided eye contact. "Yeah . . . you know . . . just a little sick."

"You're back with Eddy again."

Cissy looked up. Her jaw jutted out in a defensive manner, and her dark eyes seemed to flash with artificially enhanced brilliance.

"You back on crank too?" Sedonia said.

Outside, a car horn blew. Apparently Eddy was growing impatient.

Cissy jumped up. "I gotta go."

"Cissy . . ." Sedonia began, struggling for words. "You can't go back to that shit. I need someone I can depend on."

Cissy acted as if she hadn't heard. Instead, she turned and started toward the door.

"Cissy," Sedonia called after her, "you've left me no choice. I have to let you go."

The horn blew again, and Cissy darted out the door.

Sedonia stood in front of the mirror in the small office bathroom. Five o'clock had finally arrived, and she was applying fresh makeup, more than she usually used. Brad had suggested an after-work dinner today, rather than lunch later in the week. Needing to shore up her relationship with her primary client, Sedonia had no choice but to agree.

Raul called out from the office, "Okay, Sedonia, I'm going out to the job site and get the workers."

Sedonia opened the bathroom door. *"Bueno, Raul. Hasta mañana."*

Raul responded with a smile and a wave. Sedonia had informed him that she'd fired Cissy. He'd been sorry that Cissy hadn't worked out; he'd grown to like her before she started calling in sick. However, he was relieved when Sedonia authorized him to find a replacement. He'd told her Paco was available. It had been more than a year since Sedonia had run into Paco in Juan's Beer Garden. Hopefully, he was still as reliable as when he'd worked for her father.

Sedonia heard Raul pull away, and then looked back in the mirror. Fresh makeup hadn't masked her fatigue. Somehow, she had to make it through the next two or three hours. The phone rang in the office. What now? she thought irritably as she hurried to answer it.

"It's me," Jimmy said.

"Hi," Sedonia said. "Listen, I've got a business dinner in a few minutes. Can I call you back?"

"Call me back?" Jimmy exclaimed. "The Filipino's in town."

"What Filipino?"

"I don't know what his name is, but he must be strong. I heard last night he was playin' Nine-Ball for $5,000 sets."

"At Buster's?"

"Naw. Place called Parker's in Houston. Ever been there?"

"Never heard of it."

"It's on Washington Avenue, a few blocks west of downtown. There used to be a poolroom there called T. J. Parker's, but it closed down years ago. I don't know if these are the same people, or not."

"Are you going to be playing this Filipino there?"

"Depends on what kind of weight I can get. Could be me playin' him . . . or could be you."

"Jimmy, I can't make it. I'm having dinner tonight with my most important client. Besides, I'm exhausted from last night."

"Exhausted? We got back early."

"What time did you wake up?"

Jimmy laughed. "About an hour ago."

"I'll go with you tomorrow night," Sedonia said.

"Tomorrow night! Hell, the Filipino may be in Chicago tomorrow night."

"Jimmy, I've *got* to make this dinner."

"Action won't start until about 10:00 or 11:00. Come by when you're done with the dinner. I'll see you there." He hung up.

Gustavo, the proprietor of *Restaurante Merida,* beamed as he led Sedonia over to a corner table where Brad was sitting. Brad stood up and pulled out a chair for her as she approached. "Good to see you," he said.

"And good to see you," she said as they sat down.

"What can I get you to drink?" Gustavo said.

"Corona con cal," Sedonia and Brad replied in unison.

Gustavo grinned. "No surprise," he told Sedonia. "Just like your father." Then his expression grew serious. "I wish he was here with us this afternoon."

"Gracias, Gustavo," Sedonia said.

Brad cleared his throat. "We all miss him."

Gustavo's smile returned. "But now it is good to see you two . . . together." For a moment, everyone seemed slightly embarrassed. Then Gustavo gave a quick nod and left with their drink order.

"So," Brad said, "what's new? Haven't heard from you lately."

"Sorry about not calling with the project update on Friday. I got busy."

"How'd you do in that pool tournament?"

"Finished second."

"Congratulations," Brad said. "But you don't sound too happy about it."

"Should have won."

Brad chuckled. "Golf got you used to winning, didn't it?"

"Yep," she said. "But this is a whole new game."

Gustavo returned with their Corona and limes, plus a basket of fresh, still-warm tortilla chips. The three of them chatted for a few minutes, then Gustavo left to tend to his other customers. Sedonia and Brad sipped their beers, munched on chips, and lapsed into a comfortable silence, both surveying the crowded, brightly-decorated restaurant. What a contrast in men, Sedonia thought. She was attracted to Brad, as she'd been when she was a teenager. He seemed familiar, strong, and dependable. Jimmy, on the other hand, was strange, exciting, and potentially dangerous. Yet as dissimilar as they were, they had one thing in common: she was dependent on each. Brad provided stability for her business. Jimmy provided access to pool competition.

"Something wrong?" Brad said.

"Wrong?"

"Yeah. You're frowning."

She smiled and shook her head. "Thinking about business. And speaking of business, what projects do you have coming up?"

Gustavo brought their bill, and Sedonia snatched it away from Brad, saying "*I* invited you, remember?"

"Okay," he said with a grin, "but next time's on me."

From his manner, she sensed his interest was personal, not business. When she didn't reply, he said, "You still seeing someone?"

Sedonia hesitated, sorting through mixed emotions. It would be unfair to encourage Brad, since she intended to continue seeing Jimmy. Brad would never understand her desire to play pool. It was more than a desire; it was a need. It was a need she didn't fully understand herself. He'd touched on it earlier. Golf *had* got her used to winning. Finally she replied, "Yeah, I am seeing someone."

Brad responded with a forced smile and a nod of resignation.

Gustavo returned with her change. The three chatted for a few more minutes, then Sedonia and Brad left the restaurant. They crossed the parking lot in awkward silence. When they arrived at Sedonia's Miata, Brad didn't stop; instead he simply nodded and said, "Thanks for dinner."

Sedonia climbed into her car and fiddled with her keys, giving Brad time to precede her out of the parking lot. He passed without so much as a glance in her direction. She heaved a sigh and started her car. During the interminably long workday, she'd looked forward to going straight home and to bed. Now, she realized her need to play pool had come at an extremely high price. She watched Brad pull out of the parking lot and head toward Nassau Bay. Moments later, she pulled out, and headed toward Houston.

An elevated section of the I-45 Freeway carried Sedonia through downtown Houston. It was after 10:00. The surface streets below were almost deserted, and night lights encased the city in a shadowy glow. Despite local politicians' attempts to centralize Houston into a mini New York City, most residents still fled to the suburbs each evening, turning downtown over to a relatively small contingent of night people—custodians, indigents, and transgressors.

Sedonia felt surprisingly alert as she looked for the Memorial Drive / Houston Avenue exit ramp. Either she'd gained a second wind, or perhaps adrenaline was overriding the fatigue she'd experienced throughout the day. As she swung north, passing along the west side of the city, she spotted a sign indicating her exit. She descended a steep ramp that led to Houston Avenue, and then turned left onto Washington Avenue.

The immediate neighborhood was in transition. Brick buildings, one to four stories high, and most more than 50 years old, lined both sides of the poorly-lit, two-lane street. Many of the buildings were boarded up, but others had been gentrified into loft condominiums. Small businesses—used car lots, coffee shops, bail bond companies—appeared to be struggling for survival. Sedonia passed a small grocery and a drugstore, each with black bars protecting dusty front windows. Next came a thrift store, the Salvation Army, and an indigent care clinic.

Every few blocks, she approached a traffic signal. She slowed and accelerated, trying to time her arrivals so she didn't have to come to a complete stop on the nearly deserted street. Uncomfortable in these surroundings, she considered turning around and heading for home. Then ahead on the right, she spotted Jimmy's black Z-28, parked at the curb in front of an old two-story building.

A small painted sign above the entrance simply read, "Parker's." Jimmy had parked at the curb, in what during the daytime was a No Parking zone. Sedonia pulled in behind him, and shut off her engine. The large front windows of the poolroom had been covered with white paint, preventing a preview of what awaited her. She gave a wry smile. No, Brad would never understand.

Moments later, cue case slung over one shoulder, she stepped through the front door and into a grimy bar and grill. No one was working behind the U-shaped counter, and the only patron was a disheveled old man slumped in the corner booth, apparently asleep. Through an open doorway, Sedonia had an oblique view of unoccupied pool tables.

She again momentarily considered turning around, but her legs seemed to propel her forward of their own accord. She hesitated in the doorway, finding herself looking into a stark room, with a bare concrete floor. Then she started down the aisle that ran between two rows of aging Brunswicks. The tables were scarred and their felt was faded. Only the last two were occupied. Jimmy was shooting on the left, and a short, swarthy young man—apparently "the Filipino"—was shooting on the right. Jimmy's grating voice carried the length of the room; he was badgering for weight.

A dozen railbirds, all men, perched on stools along the far wall. They watched with interest as Sedonia approached. A decade-old news story flashed into Sedonia's mind: a lone woman who'd been raped by customers in a Boston bar. Now Sedonia was glad Jimmy had his pistol nearby.

A middle-aged man, with a shock of gray hair, stood up and demanded, "How'd you get in?"

Before Sedonia could reply, Jimmy said, "She's my player."

Laughter circulated among the railbirds, apparently thinking he was joking. Sedonia walked over to him.

"Shit," the man said, "I forgot to lock the door." Apparently he was the proprietor. He hurried toward the front.

Jimmy turned to Sedonia and said in a voice low enough that only she could hear. "I can't get any weight out of him. And I can't beat him without it."

"You sure?" Sedonia whispered. Not only was Jimmy a renowned road player, but she was surprised his ego would allow him to admit he wasn't as good as someone else.

"The Filipinos that come to the States are all strong. Must be something in the water over there. Two nights ago, this guy came in here and robbed Cannonball for over $10,000. I only give Cannonball the eight, so I know I can't beat this guy without any weight."

Sedonia looked around the stark surroundings, finding it difficult to believe people played for that amount of money in here.

"If we can get him to give you the right weight, though," Jimmy continued, "I think you can take him."

"How much would we be playing for?"

"Let me handle that. You go ahead and get warmed up. Use the table I was playing on. But just shoot straight-in shots. Don't show 'em a lot." He walked over to where the Filipino waited with another man, who also looked Filipino. He apparently was the stakehorse.

Sedonia heard a brief, angry exchange from the bar and grill, and then a door slam. The proprietor reappeared, shaking his head. Apparently the sleeper had been reluctant to leave.

Sedonia felt self-conscious under the intense male scrutiny, and her hands shook slightly as she screwed her stick together. However, after she'd spread the balls across the table and begun shooting, her nervousness passed. As Jimmy had instructed, she attempted only easy shots, concentrating on good mechanics and studying how the cue-ball reacted on the worn felt.

Jimmy argued with the two Filipinos for several minutes, frequently raising his voice. Finally he returned and said, "Feel like you're in stroke?"

"Yeah, I guess so," Sedonia said. "What we playing for?"

Jimmy turned back to the others. "Okay, race-to-5 for $1,000." Then he told Sedonia, "He won't give any weight, because no one's seen you play before."

"If he won't give me any weight, then maybe you ought to play him."

He studied her for a moment, then said, "Let's see how this goes. It's just for a thousand."

"Just a thousand?" Sedonia echoed. It was the most she'd ever played for, and Jimmy made it sound as if it were spare change.

"That's the least he'll go for," Jimmy said. "We'll see how you do in this short set. First, though, we need to move him off that table. He looks too comfortable there." Jimmy turned and called out, "We wanna play on *this* table."

Another argument ensued, dragged out by the need to translate everything to and from the Filipino. Finally he and his camp grudgingly agreed to change, and everyone repositioned themselves so that they now encircled Sedonia's table. The railbirds looked similar to those who followed the action at Buster's—a mix of blue- and white-collar types. Jimmy brought over stools for himself and Sedonia.

The Filipino held up a quarter, and Sedonia said, "Heads." The coin came up tails. Sedonia noted her hands were steady as she racked for the first game. Fatigue once again provided a tranquilizing effect. Now the trick would be to maintain focus.

The Filipino inspected the rack, and nodded his approval. Sedonia extended her hand and said, "My name is Sedonia."

He frowned and shook his head that he didn't understand.

"Sedonia," she said, pointing to herself.

He responded with an uneasy smile, and as they shook hands he pointed to himself and said, "Lito."

"Good luck, Lito," she said, and then felt slightly embarrassed. Unlike players in amateur leagues and semipro tournaments, gamblers at this level probably didn't wish each other good luck. She walked over and sat down on a stool beside Jimmy.

He leaned over and whispered, "No stall. Shoot your best shot."

Lito was a couple of inches shorter than Sedonia, and slight of build, but he broke with an exaggerated stroke and a full follow-through. There was a resounding crash, and balls scattered about the table. Three balls found pockets, including the gold-striped 9-ball. One shot, and Sedonia trailed 1 to 0 in the race-to-5.

He made two balls on the next break, and had no trouble quickly pocketing the remaining seven. Sedonia was behind, 2 to 0, and hadn't yet been to the table.

The third game was similar, beginning with three balls on the break. Lito's stroke was compact and his cue-ball positioning was impeccable. He appeared almost nonchalant as he worked his way around the table. Finally he lined up on the 9-ball, and then made it in the corner pocket. Sedonia trailed 3 to 0 and still hadn't had a shot.

She racked for the fourth game and returned to her stool. While Lito prepared to break, she leaned over and whispered to Jimmy, "Time for me to come off my stall?"

He turned and frowned, and then chuckled and shook his head. "He's gotta miss sooner or later."

Their light moment was cut short. Lito made the 9-ball on the break.

Sedonia looked back at Jimmy. "This is getting ridiculous."

Jimmy just shrugged.

After racking for the fifth game, Sedonia returned to her stool. For the first time since she'd begun playing serious pool, she realized how important the break could be. In matches before tonight, there was a high probability that her opponent would miss at least once during a game and give her a chance to get to the table, where she was likely to run out. But not tonight. Her confidence in her game wavered. She realized her shoulder wouldn't allow her to do what Lito was doing: break hard repeatedly.

On his fifth break, the blue 2-ball rolled into the corner pocket. However, for the first time the other eight balls hadn't spread out across the table. Sedonia chalked her cue and admonished herself to take her time when she got her chance to shoot—to simply concentrate on making one shot at a time. The pep talk proved unnecessary. Lito ran seven balls, then closed out the match by banking the 9-ball the length of the table and into the corner pocket. He'd taken the set 5 to 0, without giving Sedonia a single shot.

Jimmy gave a disgusted shake of his head, then walked up to the table and counted out ten $100 bills. "We want some weight this time!" he demanded.

Lito's stakehorse translated for him. Lito said something in Filipino, and his stakehorse laughed, then turned to Jimmy and said, "Lito say he can't give her no weight. He still ain't seen her shoot!"

The railbirds roared at the remark, and even Sedonia had to smile. Jimmy looked livid. He walked over to the Filipinos and began negotiating in earnest, his strident voice rising above the others. Sedonia only heard pieces of the exchange, but she got the impression they weren't taking her seriously.

Finally, Jimmy came over and said, "You've got the 'wild eight' in this next set."

Sedonia was surprised at getting the "wild eight," feeling it would give her a significant advantage. In effect, she would have two "money balls." While Lito still had to sink the 9-ball to win, she could win by sinking either the 8-ball or the 9-ball. Of course, weight was of no value, if Lito kept her off the table.

"How much are we playing for?" she said.

"Two thousand, and it's race-to-9."

Lito returned to the table and held up a quarter.

"Uh . . . tails," Sedonia said, departing from her usual practice of calling "heads." The coin came up heads. With a disgusted shake of her head, she racked for the first game of the new set.

Lito ran the rack, and the one after that. Sedonia was down 2 to 0 in the race-to-9. Two games into the second set, and she still hadn't had a shot. Starting the third game, Lito's break sounded solid, however, he failed to pocket a ball.

"Take your time," Jimmy whispered.

The cue-ball was in the middle of the table; the yellow 1-ball within an inch or two of the end rail. Sedonia's only two options were to attempt a razor thin cut into the corner pocket, or play a safety. After having to sit and watch seven straight games, she wanted to make a ball. She leaned down. *One, two, three* . . . Abruptly she straightened up, aborting her shot routine. She heaved a sigh, took a wistful look at the corner pocket, and then resorted to a safety.

She executed it perfectly, barely tapping the 1-ball, then rolling the cue-ball back down to the other end of the table and hiding it behind several other balls. Lito attempted a jump shot, and the cue-ball bounced once on the table, and then onto the concrete floor. Jimmy jumped up from his stool and fielded it on the fourth bounce. Before handing it to Sedonia, he wiped it off on his shirt front.

"Okay," he said, "play it smart and—"

Sedonia cut him off. "Don't talk to me while I'm playing."

He responded with a quizzical look, then went back to his stool.

Sedonia returned to the table with ball-in-hand. She determined the sequence in which she was going to shoot the balls, and then went to work. Her first stroke felt awkward; she'd sat and watched too long. Nevertheless, the 1-ball dropped into the corner pocket, and she felt more comfortable as she made the blue 2-ball in the side. By the 5-ball, she was in stroke and the distractions of the surroundings were partitioned from her thoughts. The green 6-ball and the maroon 7-ball went into corner pockets, and then she made the black 8-ball in the side. She was about to call the gold-striped 9-ball in the corner, when Lito approached the table and began pulling balls from the pockets.

"You've got the 8-ball, wild," Jimmy hissed.

Sedonia had forgotten that with the weight she'd been given, for her making the 8-ball was as good as making the 9-ball. She smiled. Now that she'd finally broken his string of wins, this ought to be easy.

An hour and a half later, Sedonia was on-the-hill, leading 8 to 4 in the race-to-9. Breaking at three-quarter speed, she'd managed to make at least one ball each time, and then had taken full advantage of having been given the "wild eight." At one point, she'd run off five straight games.

But now in the thirteenth game, she scratched on the break. She pulled up her stool and watched Lito return to the table. He had no trouble running the rack, and then the next. Although he'd given up significant weight, he was coming back and making a match of it.

Lito broke again, and began working his way around the table to what would be his seventh win. Sedonia glanced at her watch: 1:35. She looked up in time to see Lito make the 3-ball, but leave himself with poor position on the 4-ball. He surveyed his next shot from all angles, then played a safety, leaving the 4-ball in front of the corner pocket and sending the cue-ball down to the other end of the table.

Sedonia studied the shot he'd left. The gold-striped 9-ball partially blocked the path between the cue-ball and the 4-ball. Other balls prevented her from kicking the cue-ball off either side rail. She considered trying to jump over the 9-ball, but was reluctant to attempt it, since jumps were low percentage shots. If she missed here, it might well be her last shot of the set.

Sedonia walked over to where Jimmy was sitting and sprinkled some talcum powder onto her bridge hand. Jimmy, who hadn't spoken in almost two hours, looked grim.

"I need my golf clubs," Sedonia said, attempting to lighten the moment. "I could make this shot with a pitching wedge."

Jimmy didn't reply. "Stakehorses" also were known as "sweaters," and Jimmy was living up to the name.

Sedonia returned to the table. "Four-ball in the corner," she said. She imagined a line, just to the right of the 9-ball, elevated the butt of her cue stick, and aimed at the lower left side of cue-ball. *One, two, three . . . jab!* Driving the cue-ball down, produced a hard low-left spin. The force of the blow started the cue-ball off to the right, but then as it passed the 9-ball, the felt caught the spin and brought the ball back to the left in a sweeping curve, and into the 4-ball.

"Yes!" Jimmy shouted. A murmur went through the railbirds.

Sedonia meticulously chalked her cue tip to give her adrenaline a chance to normalize before she resumed play. The rest of the balls were positioned for a run-out. Moments later, she said, "Eight in the side."

Lito responded with a dismissive wave, and then turned and began speaking in earnest to his stakehorse. He still had his back to her, when she pocketed the 8-ball, closing out the match 9 to 6. She and Jimmy now were ahead, $1,000.

A smiling Jimmy went over and collected. The two Filipinos and a couple of the railbirds, who apparently also had lost on the match, appeared angry. Jimmy badgered for a rematch, but the Filipinos shook their heads.

"We only play for $5,000," said the Filipino who served as translator. "And no weight. Lito say, she too good. No weight."

Lito unscrewed his stick, and Sedonia checked her watch: 1:55. She felt relieved that she wouldn't have to play any more tonight. Fatigue had abruptly set in. She'd had little sleep the night before, and now had a one-hour drive back to the coast. While Jimmy continued to badger the Filipinos, she unscrewed her stick and took the opportunity to go to the ladies room.

When she returned, Jimmy was screwing her stick back together and Lito was racking the balls.

Jimmy handed Sedonia her stick and said, "Race-to-9, $5,000."

Sedonia felt a pang of apprehension. "We're playing some more? What weight do I get?"

"Alternate breaks. You break first, and then the break alternates, no matter who wins the game."

"That's all I get?"

"He won't give us anything else. He knows you're too good."

"Jimmy, I don't know . . ."

"The bet's made. Don't hold anything back." His expression was grim as he returned to his stool.

Sedonia walked down and checked the rack. The balls were tight. She returned to break end of the table and tried to collect her thoughts. She'd thought she was on her way home, instead she had at least another two hours of pool ahead of her. And for $5,000! Protect the shoulder, she told herself. Three-quarter speed break. *One, two, three . . . stroke.* The balls spread out, but nothing fell.

As Lito took the table and Sedonia pulled up her stool, Jimmy hissed through clenched teeth, "Damn it, Sedonia! Break the fuckin' balls!"

Lito had no trouble running the rack. Then after Sedonia racked for the second game, Lito broke and ran. He was ahead, 2 to 0, in the race-to-9.

It was Sedonia's turn to break, and as Lito racked, Jimmy opened his large cue case and pulled out a stick. "Here," he said, "use my break cue. It's twenty-two ounces."

Sedonia screwed the heavy break cue together as she walked back to the table, puzzled by Jimmy's behavior. Beads of perspiration had formed on his forehead. Five thousand dollars was a lot of money, but surely he'd gambled for higher stakes. Why was he was acting as if it were a matter of life and death?

Sedonia abruptly turned and walked back to where Jimmy was sitting. She leaned forward and whispered, "Can you cover the bet if we lose?"

"Get back there and break."

"Can you?" she insisted.

"No, damn it!" he hissed. "I've only got $3,700."

"Tell them." She started to step away.

Jimmy grabbed her arm and pulled her back. "It's too fuckin' late! Now go play."

Sedonia's legs felt weak as she returned to the table. She glanced to her left and saw Lito and his backers, watching her with frowns. She chalked her cue and remembered how breaking hard during her match with "Austin" Danny had caused her shoulder to flare up to an unbearable level. That night, she'd been able to quit between sets. And that night, she'd had Buster to protect her. Tonight, it was early in a set, and there was no quitting. And tonight, she was the only woman in the room. Again she remembered the lone woman in the Boston bar. Could she count on Jimmy?

One, two, three . . . stroke! A stab of pain and a resounding *crack!* An instant later, the gold-striped 9-ball disappeared into the corner pocket. Nine on the break. The score was 2 to 1.

As she racked for Lito's break, the familiar dull ache began to spread across her right shoulder and lower neck. When she returned to her stool, Jimmy hissed, "Why didn't you break like that the first time?"

"My shoulder, damn it!"

"Christ! I forgot about that. Do you have something for it?"

"I've got some pain pills. They're in my purse, under my car seat."

"Gimme your keys. I'll go get 'em."

Sedonia reluctantly handed over her keys. Jimmy grabbed the proprietor, and they hurried toward the front of the building. Lito looked around in annoyance at the disturbance, but then broke and began what looked as if it would be a break-and-run.

Jimmy returned just as Lito made the 9-ball. The score now was 3 to 1. Jimmy handed Sedonia six hydrocodone tablets.

"Time out," Sedonia said.

As she started toward the ladies room, she heard grumbling from Lito and his backers. Then Jimmy said something that evoked a round of male laughter. Sedonia heard the word Midol, and shook her head in annoyance.

The restroom was small—a sink and a single stall. Sedonia studied the pills in palm of her hand. The pain in her shoulder was bearable, but she would have to break another half-dozen times. And she *had* to win. She took one pill, hesitated, then took a second. The rest she folded into a paper towel, and put it into a front jeans pocket. She leaned over the sink and stared at her fatigued reflection in the mirror, stalling as long as she could, trying to allow time for the pills to take effect.

The door suddenly opened and Jimmy said, "You okay?"

"Go away."

"We gotta have this set," he said, urgency on his tone.

She heaved a sigh, and then pushed past him. "I'll do the best I can."

When she broke for the fifth game, the stab of pain and the residual ache were worse than before. The pills hadn't taken effect. However, she'd made two balls.

"Get me something to drink," she told Jimmy. "No alcohol. Something with caffeine."

She made three balls, and then resorted to a safety that Lito couldn't counter. After he missed, she returned to the table and ran the rest of the balls. She now trailed, 3 to 2.

In the sixth game, Lito broke and ran six balls, then for the first time missed a relatively easy shot. Sedonia ran the rest, making the score 3 to 3. Not only was the set even, but Sedonia had regained the edge that she'd forfeited by losing the first game. If each player won their break games from now on, she would reach nine games before he did.

The next eight games dragged on for two hours. Lito's earlier nonchalance had been replaced by total concentration. Now he studied each shot, and frequently resorted to playing safeties. The pain in Sedonia's shoulder had lessened, but maintaining concentration was becoming increasingly difficult. She was playing for stakes that she and Jimmy couldn't cover; nevertheless, she had trouble keeping her eyelids from closing for seconds at a time.

"Your shot!" Jimmy snapped.

Sedonia rose unsteadily to her feet. She evidently had dozed for a moment. As she approached the table, she glanced down at her watch: 4:05. She looked back at Jimmy. "What's the score?"

"It's 7 to 7," Jimmy said, exasperation in his tone.

"Time out," Sedonia said, and started toward the ladies room.

Lito snarled something in Filipino, then walked over and dropped onto his stool. He appeared frustrated by the delay; however, he seemed as energetic now, as he'd been six hours ago.

Sedonia closed the restroom door behind her, but it immediately flew open and Jimmy pushed his way in. "Here!" he said, handing her a pill.

"What is it?" Sedonia said, her words slurred. It was difficult to think, much less to talk.

"Black molly. You're falling asleep between shots. This'll pick you up."

"I don't use stuff like that. Besides, I've already taken pain pills."

"You don't use amphetamines," he said with heavy sarcasm, "but pain pills are okay?"

"Just . . . leave me alone."

"Damn it, Sedonia, this is serious shit. These people don't take IOUs!"

"*I* didn't get us in this situation. *You're* the one who made the bet."

"Yeah, and it was stupid, because *I'm* not the one who's playing. But I figured you could pull it off. If you lose, we can't pay. Do you understand that? You cannot lose!" He forced the amphetamine into her hand.

"Get out of here," she said.

"Swallow it."

"I will!" she said, giving him a push. "Now get out. I have to use the toilet."

He reluctantly left, closing the door behind him.

Sedonia stared at her reflection in the mirror, barely able to keep her eyes open. If only she could lie down and sleep. She wet a paper towel and wiped her face. It felt cool and momentarily refreshed her. She walked over to the toilet, dropped in the amphetamine, and flushed.

A few minutes later, she assumed her stance at the break end of the table. She was surging—short periods of clarity, punctuating a general mental blur. She leaned over the table and told herself, full force break. *One, two, three . . . stroke!* A momentary stab of pain, then the exhilarating sight of the gold-striped 9-ball rolling into the far corner pocket. She was on-the-hill, 8 to 7.

As she racked for Lito's break, a wave of fatigue swept over her. She hesitated, staring down at the balls. She'd racked for Nine-Ball thousands of times, but suddenly she couldn't remember the order in which the balls had to be placed. Abruptly, her mind cleared, and she quickly completed the rack.

She returned to her stool and started to sit down, but then decided she'd stay more alert if she remained standing.

Lito broke-and-ran. The set was now hill-hill.

Sedonia waited at the break end of the table, while Lito racked for the seventeenth and final game. She took several deep breaths, trying to get more oxygen to her muddled brain. Lito lifted the triangle, and waited for her to inspect the rack. Rather than expend the energy, she simply nodded that it was acceptable.

"Okay, babe," Jimmy exhorted from the sideline, "race-to-1. Bring it home!"

One, two, three . . . stroke! There was a sharp *crack!* but the balls responded sluggishly, as if due to a loose rack. At the last moment, the orange 5-ball tapped the blue 2-ball into the side pocket. Sedonia's relief was only momentary. The yellow 1-ball sat in front of the corner pocket, but the maroon 7-ball blocked the cue-ball's path, and other balls prevented Sedonia's trying a curve. She studied the shot, then took her stance and prepared for a jump shot.

"Push out!" Jimmy said, calling for her to open the game with a safety.

Sedonia stepped back and surveyed the table again. Nine-Ball rules didn't require that a player hit the object ball on the first shot after the break, so Sedonia was allowed to "push" the cue-ball anywhere on the table. Then it would be Lito's option either to take the next shot, or require her to shoot again. Sedonia took another deep breath. Play safe, or go for it now? A similar decision on final hole of the U. S. Women's Amateur Golf Championship flashed into her mind, when her coach had exhorted her to play it safe. Now, Sedonia looked over at Jimmy, sweating with the other railbirds.

"Push out," he repeated.

Sedonia shook her head. "Gonna grip it and rip it."

Jimmy frowned, then shook his head and covered his eyes.

Sedonia turned back and resumed her stance. She lined up the shot, and then elevated the butt of her cue stick. *One, two, three . . . jab!* She drove cue-ball into the slate, it jumped the 7-ball, tapped the 1-ball into the corner pocket, and came to rest in perfect position on the red 3-ball. Sedonia's mind was clear as she walked down to the other end of the table to determine how she wanted to play the remaining balls. They were clustered closer than she liked, but all were makeable. She smiled. She was in control.

Working her way around the table in dead stroke, her shots were crisp, her position precise. Finally, the cue-ball came to rest in the middle of the table, leaving her an easy shot on the set-deciding 9-ball. She looked over at Lito.

The Filipino stood up, walked over, and raked the 9-ball into the side pocket with his cue stick. He'd conceded the final shot of the set.

Jimmy rushed over, gave Sedonia a quick hug, and then hurried over to Lito's backer to collect his bet.

Sedonia unscrewed her cue stick and prepared to leave. Jimmy returned and said, "They want to go again. This time for $10,000."

Sedonia checked her watch: 5:17. "You're insane," she said. "I'm going home."

"C'mon, babe," Jimmy pleaded, "we'll clean these guys out. You and 'molly' can play for days."

"Molly is somewhere in a Houston sewer," Sedonia said as she slung her cue case over her shoulder.

"In the sewer?" Jimmy said in obvious disbelief.

"Yeah, and I'm going home." She turned to the proprietor. "Unlock the front door."

Leaving a perplexed Jimmy behind, she followed the proprietor past the unoccupied pool tables and through the deserted bar area. The early morning light momentarily blinded her as she stepped onto the sidewalk and started toward her car, parked at the curb. Washington Avenue was deserted, except for a dusty brown Pontiac Firebird heading in her direction. As she unlocked her Miata, the Firebird slowed. Sedonia quickly jumped into her car and locked the door. The Firebird passed, and she saw the hard countenance of Audri Krump, gazing back at her through the side window. Audri's boyfriend, Cannonball, was driving. He turned into an alleyway that ran alongside the poolroom.

Sedonia started her car, and made a U-turn. As she headed toward downtown Houston and the Gulf Freeway, she turned the air-conditioner on full blast and directed the vents so the frigid air hit her face. A smile formed. She was exhausted, but recalling the thrill of the final game would keep her alert enough for the drive home.

Later that morning, Sedonia tried unsuccessfully to work an incessant ringing into a tortured dream. Then forcing her eyes open to narrow slits, she located the alarm clock and pounded on the snooze bar. The damned noise wouldn't stop! Finally she realized the ringing came from the nearby phone. Her mouth was dry, and she barely could choke out, "Hello?"

"Sedonia?" said a male voice with a Spanish accent.

"Yes. Who is this?"

"Emilio."

Sedonia raised up in bed on one elbow. She'd had no contact with Emilio in more than a year, since the night he'd threatened to assault her in Willie O's parking lot. "What do you want?" she demanded.

"My *tio*, Raul, is in the hospital."

Sedonia sat up and said with alarm, "Raul's in the hospital?"

"Yes. He fell down."

"At work?"

"Yes."

"When? What happened?"

"Late yesterday afternoon. He fell off a ladder and hurt his leg. They think it is cracked. He also hit his head, and he had bad headaches last night. I made him go to the hospital. They will do more tests today."

Sedonia looked at the clock: 10:03. She'd slept less than four hours. She swung her legs over the side of the bed, rubbed her eyes, and tried to clear her brain of sleep deprivation and hydrocodone hangover. Her father had never carried health insurance on their workers, even Raul. Instead, he'd set up an escrow account to cover emergencies, but Sedonia had tapped that fund long ago to cover operating expenses. *Damn it!* Then she remembered her share of the previous night's winnings: $3,000. She needed to get hold of Jimmy right away.

"Sedonia?" Emilio said.

"Yes, I'm still here. What hospital is Raul in?"

"Clear Lake."

"Okay, tell him I'll come by as soon as I can."

"Sedonia," Emilio said, "I will come in and work in my uncle's place."

"Don't be ridiculous! I never want to see you again."

"Please, Sedonia. He is afraid he will lose his job. I must do this for my *tio*."

"Forget it," she snapped. "And he is *not* going to lose his job."

"But—"

She slammed down the receiver.

Two hours later, Sedonia paced her office, sipping her third cup of coffee since arriving. She'd telephoned the hospital and learned that Raul was still having tests run, and it would probably be mid afternoon before he could receive visitors. Then she'd tried to track down Jimmy. There'd been no answer either at Microtel or at Parker's Billiards. She'd left a message with the hotel desk clerk for Jimmy to contact her as soon as he arrived, day or night.

She returned to her desk and tried to collect her thoughts. Her paint crew already had been shorthanded, and they were behind schedule on Brad's project. Now her painters were working unsupervised. She needed to get out to the jobsite herself, but someone had to cover here at the office. She switched on her PC. Maybe she could afford a temporary clerk, who at least could keep the office open and answer the phone.

She brought up the operating account. After she made this week's payroll, there would be less than $2,000, and she didn't know how much Raul's hospitalization was going to cost. Damn it! She needed that $3,000 she'd won last night.

She brought up Brad's account: slightly more than $22,000. She couldn't use that, though. It was strictly for his projects. No way, she told herself when the temptation recurred.

The crunch of a vehicle pulling into the parking lot drew her attention. She jumped up, hoping to see Jimmy's black Z-28, but then shook her head in disbelief. A scowling Emilio climbed out of his blue Silverado pickup.

When he burst through the door, Sedonia's hand was resting on the telephone receiver. "Get out of here!" she said. "Or I'm calling the Seabrook Police!"

"I don't mean you no trouble. You didn't let me explain."

"Get out. Now!"

Emilio lowered his head. "I'm sorry about that night. I was drunk."

"That's no damned excuse."

"I know," he said. He looked away in obvious embarrassment, then turned back with moist eyes. "Please, Sedonia. You don't have to pay me nothing. I just work in my *tio's* place. He told me, his workers know what to do. They just need someone to watch them, and be sure they keep working."

Sedonia shook her head, recalling when she'd first met Emilio and shaken his pool-hustler's soft hand. "Have you ever worked a day in your life?"

He hesitated, then replied, "In Mexico. Yes."

The phone beneath Sedonia's hand rang, causing her to jump. She automatically picked up the receiver and said, "Forbes Painting."

"It's Brad, Sedonia. I'm out at the job site. What's the story on Raul?"

Sedonia slumped back in her chair. Now she had Brad to deal with. She felt like giving up, but leaned forward again and said, "He's in the hospital. As I understand it, when he went back out there late yesterday evening, he fell off a ladder. They're running some tests, and I should know more this afternoon. I don't know how long he'll be off work."

Brad didn't respond for a moment, then said, "I hate to put more pressure on you at a time like this, but I've made commitments. We need to get back on schedule. If it looks like you're going to be short-handed, I'm afraid I'll have to make other arrangements."

Sedonia winced, then looked over at Emilio, whose shoulders were slumped. "I'm taking care of things, Brad," she said. "Raul's nephew is here in the office right now, and . . . he's about to head out to the job site."

Emilio looked her in the eye, held up a clenched fist, and said softly, "I won't let you down. I promise you."

Sedonia responded with a resigned nod, and continued with Brad, "And I'll be on-site too, soon as I get things reorganized here."

"Okay," Brad said. "What hospital is Raul in?"

"Clear Lake."

"I'll try to get by there and see him this afternoon," he said. "Talk to you later." He hung up.

Sedonia rubbed her tired eyes and told Emilio, "To get to the job site—"

"*Tio* told me where it is." He interrupted, then turned and headed for the door, as if to get away before she changed her mind. He paused in the doorway long enough to call back, *"¡Gracias!"*

The usual *"de nada"* caught in Sedonia's throat. She couldn't bring herself to tell him that the concession she'd made had been "nothing."

By early afternoon, Sedonia still hadn't heard from Jimmy. She tried Parker's Billiards again, and this time a gruff male voice finally answered the phone, but told her that Jimmy had left a short while earlier. She tried Microtel again, and left another message that it was imperative that Jimmy contact her right away. Then she tried the hospital to get an update on Raul's status. The nurse on his floor said he was having more X-rays.

Sedonia rubbed her eyes. If she was unable to locate Jimmy, where could she turn? Her only real friends were Hannah and Buster. Growing up, she'd always had a large number of acquaintances, but the relationships had been predicated on specific activities, such as golf, sailing, and music. Her only true friend had been her father. And now the only people she considered friends were pool players. But she wouldn't feel right turning to Hannah or Buster for money.

She folded her arms and rested her head on the desk. Her seven-year-old Miata might bring $5,000, but that would take time. Plus, she'd need to replace it with a pickup truck, so selling her car would be of no help. She still had a thousand-dollar certificate of deposit from a birthday several years ago. It must be worth about $1,500 now. She could cash that in tomorrow morning, if she needed to apply it to Raul's medical expenses. Her eyelids closed, and her mind immediately drifted into disjointed images.

Oyster shells crunched in the parking lot. She jumped up, and through the window saw Jimmy climb out of his black Z-28. He was dressed in the same polo shirt and jeans he'd worn the night before.

Sedonia met him at the doorway. "You got my message."

"Huh? What message?"

"Never mind. I need my $3,000."

"I don't have it. I need to borrow some money from you."

"What do you mean, you don't have it!"

"They cleaned me out. Right after you left, Cannonball came in. Black bastard shot like God. I was backing the Filipino, but after you got done with him, he couldn't hit shit. Hell, I think *I* could have beaten him."

Sedonia stared at Jimmy in disbelief.

"Loan me $1,000," he said. "I gotta get to that Filipino again, before he blows town."

"I don't have $1,000!"

"Okay, then at least loan me $300 to cover this week's rent."

"God damn you, Jimmy!" She turned away, and strode over the window, trying to regain control.

She felt his hands on her shoulders. She turned and he took her in his arms.

"What's going on?" he said.

She sighed, and gave him a brief explanation of the jeopardy she was in. Then she pushed him away, and walked over and sat down at her desk. Jimmy pulled up a chair across from her.

"What can I do to help?" he said.

"Are you really broke?"

"Yeah. Most of what I won at the South Padre Island tournament, I lost in Corpus Christi on the way up here. Then this morning I lost the rest of it."

"Don't you have money in New Orleans? I need my $3,000!"

"I was busted at home, babe. That's the reason I'm on the road."

Sedonia rubbed her tired eyes. "Damn it," she said. "I need to go out and inspect the job site. I need to go over to the hospital and check on Raul. And I can't leave this God-damned office unattended."

Jimmy looked around. "I can keep an eye on things here."

She dismissed the suggestion with a quick wave.

"Seriously," he said.

"This is a business, Jimmy, not a pool hall."

"I've been in business before."

"You?"

He responded with a quick laugh. "Worked in a bank. Only legitimate job I ever had. My ex-wife's father was the manager. Marriage didn't last long. Job was even shorter."

Down as she was, still Sedonia had to chuckle. She could imagine Jimmy as a car salesman, but not as a banker. "What did you do there?"

"Clerk. Set up customer accounts, handled electronic transactions, stuff like that. Don't worry; I know how to answer a phone and talk nice to customers."

Sedonia reconsidered his offer, and finally said, "If you could look after things here for the next four hours—just answer the phone and take messages—it would be a big help. But aren't you exhausted from last night?"

"Me and 'molly' are fine," he said. "We'll look after things here."

Sedonia heaved a sigh; she had no choice. "Okay," she said. She took her purse out of the desk drawer, and then got up and crossed the room. At the front door, she turned back and said, "Jimmy, I need that $3,000 right away. My business is riding on it."

He nodded. "I just gotta find a stakehorse, so I can get back in the game before the Filipino leaves town. Him and his buddy are still loaded. I can win our money back. No problem."

"No problem," Sedonia muttered, and then stepped outside and closed the door behind her. As she descended the stairs and started across the parking lot, she shook her head. No problem. One pool hustler who had threatened to assault her was supervising her paint crew, and now another on amphetamines was overseeing her office. No problem.

Chapter 17

Sedonia sat on the bare living room floor, applying a final coat of enamel to the baseboard. A *ranchero* blasted from Luis' boom-box in the dining room, where he and Emilio were rolling wall paint. As Sedonia dipped her brush into the can, she thought she heard a car horn. She paused, wiping perspiration from her eyes with the back of one hand. When she didn't hear the horn again, she resumed her task. She hadn't lost the delicate touch she'd acquired during her high school summers. The only trim she couldn't manage now was the crown molding that ran along the ceiling, since it required raising her arm above shoulder height.

The *ranchero* ended, and was followed by a romantic ballad. After several days of working with her crew, Sedonia had re-familiarized herself with the Latino radio station's limited selection. When she'd worked for her father, she'd learned much of her Spanish by singing along. Now, she began harmonizing with Marco Antonio Solis' *Mi Último Adiós*, but a familiar voice interrupted her.

"Hey, lady!"

Sedonia turned and saw Hannah grinning down at her from the doorway. Sedonia glanced at her paint-flecked watch: 12:05. She'd lost track of time. *¡Almuerzo!* She called out as she struggled to her feet. *¡Una Hora!*

The radio in the dining room switched off, and there was general shuffling throughout the house as her crew wrapped up their immediate tasks and prepared for a one-hour lunch break.

Emilio paused in the doorway and said in mock servitude, *"Gracias, jefe. Gracias."* Sedonia raised her paintbrush as if to throw it, and Emilio grinned and hurried toward the front door.

"What did he call you?" Hannah asked as Sedonia walked over.

"*Jefe*. Means 'boss'. He's just being a wise guy. He's the pool player I told you about."

"The one . . . in the parking lot?"

"Yeah. He's paying for it now, though. I'm working his butt off. You should have seen the blisters he got on his hands the first day he was out here." Sedonia pulled off a pair of rubber gloves. "Now he wears these too."

"Let me take you to lunch . . . *'jefe'*."

"I can't leave the job site, Hannah."

"C'mon, it's Friday."

"We're still a week behind schedule. But if you want to eat here, the 'roach coach' is due any minute."

"The *what* is due any minute!"

"Sandwiches and stuff. C'mon."

As they stepped outside, the canteen truck pulled up. Sedonia and Hannah got in line behind Emilio and two workers from a project down the street.

"What's the house specialty?" Hannah whispered.

"Roast beef and cheese sandwich, chips, and a Coke," Sedonia said.

"Okay. I'll trust your judgment."

Sedonia stepped up to the counter, and the young woman who operated the truck said, "You're a mess. And that pretty little car of yours is too."

Sedonia looked over at her Miata. Earlier that morning, a developer had leveled the vacant lots across the street, sending over clouds of dust. "Thanks, Mary," Sedonia replied. "Every little bit of encouragement helps."

Mary laughed, then said, "You want your regular?"

"Yeah, and she'll have the same."

"Where's that good looking contractor of yours?" Mary said as she handed over their order.

Sedonia paid. "Haven't heard from him today. When I do, I'll tell him you were looking for him."

"He *knows* that," Mary replied.

Sedonia laughed. "See ya, Mary," she said.

"See ya."

As Sedonia and Hannah walked away, Sedonia said, "We can eat in my car. It's too hot there in the house."

"Are you kidding?" Hannah replied. "If I did manage to squeeze into your car, I'd never be able to get out. Let's use mine."

"I'm pretty dirty."

"C'mon," Hannah said.

A few minutes later, with the Cadillac running and its air-conditioner blowing, the two women settled back.

"How's your foreman doing?" Hannah said between bites of her sandwich.

"Raul's doing better. He's still having headaches, though, and he'll have to wear a walking cast for a while. But they gave him the okay to return to work next week. Instead, of course, he showed up this morning. But I had Emilio take him back home. Raul's terrific. Don't know how I'd manage without him."

"You look happy," Hannah said, "in spite of your business problems."

Sedonia thought for a moment. "You know, I guess I am happy…happier than I've been in a long time. I've let things go for more than a year, ever since Dad died. I hurt my business, but now I feel like I'm back on track."

"How about 'French Quarter' Jimmy?" Hannah said with a knowing smile. "Is he the source of some of this new-found happiness?"

"Hannah!" Sedonia protested. Then she said, "He's been a big help, overseeing the office for me, but we don't see much of each other. He leaves at five o'clock and heads straight for his motel. He sleeps for a few hours, then goes out and plays pool all night."

"Don't know how he keeps going with a schedule like that," Hannah said.

Sedonia didn't mention Jimmy's reliance on "molly," she just replied, "I can't keep up with him. He keeps asking me to go along, but after a day out here, I've barely got the energy to eat dinner. I'm in bed by 8:00 every night."

"And all alone, poor thing," Hannah teased. "Well, what about in the future?"

"Next week, after Raul gets back?" Sedonia looked over at the house on which she'd been working, then turned back to Hannah. "I've decided to let pool go, and concentrate on running my business."

"You're kidding!"

"Nope. Pool's taking up too much of my time."

"But you're so good at it. You've got more talent than anyone I've ever seen. And I think you've just scratched the surface."

"I appreciate your saying that," Sedonia said, "but pool's hard on my health, as well as my business."

"Is your shoulder giving you that much trouble?"

"Sometimes it's pretty bad." Sedonia said. She didn't mention Parker's Billiards, where she'd resorted to pain pills and almost risked an amphetamine. "Also, I haven't been able to keep up with my regular fitness routine."

"How about league play? Can I talk you into playing with the Cue-Ts again next session?"

"I don't know. I'll have to see if I can work it in."

"And Jimmy?" Hannah said. "Is he in your future plans?"

Sedonia sighed. "He might be, if he's not just passing through. I think there might be more to him than meets the eye."

"I *like* what meets the eye."

"Seriously, Hannah, I don't know what to make of him. I gotta admit, there's definitely some chemistry. And I keep thinking, if he hadn't grown up under the circumstances he did . . ."

"You think he's salvageable?"

Sedonia responded with a wry smile and shake of her head. "We women do that, don't we? Try to 'salvage' men. When I was going with a musician, my dad warned me about what he called 'fixer-uppers'. And he wasn't talking about houses."

A white Ram pickup stopped across the street, interrupting their conversation. A grinning Brad climbed out.

"Who is *that* guy?" Hannah said, sounding almost awestruck.

"Definitely not a fixer-upper," Sedonia said with a faint smile.

That evening, after closing down the job site for the day, Sedonia arrived at her office. The parking lot was empty. She pushed open the door and discovered the afternoon mail lying on the floor beneath the letter slot. Jimmy apparently had left early. Sedonia suspected he was in his motel room, resting up for a long weekend of pool. He'd better win; she needed the $3,000 he owed her, though she planned to reduce it by $1,000 in appreciation for his looking after the office.

She dropped into the chair behind her desk and threw the mail into her "In" basket. Most of it appeared to be bills; they'd hold until Monday. She leaned back in her chair, tired but satisfied.

She and her crew had accomplished a lot this week. Hannah had stayed long enough to meet Brad, and then with a clandestine wink that only Sedonia had seen, she'd gone on her way. Brad inspected the progress on his house and was pleased with the quality of the work and the knowledge that they were getting back on schedule. After he left, Sedonia called the crew together and passed along his comments. She asked for volunteers to come in the next day, even though they normally didn't work on Saturdays. Everyone, including Emilio, said they were willing to work.

Sedonia smiled. It had been a productive week, and Raul would be back on Monday. She wondered if Emilio would want to continue working for her. Probably not. He'd certainly worked hard in his uncle's absence, though.

Thinking about the following week, she decided she'd have Raul stay in the office for a while, while she continued to go out and work with the crew. Not only would it give Raul a chance to recover fully, she'd enjoyed being out there. She needed the physical exertion. She suspected she'd gained at least ten pounds since she'd quit jogging. She hadn't risked getting on a scale to find out.

She switched on her PC. Although she'd spoken with Brad five hours earlier, she still wanted to check his account balance and give him the Friday update before she headed for home. The phone rang, causing her to jump.

"Forbes Painting."

It was Hannah. "Have you heard?" she said.

"Have I heard what?" Sedonia said with a smile, expecting a typical Hannah quip.

"About Cissy." Hannah's tone was unusually subdued.

"What about her?" Sedonia said. She anticipated hearing that Cissy was back in jail.

"She's dead, Sedonia. Buster just called me. He tried to reach you all day there at the office, but kept getting your recording."

"Cissy's dead?" Sedonia said in disbelief. "Are you sure?"

"I'm sure. I called the funeral home."

"But how? What happened?"

"She overdosed, two days ago. That piece of crap, Eddy, didn't notify any of her friends. Buster saw a little write-up in *The Citizen*. They're burying her tomorrow morning at Forest Park Cemetery on the Gulf Freeway."

Sedonia was too stunned to speak. "Oh, Hannah," she said finally, her voice breaking, "I had to fire Cissy."

Hannah didn't respond for a moment, then said, "Cissy's problem was dope, not her job."

"I didn't even try to talk to her . . ."

"Sedonia, stop it. You gave her a chance in Las Vegas. You gave her a job. You're not responsible for her weakness."

There was another long pause, before Sedonia said, "Will there be a funeral service for her?"

"Just an informal gathering at the gravesite. The funeral director told me that her only known relative was an aunt in Illinois. He's not sure if she's coming. I'm going to call Flora and Vicky and let them know."

"What time is the funeral?"

"Nine o'clock."

"Okay. I'll see you there."

After they'd hung up, Sedonia sat for a long time, trying to fathom the fact that Cissy was no longer alive. She couldn't. Sedonia's life had been touched by only two deaths. Cissy's passing was as unfathomable as her father's had been, the year before.

Tears formed, and Sedonia opened her purse to get a package of Kleenex. She saw the hydrocodone that Cissy had given her. Sedonia closed her eyes, recalling the night following her father's death and her shoulder injury, when she'd sat on her balcony with a bottle of scotch and a container of prescription pain pills. At the hospital the next day, the doctor told her that she'd managed to dial "911" before losing consciousness. But even now, she had no recollection of having done so. She lowered her head and her sobs broke the silence of the office.

Finally she looked up, grabbed the bottle of hydrocodone, and fired it into the metal wastepaper basket in the corner. The bottle shattered, leaving white pills lying among the shards of glass. *Never again!*

Sedonia wiped her eyes, then reached over and switched off the PC. No need to check Brad's account tonight. She couldn't bear the thought of having to talk to anyone, particularly someone outside her circle of pool-playing friends. Brad wouldn't understand.

The following morning, Sedonia drove south on the Gulf Freeway feeder road, past a service station, a dirt-bike dealership, and then a monument works, with sample headstones on display. The route to Forest Park was all too familiar; she'd visited her father's gravesite several times during the past year. She turned into the cemetery, passing through a black wrought iron gate, swung open for visitors. A hearse and four cars, including Hannah's Cadillac, were clustered off to the left.

Sedonia turned down a narrow lane, and pulled in behind Hannah's car. As she climbed out, she checked her watch: 8:59. She'd arrived on time. Hannah, Flora, and Vicky stood on the near side of the open grave. A man in a dark suit, apparently the funeral director, and a middle-aged woman Sedonia didn't recognize, stood on the far side. The plain, gunmetal-gray casket already had been lowered.

Hannah walked over and met Sedonia with a hug. "It's so sad," Hannah said, her voice breaking. "She was only 27."

Sedonia nodded, and then said. "Is that Cissy's aunt?"

"No, a neighbor. She lives in the apartment next-door. She's the one who found Cissy. The aunt couldn't make the funeral."

"And Eddy?"

"No sign of him. Probably stoned, or just doesn't have the guts to show his face."

Hannah took Sedonia's elbow and led her to the gravesite, where Sedonia exchanged hugs with Flora and Vicky. Then they all took their positions at the side of the grave.

Sedonia heaved a sigh, trying to remain composed. She looked about. Late summer temperatures had burned the cemetery grass a yellowish brown. Two seagulls squawked overhead. Sedonia followed their flight as they headed in the direction of Galveston Bay. A few hundred yards down the feeder road stood Champ's Billiards. That seemed appropriate. Sedonia recalled that Sunday afternoon, when she'd gone to Champ's, looking for someone named Emilio. In the first pool game she'd witnessed, Cissy had been one of the competitors. That now seemed so long ago.

The funeral director interrupted her sad reverie. "Would someone like to say a few words?"

Flora and Vicky shook their heads, obviously too shy.

Hannah sighed. "I don't know what to say. I just knew Cissy from pool."

There was a long silence, then Sedonia cleared her throat. "I met Cissy last year. I also knew her, mainly just from pool. We were teammates." A lump rose in Sedonia's throat, and she had to pause before she could continue. "I saw her . . . struggle with life. I saw her . . . give in." Sedonia's voice broke and her tears flowed. "I should have been her friend!"

Hannah put a comforting arm around her shoulder. "A few months ago," Sedonia continued, "we were in Las Vegas. I can picture Cissy now . . . walking among the hundreds of pool tables. She was alone. Alone, like she is now . . . lying among all these tombstones."

Flora sobbed, and Vicky placed an arm around her shoulder to console her.

Sedonia cleared her throat again, and then paused to look at each of her former teammates. "When we think of Cissy," she said, "we shouldn't dwell on her struggle, her defeats. We should remember instead, that time when we saw her at her best. Remember that determined jut of her chin, and what she taught us about 'heart'. Remember her, as she wanted to be remembered. Remember her in Las Vegas. Undefeated!"

After the funeral, Sedonia returned to her office. Hannah had suggested that they all get together for lunch, but Sedonia had begged off, saying her painting crew was working overtime, and she needed to join them. Flora and Vicky also had declined. It was evident they wanted to get this tragic episode behind them.

Now, sitting behind her desk, Sedonia listened to the brisk flow of late morning traffic on Waterfront Street. Saturdays were particularly busy for the nearby seafood markets. She heaved a sigh, and then shook her head. She needed to fight through this depression. First, she'd check Brad's balance and be sure the account payables were up to date, and then give him a call. After that, she'd change into the work clothes she'd brought along, and get out to the job site.

She switched on her PC, and while the system came up, she leafed through several invoices that needed to be paid. They totaled almost $8,400. The cursor began to blink, and she brought up the account she shared with Brad. She frowned. The balance was $347.91. She clicked on "Account History" and discovered $22,000 had been transferred out of the account, late Thursday afternoon. Brad must have withdrawn the funds to cover another need. But why hadn't he mentioned it yesterday at the job site?

She looked at the transaction again. The number of the receiving account wasn't Brad's. She went back through the history file and couldn't find the number there either. Suddenly her eyes widened. The pile of mail on the floor. Buster had only received her recording. Jimmy hadn't been in at all yesterday!

Sedonia lifted the mouse pad. The Post-it note was there, where Brad had written their joint account password, "Acropolis." She grabbed the phone and called Microtel. Jimmy had checked out on Thursday morning. *That bastard!*

Sedonia stared out her office window. The seafood market across the street had closed for the day, and the nighttime hubbub from Kemah's Restaurant Row drifted across the channel. Off to the left, she could see the top of the Ferris wheel, entertaining carefree Saturday night patrons.

The phone on her desk rang, and Sedonia quickly turned and grabbed the receiver.

It was Buster. "Near as I can tell," he said, "Jimmy's blown town. He dropped a bundle at Parker's on Thursday night and Friday morning. A couple of Filipinos took him for maybe $20,000."

"Damn that son of a bitch!"

"I called every poolroom I could think of," Buster continued. "Only one person saw him after he left Parker's. A barmaid out on I-10 East."

"I-10 East?"

"Yeah, joint called Blue's. She said a guy was leaving, just as she came on duty last night. From her description, I'm positive it was Jimmy. She said he looked like a walking ghost, and he'd apparently dropped $1,000 just before she got there. He went nuts and wanted to flip a coin for the $1,000, double or nothing. The other guy refused, and Jimmy offered to put up $1,500 against $1,000. Crazy bet, giving weight on a coin flip. Sounds like Jimmy, though. The other guy took him up on it, and Jimmy lost the flip. Barmaid said Jimmy was barely able to cover the bet."

"He's lost it all," Sedonia said, dejected. "And I-10 East will take him back to New Orleans."

"Better call the cops."

"Brad will have to do that," she replied in a monotone. "It's his account. I'll have to let him know . . ."

"I'm sorry, kid," Buster said. "I wish I could help you out. I could stake you to some pool matches, but we'd never be able to run it up to $20,000 by Monday morning."

"I appreciate your trying to find Jimmy for me," she said. "I'll talk to you later."

"Wait a minute!" Buster said. "You gonna be all right?"

"I gotta go, Buster. Thanks again." She hung up.

She dialed Brad's number, hoping he wasn't available. He was. She forced herself to maintain a matter-of-fact tone as she briefly recounted what had happened to his account.

After she finished, there was a pause, then Brad said, "I don't understand how this guy got access to my account, and how he managed to transfer the funds."

"I kept that slip of paper with the password under my mouse pad. He must have found it. And he used to work in a bank. He must have a personal account he can transfer funds in and out of, when he's on the road."

"*Who* did you say this guy was?"

Sedonia took a deep breath. "He was . . . someone I play pool with. He was covering the office for me, while Raul was out."

"Is this also the guy you told me you were seeing?"

"Well, yes, but—"

"You told me the other day that Raul's nephew was going to be covering for him. Why didn't you let the nephew take care of the office?"

For a moment, Sedonia couldn't bring herself to reply. Finally she said, "Raul's nephew is a pool player too."

"Good grief! What kind of business are you running there? A painting service, or a pool hall?"

"Brad, I'm terribly sorry about this. I'll see that you get your money back. I just need time to—"

"Sedonia, first thing Monday morning, I'm going to report this embezzlement to the authorities. And the following Monday, if you haven't made arrangements for full restitution of my $22,000, I'm going to have George Huff take over my projects. And then I plan to have my attorney take action against you and your company."

Sedonia felt overwhelmed, but managed to say, "I understand."

Brad hung up.

An incessant pounding on the front door awoke Sedonia on Sunday morning. Her bedside clock radio read 8:17. She'd struggled with insomnia all night, and the last time she'd looked, it had been after three. Now she dragged herself out of bed, and padded across the bedroom and down the narrow hallway to the front door. Through the peephole, she saw Hannah.

Sedonia opened the door. "What are you doing here?"

"Are you all right?"

Sedonia shook her head. "Not really. C'mon in."

She led Hannah into the kitchen, and said, "Make yourself some coffee. I'll be back in a minute."

She returned a short while later, having pulled on jeans and a T-shirt. Hannah handed her a cup of coffee. "Buster told me Jimmy ripped you off."

"C'mon," Sedonia said, "let's talk on the balcony."

There was no wind, and the bay lay placid. Sedonia watched a solitary rower propel his racing shell past her balcony. She shook her head, and turned to Hannah. "You know, there was a time I used to get up and work out for an hour every morning—stretching, jogging."

Hannah responded with a sympathetic smile, then said. "Buster called me about an hour ago. He said he talked to you last night, and was worried about you. He said you sounded really . . . depressed."

Sedonia studied Hannah's expression. Had she, or Buster, somehow heard about her overdose of pain pills last year? No, probably they were just two concerned friends. Sedonia sighed. "Dad warned me about 'fixer-uppers,' but damn, Hannah, I didn't think Jimmy was a flat-out crook."

"He didn't strike me that way, either. What happened?"

Sedonia recapped the embezzlement, and when she was done, Hannah muttered, "That son of a bitch."

The rower passed in the opposite direction. Sedonia and Hannah watched in silence. When he was out of sight, Hannah turned and said, "What are you going to do?"

Sedonia responded with a resigned shake of her head. "I don't know. Brad's mad, understandably so. He's not only lost $22,000, but there's the other thing too."

"What other thing?"

Sedonia sighed. "I've known since last year that Brad was interested in me. But because of pool, I've . . ."

"Strung him along?"

"Yeah, strung him along. But I wasn't trying to take advantage of him. I was interested too, but playing pool . . . became so important."

"Kid, you've made a mess."

Sedonia responded with a rueful nod.

"Well, I don't have $22,000 to give you, but I had an idea just before I left the house." She picked up her cell phone. "Lemme check my voicemail." She dialed, listened for a moment, and then nodded. She switched off her phone, and said, "That was a friend of mine at the WPBA. I'd left her a message, and she returned my call. They've still got three unfilled qualifier spots in L.A. this week. Just give me the word, and I'll get you entered."

"What are you talking about?"

"The Los Angeles stop on the WPBA tour. You qualified at Big Ernie's, remember?"

Sedonia's eyes widened. "What's the payout?"

"First place is $12,000."

Sedonia shook her head. "Even if I got lucky and won it, that's not enough. I need almost twice that amount."

"I'll stake you to $1,000. I bet Buster will match it. There's lots of gamble around any large tournament—in the practice rooms and in nearby pool halls."

Sedonia's hope rose. "Remember in Las Vegas, when Jimmy told us about a poolroom in some town near Los Angeles?"

Hannah smiled. "Now we're on the same page. The poolroom was Tough Times, in Bellflower. It's well known."

"Hannah this is crazy," Sedonia said with a dismissive shake of her head. "With all that's going on here, I can't just fly to Los Angeles to play pool . . . can I?"

Chapter 18

Sedonia walked down the Southwest Airlines concourse. Hannah had dropped her off at Houston Hobby Airport two hours early. Sedonia had wanted to ensure she'd be able to get through the security check, and also get a good seat for the four-hour, one-stop flight to Los Angeles. The airline clerk had informed her that security regulations required that she check her cue case, rather than carry it on board, so she'd also checked her single suitcase. Locating her luggage at LAX would be a hassle, but at least now she wasn't burdened with carry-on items.

She arrived at her assigned departure gate and discovered two dozen people already scattered throughout the waiting area. Most were reading, a few business types were laboring over laptop computers, and a young couple with backpacks were leaning against each other, dozing.

At the end of an aisle, she found a seat that offered a view of the runways. She settled back in the vinyl and chrome chair, and heaved a sigh. For the first time since learning of Jimmy's embezzlement four days ago, nothing required her immediate attention.

Ahead, lay the unknown. She would be competing against the top women professionals in the world. Plus, between matches, she somehow would need to get matched up, so she could gamble with other top players—men or women. The future of her business depended on it, and the uncertainty brought a pang of anxiety.

Then her thoughts shifted to what she'd left behind, which was equally disturbing. Brad had contacted the Seabrook Police Department on Monday morning, and by mid afternoon they were in Sedonia's office getting a full account of the embezzlement. Raul, who had returned to work that morning, was dismayed at what had taken place during his absence. At the first opportunity, he'd hobbled out of the office to seek refuge at the job site.

Sedonia sighed. What a mess she'd made of things. She'd allowed Jimmy into her life, and he'd betrayed her and placed her business on the brink of ruin. And Brad, who she'd kept at a distance, now was fed up with her and about to file suit.

A gruff male voice interrupted her musing. "Excuse me, miss."

Sedonia was startled, and looked up to see two uniformed airport security officers standing beside her.

The older man held out two claim checks. "Is this your luggage?"

Disconcerted by his stern demeanor, Sedonia checked the numbers against the stubs that the check-in clerk had stapled to her ticket envelope. "Yes."

"Would you come with us please?" the older officer said.

Sedonia stood up. "What for?"

"Come along," he said gruffly, this time taking her by the elbow.

The other passengers watched with interest as the two officers led her out of the waiting area and back up the concourse.

"Where are we going?" Sedonia said.

"Security office," the older officer said.

"What's this about?"

"We want to ask you some questions."

Sedonia's mind raced. The only people who knew she was going to Los Angeles today were Raul, Hannah, and Buster. One of them must have told the authorities. Surely the Seabrook Police hadn't been watching the airport, not for a $22,000 embezzlement. And yesterday, they hadn't told her she couldn't leave town. Damn it! Why hadn't she contacted her father's lawyer!

They arrived at a makeshift office near the carry-on baggage checkpoint, and the officers ushered Sedonia inside. Another officer, a young woman, and a middle-aged woman in business attire were waiting. On a table lay Sedonia's small suitcase and her cue case.

"I'm the airport manager," the older woman said. "Is this your luggage?"

"Yes, it is," Sedonia said, then scanned the faces directed toward her. What was going on here?

"Open it, please," the airport manager said.

Sedonia stepped over and grasped the zipper on her suitcase. She frowned. What were they looking for? She just had regular travel items inside.

"The other one," the gruff officer said.

"It's just a cue stick," Sedonia said. Surely they'd seen players traveling with cue cases before. She reached over and started to unzip the top of the case, so she could withdraw her stick.

"That compartment down at the other end," the officer barked.

"I don't use that pocket—," Sedonia began, then thought, *Oh no!* She turned to the officer. "Listen, that was given to me as a joke."

"Open the compartment," he demanded.

Sedonia felt blood surge to her face as she opened the utility pocket and withdrew the box that contained the Silver Bullet vibrator she'd been awarded at the Montrose District tournament.

The young woman officer burst into laughter, and the other three turned to her. She walked over and whispered into the older woman's ear. The airport manager frowned, then cupped her hand over her mouth to suppress a laugh. She turned to Sedonia. "Thank you, miss. That will be all. This . . . object showed up on our X-ray equipment, and these men didn't know what it was."

"That was a gag gift. I forgot I put it in there."

"That will be all, miss," the airport manager said again, obviously struggling to keep a straight face.

Sedonia exited the office, and as she headed back down the concourse, she disposed of the vibrator in the first trash receptacle she passed. She was still red-faced when she arrived back in the waiting area. At least twice as many people were there now, and her seat by the window had been taken. Several people, who had seen her escorted out, now looked at her with curious expressions. She found a seat across from the young couple who were still dozing. She couldn't stop blushing.

Sedonia stood in front of the Best Western Hotel, waiting for her cab. Afternoon rush-hour traffic jammed Century Boulevard, and off to her right, the 405 Freeway moved at a crawl. Overhead, a procession of jets lumbered in and out of LAX. A storm in the northwest had disrupted schedules, and air traffic was bottlenecked throughout Southern California. Earlier this afternoon, Sedonia's flight had circled for almost two hours before getting clearance to land.

She shifted her cue case from one shoulder to the other. Due to arrival delays, the tournament director had left messages at the players' hotels that this evening's pre-tournament meeting was being postponed until 9:00 tomorrow morning. That left this evening free for Sedonia to get matched up at Tough Times. She'd accompanied Emilio and Jimmy on forays into icehouses, taverns, and poolrooms, and she'd seen a number of road players pass through Buster's, but would she be able to hustle pool herself?

A Yellow Cab pulled up, and she climbed inside.

"Where are you going?" the driver said. From his appearance and accent, she surmised he was an Arab.

"Hollywood Park Casino first," Sedonia said. "I just want to drive by, so I can see where it is. Then take me to Bellflower. Do you know where Tough Times Billiards is?"

The driver responded with a curt nod. Then, as if to discourage further conversation, he switched on a cassette player that was strapped to the dashboard. The music, discordant to Sedonia's ear, confirmed his nationality.

On her earlier cab ride from the airport, the one-mile stretch of Century Boulevard between LAX and her motel had featured modern, medium-rise office buildings. On this stretch of Century, however, aging one- and two-story buildings, housing small businesses, lined both sides of the street. An unkempt neighborhood was visible down the side streets.

A mile or so from her motel, they approached Hollywood Park Race Track. In a corner of the expansive parking area stood the Hollywood Park Casino, which reminded Sedonia of the older gambling establishments in Las Vegas. Announcements scrolled across a gaudy electronic billboard, touting blackjack and poker specials. There didn't seem to be anything "Hollywood" about this racetrack and casino complex. Any original glamour had long since faded.

They stopped at a red light and the driver turned and gave her an inquiring look.

"Okay," she said. "Let's go to Bellflower."

The traffic jam on the 405 Freeway delayed them for half an hour, but then California 91 East moved more quickly. As they exited the freeway and started down Bellflower's main street, the passing scene reminded Sedonia of the refinery town of Deer Park. The architecture of these surrounding two- and three-bedroom houses was slightly different—California stucco versus Texas wood-frame—but this town had the same middle-age feel. And the founding fathers of each had given their blue-collar communities poignant and inappropriate names.

The driver pulled into the parking lot of the two-story building that housed Tough Times Billiards. Sedonia paid the $32 fare and tipped him $5. He pulled away without a reply. As Sedonia walked toward the entrance, she regretted having not rented a car at LAX. She'd thought she'd be able to walk from her motel to the Hollywood Park Casino, but after viewing the neighborhood, she realized she couldn't. She also hadn't anticipated it would be such a long drive to Tough Times. By the time she got back to the motel tonight, she would have spent almost $100 on cab fare. Damn it. She needed to make money here, not find ways to waste it.

Sedonia entered the poolroom. A swarthy man in his thirties, who weighed perhaps 300 pounds and looked like a sumo wrestler, sat perched on a stool. He nodded to Sedonia as she passed, and she responded with a hesitant smile. A 6' x 12' snooker table stood off to her left. Four men interrupted their game to watch her walk by. She paused to get her bearings.

Thirty or more tables filled the room, but only a few were occupied. On the far right, there appeared to be a smaller room behind a dividing wall.

Sedonia checked her watch: 6:30. If gamblers here were like those at Buster's, they probably wouldn't arrive for a couple of hours. Good. That would give her a chance to practice and get comfortable in the strange surroundings.

"You lost?" said a husky voice behind her.

Sedonia turned. The man who had been sitting by the door lumbered up. "Uh . . . yeah," she said. "This is the first time I've been here. Who do I see about getting a table?"

"Pick any one you want," he said. "I'll bring you the balls."

The man had a slight accent she didn't recognize; it wasn't Spanish. She looked around again. The tables were all Brunswick Gold Crowns and in fair condition. She walked over to the closest one and waited for him to return.

He came back with a tray of balls and said, "You here to gamble?"

"Uh . . . yeah."

"How much do you play for?"

Sedonia hesitated, wishing she'd paid more attention to Buster's and Jimmy's pre-match negotiations. She always relied on their handling that. She had ten $100 bills folded in each hip pocket. Hannah and Buster had each staked her to $1,000. "Uh . . . I don't know," she said. "I mean, I'm new here, and I don't know anybody's . . . speed. Maybe, $100 a game . . . err, set?"

He smiled. "Which is it? A game, or a set?"

"Set."

He handed her the tray of balls. "Take that table in the corner. I'll match you up when the regulars get here."

"Thanks."

With a smile, he turned and walked back to his post near the door, and Sedonia headed for the back of the room.

The corner table had cushioned stools lining two sides, probably to accommodate railbirds. As Sedonia screwed her stick together, she realized she hadn't asked what the hourly pool rate was. But, it didn't matter. Whatever it was, she'd have to pay it. In Buster's parlance, she wasn't here to "play" people, she was here to "rob" them.

A few minutes later, she was focused on her usual practice routine, when a reedy voice interrupted her. "What's your game?" A thin young man in baggy jeans and a faded flannel shirt had walked up.

"Nine-ball."

"Race-to-5 for $20 a set?"

Sedonia pulled a coin from her jeans. "Call it."

* * *

Her opponent counted out four $20 bills and dropped them on the table. He'd gone double or nothing in the last two race-to-5 sets, and now was down $160. Sedonia had dumped a couple of games in each set, to keep him hopeful of winning and to avoid showing her speed to the railbirds who'd gathered during the session.

Her opponent unscrewed his stick, and Sedonia said, "Let's go again. I'll give you the 8-ball, wild."

He inserted his cue stick into its case. "I'm busted."

The half-dozen railbirds settled their side bets. Sedonia guessed that those backing her probably had made more money than she had. That was a disadvantage of not having someone like Jimmy with her, handling side action.

The man who had assigned Sedonia the table had watched the final set. Now he walked over and said, "You wanna gamble some more?"

"Yeah," Sedonia replied, "but can you match me up for higher stakes?" A three-quarter speed break had been enough to win her first session, and her shoulder felt fine. Now she needed to raise the ante.

"Bring your stuff," he said, gesturing with a quick jerk of his head that she should follow him. He started toward the front of the room.

Sedonia grabbed her stick and cue case and caught up with him. "Do I need to pay for my table time?"

"It's covered," he said.

They crossed the room, weaving through the dozens of tables. Games now were in progress on all of them, and Sedonia and her escort frequently had to pause, so as not to disturb a shooter.

At the front of the room, they stopped at the dividing partition she'd noticed when she'd first arrived. A smaller room lay before her, with a dozen pristine Brunswick Gold Crowns, each with new Simonis cloth. Custom bleachers lined the partition wall. Only one table was occupied. In the far corner, a young woman was nonchalantly hitting balls, while bantering with a dozen spectators who were seated in the bleachers. Holding court as she was, she reminded Sedonia of a female Jimmy. The railbirds from Sedonia's earlier match filed past and joined the other spectators.

"This is the tournament room," her escort said. "Best players play here. You want me to match you up?"

Sedonia smiled. That was exactly what she wanted. "Will I be playing her?"

He nodded. "Her name's Bonnie. She's the SCWBT champ. She'll be playing in the WPBA tournament tomorrow in L.A."

"What's SCWBT?"

"Southern California Women's Billiard Tour. Bonnie plays out of this poolroom."

Sedonia surmised the SCWBT must be the local equivalent of the Hunter Classics Tour, so this woman must be strong. Plus, she was playing in her home poolroom.

"Match me up." Sedonia said. Then as they started toward the back of the room, she asked, "What's your name?"

"Rami."

"Rami," Sedonia repeated. "Good name. I haven't heard it before."

"I am Samoan."

"My name is Sedonia."

Rami smiled. "Sedonia is a good name too."

Bonnie stopped shooting and leaned on the table, watching Sedonia approach. Bonnie was thirty or so, attractive, with a hard edge. She looked as if she'd grown up in poolrooms. With a tight smile that bordered on a sneer, she said, "These guys tell me you've been kickin' ass next-door."

Sedonia withdrew her cue stick, and slid her case under the table for safekeeping. With a tight smile of her own, she said, "Do you play Nine-Ball?"

Less than two hours later, Bonnie unscrewed her stick. She'd dropped three $200 sets, and her jaw was clenched. Sedonia didn't risk trying to coax another set out of her. In the first, Sedonia had been cautious and had won, 5 to 4. In the second, she had to dump two games to keep the scores reasonably close, 5 to 3. Then in the final set, Bonnie's game unraveled. Sedonia dumped two games, but the score wound up 5 to 2. And again, Sedonia had been able to avoid risking her shoulder with a full-force break.

Now, with forced nonchalance, Bonnie said she had to leave early to rest up for the WPBA tournament in the morning. She disappeared around the partition.

Sedonia looked over at the spectators. All were men. Four were speaking among themselves in what Sedonia thought she recognized as Filipino.

"Hey, Florante," Rami called out. "You gonna play tonight?"

One of the Filipinos pulled himself away from their conversation, and said to Sedonia, "Race-to-9. One thousand dollars?"

"What weight will you give me?"

"No weight," Florante said. "You too strong!"

His smirk conveyed that he wasn't actually concerned that she was too strong. "I need some weight," she said. "You've seen me play, but I haven't seen you."

He responded with a mirthless laugh. "I see you play, yes. But I no see your best game."

Sedona hesitated. He'd probably recognized that she'd dumped games during her last match. "I gotta have the 8-ball, wild," she insisted.

He shook his head, then turned his back on her and resumed talking in Filipino to his friends, as if to indicate the negotiations were closed. Sedonia had seen road players behave similarly. Often it was just a ploy. She checked her watch; it was a little past midnight. These guys probably would play all night, while she had to be at the Hollywood Park Casino in less than nine hours. She needed to win a quick set, and then get out.

"Race-to-9 for $2,000," she said, doubling the bet. "But I get the 8-ball, wild."

Momentarily, Florante seemed interested, but then smiled and shook his head again. "Two thousand, okay. But no weight."

Sedonia pulled her cue case from under the table, and unscrewed her stick. She said to Rami, "Could you call me a cab? I'm in that WPBA tournament too." She was bluffing that she was leaving. If Florante didn't offer her weight by the time she reached the end of the partition, she planned to turn around and play the match with no weight. She slung her cue case over her shoulder and started toward the front of the room.

"I give you the eight," Florante said, "but not wild."

"Eight and alternate breaks," Sedonia said. Alternate breaks would ensure this guy didn't take off on a long game run, as Lito had done in their first set at Parker's.

Florante opened his cue case and withdrew his stick.

Sedonia pocketed the game-winning 8-ball, putting her ahead, 7 to 3 in the race-to-9. She pulled up her stool, and checked her watch: 1:37. This match was dragging on longer than she wanted; the WPBA player meeting was a little more than seven hours away.

Florante was strong, but after overcoming early jitters, Sedonia now experienced the familiar feeling of being in control of the match. She was over-hitting balls at times, not allowing for the fast roll on the new Simonis cloth, but she was playing smart and leaving Florante with poor shots whenever she had to relinquish the table. For the past few games, Florante had griped about having given her weight. Sedonia just smiled, knowing he already was negotiating for no weight in the next set.

Rami racked for the eleventh game. Sedonia had discovered that racking was a service he provided for both competitors in high stakes games. Sedonia was sure it saved a lot of arguments. Not only was he neutral, but she couldn't imagine anyone would take the huge man to task for a loose rack.

Florante assumed his stance to break, then abruptly straightened. An unassuming looking man, mid thirties and also apparently Filipino, had entered the room and was walking toward them. Florante and most of the railbirds seemed to acknowledge this new arrival with deference. Even Rami responded with a smile and polite nod. Sedonia felt she'd seen the man before, but couldn't remember where or when.

She yawned; it was 3:37, Nassau Bay time. The sharp *crack!* of Florante's break returned her attention to the table. Balls flew about the table, but nothing fell. Sedonia sprang from her chair. She needed to get out, and get going. She ran the rack, making the score 8 to 3. Then she broke-and-ran the final rack to win the set.

"Next set, *you* give *me* weight," Florante demanded as the 8-ball disappeared into the side pocket.

Sedonia shook her head and pulled her cue case from underneath the table. "I gotta go," she said as she unscrewed her stick.

"You can't quit me now," Florante cried. "Not after one set!"

Sedonia ignored his tirade. She needed to get back to her motel. Rami was holding the stakes. Sedonia slung her cue case over her shoulder and walked over to where he was talking to the late arrival. "I need to go, Rami," she said.

Rami handed her $4,000 in one-hundred dollar bills. Then he said, "Victor would like to play you now. Five thousand dollar sets. We have another room upstairs."

Sedonia swallowed. Five thousand dollar sets! She'd won almost $3,000, and still had the $2,000 she'd come in with. "Maybe some other time," she told the new arrival. "I've got a tournament in less than seven hours."

The Filipino responded with a curt nod, then turned and resumed his conversation with his companions.

Sedonia asked Rami, "Can I get you to call me a cab?"

"Sure," he said. "Let's go."

They left the tournament room, and then passed through the main room. Although it was after 2:00, more than half of the tables still were occupied. Rami paused at a service counter and placed a call for Sedonia's cab, then escorted her outside.

The night air hit Sedonia like a splash of cold water. Temperature and humidity both felt as if they were in the 50s—such a difference from a summer night on the Texas Gulf Coast. Rami didn't go back inside. Apparently he planned to ensure she had no problem getting on her way. She was glad; she'd had bad experiences in poolroom parking lots. She looked around. Bellflower Boulevard was deserted in both directions.

"Oh," she said suddenly. "I never paid for my pool time."

"It's covered when you gamble in the tournament room, or upstairs."

"Well, thanks. By the way, who was that guy back there? The one who came in late?"

Rami frowned, as if not sure she was serious, then said, "Victor Morella."

"*That's* where I've seen him. *Billiards Digest.*"

Rami nodded. "He is the No. 1 player in the world."

"And he plays here?"

"All the time. He goes back to the Philippine Islands a lot, but when he's in the States, this is his home poolroom."

"And he wanted to play me?" she said in disbelief.

"You got a sweet stroke," Rami said with a smile. "Do you shoot that good all the time, or did you just have a good night?"

"That's . . . pretty much my game," she said. Actually, she knew she'd played better at times.

"That guy you just robbed back there," Rami said, "most people put him in the top twenty."

Sedonia was surprised, but she knew better than to judge relative ability on just one match. Car lights down the street drew her attention. She suspected it was her cab, and turned to Rami. "I appreciate your looking after me this evening. I'm not . . . that experienced in . . . gambling."

"Hustling," he corrected with a smile. "You did good. Call me after your tournament, and I'll see if I can match you up with Victor. I want to see how you do against him."

Sedonia nodded, then said, "It seems like a lot of strong players come from the Philippines."

Rami seemed to study her comment for a moment, then said, "Probably, because it is a very poor country. Filipinos learn to play, and to gamble, very early. And when they gamble, they're usually gambling for everything they have."

The cab pulled up to the curb, and Sedonia extended her hand. "Thanks again, Rami."

"Call me when you want to play again," he said as he enveloped her hand in his own, surprisingly soft grip. Then he handed her a business card that advertised the poolroom.

As the cab pulled away, she was still thinking about what Rami had said about Filipino players gambling for everything they had. She knew what that was like.

Chapter 19

Sedonia stood at the doorway of the Best Western shuttle as it pulled up in front of the Hollywood Park Casino. She impatiently checked her watch: 9:08. The player meeting would already have started. The door opened, and she jumped down and hurried toward the casino entrance. The glass door opened automatically. She entered the high-ceilinged, expansive room and looked around for some indication where to go. She spotted a uniformed security guard.

"Can you tell me where the pool tournament is?"

He smiled. "All the way to the back of the casino, and up the escalator."

At that moment, three women walked past, carrying cue cases and heading in the direction the guard had indicated. Sedonia fell in behind them, relieved that she wasn't the only one who was running late this morning.

Dozens of green-felted card tables lay off to the right. Most were unoccupied at this hour of the morning. She passed a lounge on her left that featured TV sets and tote boards. Apparently, later in the day this area would offer pari-mutuel betting on horse races. The lounge was deserted now, though.

She arrived at the escalator, feeling over-dressed. The three players in front of her wore jeans. While selecting her clothes that morning, Sedonia had considered casual khakis, but then remembering the semiformal attire that professional players wore during their TV matches, she'd settled instead on navy blue slacks.

As the escalator arrived at the mezzanine, she told herself to quit worrying about clothes. She was here; that was what mattered. She took a couple of steps off the elevator, and then froze. Dozens of players with cue cases were milling about, but most were *men*! In front of her, several players were talking to three people stationed behind a long counter. A young Asian woman was available, and Sedonia hurried over. "Is this where you check in for the pool tournament?"

"Yes, it is," the woman said with a smile. "Are you playing singles or team?"

"Team? I didn't know they had teams?"

"Are you APA?"

"APA?" Sedonia said, confused. "I don't know what that is."

"You're not a member of APA?"

"I just told you," Sedonia said, growing flustered, "I don't know what APA is! Isn't this where the WPBA tournament is being held?"

"Oh, I'm sorry," the woman said. "There are two tournaments here this week. This is check-in for APA—the American Pool Association. It's an amateur league. The WPBA pros are here too. Just pass through the APA area on my left, and then go all the way back." She checked her watch. "I think they were supposed to be meeting at 9:00. You're late."

"I know," Sedonia said in a worried tone. "My shuttle was late." She hurried through the open doorway the woman had indicated. Forty or fifty bar-boxes filled a large exhibition hall; men and women were practicing on most. She quickly crossed the room, and as she passed under the Exit sign, she glanced down at her watch: 9:14. Since she'd been a late addition to the tournament, she was afraid she might have to forfeit her place for not arriving on time. Surely she hadn't come all this way for nothing!

She entered a long, narrow pavilion. Six unoccupied pool tables stood side by side in front of her, surrounded by empty spectator bleachers. At the other end of the room, a neatly-dressed, gray-haired man was standing on a chair, looking down at dozens of women gathered in a semicircle in front of him.

Sedonia started toward the group, but a young woman with a clipboard intercepted her. "Name?"

"Sedonia Forbes."

The woman scanned a list. "I don't see you here. Were you a late entry?"

"Yes. A friend registered me on Sunday. I'm the regional qualifier from the Hunter Classics in Texas."

The woman checked her list again. "You're not on this list."

"*Somebody* must know about me," Sedonia said, desperation in her tone. "They left a message for me yesterday at my hotel, about the players' meeting being postponed until this morning."

The woman rechecked her list, and shook her head. She looked distracted. "With the flight delays and all, it's been confusing. Have you paid your $500 entry fee?"

"No," Sedonia said.

"Since you're late, it'll have to be in cash.

Sedonia peeled off five of the $100 bills she'd won at Tough Times the night before, and handed them to the woman.

"Sorry for the confusion," the woman said. She went over to a 4' x 8' bulletin board and made an entry on a large tournament bracket sheet.

Sedonia heaved a sigh of relief. This was the place. She was on the board. Now, if she could just stop perspiring.

The man raised his arms and said, "Okay, ladies, lets get started." He introduced himself as the WPBA tournament director, and then said, "A number of players, particularly those coming from the east, still haven't arrived. Those of you who came through LAX understand the problem. But we're going to go ahead and start the tournament with those of you who are here. You'll match up with the same people you were scheduled to play, but your start times will probably be different. Look over the board and see if you have any questions. If not, those of you who have matches scheduled for 10:00, report to your tables right now."

Sedonia and the others studied the board behind him, which displayed the 32 pairings of 64 players. The chart was divided into four brackets, labeled A, B, C, and D. Sedonia found her name at the bottom of bracket A. Her match would be on table No. 6 at 10:00, and she'd be playing someone named Brandi White. The name sounded familiar. Sedonia reached into her pocket and pulled out the page from *Billiards Digest Magazine* that showed the ranking of WPBA players. Brandi was listed at No. 14.

Sedonia scanned the rest of the players in bracket A. She winced, and then winced again. The name at the top was Margaret Faulkson, the No. 1 ranked woman player in the world. And several names below hers she saw Audri Krump, the woman who had defeated her for the Hunter Classics championship. Sedonia shook her head. She'd come here needing to win this tournament, but now she wondered if she'd even survive bracket A.

Trying to push defeatist thoughts from her mind, she checked the rest of the tournament pairings. The Top-20 professionals had been distributed evenly throughout the list of 64 names, so they wouldn't knock each other out of the tournament in the first few rounds. Five of the Top-20 professionals were seeded in each of the four brackets. The two women who had so impressed Sedonia in Las Vegas, Jeanette Lee and Ewa Laurance, were brackets B and D. Also, perennial favorites, Allison Fisher and Karen Corr, were in brackets C and D. Sedonia heaved a sigh. It probably wouldn't have made any difference which bracket she'd been assigned. The players in each were strong.

Sedonia settled back in her chair, while her first opponent, Brandi White, shot a final rack of practice balls. Sedonia had shot for five minutes to get a feel for the 9-foot Diamond Pro. She'd verified she was still in stroke, as she'd been just seven hours earlier at Tough Times. Then she'd relinquished the table, not wanting to put unnecessary wear on her temperamental shoulder.

Name placards hung from a wire above the tables and indicated the pairings. A placard on the next table read "Audri Krump." Audri's first opponent was warming up, but so far there was no sign of Audri.

Sedonia turned her attention back to Brandi. She was perhaps forty, and displayed a short, efficient stroke as she worked her way around the table. They had chatted briefly, and Brandi had mentioned she was a twelve-year veteran on the WPBA tour.

Movement at the next table drew Sedonia's attention. Audri swaggered up. She uncased her stick, screwed it together, and told her opponent she wanted to hit some balls. The other woman frowned at the gruff request, which had sounded more like a demand, but then nodded and relinquished the table.

"Hello, Audri," Sedonia called over.

Audri acted as if she didn't hear. Sedonia suspected she already was in intimidation mode. Sedonia had seen men players, like Jimmy, use it on each other. Audri had used it successfully against her at the Hunter Classics tournament.

Sedonia turned away, trying to block out her mounting pre-match jitters, and looked about the pavilion. The bleachers were less than half filled, probably because of the hour. Most of the spectators were men, and many had cue cases slung over their shoulders. Apparently they were competitors from the APA tournament next door. Sitting at the top of the bleachers by himself, Sedonia spotted Cannonball. He appeared bored with the proceedings.

"Okay, ladies!" announced the tournament director. "It's time to . . . rack and roll!"

His enthusiasm was greeted by a polite smattering of applause from the spectators. Starting with table No. 1, he began introducing the twelve competitors for the first six matches. The marquee players were conspicuously absent in this opening session. Sedonia suspected they were being saved for later in the day, when there would be a larger crowd.

As the director announced the players, Sedonia studied how the touring professionals acknowledged their introductions. Most responded with etiquette similar to that used in golf tournaments. However, when Audri was announced, she half rose, and then dropped back into her chair, as if these formalities were an annoyance.

Sedonia was the last player introduced. "And on table No. 6," the director said, "from Nassau Bay, Texas . . . representing the Hunter Classics regional tour . . . playing in her first WPBA event . . . Sedonia Forbes!"

Sedonia's pulse accelerated. The last time she'd been formally introduced for a contest had been before teeing off for her final golf tournament. Now, she stood, took a step forward, and acknowledged the ripple of applause with a quick wave. Then as she turned, someone emitted a loud wolf whistle, and several copycats followed suit. Sedonia sat back down, irked by the nature of the acclaim.

"Ready to lag?" Brandi said.

Sedonia jumped up and joined Brandi at the break end of the table. She'd forgotten that in WPBA tournaments, the players lagged for the first break, rather than flipping a coin. The lag called for the competitors to simultaneously each shoot a ball the length of the table and kick it off the far end rail. The object was to see who could come closest to the near rail on the return trip. Brandi's ball came within an inch of the rail; Sedonia's stopped almost a foot away.

As Sedonia walked to the other end of the table to rack the balls, she made a mental note to practice lagging at the first opportunity. Underneath the table, instead of the usual wooden triangle, she found a bulky metal and plastic device known as a Sardo Tight Rack. She turned to Brandi and said apologetically, "I've seen these on TV, but I don't have any idea how to operate one."

The amiable professional came over and showed her how to align the device on the table, roll the balls into it in the correct order, and then push down on the two handles that pressed the balls into position. Brandi straightened up. "A perfect rack, every time," Brandi said, mimicking the Sardo Tight Rack television commercial.

"Thanks," Sedonia said, and returned to her chair. She noticed a large number of spectators, primarily men, had changed bleacher seats so they could watch her match. Several more were on the way. As Brandi chalked her cue, Sedonia heaved a sigh. She'd gotten off to an inauspicious start this morning. First, she'd arrived late. Then she'd discovered her nemesis, Krump, and the No. 1 player in the world, Faulkson, were in her bracket. Now she'd found she didn't know how to lag, or even how to rack. And a growing number of spectators were looking at her as if they were dogs, and she was a hamburger.

Brandi opened first game of the match with a soft break. Sedonia's eyes widened as the yellow 1-ball rolled slowly into the side pocket. The significance of "a perfect rack, every time" hit her. Brandi had broken with only half speed, yet she'd made a ball, the others had spread out reasonably well, and the cue-ball had come to rest in the middle of the table. If Sedonia could master that break, she might be able to protect her balky shoulder throughout the tournament.

Brandi made three more balls, then missed a thin side-pocket cut on the orange 5-ball. Sedonia stood up, sprinkled some talcum powder on her bridge hand, and walked over to the table. The 5-ball was in front of the side pocket, and the other four balls presented no problems. Yet she hesitated, marshalling her thoughts. She'd be playing against pros here, but she reminded herself that the last pro she'd faced, at Duke's Billiards in Houston, she'd beaten, 9 to 0. And just seven hours ago, she'd similarly "robbed" a Top-20 male player. A Filipino, no less. With the trace of a smile, Sedonia leaned over the table for her first shot. These other women might be here to play. She was here to win.

An hour later, Sedonia pocketed the gold-striped 9-ball to close out the match, 9 to 3, and the crowd responded with an enthusiastic round of applause and whistles.

Brandi came over and shook hands. "Good match," she said. "You play very well."

"Thanks," Sedonia said. "Good luck the rest of the way."

Sedonia felt self-conscious as the tournament director announced her victory over the public address system. She unscrewed her stick, feeling as if all eyes in the pavilion were on her. As she opened her cue case, she heard the announcement that Audri Krump had won on table No. 5.

"Audri and Sedonia," the director continued, "don't go anyplace. You're up on table No. 2. Right now."

There was general shuffling of feet through the bleachers, as most of the spectators who had watched Sedonia's match on table No. 6, now moved down to table No. 2. Sedonia fell in behind Audri's odd rolling gait.

When they arrived, the director met them and said, "You've got time to shoot one warm-up rack each."

Audri took over the table, as if it were her due. Sedonia took a deep breath, pulled up a chair, and vowed not to let Audri's sharking get to her. Audri spread the balls out on the table and began pocketing them in Nine-Ball order. Her technique was as awkward as Sedonia remembered from the Hunter Classics tournament, but she ran all nine balls without missing. Sedonia got to her feet and walked over to the table.

"I'm not done yet," Audri growled.

"One warm-up rack, each. That's what the man said."

Audri glowered, then bumped shoulders with her as she lumbered past. She pulled up a chair and fixed Sedonia in a menacing gaze. Sedonia's hand shook slightly as she pulled the balls from the pockets and spread them across the table. She lined up on the yellow 1-ball, and miscued.

She took a deep breath and chalked her cue. Buster had cautioned her long ago about players wanting to instill fear in their opponents. Sedonia leaned over and lined up on the 1-ball again. *One, two, three . . . stroke.*

It rolled into the center of the corner pocket. She worked her way around the table, driving balls into the pockets, and fear from her mind.

Sedonia was on-the-hill, 8 to 2. During the first part of the match, Audri had employed her arsenal of sharking tactics—talking to spectators, not remaining seated while Sedonia was shooting, arguing over nonexistent issues, calling for tournament director rulings, and muttering and beseeching the pool gods while she lumbered around the table.

But Sedonia had seen it all before, much of it employed by Jimmy. The Sardo Tight Rack prevented Audri from manipulating Sedonia's breaks, as she had in the Hunter Classics tournament. And an honest rack was all Sedonia needed. She'd run the last three.

Now, as Audri racked for the eleventh game, she seemed detached, as if she'd already conceded the match. Sedonia felt a pang of sympathy for her as she shambled back to her chair, but then forced the emotion from her mind. She placed the cue-ball near the right rail, and executed the half-speed break she was trying to develop. The yellow 1-ball rolled slowly into the side pocket, and the others fanned out across one end of the table. The cue-ball was in good position on the blue 2-ball. *One, two, three . . . stroke.*

A few minutes later, Sedonia drew a ripple of applause as she made the 8-ball in the side and left herself in perfect position for the potential game winning shot. Then as the 9-ball dropped, the crowd erupted with cheers and whistles.

Audri stood up and snarled, "Didn't take you long to become a crowd favorite." She unscrewed her stick without offering Sedonia the customary handshake.

The tournament director hurried up, as if he sensed the antagonism between the two players, or perhaps he'd seen Audri's behavior before. Sedonia was standing between them as he raised his microphone. "Okay, ladies and gentlemen," he said. "We have our first winner of two matches. And she's a regional tour qualifier. Sedonia Forbes!"

Most of the spectators had watched Sedonia's match, and they gave her another enthusiastic ovation. Sedonia responded with a smile and a quick wave. When the crowd quieted, someone let loose with a loud wolf whistle, followed by another round of copycat whistles.

Sedonia's smile faded and she lowered her head. She'd worked too hard to have her victory cheapened in this manner. "Damn it," she said softly.

Audri cleared her throat, and said in an aside, "Don't let them harddicks get to ya."

Sedonia turned and looked at her. Had Audri really said that?

A trace of a smile momentarily broke Audri's hard features. "You got game," she said, "as well as looks."

Before the stunned Sedonia could reply, Audri's smile vanished. She turned, grabbed her cue case, and shambled out of the playing area. Standing in a passageway between the bleachers, Cannonball was waiting.

Sedonia arrived back at her hotel room at 3:20 that afternoon. She laid her cue case on the credenza, kicked off her flats, and stretched out on the king-size bed. She was exhausted. She'd even dozed off a couple of times during the 15-minute shuttle ride from the casino. She'd had four hours sleep last night, and had been on her feet most of today.

Now she stretched and felt a slight ache in her right shoulder. Not surprising. Since this time yesterday, between Tough Times Billiards and the Hollywood Park Casino, she'd played something like 100 games of Nine-Ball. But at least here in the tournament, with the Sardo Tight Rack, she didn't have to break hard.

She yawned, and risked closing her eyes. She had another match at 10:00 p.m. Just before she'd left the casino, the tournament director had made an announcement that the skies had cleared in the northwest, and air traffic was returning to normal at LAX. He promised that by tomorrow morning, the remainder of the players would have arrived and tournament would get back on schedule.

Sedonia dozed for a moment, and the telephone rang. She reluctantly sat up and answered it. Raul was checking in for the evening. She'd left her cell phone with him, and he was calling from his van. She had trouble hearing him over the road noise.

"Mr. Landry comes by in the morning and in the afternoon," he said. "And today he had Mr. Huff with him."

"That vulture," Sedonia muttered.

"What?"

"Nothing, Raul. Just keep working, as if they're not there. Brad gave me until Monday. Can you get volunteers to work on Saturday?"

"Do we have money to pay them?"

"Enough to cover this week, including Saturday," she said. "I know this is tough on everyone. Just . . . do the best you can. That's what I'm doing here."

"Is everything . . . going okay there?"

"Too early to tell, Raul. Listen, I'm having trouble hearing you. I'll call you tomorrow."

After they hung up, Sedonia lay back again and took stock of her financial situation. She had barely enough money in the bank to meet this week's payroll, and she'd won enough at Tough Times to pay back the

$2,000 Hannah and Buster had advanced her. She had enough additional cash on hand to cover her expenses here during the week, and she had a plane ticket home. But, she owed Brad $22,000. In simplest terms, for the next four days, at the tournament and later at Tough Times, she'd be playing to save her company and the jobs of her employees. Pretty simple. Like hell it was.

Sedonia reentered the pavilion, cue case slung over one shoulder. After a four-hour nap, an hour of stretching and stationary bike riding in the hotel fitness center, a shower, and dinner at a nearby Carl's Jr. Restaurant, she felt healthy for the first time since arriving in Los Angeles.

The 8:00 p.m. matches were still in progress on all six tables, and the bleachers were almost full. Most spectators were watching the match on table No. 1, between the top-ranked Margaret Faulkson and a young regional qualifier.

Sedonia had half an hour before her next match, and she looked around for a spot to watch Margaret play. On the top row of bleacher seats, she spotted Audri and Cannonball. There were a couple of empty seats on the row in front of them. Sedonia headed up the aisle stairs.

She nodded to Audri as she took her seat, then said, "Have you played again?"

"Yeah. It gets real busy on the one-loss side. I beat a regional qualifier from New Jersey. You're up against another qualifier at 10:00. You oughta beat her easy."

Sedonia turned to Cannonball. "My name's Sedonia."

"I know who you are," he said with a chuckle. "You that gal that robbed Lito last week at Parker's. Then Lito robbed that 'French Quarter' boyfriend of yours, big time."

"Jimmy's *not* my boyfriend."

"Not no more, ya mean," he said with a grin. "I heard tell, last night you was robbin' folks at Tough Times, too. What you got against them Filipinos?"

"I love Filipinos," Sedonia said with a laugh. "They've got lots of money." As she turned back to watch the games in progress, she wondered where that burst of bravado had come from. Spending too much time with pool players, she supposed.

The counters on the wire stretched above table No. 1 indicated Margaret was ahead 7 to 1 in the race-to-9. Sedonia had seen her in televised matches, but she was even more impressive in person. Stocky, red-haired, pale-skinned, she moved around the table, a study in concentration. When shooting, she leaned over the table in the manner of British

Snooker players—legs side by side and spread apart, rather than the American style of one behind the other. While her stance seemed awkward, her stroke was smooth and consistent. As she pocketed balls and moved from one rack to the next, she lived up to her nickname, "The Queen of Cue."

Sedonia turned back to Audri. "Have you ever played Margaret?"

"Two years ago. Just before I went to prison."

"How'd you do against her?"

"She killed me. Her reputation got me too tight. You couldn't have stuck a greased needle up my ass."

Sedonia laughed.

"Margaret's strong," Audri said. "You might be able to stay with her, though."

Sedonia turned back to watch the match. A man and a girl, perhaps ten years old, stopped in the aisle beside her. She scooted back to let them pass, but instead the man said, "My daughter's collecting autographs." The little girl shyly extended an autograph book and a pen.

"Well, thanks for asking me," Sedonia said. At the U.S. Women's Amateur Golf Tournament, she'd signed numerous autographs for young girls. Now she was pleased to be signing one for pool. She wrote, "Best wishes. Sedonia Forbes."

When she returned the book, the little girl read what she'd written, and frowned. "What's your other name?" she said.

Sedonia was disappointed, and embarrassed. Apparently the father had confused her with one of the well-known players. "I'm afraid that *is* my name," she said.

"No, I mean your other name," the girl insisted. She flipped back a page and pointed to another autograph: "Jeanette Lee—The Black Widow." Next to it was "Ewa Laurance—The Striking Viking." Sedonia turned another page and saw two more autographs: "Allison Fisher—The Duchess of Doom" and "Karen Corr—The Irish Invader."

"I'm sorry, honey," Sedonia said, "I don't have another name."

"C'mere, kid," Audri snarled.

Sedonia grew concerned as the little girl climbed two stairs, and started down Audri's aisle. Audri took the child by the shoulders, pulled her close, and said something in her ear.

The little girl stepped back, turned, and said to Sedonia, "She says you're the Bay . . . something." She turned back to Audri. "What did you say her name was?"

"Bay Area Bomber. That's what they call her in Texas."

The little girl handed Sedonia the autograph book again. Sedonia took it, hesitated, and then dutifully entered "The Bay Area Bomber" next to her signature. As she handed the book back, she pointed to Audri and told the little girl, "Get that lady's autograph too."

"What's *her* name?" the little girl said.

Sedonia smiled. "The Intimidator."

The escalator carried Sedonia down to the casino. As she stepped off, she checked her watch: 11:20 p.m. Her 9 to 2 win had taken little more than an hour. She was through for the day, but wanted to hang around until the rest of the 10:00 p.m. matches concluded, so she could see who else was still playing on the winners' side, and what time the next day her first match would be.

An open restaurant occupied an area to the left of the escalator. Only two tables had customers. Sedonia walked up, and the hostess told her she could sit wherever she liked. Sedonia picked a vantage point that offered a view of the casino below. She laid her cue case on the table and sat down. She'd learned that California's gambling laws allowed only card playing and pari-mutuel betting. Without noisy slot machines, this casino seemed strangely subdued.

The door to the ladies room opened, and Margaret Faulkson emerged. She stopped at Sedonia's table and said with a pleasant British accent, "How are you doing in the tournament?"

"Still on the winners' side, 3 and 0," Sedonia said, enjoying the opportunity to speak with the billiard celebrity.

A waitress interrupted them, offering Sedonia a menu.

"I'm not eating," Sedonia told the waitress. "I'd just like a Dewar's and water." Then she asked Margaret, "Would you care to join me?"

Margaret smiled as she pulled up a chair. She ordered a gin and tonic, and the waitress left with their order. "I watched the end of your last match," Margaret said. "You're quite good."

"Thanks," Sedonia said, flattered. "How are you doing so far?"

Margaret smiled. "I arrived late, but drew a first-round bye, and they worked me into two matches this evening. So I'm 3 and 0 also, and through until 2:00 tomorrow."

The waitress brought their drinks, and Sedonia insisted on paying. Margaret agreed, as long as the next round was on her.

"How'd you get into pool?" Sedonia said.

Margaret responded with a brief account of growing up in Oxfordshire, England, learning Snooker in local clubs, and going on to win three World Championships in Europe. "Then, my mum died," she concluded, "and I decided to come over here and try my luck at Nine-Ball."

"And now you're the top-ranked WPBA player."

Margaret nodded. "The transition from a 12-foot Snooker table, to a 9 foot Nine-Ball table, was easier than if it had been reversed."

Sedonia smiled, enjoying Margaret's British accent. She pronounced "Snooker" as "Snooooker," and "been" as "bean."

"You've got a beautiful smile, luv," Margaret said.

Sedonia felt self-conscious under the celebrity's scrutiny.

"Tell me about yourself," Margaret said.

Sedonia admitted she'd been playing pool for a relatively short time—league pool, a semipro tournament, and matching up with men players. She didn't mention Jimmy specifically, or the circumstances that had brought her to Los Angeles.

"It's remarkable how much you've learned," Margaret said.

"I've been lucky. I've made friends with people who know the game, and have been willing to coach me."

"And modest too," Margaret said with a smile. "Do you have an equipment sponsor?"

"No," Sedonia said, nodding toward her plain Naugahide cue case.

"I noticed," Margaret said, still smiling and studying her. "You're quite attractive. I might be able to help you promote yourself."

"I'd appreciate that," Sedonia said. She was growing increasingly uncomfortable under Margaret's gaze. She wondered if maintaining eye contact was a British norm. "I noticed your technique is different than we use here."

"My 'technique'?" Margaret said.

"Your . . . stance."

"You mean, the way I sort of . . . thrust out my butt?"

"Yeah," Sedonia said. Every topic of conversation seemed to increase her discomfort.

"Where are you staying?" Margaret said, abruptly changing the subject.

"Best Western, down the street."

"Good Lord," Margaret said. "Best Westerns are so . . . functional." She took her eyes off Sedonia and gazed down at her drink for a moment. Then she raised the glass to her lips and drained it. "I have a suite at the Crowne Plaza," she said, standing up. "It's much more comfortable there. Come along. We can discuss my stance further. I'll instruct you on how we English bend over . . . and all manner of other things."

"Uh . . . no thanks," Sedonia said, now certain that this conversation was too much like the ones she'd had with Miss Mickelson. "I'm tired, and need to rest up for tomorrow."

"You're sure, then?" Margaret said, pique in her tone.

"I'm sure."

"Well, then," Margaret said. "I'll see you tomorrow at 2:00."

"At 2:00?"

Margaret turned, and as she walked away, she looked back over her shoulder and said, "Check the tournament board, luv."

At 1:45 the next afternoon, Sedonia felt tense as she stepped off the casino escalator. Concern over this next match had prevented a good night's sleep, and then she'd had a long morning to kill. She'd worked out in the exercise room, then passed the remainder of time in the Best Western lobby, reading a paperback novel.

Now she crossed the mezzanine and entered the exhibition hall, where the APA amateur tournament was in full swing. She paused to watch for a moment. The scene seemed so familiar. Men and women of all ages occupied the four dozen bar-boxes. Polo shirts and blue jeans were standard attire. The players here displayed the same intensity as those she'd competed against in the rival BCA league. She smiled, remembering how dejected she'd been over her performance in the BCA national tournament in Las Vegas. Yet, here she was. In fifteen minutes, she'd be playing the top woman professional in the world. She took a deep breath, and continued across the room.

Inside the pavilion, two games were still in progress from the noon session. Table No. 1, where she and Margaret were scheduled to play, was unoccupied, but the bleachers surrounding it were full. Sedonia realized the fans weren't here to see her; they were here to see The Queen of Cue.

A railing separated the playing area from the bleachers, and as she passed through an opening that served as the gate, she saw Margaret standing off to one side, talking to a balding young man who was holding a tape recorder.

Sedonia screwed her stick together and walked over to the tournament director. "Okay if I hit some balls?"

"Sure. Margaret's already warmed up. We'll get started as soon as she finishes that interview."

The director and Margaret returned a few minutes later. Warming up had done little to quell Sedonia's pre-match jitters.

"Margaret," the director said, "I'd like you to meet Sedonia Forbes."

Margaret flashed an artificial public relations smile, and extended her hand, neither acknowledging nor denying they'd met before. Sedonia simply nodded as they quickly shook hands. They each mouthed the obligatory, "Good luck."

The director introduced them over the P.A. system. He identified Sedonia as a regional qualifier from Texas, and the spectators responded with polite applause and a couple of wolf whistles. Then he went into a litany of

Margaret's many championships, both in Europe and the United States, which drew an appreciative ovation. "Good luck, ladies!" he concluded.

Margaret won the lag for the first break. Sedonia racked, then took her seat. She massaged her shoulder. It had held up well under the rigors of the past two days, but it had stiffened and become tender during the night. Four Advil tablets now rumbled in a stomach already uneasy with a case of nerves.

Margaret made two balls on the break, and Sedonia sat back, awaiting her first opportunity to get to the table. Margaret ran the rack. Then she also ran the second. In the third game, she ran down to the 6-ball, but failed to get the position she wanted for her next shot. She recovered by executing a perfect safety. Sedonia managed to hit the maroon 7-ball, but had no chance of pocketing it. Margaret finished that rack, and then ran the next two.

Sedonia racked for the sixth game, trailing 5 to 0 in the race-to-9. Margaret had only allowed her to the table once, and that had been for an impossible shot. Sedonia slid the Sardo Tight Rack under the table and headed back to her seat. As she passed the other end of the table, Margaret said in an aside, "You give excellent rack, luv."

Sedonia hesitated and glared back at her, causing a stir among the spectators. Then she returned to her seat. Margaret made three balls on the break, and quickly pocketed three more. Then she turned down a makeable corner shot on the maroon 7-ball, and instead executed a brutal safety.

Sedonia walked up to the table, frustrated. Margaret wanted to humiliate her. Sedonia's only possible shot was to kick off the side rail. She half-heartedly lined up the shot, and put too much topspin on the cue-ball. It flew off the table and bounced across the floor. The tournament director retrieved it, and Sedonia went back to her seat, red-faced.

Margaret returned to the table with ball-in-hand. She made quick work of the remaining balls. Then she ran the next rack. Sedonia watched with clenched teeth. She now trailed, 7 to 0. In pool vernacular, she was being "tortured." She now fully understood the term.

In the eighth game, Margaret appeared to be on her way to another run-out, but then lined up on the gold-striped 9-ball and missed an easy shot in the corner, leaving the game winner wide open for Sedonia. The shot itself, and Margaret's theatric display of disappointment, seemed intended to ensure that the audience knew she'd missed on purpose—that she'd thrown a sop to the overmatched, regional qualifier.

Sedonia barely looked at the 9-ball as she drilled it into the corner pocket. For an instant, it looked as if the cue-ball might follow, but it stayed up, and the score was now 7 to 1.

Margaret racked for the first time. Seething, Sedonia ignored the fact that it was a "perfect rack," and broke with all the force she could muster. A stab of pain shot through her shoulder. Balls scattered, and four found pockets. The last one, unfortunately, was the cue-ball. Margaret returned to the table with ball-in-hand, shaking her head as if sympathetic to Sedonia's plight. Then she ran the remainder of the rack, and the following rack, for a 9 to 1 victory.

"Okay," the director said over the P.A. system, "let's hear it for Sedonia Forbes, playing in her first professional tournament."

The crowd responded with scattered applause, and Sedonia managed to quell her frustration and acknowledge the spectators with a quick wave. Be graceful in defeat, her father had taught her, regardless of how it rips your guts.

Margaret walked over, and again flashed a public relations smile. But as they shook hands, she said under her breath, so only Sedonia could hear, "You've still a lot to learn, luv. Next time, I suggest you not turn down my offer of . . . instructions."

A short while later, Sedonia stood in front of the tournament board and discovered firsthand what Audri had meant when she'd said, "it gets real busy on the one-loss side." Sedonia was scheduled to play again in 45 minutes, on table No. 4, and would be going against the 17th ranked player on the WPBA tour. Since this was double-elimination, one of them would be knocked out of the tournament at the conclusion of this match.

Sedonia studied the board, assessing her chances. In the championship match, two days from now, there would be only one undefeated player; her record would be 6 and 0. She would then play the winner of the one-loss side, whose record would be 8 and 1. Sedonia slowly shook her head. To win the one-loss side and reach the championship match, she'd have to defeat her next five opponents. And in addition to the three extra matches, competition would grow increasingly tough, as lesser players were eliminated from the tournament.

She turned and headed toward the playing area, still trying to collect her thoughts. She needed to develop a strategy for the remainder of the tournament. In other sports, a coach came in handy at a time like this. Too bad Buster wasn't here. Maybe she needed to hear his "fear" lecture again.

She entered the playing area and walked over to table No. 4. A slight young woman, with short hair colored so lightly it was almost silver, was already warming up. Sedonia nodded a greeting, and then opened her cue case and took out her stick. The tournament director came over and hung placards with their names over the pool table. Her opponent's looked unpronounceable—something Scandinavian.

As Sedonia watched the woman shoot, her thoughts were still on her own game. In golf, and in other sports, the adage was: don't try to get it back, all at once. She needed to take that to heart. From here on, she needed to forget about the championship match. She needed to take it one shot at a time, one game at a time, one match at a time. That's what she should have done when she fell behind against Margaret.

The woman at the table pocketed the 9-ball, and began spreading out the balls again, as if she were going to play another rack. Sedonia stood up, and walked over to the table. She'd start by instilling some fear into this woman, whatever the hell her name was.

The woman leaned over the table to shoot, but Sedonia grabbed the cue-ball and said, "I'm up."

Sedonia hung her wet bath towel over the shower curtain rod, and then slipped into her T-shirt nightgown. At the sink, she ran a glass of water, and then washed down two Advil tablets to reduce the shoulder inflammation, followed by two Tylenol P.M. capsules to mask the ache and to help her sleep.

As she padded into the other room, she checked the clock-radio: 8:47. She set the alarm for 6:00 a.m., and then pulled her address book out of her purse.

A few moments later, a familiar voice said, "Buster's." In the background, she heard the equally familiar sounds of the poolroom.

"Hi. It's Sedonia. Got a minute?"

"Hang on," Buster said. He put her on hold, and when he picked up again, the background noise was gone. He'd apparently gone into his office to take the call. "You still in L.A.?"

"Yeah," she said, then gave him a brief summary of the night at Tough Times.

"That Florante passed through here a while back," Buster said. "Hang on."

Sedonia heard the sounds of the poolroom again, then Buster shout, "Monk!"

A few moments later, Buster came back on the phone. I just checked with my expert. Monk's seen you both play, and he said Florante shouldn't have given you the 8-ball. He says you should have given Florante the breaks."

Sedonia and Buster laughed together. "That's the kind of encouragement I need," she said. Then she recapped her five tournament matches. "So," she concluded, "I'm 4 and 1 in matches, and I'm guaranteed to finish no worse than 9th to 12th. But that only pays $2,500."

"If you weren't so hard up for money," Buster said, "that already would be a damned good first tournament. And your one loss was to Margaret?"

"Yeah, but she tortured me, 9 to 1."

"Well, you ain't the first gal she's tortured, and you won't be the last. She's strong. And at least she didn't shut you out."

"She dumped the one game I won."

"That was nice of her."

"There's nothing nice about that bitch," Sedonia said.

Buster chuckled. "That's the attitude you need to have, the next time you play her."

"If there is a next time."

"You came back and won the next match, right?"

"Yeah, 9 to 4. She was just ranked No. 17, though."

"*Just* No. 17," Buster said in a teasing manner.

"I mean . . ."

"I know what you mean, kid. And that's a good sign. You don't fear those pros. You've still got your confidence. How's your shoulder holding up?"

"It's bothering me a little. I'm lucky, though. They're using the Sardo Tight Rack here, so I don't have to break hard. But I haven't developed a good, soft break. I only make a ball about a third of the time."

"What are they rackin' on the spot? The 1-ball, like we do here? Or are they pushin' the rack forward, so the 9-ball's on the spot?"

"The 9-ball."

"Try this then. Instead of breakin' from the right side of the table the way you usually do, break from the left. Put the cue-ball right behind the head string and about three inches off the rail. Use draw, and hit the 1-ball slightly left of center, and watch where it goes. If the 1-ball hits the rail short of the side pocket, then shoot a little harder. If it goes past the side pocket, shoot a little softer. Play around with the speed until you figure out what it takes. You ought to be able to pocket the 1-ball in the side almost every time."

Sedonia repeated the instructions, and then said, "I'll try it tomorrow morning. I'd already planned to go in early to practice breaking. I need to work on lagging too. If you don't win the lag for the first break here, you may not get to play at all."

"Anything else I can help you with?"

Sedonia knew he needed to get back to work. "It's gonna be tough from here on," she said. "*All* these women are strong."

"So are you, kid. So are you."

"Thanks, Buster." There was a pause. Finally she said, "I'll let you go. I just . . . needed somebody to talk to."

"Kick some ass, tomorrow, kid. Just wish I was there."

"Me too . . . coach. Me too."

Chapter 20

The following night, Sedonia strolled through the casino, killing time before her 8:00 p.m. match. Her early morning practice session had gone well. She'd had immediate success applying Buster's tips on breaking, and then she'd spent a half-hour practicing her lag shot. After that, she'd worked on her defensive game—shooting safeties, then shooting her way out of them. Everything she'd practiced worked for her later in the day; she'd won her morning match, 9 to 5, and her afternoon match, 9 to 6.

Now, she paused at a railing and looked about the casino. A large Saturday night crowd occupied the dozens of card tables below and filled the pari-mutuel lounge behind her. Again she was struck by how quiet the expansive room was. With no slot machines, it seemed more like a clubroom than a casino. She sighed, feeling listless. She'd been on the premises for almost 12 hours. The between-match boredom was as taxing as the competition itself.

She turned, looking for a place in the lounge to sit down, but then saw a familiar figure coming down the escalator—Bonnie, the young woman she'd gambled with at Tough Times. Bonnie exited the casino through a side door. Curious, Sedonia followed, and a moment later found herself in the valet parking area.

A Hollywood Park grandstand loomed in front of her, and the track announcer was droning on about the next horse race. Small clusters of pool players stood around the asphalt parking lot, smoking, which was prohibited inside the casino. Bonnie stood by herself.

Sedonia walked over. "You still alive in the tournament?"

Bonnie took a long drag off her cigarette, and shook her head. "I went two and out on Thursday. Just came back tonight to gamble with some of the APA amateurs. How about you?"

"Won three, then Margaret beat me, and I won the last three. I play again at 8:00, against Inger Ruud."

"Inger's strong," Bonnie said. "I've played her before."

Sedonia nodded. "I have too." She didn't mention that at Duke's Billiards in Houston, she'd tortured Inger, 9 to 0.

Bonnie frowned through a cloud of cigarette smoke. "You ever play WPBA before?"

"No. First time."

Bonnie raised an eyebrow, then said, "So, at 6 and 1, what are you guaranteed?"

"Fifth and sixth place. It pays $4,000."

"You plan to bring some of that bread back to Tough Times? Not that I want to play you again."

Sedonia nodded. "I'm gonna see if Rami can match me up there tomorrow night, regardless of what happens here."

"Who are the big names still in it?"

"Margaret Faulkson, Karen Corr, and Allison Fisher. The other top players, like Jeanette and Ewa, have either knocked each other out, or gotten upset by nobodies like me."

"You ain't gonna be a 'nobody' for long," Bonnie said, "not the way you're playin'. She ground out her cigarette on the asphalt. "You think you can win this thing?"

"Trying not to think about it. Just taking it, one game at a time."

Sedonia racked the balls for Inger, and then returned to her seat. She glanced up at the scoring counters on the wire stretched above the table. After jumping to a 3 to 0 lead in the race-to-9, she'd now fallen behind, 4 to 3. Although Inger was only No. 19 in the WPBA rankings, she was having an exceptional tournament, having knocked off several higher rated players. After losing the first three games to Sedonia's aggressive style of play, Inger had changed tactics. For the last four games, she'd stalled and played frequent safeties, successfully curtailing Sedonia's momentum and pulling into a one-game lead.

Now Inger was delaying the match again, meticulously dressing the tip of her break cue. Sedonia glanced around at the crowd. Inger's traveling companions, Kari and Gunnar, and several other WPBA players were watching this quarterfinal match from reserved seats.

Sedonia heaved a sigh. She knew what she had to do, but hated to do it, since she was a newcomer, playing in her first professional tournament. She stood up and called, "Time out." Then she walked over to the tournament director. "Put us on the clock," she said.

"We *are* running slow tonight," he said. "But I generally don't put players on the clock, if it's the last match of the night. And I don't remember the last time a player *asked* to go on the clock."

"I'm asking. We're more than an hour into the match, and we've only played seven games. Inger used these same stall tactics in Las Vegas, and you put her on the clock there."

A look of displeasure crossed the director's face, but he raised the microphone and addressed the audience. "The allotted time for games in this tournament is one hour and forty-five minutes. WPBA rules state that if midway through the allotted time, less than eight games have been played, and neither player has won seven or more games, both players will be put on a 30-second clock."

He turned to Inger and Sedonia. "Ladies, you now must shoot within 30 seconds. You are allowed one extension per game. This extension entitles you to an additional 30 seconds. Resume play."

Inger shot an angry look at Sedonia. Then she turned to the professionals in the reserved section and shook her head, showing her displeasure. From the expressions on their faces, Sedonia sensed she'd alienated them—probably because this was her first tournament and Inger was established on the tour. The hell with them, she thought. Inger had sharked her with slow play; she'd shark Inger with fast.

Inger walked down to the other end of the table and inspected the rack. "Re-rack," she said, loud enough to be heard throughout the pavilion.

A titter went through the crowd. Now Sedonia shook *her* head. Inger's calling for a re-rack of a Sardo Tight Rack was nothing but more sharking. Sedonia didn't move to comply; instead, she simply looked at the tournament director. Finally he walked over and inspected the rack. He heaved a sigh of exasperation, but rather than take sides in the dispute, he re-racked the balls himself. Then he switched on his microphone and said through clenched teeth, "For the remainder of this match, I will rack for both players. Resume play, ladies."

Inger broke and failed to make a ball. Sedonia sprang from her chair and surveyed the table. It would be an easy run-out. She was back in control.

Twenty minutes later, Sedonia sank the final 9-ball in the side pocket. The applause was polite, but the gamesmanship between the two players had dampened the crowd's enthusiasm. Even the usual wolf whistles were missing.

Sedonia walked over to where Inger was putting away her cue stick, and extended her hand. "Sorry things got so tense."

"Tense, yes," Inger said. Then she accepted the extended hand. "You play very good. My only chance to beat you was to slow things down."

"And to beat you," Sedonia said, "I had to speed things up. No hard feelings?"

"No hard feelings," Inger said. "Good luck tomorrow."

Down on table No. 3, the final match of the night also concluded. The director thanked the spectators for their attendance, and encouraged them to return for the semifinals and finals, beginning at 1:00 the following afternoon. "Get here early and get a good seat," he concluded. "You'll have a chance to be part of history. ESPN will be doing their first *live* telecast of a WPBA tournament."

Later that night, Sedonia had showered and taken her nightly ration of Advil and Tylenol P. M. She walked over to the window and stared out at the night. Traffic was light along Century Boulevard and the 405 Freeway. She closed the drapes, and went over and sat down on the edge of the bed. She was tired from having spent 14 hours at the casino, but pleased with her success. She glanced at the clock; it would be almost 1:00 a.m. in Nassau Bay. It was late to be calling anyone, but she decided she would anyway.

A few moments later, a man's sleepy voice said, "Hello."

"Hi. Sounds like I woke you up. Sorry. This is Sedonia. Can I talk to Hannah?"

A moment later, Hannah came on the phone, sounding more awake than her husband. "How's it going, kid?"

"Sorry to wake y'all up, Hannah. I just wanted to talk to somebody. I bugged Buster last night, so tonight it's your turn."

"Not a problem," Hannah replied. Then she said, "Shut up and go to sleep!"

"What?"

"I was talking to my husband," Hannah said with a laugh. "I spoke to Buster this afternoon, and he said you were doing real well there. How'd it go today?"

"I won three more matches. I'm in the semifinals."

"That's great!" Hannah said. Then in an aside, "Put the pillow over your head, or go sleep on the couch."

Sedonia laughed, then said, "As it stands right now, I'm guaranteed no worse than 3rd place. It pays $7,000."

"Fantastic!"

"Yeah, but still way short of $22,000."

"What's the latest on that problem?"

"Not much new. I spoke with Raul a couple of days ago, and he told me that Brad stops by the job site a couple of times a day. And Huff, that vulture who's waiting to take over, has been by there too. I've just got until Monday to come up with the money."

"What's the name of Brad's company?"

"Coastal Construction. Why?"

"Just wondered. You realize, of course, Monday is day after tomorrow."

"I know. The semifinal match is at 1:00 tomorrow afternoon. If I win that, then I play Margaret in the finals at 3:00. She won the winners' bracket. But whether I win or lose, my only chance to raise the money I need is to go back to Tough Times tomorrow night and see if I can match up with some of the high rollers there."

Hannah chuckled.

"What's funny about that?" Sedonia said.

"Sorry, kid. But last year, I had to twist your arm to get you to play league pool. Now, tomorrow you'll be competing for a WPBA championship, and you're already making plans for high stakes games that night."

Sedonia sighed. "You're right. What a difference a year makes. Last year I owned a company, free and clear, and now I'm about to lose it."

"By the way," Hannah said, "I'm sure you've heard. ESPN's carrying the semifinals and finals tomorrow. Four-hour, live telecast, 3:00 to 7:00 our time."

"Thanks for reminding me. I was trying to forget about that."

"I'm sorry," Hannah said with a laugh. "Have you had a chance to get over to Redondo Beach?"

"No. There hasn't been enough time between matches. All I've seen is the seedy neighborhood between this hotel and the casino, and of course, beautiful downtown Bellflower."

"That's too bad," Hannah said. "Redondo was a great place to grow up. And the ocean there, it's . . . good for the mind. Wish you could have seen it."

"Me too, Hannah."

"I'd move back there in a heartbeat," Hannah said, "except I love this Texan, snoring beside me."

"Glad he got back to sleep," Sedonia said, smiling at her mental picture of the bedroom scene, 1,500 miles away. "I'd better let *you* get back to sleep too."

"You too, kid. Get some rest. Big day tomorrow."

The cab pulled away, and Sedonia walked over to a railing that overlooked the Pacific Ocean and the Redondo Beach Pier. Twenty feet below, a paved recreational lane shadowed the shoreline for miles in either direction. A stream of walkers, joggers, skaters, and cyclists passed below, obviously invigorated by the temperate Southern California climate. What a contrast, Sedonia thought, to her spartan morning runs through Nassau Bay. She wished she could join those people down there this morning.

Across a hundred-foot expanse of unoccupied sand, a steady procession of emerald-green, five-foot waves crashed onto the beach. Surf of this quality was unknown on the Texas Gulf Coast. Here, though, the half-dozen early-morning surfers straddled their boards, waiting for sets that were even better.

Sedonia descended a steep flight of concrete stairs. Other community piers she'd seen had simply extended straight out over the water. The Redondo Beach Pier, however, was shaped like an irregular "D." The straight side was a midway, flanked by bars, restaurants, and curio shops. At this hour on Sunday morning, the businesses were closed and placards hung on the doors, saying they would open later in the afternoon. As she walked along the deserted midway, the chorus from an old Kris Kristofferson song echoed in her mind, about Sunday morning sidewalks making a person feel alone.

She arrived at the curved side of the pier. Here the deck was wide open, and a dozen people of all ages were fishing from the railing. Seagulls squawked overhead, and others strutted about the walkway, looking for morsels that might be cast aside.

She passed an Asian family, and a little girl smiled and showed off a small, wriggling fish.

"That's great!" Sedonia said. "Did you catch it?"

The little girl shook her head, and ran to a woman who was fishing at the railing. The woman looked over her shoulder, gave Sedonia a hesitant smile and quick nod, and then turned back to the ocean and the business at hand.

Farther around the curved portion of the pier, Sedonia found an un-occupied space, and leaned on the railing and looked back toward the shore. A half-dozen trawlers were moored near a row of fish grottos. Waves broke against brown, shiny boulders; seagulls cried overhead; children laughed and played nearby. Sedonia smiled as she compared Redondo Beach to the Seabrook-Kemah channel. This setting won, hands down.

She looked back at the ocean and sighed. A peaceful Sunday morning. She glanced at her watch. Hard to believe, in less than three hours she'd be locked in combat on national TV. She felt a pang of pre-match apprehension, but forced it back.

In what now seemed like another lifetime, she'd been a world-class woman golfer, winning the U. S. Amateur Championship. But her shoulder injury had denied her the opportunity to compete professionally. Now she was what? She smiled. A professional woman cueist—world class.

She turned and retraced her steps along the pier. The little Asian girl smiled again, and Sedonia waved. And again, the little girl ran to her mother. Sedonia was glad she'd gotten up early to experience Redondo Beach. Hannah had been right. The ocean here was "good for the mind."

* * *

As Sedonia rode the escalator up to her semifinal match, she looked over her shoulder at the activity below. The card tables were almost full, and the pari-mutuel lounge was standing room only. She'd spent much of the past three days here. Killing time between matches, she'd grown familiar with every recess of the casino complex. Now she felt a tinge of regret, realizing that in four hours she would leave, and most likely never return.

The escalator arrived at the mezzanine, and she stepped off and exchanged smiles and waves of recognition with the hostess in the open restaurant. She passed by spectators who were queued up in front of the ticket counter. A tournament organizer recognized her and waved her through the players' entrance.

She passed through the doorway, then stopped. The exhibition hall, where the APA amateur tournament had been held all week, now was empty. A crew must have worked all night to remove the bar-boxes. Thousands of matches had been contested here this week, but now it was if the tournament had never been played. The triumphs and defeats would echo only in the minds of the competitors.

She crossed the open expanse, passed under the Exit sign, and continued up an aisle that had been formed between two sets of bleachers. She stopped again. The pavilion also had transformed overnight. Five of the pool tables had been removed, and additional seating installed around table No. 1. A raised podium now stood in one corner, where two ESPN commentators sat chatting. A young woman wearing headphones, apparently the TV producer, was positioning cameramen at each end of the pool table. A third camera had been mounted overhead.

Sedonia made a quick, final check of her attire. She'd saved her best charcoal-gray slacks and a new white, long-sleeve blouse for today. She took a deep breath, and stepped into view of the spectators. A round of applause greeted her arrival. She entered the playing area, where her opponent was already warming up. Sedonia took a seat, and opened her cue case. The tournament director approached as she screwed her stick together.

"Where the hell have you been?" he demanded.

Sedonia stood up and checked her watch. The match wasn't scheduled to start for another fifteen minutes. Before she could reply, he turned away and switched on his microphone.

"All right, ladies and gentlemen . . . in a few minutes, we'll be going *live* . . . across the nation . . . on ESPN!" He went on to tell them not to behave as if they were in a golf gallery, but to feel free to whoop and holler for their favorite player. He wanted them to convey a sense of excitement to the TV audience. He selected fans from each of the four sets of bleachers to serve as competing cheerleaders.

Sedonia walked over to the table and introduced herself to her opponent, then took her turn at warming up. The two cameramen moved closer to the table. Sedonia felt uncomfortable with their close proximity, but reminded herself she'd had to contend with worse—Willie O's in San Leon, for example. The contrast in venues caused her to smile.

A few minutes before 1:00, the tournament director called the players over and had them stand on either side of him. They stood in silence. Finally the TV producer began counting backwards from ten. On zero, she pointed to the tournament director.

"Welcome to the fabulous Hollywood Park Casino!" he said, sounding like a carnival barker. "We're here, *live*, presenting the semifinal round of the WPBA Los Angeles Championship. We've got a real Texas shootout in store for you! From Dallas, Texas . . . a ten-year pro . . . winner of *four* WPBA championships . . . Fran Carter!"

The spectator cheerleaders did their job in coaxing an enthusiastic ovation. As her opponent smiled and waved, Sedonia felt a surge of pre-match anxiety.

"And her opponent," the director continued, "from Nassau Bay, Texas . . . playing in her *first* pro tournament . . . Sedonia Forbes!"

Sedonia stepped forward and acknowledged the ovation with a wave. As the applause quieted, someone emitted a wolf whistle, which drew laughter from the crowd and a grimace from Sedonia.

The director gave the spectators and viewing audience a quick rundown of the basic rules of Nine-Ball. In addition, because the match was being televised, the players would be on the 30-second clock, with only one 30-second extension allowed per game. If a player had not shot within twenty seconds, the director would announce "ten seconds" to warn her that her time was expiring.

When he finished, Sedonia followed Fran over to the break end of the table. After a quick handshake and exchange of "Good lucks," Sedonia and Fran leaned over the table to lag for the first break. The TV producer crouched at the other end of the table, and she frantically waved for them not to shoot. She mouthed something. Sedonia finally understood, "commercial." Seconds passed, and Sedonia turned her head, to relieve the pressure that was forming in the right side of her neck. She heard the sound of a ball being struck and saw her opponent's lag shot rolling down the table. She looked at the TV producer and saw her now frantically signaling with a chopping motion for her to shoot. Sedonia shot too hard, as if trying to catch Fran's ball, and bounced it off both rails. She'd lost the important lag for first break.

Sedonia started toward the other end of the table to rack, but the tournament director intercepted her and informed her that he racked during televised matches. She returned to her seat, while Fran prepared to break. For the first time since entering the pavilion, Sedonia had a moment to collect her thoughts. She took several deep breaths, hoping to recapture the tranquility she'd experienced that morning on the pier.

Fran miscued slightly on her break and failed to make a ball. Sedonia rose from her chair, sensing her opponent was as nervous as she was. As she started toward the table, one of the cameramen stepped to his left and bumped into her.

He turned and said with a sheepish grin, "Sorry."

Then he moved to his right, as Sedonia moved to her left. He stepped to his left, as she went to her right. Finally he remained still so she could get by. As she passed, she smiled and said, "In Texas, we call that dance the two-step." The spectators in the nearby reserved seats heard her comment and laughed.

Sedonia was still smiling when she arrived at the table, knowing that Hannah and others in Nassau Bay had witnessed that inauspicious first trip to the table. Her smile faded, and she focused on the task at hand. Most of the balls were at one end of the table, but none were touching. A possible run-out. As she concentrated on how she would work her way around the table, she partitioned from her mind the cameramen, the spectators, and the television audience. A faint smile returned as she leaned down for her first shot. *One, two, three . . . stroke.*

An hour later, Sedonia waited at the break end of the table. The TV producer crouched near the other end, holding up both palms. Behind her, the two ESPN commentators were interviewing three middle-aged men in dark business suits. Sedonia caught the eye of the tournament director and gave him an inquiring look.

He sidled over. "Visitors from the International Olympic Committee," he whispered. "Stand by. We're about ready to go again."

He resumed his position at the side of the table, and Sedonia glanced at the large digital scoreboard that had been installed for today's matches, which showed she led, 8 to 2. Finally the TV producer counted backward from ten, then pointed for Sedonia to resume play. Sedonia chalked her cue and tried to refocus after the four-minute interruption. The TV producer apparently thought Sedonia hadn't seen the signal to resume, because she began to give the frantic chopping motion for Sedonia to break.

Sedonia carefully placed the cue-ball three inches from the left rail, leaned over the table, and positioned the tip of her cue for low left english. *One, two, three . . . stroke!* The yellow 1-ball rolled slowly into the far side pocket, and the other balls scattered. The cue-ball came to rest in the middle of the table. As Sedonia chalked her cue, she hoped Buster was watching. She'd again executed the break as he'd coached her. And a couple of minutes later, the crowd erupted as the gold-striped 9-ball dropped in the corner, giving her a lopsided 9 to 2 victory in the semifinals.

Sedonia came out of the ladies room, and checked her watch: 2:17. Since her semifinal match had concluded so quickly, the TV producer and the tournament director had agreed to move the finals up to 2:30. Instead of turning left and reentering the pavilion, Sedonia continued straight and walked into the open restaurant.

The young hostess hurried over. "Congratulations! I've been watching on TV. Aren't you supposed to be getting ready for the finals?"

"I've got a few minutes. Can you let me have a small Coke?"

"Sure."

Sedonia followed the hostess over to the bar, which like the restaurant was deserted. She pulled up a stool and the hostess poured her drink. Sedonia opened her purse to pay, but the hostess said, "It's on me."

"Thanks," Sedonia said. She took two Advil tablets from her purse, and washed them down. The shoulder discomfort was slight; it shouldn't be a factor in the next match. She sipped her drink and looked at the TV set mounted behind the bar. The commentators were interviewing Vivian Villarreal, but the sound was turned down, so Sedonia couldn't hear what they were saying. She glanced to her right in time to see Margaret Faulkson step off the escalator. Margaret gave Sedonia a hostile glance as she headed toward the ladies room.

"She's good isn't she?" the hostess said.

Sedonia nodded. "Kicked my butt, 9 to 1 on Friday."

"Think you can beat her?" the hostess said.

Sedonia took a last swallow, and stood up. "Time to go find out."

She received a ripple of applause as she reentered the pavilion. The tournament director came over and said, "Where have you been? The ESPN folks want to do an interview with you."

"After the match."

"They want to—"

"I said, after the match," Sedonia snapped. She pushed past him and went over to the pool table to loosen up again.

The TV producer approached. "Watch for my signals this time. You need to—"

"After you give me a signal once, get the hell out of my line of vision," Sedonia said. Then she turned to the table and drilled the yellow 1-ball into the side pocket. The producer hesitated a moment, then moved well out of Sedonia's way.

A few minutes later, another ripple of applause went through the crowd, as Margaret Faulkson made her entrance. Sedonia didn't acknowledge her. Instead, she took a final warm-up shot, left the table, and pulled up a chair. Sal in Las Vegas had told her that women were too "buddy-buddy." There'd be none of that in this match.

Margaret spread the balls across the table, and then began pocketing them in Nine-Ball order. Sedonia watched out of the corner of her eye. Margaret's seemingly awkward stance, backside protruding, produced precision stroke after stroke. Sedonia decided when she got back home, she'd experiment with that stance herself—in private, of course.

"Something amusing, luv?" Margaret said.

Sedonia chuckled, suppressing the temptation to tell Margaret her stance made her look like a mare during breeding. Instead, she said, "I'm just enjoying the moment." Despite all that was riding on this match, and the knowledge that more pressure awaited her that night at Tough Times, she was, in fact, enjoying herself. This was the moment that she'd been denied in golf.

Margaret frowned at her reply, then turned and missed her next shot.

A few minutes later, the tournament director called them to the table, and announced. "Tonight's finals will be for the grand prize, $12,000! The challenger . . . a regional qualifier . . . from Nassau Bay, Texas . . . playing in her first WPBA tournament . . . Sedonia Forbes!" The crowd responded with enthusiastic applause, followed by the usual round of whistles.

"And our defending Los Angeles Champion . . . originally from Oxfordshire, England and now living in Wilmington, North Carolina . . . three-time European World Snooker Champion . . . two-time WPBA Player of the Year . . . and currently ranked No. 1 in the world . . . "The Queen of Cue" . . . Margaret Faulkson!"

Sedonia and Margaret exchanged public-relations smiles, handshakes, and "Good lucks," then waited for the TV producer's signal to lag for the first break. They leaned down together and struck the balls simultaneously. Sedonia's ball came within an inch of the near rail. Margaret's was closer. Sedonia took her seat, while the tournament director racked for the first game.

Margaret broke, made a ball, and then continued right where she'd left off in their Friday match. Her tailored navy blue slacks, gray blouse, and paisley gold vest contrasted with Sedonia's simple charcoal-gray slacks and white blouse. Margaret looked and played like the professional she was. She didn't allow Sedonia to get to the table until the third game, and then it was after she'd played a perfect safety. Sedonia managed to hit the object ball, but then had to relinquish the table again. Margaret ran the remainder of that rack. Then she broke and ran the next rack.

Leading 4 to 0, Margaret failed to make a ball on the next break. Sedonia returned to the table, and this time had a shot. The yellow 1-ball was makeable in the corner pocket, but the blue 2-ball was at the opposite end of the table and hidden behind the orange 5-ball. She knew conservative play called for making the 1-ball, and then playing a safety. On the other hand, the gold-striped 9-ball sat in front of the far side pocket, and she might be able to hit the 1-ball, and draw the cue-ball into the 9-ball.

"Ten seconds," announced the tournament director.

"Extension," Sedonia said. She chalked her cue stick and continued to weigh the alternatives of playing conservatively or aggressively.

"Ten seconds," the director said, indicating her extension had almost expired.

Sedonia leaned down. *One, two, three . . . stroke.* The cue-ball glanced off the left side of the 1-ball, kicked off the end rail, rolled slowly back up table, and kissed the 9-ball into the side. A cheer went up from the spectators. The score was 4 to 1 in the race-to-9.

Sedonia heaved a sigh as she prepared to break for the sixth game. She'd stopped the bleeding. Now she needed to run some racks. Her relief was short-lived. On her break, the 1-ball rattled the side pocket, but failed to drop. Margaret rose and approached the table with a tight smile. A few minutes later, she made the 9-ball. Then she ran the next rack. The score was 6 to 1.

"Time out," Sedonia said.

She grabbed her purse and headed for the ladies room. As she passed through the pavilion doorway, she heard the tournament director inform the spectators that each player was allowed one five-minute timeout during the match.

The ladies room was unoccupied. Sedonia walked over to the row of sinks, ran water onto a paper towel, and patted her eyelids. *Damn that woman!* There was no way to beat her. Sedonia felt defenseless, as she'd been on Friday. Margaret was just too strong.

Sedonia looked at her reflection in the mirror. She shouldn't have worn a white blouse; several blue chalk stains dotted the front. She dabbed at one with the damp towel, and only succeeded in smearing it. Talcum powder had rubbed off her bridge hand and onto her left pant leg. Her hair was frizzing. She shook her head. She'd looked better after an hour's run through Nassau Bay.

She opened her purse and pulled out her compact and lipstick. At least she could repair her makeup. Suddenly she began to laugh. Miss Astor! That's what Cissy had called her in Las Vegas. Miss Astor. Tears formed at the recollection. Cissy had gone 14 and 0 in Vegas. Bet Cissy could have found a way to beat this British bitch. Sedonia pushed the compact and lipstick back into her purse. The hell with makeup! She strode across the room and banged out the door.

As Sedonia reentered the pavilion, the TV producer approached, looking as if she were about to speak. Sedonia pushed by her and returned to her chair.

Margaret was waiting at the break end of the table. "Are you ready to resume?" she said.

Sedonia fixed her in an unblinking stare, and didn't reply.

Margaret broke and made a ball. She ran two more, then left herself with poor position and resorted to a safety. Sedonia returned to the table. The purple 4-ball sat in front of the corner pocket, but the cue-ball's path was blocked by the black 8-ball. The only possible way to make the 4-ball would be with a jump shot. Sedonia felt an adrenaline surge, and she stalled. She needed to gain control. She chalked her cue and looked about the bleachers, trying to relax.

"Ten seconds," warned the tournament director.

"Extension," Sedonia said, not turning to look at him. For the first time, she noticed Audri and Cannonball sitting together on the top row. A faint smile tugged at Sedonia's lips. Like Cissy, Audri could find a way to beat this woman, even if it took assault and battery. Audri gazed back at her without expression, but when Sedonia turned back to the table, she heard Cannonball's resonant voice boom, "Go now!"

Sedonia lined up on the 4-ball, elevated the butt of her stick forty-five degrees, and drove the cue-ball into the slate. It jumped the 8-ball, tapped in the 4-ball, and came to rest in perfect position on the orange 5-ball. One at a time, Sedonia cautioned herself. Take 'em one at a time. A few minutes later, the score was 6 to 2.

The next six games featured defensive play. Margaret's smug confidence began to wither under Sedonia's relentless charge. Margaret increasingly resorted to safeties, and her frustration showed as Sedonia responded in kind. In each game, Margaret eventually made a minor error in cue-ball position, which gave Sedonia an opportunity to switch from defense to offense, and run the remaining balls. After fourteen games, Sedonia had pulled to an 8 to 6 lead. She was on-the-hill in the race-to-9.

Margaret called time out. This time it was she who sought refuge in the ladies room. Sedonia sat down. Just one more game, she told herself, as she touched up the tip of her cue stick. For the first time that afternoon, she hoped Hannah or someone else was recording these matches. She'd experienced being dead-stroke before, but never like today, while mixing safeties with offensive shots. Then she pushed the thought from her mind. Being in dead-stroke was like having sex—best not analyzed too closely during the event.

She looked over at the announcer booth. The commentators were filling the five-minute interruption by interviewing two other perennial champions from the United Kingdom: Allison Fisher and Karen Corr. During the past two days, before they were eliminated from the tournament, Sedonia had taken the opportunity to watch each of them play. Now, though she couldn't hear the interview, she knew they were skillfully representing their chosen profession. On a pool table, or away from it, these women were consummate professionals.

A faint ripple of applause drew Sedonia's attention. Margaret had reentered the pavilion. As she sat down, she glanced over at Sedonia. There was no mistaking her expression. Sedonia saw fear in Margaret's eyes. *Concentrate!* Sedonia told herself. Every shot had to be precise. Miss a shot, or be slightly off with position, and she might never get back to the table.

The tournament director nodded for Sedonia to resume play, and the TV producer signaled that ESPN also was ready. Sedonia broke, and failed to make a ball. *Damn it!* That's exactly what she couldn't afford to let happen. She sat down, and watched Margaret return to the table.

The yellow 1-ball presented a long shot down the rail. The only problem on the table was the nearby purple 4-ball and green 6-ball, which were touching. And those should automatically break out when Margaret shot the 1-ball. Otherwise, the table looked like a run-out.

"Ten seconds," warned the tournament director.

"Extension," Margaret said, and continued to study her options.

Twenty seconds later, the tournament director again said, "Ten seconds."

Margaret leaned over, lined up the 1-ball, and shot. The cue-ball broke out the 4-ball and 6-ball, but the 1-ball failed to drop.

Sedonia was so stunned that for a moment she didn't react. The Queen of Cue had dogged the 1-ball. Sedonia finally got to her feet and returned to the table, then paused, taking several deep breaths. The game, the match, and the championship were hers for the taking.

"Ten seconds," said the tournament director.

This time, Sedonia didn't ask for an extension. She leaned down and lined up the 1-ball in the corner. *One, two, three . . . stroke.* It fell, and she was in perfect position on the 2-ball. As she circled the table, trying to keep her emotions in check, she had the sensation that her cue stick was a magic wand. All she had to do was point it. Finally she turned to Margaret and said, "Nine in the corner."

The crowed erupted as the gold-striped 9-ball rolled into the corner pocket, and the white cue-ball stopped in the center of the otherwise empty expanse of green.

* * *

Sedonia sat on the edge of her bed, still dressed from the afternoon matches. The WPBA's cashier check for $12,000 was propped up on the bedside table. The clock-radio nearby read 6:06 p.m. Somehow, she needed to get the check cashed, so she could gamble at Tough Times.

Her shoulders slumped. She was as tired as she'd ever been in her life. The awards ceremony and the TV interview had depleted the last of her adrenaline. All she wanted now was go to bed and sleep until dawn. But she still needed an additional $7,000, or Brad would file suit tomorrow. She opened her purse and rummaged around until she found the business card that Rami had given her on Wednesday night.

When he came to the phone, the first thing he said was, "Congratulations!"

"You heard already?"

"Yeah, Bonnie's been keepin' us posted. Hell, I made $1,000 off you."

"You bet on me?"

"Yeah, everybody figured Margaret would win, or if not her, Karen Corr or Allison Fisher. I got ten-to-one odds on you! I robbed 'em. I've seen you play."

Sedonia laughed, then said, "Listen, I need to get matched up tonight. I'm looking for $5,000 sets."

"Can't help you this week. All the high rollers left for Reno this afternoon."

"Reno?" she said, crestfallen.

"Yeah. This week's the Sands Regency Open. First place is payin' $50,000. Top players from all over the country are gonna be there."

Sedonia thought for a moment, then said, "You say it's an 'open'? Like, anyone can enter?"

"As long as you put up the $1,000 entry fee."

"You think I could still get in?"

"Like I say, as long as you got the $1,000. You want the phone number out there?"

"Yeah." He read it off, and Sedonia wrote it down.

"Good luck," he said. "Call me next time you're in town."

They hung up, and Sedonia dug back into her purse. A few moments later, a pleasant, deep voice answered the phone.

"Brad, I'm sorry to bother you on Sunday night, but I need to talk to you before tomorrow."

"I'm glad you called," he said. "About tomorrow—"

Sedonia interrupted, "I've won $12,000 today in a Los Angeles pool tournament. I can wire you that amount in the morning, either from here or from Reno. Depends on how quickly I can get on a plane."

"Reno? "

"I don't have time to explain. Just let me know if you'll take the $12,000 now, and hold off filing suit."

"Why are you going to Reno?"

"Because that's where the rest of the money is."

"Forget about Reno and—"

"Damn it, Brad," she said impatiently. "Do you want your money? Or are you trying to get even with me?"

"Neither. Now, let me talk."

Sedonia heaved a sigh of exasperation. "Go ahead."

"I saw you play today."

"You did?"

"Yeah, your podnah, Hannah, called me bright and early. Had me meet her at Buster's this afternoon."

"You? At Buster's?"

"Yeah. Buster's a good guy, isn't he?"

Sedonia responded with a wry smile and shake of her head. Brad, sitting in a poolroom with Hannah and Buster, watching her play on TV. What a picture!

Brad continued, "Hannah told me I was a shit for heaping all that pressure on you."

"She did?"

"Yeah, but I already knew that."

"I cost you $22,000," Sedonia said, suddenly in the unusual position of defending him.

"Nope, no excuse," he said. "If it had just been about the money, I'd never have filed suit. If for no other reason, just out of respect for your father. No, I was . . . jealous."

Sedonia kicked off her flats, propped up two pillows, and pulled her legs up on the bed. A warm glow spread through her body. "Keep going," she said.

"I didn't fully understand about this pool business, and . . . those guys you've been running around with. Hannah explained it to me . . . kinda. Anyway, there's not going to be any lawsuit. So forget about the money. Come on home, and let's start over."

Sedonia suddenly grew aware of the tears flowing down her cheeks. He'd been honest, and so should she. "You had every right to be mad at me. And I can't tell you how much I want to start over."

"Come on home," he said again. "I'll meet you at the airport."

"That sounds wonderful," Sedonia said. "Thanks, Brad. Thanks for . . . being you." She hesitated, then said, "I'll call you from Reno, as soon as I know my return schedule."

"Reno? I told you to forget about the money."

Sedonia smiled. "It's not about money any more."

Chapter 21

The following afternoon, Sedonia stepped off the Reno Sands Regency elevator and entered the hotel lobby. Noisy slot machines occupied every available space, even directly across from the check-in counter. Several guests had their luggage stacked beside machines, apparently taking the opportunity to get in some last-minute gambling while they waited for the next airport shuttle.

Sedonia descended a short flight of stairs, and then followed a press of people along a narrow corridor that ran through a row of sundries shops. The clamor increased as she entered the casino. She made her way along the winding main aisle, past the green-felted gaming tables and through the maze of slot machines. Shrieks and groans of winners and losers punctuated the general din. How different this was from the subdued atmosphere of the Hollywood Park Casino.

Finally she came to a wide carpeted stairway that led up to the mezzanine. The casino noise subsided as she climbed the stairs. At the top, she found herself in a spacious foyer, with doors leading to conference rooms. She walked over to the closest and looked inside. A single row of metal folding chairs surrounded six, 9-foot Diamond Pros. Players occupied four of the tables, and railbirds surrounded the one in the far corner. She surmised this was the room where players would practice and gamble throughout the week.

She continued down to the next door, and stepped inside the tournament room. Ten 9-foot Diamond Pros were arranged in two rows of five. The only occupant was a table mechanic, who was doing some final leveling. Bleachers and cushioned reserved seats surrounded the playing area. The walls and carpeting were decorated in various shades of conference-room beige. The surroundings were larger than either the Hollywood Park Casino pavilion or the Las Vegas penthouse, but this venue felt more like a regular poolroom.

Sedonia returned to the foyer. Off to the right, a gray-haired man sat at a table. A banner strung across the wall behind him read:

$175,000 Open Nine-Ball Championship
$50,000 Top Prize

Sedonia approached him. "Are you registering players?"

"Sure am," he responded with a pleasant smile. "I'm the tournament director. Which player are you looking for?"

Sedonia pulled ten $100 bills from her jeans pocket. "I'm the player."

"Sure you're in the right place, honey? The women's tournament was last week in Los Angeles."

Sedonia handed him her entry fee. He hesitated, then opened a binder and flipped through three pages of signatures. He handed her a pen and pointed to the next blank line. Sedonia signed her name next to the number "94." As she returned the pen, she said, "How many players are you expecting?"

"Hope to have 128," he said. He turned the binder so he could read her signature, then looked up. "Sedonia Forbes, huh? You the gal who knocked off Margaret in Los Angeles?"

Sedonia nodded, noting he'd simply said "Margaret"—no last name had been necessary.

He leaned back, as if appraising Sedonia in a new light. "Well, you must be pretty strong, because Margaret's tough to beat. You'll be the only gal in *this* tournament, though."

"Will there be a players meeting?"

"No, but about 9:00 tonight, I'll post the brackets and start times."

"Can I see who else has entered so far?"

"Sure," he said, and turned the binder so she could read it.

Sedonia started with the first page, scanning the names. Most of the top players in the country were here, including Efren Reyes, Johnny Archer, Earl Strickland, Cory Deuel, Jose Parica, and Jeremy Jones. At the bottom of page two, she found the No. 1 player in the world, Victor Morella—the Filipino who had arrived late at Tough Times last week. Sedonia turned to the third page and, near the bottom, found the name she was looking for: James Dupre. Just as she'd suspected, there was no way "French Quarter" Jimmy would skip a possible $50,000 payout.

A little after 9:00 p.m., Sedonia returned to the mezzanine, this time carrying her cue case. A dozen men were gathered around two 4' x 8' bulletin boards that held the tournament bracket sheets. However, no sign of Jimmy. Maybe he was in the practice room.

The players were laughing and talking among themselves as she approached, but quieted as she worked her way to the front of the group, so she could see the pairings.

"You're the young lady who won in Los Angeles," said a distinguished, middle-aged man to her right.

"Yeah, that was me."

"I watched it on TV. You play excellent pool. Unfortunately, tomorrow morning I'll get a firsthand look at your game." He pointed to the second pairing on the sheet in front of them. "You and I play at 11:00."

Sedonia nodded, but the pairing right above theirs had drawn her attention. Victor Morella had received an opening-round bye, and would be waiting to play the winner of Sedonia's first match. She sighed. This draw was even worse than in Los Angeles, where she'd had to face Margaret in her fourth match.

She scanned the rest of the pairings. The tournament had drawn a few less than 128 players. The top-rated men had been seeded across the brackets. Most, like Victor, had received byes in their opening matches. She didn't see Jimmy's name on the first board, and moved over to the second. She found him near the top; he also played at 11:00.

Sedonia crossed the foyer, aware of the attention she was drawing, and entered the practice room. No sign of Jimmy. Only two of the six tables were in use. On one, a player was practicing by himself. On the other, two players appeared to be gambling, but judging by the bored expressions of the three railbirds, it must be a low stakes match. Apparently it was too early for the high rollers, or maybe they were doing their gambling in the casino this evening.

Sedonia walked over to an unoccupied table and opened her cue case. As she screwed her stick together, she wondered if Jimmy knew she was here in Reno. If so, he might be avoiding her. More likely, though, he probably was in a neighborhood poolroom, hustling locals like he'd done in Las Vegas. She chalked the tip of her cue, undecided how she would handle the scene when she encountered him. Calling the Seabrook police was an option. Maybe they could handle things through the Reno authorities. But then she shook her head. Having an opposing player thrown in jail on the first day of the tournament probably wouldn't be a good idea.

Sedonia tested her shoulder with a few long shots. Slightly stiff, but no pain. If she was lucky enough to stay alive in the tournament, it would be a long four days. She chalked her cue again, and decided to postpone any decision about Jimmy. Tonight, she'd practice for an hour, just to ensure she stayed in stroke, and then get to bed early.

* * *

Sedonia entered the tournament room at 10:45 the next morning, right on schedule. She'd prepared herself as well as she could. Before going to bed the night before, she'd laid out a regimen designed to meet the rigors of the next four days. After a good night's rest, she'd awakened early and worked out in the hotel's 17th floor exercise room, going through her stretching routine and putting in 30 minutes on a stationary bike. After a long, hot shower, she'd had breakfast in Mel's Diner on the 1st floor, and then killed time over coffee, so she wouldn't arrive too early for her first match.

Now as she walked toward table No. 5, she looked around the room. No sign of Jimmy, but she saw her distinguished-looking opponent smiling as she approached.

"Good morning," he said. "I was just warming up." Although he obviously was in mid rack, he raked the balls down to the break end of the table, politely indicating that Sedonia could warm up. "I hope you'll go easy on me," he said. "I probably don't belong here. Last month I won the La Costa Country Club championship, and my daughter thought it would be fun if I entered this tournament."

"Right," Sedonia said, not buying his modesty. She hadn't run into a pool player yet, who didn't understate his ability before a match.

"That's my daughter over there," the man said. A smiling, slightly over-weight young woman waved to them from the reserved seats.

Sedonia returned her wave, then went to work on a practice rack. As she circled the table, pocketing balls with ease, she experienced a sense of well being, and an excitement in knowing she was about to compete against the best pool players in the world. Then she looked across the room and saw Jimmy arrive on table No. 1. They made momentary eye contact, before he looked away. Sedonia felt a surge of anger, and continued to watch him as he screwed his cue stick together. Eleven in the morning was early for him. He looked as if he'd spent the night in a dirty clothes hamper. She shook her head. What had she ever seen in him? She returned her attention to the practice rack.

"I told you I didn't belong here," the man said as he and Sedonia shook hands after her 9 to 1 victory.

"You didn't play poorly," Sedonia said. "I've just been in stroke this past week, and I didn't give you a chance to shoot."

"Could we get a picture before you go?" he said.

"Sure," Sedonia replied. The man's daughter came over with a digital camera. Sedonia posed first with the father, and then with the daughter.

"And would you autograph my program?" the daughter said. Sedonia signed her name, but this time, with the trace of a smile, left off "The Bay Area Bomber."

"Good luck the rest of the way," the father said.

"You too," Sedonia replied.

She walked down to the other end of the room and found a place between the bleachers, overlooking table No. 1. The score markers strung above the table indicated that Jimmy was ahead, 5 to 2. He was strutting around the table in his usual cocky, intimidating manner, when he looked over and saw her. He miscued on his next shot.

Sedonia regretted not being able to hang around and see if she could completely unhinge him, but she needed to prepare for her next match, which would be at 1:00 against Victor Morella.

Victor was completing a warm-up rack when Sedonia arrived for their match. She looked around the room as she pulled her cue stick out of its case. Only a third of the bleacher seats were filled. Many fans probably were still at lunch. She screwed her stick together, and then walked over and extended her hand. "I'm Sedonia Forbes."

Victor conveyed intensity, even when he wasn't competing. Dark eyes bored out of a pale complexion, and a shock of straight, black hair couldn't be controlled. As they shook hands, he said, "Florante told me to watch out for you. He said you shoot like a man."

He'd said it without relaxing his intense expression, and Sedonia wasn't sure if he was serious or kidding. "Naw," she said, "I'm just a girl." Her attempt at a modest quip fell flat. She sounded too much like the man she'd played that morning. Victor began pulling balls out of the pockets, as if he planned to shoot some more. Sedonia stepped forward. "My turn." With a half-smile, he relinquished the table.

As Sedonia worked through the practice rack, she tried to settle her pre-match nerves and psyche herself up. She felt good and was in stroke. She'd had an ideal first match, where as Victor had drawn a bye. It might take him a game or two to get warmed up. On the other hand, he was the top player in the world . . .

The tournament director's voice came over the P.A. system, "All right gentlemen . . . make that lady and gentlemen . . . lag for first break."

Victor won the lag by less than an inch. Sedonia pulled the Sadro Tight Rack out from under the table, then remembered that in this tournament, the person whose turn it was to break, racked for himself. The intent was to eliminate player complaints about not receiving fair racks.

Sedonia settled back in her chair, interested in observing Victor's break technique. He lined up on the cue-ball, exactly as Buster had recommended. But he broke hard, making not only the yellow 1-ball in the side, but two others as well. Then he worked his way around the table, efficiently pocketing the remaining six. He led 1 to 0 in the race-to-9.

Victor again broke hard, and again made three balls on the break. Sedonia looked around the room, and her confidence wavered. The men on the tables nearby also were breaking hard. She hadn't noticed this in her previous match, since she'd only allowed her opponent one opportunity to break. A few minutes later, Victor made the 9-ball in the corner." The score was 2 to 0.

On Victor's third break, he made four balls. Sedonia heaved a sigh. Clearly, the Sardo Tight Rack wasn't going to be the equalizer that it had been in Los Angeles. If she broke easy here, it would put her at a one or two ball disadvantage. That is, *if* she ever got a chance to break. Moments later, Victor made the 9-ball in the side.

In the fourth, fifth, and sixth games, she studied his style. His stroke was compact, smooth, and consistent. His position play was only average, but this was offset by his concise shot making. Finally, late in the sixth game, he got too far out of position and missed the maroon 7-ball in the side.

Sedonia turned her back to the table and sprinkled some talcum powder on her bridge hand. The bleachers had filled, and the man and daughter from her morning match sat nearby in reserved seats. The man caught Sedonia's eye and pointed to the score makers strung above the table. Sedonia could only respond with a wry smile and shake of her head.

As she approached the table, she remembered how her first match against Margaret had gotten away from her. Now she forced herself to concentrate on making one ball at a time. She ran out, making the score 5 to 1 in the race-to-9.

She racked, then went around to the break end of the table. Since changing to her new break, she'd consistently made a ball, and sometimes two. But now, to compete with these men, it seemed necessary to break harder. She assumed her stance, and leaned down, still indecisive. As the cue stick went forward, she held back at the last instant, causing her to miscue slightly. Nothing fell; she'd allowed Victor back to the table.

He ran that rack, and then the next, making the score 7 to 1. He made three balls on the next break, but scratched. Sedonia returned to the table, and again collected her thoughts and told herself to concentrate on each shot. The balls weren't spread out enough for a run-out. She made two balls, then settled for a safety. Victor missed, and Sedonia returned to the table and made the rest. The score was 7 to 2.

Using her soft break in the tenth game, she made the yellow 1-ball in the side. The other balls, however, remained at the rack end of the table.

Sedonia and Victor traded a half-dozen safeties before Sedonia finally managed to get out.

She used her soft break again, but this time the 1-ball stuttered in the side pocket, and failed to drop. Victor ran the rack. The score was 8 to 3; he was on-the-hill.

As Victor racked for the twelfth game, Sedonia sat on the sideline, hoping for a miracle that would get her back to the table. She was playing well; she just wasn't getting to play enough. The crash of his break snapped her attention back to the table. The cue-ball bounced several times, but stayed in play. When the object balls finally came to rest, four had found pockets. He easily made the remaining five.

Sedonia heaved a sigh, then got up and walked over and congratulated him. As she unscrewed her stick, the man and his daughter came over to offer their condolences.

"You beat me, 9 to 1, and he beat you, 9 to 3," the man said. "Just imagine what he would have done to me!"

Sedonia forced a smile. The man had meant well, but he'd insinuated that Victor was much stronger than she was. She knew she couldn't afford to accept that.

She walked over to the bulletin board, and watched an official enter her name on the one-loss side. Her next match would be at 7:00 that night. As had been the case in Los Angeles, being sent to the one-loss side meant she'd have to play several extra matches to have a chance to win this tournament.

Before heading for her room, she scanned the other board. Jimmy also had lost his second match.

Sedonia sat at the small hotel-room desk, waiting for Raul to answer the phone. She glanced over at the clock-radio on the bedside table: 3:43 p.m. She still had three hours before reporting for her next match.

The line clicked. "Forbes Painting. Can I help you?"

"*Hola, Raul.* How's everything going there?"

"No problems," he said cheerfully. "I was just locking up." He gave her a rundown on current projects, and concluded by telling her that their operating account still had a balance of more than $7,000, from the $10,000 she'd deposited from Los Angeles. He said that Brad still stopped by at least once a day, but now he seemed very happy. And Mr. Huff had never come back.

They chatted a bit more, then Sedonia said, "Okay, Raul, I'll let you go. I'll be home no later than Sunday."

After they'd hung up, she smiled. She missed the daily activities of her business, and the people who worked for her. For the first time since the death of her father, she realized how much she'd taken for granted.

That night, Sedonia's opponent stalked out of the tournament room without offering the obligatory handshake, after she eliminated him from the tournament by the surprisingly one-sided score of 9 to 2. She wasn't surprised by his behavior. He was a top-rated player, but had the reputation of being a hothead. His unofficial nickname was "Crying John."

She went over to the scorer's table and reported her win. The young woman tallying the scores said, "Way to go!" She entered the match score on the bracket sheet, then told Sedonia she didn't play again until 9:00 the next morning. Her opponent's name was already written in. A tight smile formed on Sedonia's lips. Small world.

A reporter from *Billiards Digest Magazine* walked up and thrust a tape recorder microphone in front of her face. "How does it feel to knock off one of the top male players in the country?"

"I'm pleased with the win," Sedonia said. "It means I get to come back tomorrow."

"But with more than a hundred men in this tournament, do you really think you can win it?"

Sedonia sensed he hoped to lead her into making a battle-of-the-sexes comment, so she cut short the interview with, "Ask me on Saturday night. If I'm still around."

She turned her attention to a dozen spectators waiting near the entrance, and dutifully signed each autograph book, program, and scrap of paper offered her as she made her way toward the door. Signing the round surface of a cue-ball proved tricky, but she managed a fairly legible signature. She noted she seemed to have an equal number of men and women fans.

When she'd signed the last autograph, she crossed the foyer and entered the practice room. Railbirds again crowded around the far corner table, sweating the action. In their midst, sat Jimmy. His strident New Orleans accent rang out above the others. He didn't see her until she arrived at the next table, which was unoccupied. When he spotted her, he initially looked away, then looked back with a sneer, as if to mask his discomfort.

Sedonia maintained eye contact as she laid her cue case on the table, withdrew her stick, and screwed it together. The dozen or more men around the other table grew quiet, seemingly aware that something was up. Even the two players interrupted their game. Sedonia reached into her left front slacks pocket and pulled out a fold of $100 bills and laid ten of them on the table.

A grizzled railbird sidled up to her. "I'm called Snaggletooth," he drawled, then grinned as if to validate his claim. "What kinda action you lookin' for?"

Sedonia ignored him, and pointed to Jimmy. "I want to play you."

Jimmy didn't respond.

Sedonia said, "Nine-Ball, race-to-9, $1,000."

Jimmy glared.

"No gamble?" Sedonia pressed. "Or no balls?"

Jimmy jumped to his feet. "Make it $2,000!"

Sedonia felt her pulse accelerate. "How about $3,000?" she said.

Jimmy hesitated, and the railbirds started to woof. "Make it $4,000," he said.

Now Sedonia hesitated. She'd planned on at least two sets, but Jimmy had raised the stakes quicker than she'd anticipated. If she lost, she'd barely have enough money to cover her expenses for the next three days. But this wasn't about money. And it wasn't about competition. She wanted to beat this man. Beat him bad!

Sedonia again pulled out the fold of $100 bills, counted out another $3,000, and dropped them on the table. "Tournament rules," she said, "including rack for yourself."

Jimmy nodded. "Snag'll hold the stakes." They each gave their $4,000 to the railbird called Snaggletooth. Jimmy screwed together his cue stick and walked over to the table where they'd be playing. If he was still uncomfortable over the embezzlement, he did a good job of not showing it.

The set concluded on the other table, and interest in the room now turned to this new match-up. Jimmy launched into his usual, obnoxious woofing with the railbirds; however, Sedonia noticed he wasn't taking side bets. Possible indication of fear?

Jimmy wanted to flip for first break, but Sedonia insisted on tournament rules, and she easily won the lag. Her hands were steady as she rolled the balls into the Sardo Tight Rack. Jimmy continued to drone on with the railbirds, but Sedonia partitioned him out and collected her thoughts. She'd been in stroke for more than a week, and at this moment she was more than warmed up. She'd just tortured a top professional. Her shoulder felt okay. She'd broken hard twice in her just-completed match, then she'd been able to coast to victory with soft breaks. *This* was the match-up she'd come here for. She'd do whatever it took.

A hard break pocketed the yellow 1-ball in the side, plus two others. Sedonia picked up where she'd left off in her nine o'clock tournament match. In twenty minutes, she was up 4 to 0 in the race-to-9, and Jimmy had yet to get to the table. On the last break, her shoulder had sent a warning twinge, so for the fifth game, she went to half-speed, but still pocketed the 1-ball. She glanced over at Jimmy as she chalked her cue. His chatter had ceased, and now he stared at the floor. He looked defeated. Sedonia lined up on the blue 2-ball in the corner, then shifted her aiming point slightly to the left. The ball went where she shot it, failing to fall.

Jimmy jumped to his feet. His cocky strut was back, and he resumed his banter with the railbirds. Sedonia pulled up a stool and looked around. The number of spectators had grown while she'd been shooting. Apparently, word of the match-up had spread across the mezzanine. Now, three or four dozen people surrounded the table.

As Jimmy worked his way through the rack, Sedonia remembered the first time she'd seen him play, hustling a local player in Buster's back room. Firing fast and loose, he'd displayed intimidating skill and confidence. Here, he still was firing fast and loose, but she knew that during the past several months she'd competed against better players. She'd beaten better players.

Jimmy ran three racks, then attempted a jump shot, when prudence called for playing a safety. He missed the shot and left Sedonia with perfect position. Still, he strutted back to his seat, as if confident he was back in the match.

Sedonia finished the rack. Then still relying on her slow break, she ran the next, making the score 6 to 3. Once again, Jimmy grew quiet on the sideline. In the middle of the tenth game, Sedonia again aimed slightly off line, missed the shot, and allowed him back to the table.

He rose to his feet, more slowly this time, as if wary. Rather than firing fast and loose, he began to study each shot. He finished the rack, and then ran the next two, tying the score at 6 to 6.

Sedonia drew a deep breath, apprehensive for the first time in the match. Maybe she'd gone on her stall too early. In the thirteenth game, Jimmy broke as hard as seemed humanly possible. The cue-ball flew off the table and crashed into the wall. "Motherfucker!" he screamed.

Sedonia retrieved the cue-ball, and then waited until Jimmy returned to his seat. As she surveyed the table, he continued swearing in the background. She took a deep breath and released it. Four balls were down, and the rest should be easy. She needed to get out from here. Jimmy was too strong to allow him back to the table. But, he hadn't displayed his usual confidence during the match, and if she won the last three games and he lost 9 to 6, he might not play again.

She suppressed a smile. She knew what to do. First though, she needed to get on-the-hill. Now, she too began to study each shot, as if she were uncertain. She finished the rack, and then, with a soft break, made the yellow 1-ball in the side pocket, and ran the rack. She was on-the-hill, 8 to 6.

She racked the balls, then went to the break end of the table. She took a deep breath. This was going to hurt. Possibly it would eliminate her from the tournament, but to keep this match going she had to risk it. She placed the cue-ball next to the right side rail, then leaned over the table and gritted her teeth. *One, two, three . . . stroke!* She broke with all the force she could muster and felt a stab of pain. Balls seemed to fight for pockets, and the cue-ball came to rest in the middle of the table.

Sedonia let her right shoulder droop, and with her left hand she massaged the area above the shoulder blade. The ache passed, but she continued to rub. She walked around the table assessing the layout, every once in a while shrugging and massaging her shoulder. When she began to shoot, she shot more softly than usual and took longer between shots. Finally the cue-ball drifted down the table and left an easy shot on the gold-striped 9-ball. She slow-rolled it into the corner pocket, winning the set, 9 to 6.

Snaggletooth paid her off, and while she counted out eighty $100 bills, Jimmy had to be separated from a railbird who'd gotten too explicit in his jibes about Jimmy's losing to a "split-tail."

Sedonia gave a confirming nod to Snaggletooth that all $8,000 was there. Then she turned to Jimmy. "Let's go again. Same way."

He shook his head.

She rubbed her shoulder.

"One thousand," he said, uncertainty in his voice.

"*One* thousand?" Sedonia said, loud enough for all the spectators to hear. "I thought you had gamble."

Jimmy looked around, then approached her. He hissed through clenched teeth, so those around them couldn't hear, "I don't have $4,000."

Sedonia took a step back and again played to the spectators. "Try that lame excuse on somebody else. You stole $22,000 from me. Remember?"

He closed the space between them, and again hissed, "I lost it all in Houston. That's the reason I hauled ass back to Nevada, to try and win enough to pay you back."

"How much do you have?"

He hesitated, then said, "About $3,000, but I need $2,700 of that to get my car back."

"Get your car back?"

"I had an oil leak crossing the desert. Engine blew in Carson City. Car's still there."

"I'd feel sorry for you, if you weren't such a crook."

"I said, I was gonna pay you back!"

"*When* did you plan to do that, Jimmy? Sometime next month, after I'd lost my business?" He looked down at the pool table, as if hoping she'd end this confrontation. Instead, she said in loud voice, again playing to the dozens of people standing around, "Four thousand dollars . . . or get off the table!"

She saw hatred in Jimmy's dark eyes. Remembering his shady past, she wondered if she'd pushed him too far.

Jimmy whirled. "Snag! Stake me to a dime."

"I dunno, Jimmy," Snaggletooth drawled. "I think this gal's too strong for you."

Sedonia watched Jimmy's response, and thought she saw a hint of relief on his part. Not having enough to cover the bet, he could get off the table and at least save a little face. She turned to Snaggletooth. "Same as last time, but I'll give him the 8-ball."

Snaggletooth studied her offer of weight for a moment, then counted out ten $100 bills.

Jimmy hesitated, then gave a shrug, as if trying to convey the stakes were of no consequence. His gesture fell short. He counted out thirty $100 bills, which appeared to leave him with only a few smaller bills, which he returned to his pocket. As he and Sedonia prepared to lag for first break, she looked over at him and sensed his fear.

Sedonia won the lag by a couple of inches. Then, as she'd done in the last game of the previous set, she opened this game, breaking with full force and making three balls. Again she felt a stab of pain, but this time she gave no indication. Instead she chalked her cue, and looked at Jimmy and smiled. He glowered back at her, slowly shaking his head. At that moment, he no doubt realized she'd sucked him into this second set, by making him think she was injured. The shark had reacted instinctively to what he'd thought had been the sight of blood.

She turned her attention to the table. Three balls were down, and the rest looked good. *One, two, three . . . stroke.*

"You sandbaggin' bitch!" Jimmy said through clenched teeth. "You were on a fuckin' stall!"

"Wasn't that what you tried to teach me, Jimmy?" Sedonia said, then counted out the eighty $100 bills Snaggletooth had given her. She slipped the $8,000 into her slacks pocket, with the $4,000 from the first set, and began unscrewing her stick.

Jimmy pulled a small fold of bills from his pocket and quickly counted them. Then he said, "One game for $200."

Sedonia shook her head.

"You can't quit me now!" Jimmy bellowed, his face turning crimson.

"Got to rest up for tomorrow morning," Sedonia said, slipping her stick into its case. "Got a big match at 9:00. You and me."

From the expression on Jimmy's face, it was evident he hadn't checked the tournament board in the past few hours. Sedonia headed toward the doorway, and the spectators smiled as she passed. As she entered the foyer and headed for the stairs, she heard Jimmy's strident voice rise again. "Who wants to flip for $200? Nobody? Nobody's got any gamble? I'll put up $200 against $100! One flip of a coin!"

Sedonia turned off the bathroom light, and crossed the room. As she turned down the bed covers, she glanced at the clock-radio: 11:07 p.m. She sighed, knowing sleep would be impossible. She was still too keyed up after her match with Jimmy. Something akin to melancholy swept over her. Homesickness? Perhaps. She'd been on the road for more than a week.

She walked over to the small desk and considered calling Hannah or Buster, even though it was past 1:00 a.m. in Nassau Bay. No, Hannah or Buster wouldn't do. She picked up the receiver.

Moments later, a sleepy, deep voice said, "Uh . . . hullo."

"Hi, Brad. I'm . . . sorry to wake you. I just . . . you know . . ."

"When the hell you comin' home?"

Sedonia felt a warm glow. That was the response she needed to hear. "I've got reservations for Saturday night, after the tournament finals. I'm scheduled to leave here at 9:00 p.m. my time, and arrive Houston Hobby at 3:00 a.m. your time."

"I'll be there to pick you up."

"Not at three in the morning," she protested with a laugh.

"I said, I'll be there."

Sedonia smiled. She knew how she felt, and what she wanted to say, but settled for, "Thanks, Brad. I'm . . . really looking forward to seeing you."

They talked for a while. She described Reno and the tournament, but didn't mention Jimmy. She concluded, saying, "The competition here is unbelievably tough. The $50,000 first place money has attracted the very best players. Soon as I lose again, I'm out of the tournament. I could be on my way home as early as tomorrow."

"Damn," Brad said with a chuckle, "you're puttin' me in a position where I kinda hope you lose."

Sedonia smiled again, and was at a loss for words. "I'll let you get back to sleep," she said finally. "I need to get some rest myself. I just wanted . . . to talk to you."

"Call me anytime," he said. "I mean *anytime*. And seriously, good luck out there. Just wish I was with you."

After they hung up, Sedonia opened the drapes and gazed out the window. Her 14th floor room overlooked a railroad track that ran through Reno's cluster of aging hotel-casinos. Nearby, gaudy neon signs flashed above Fitzgerald's and Harold's. And far beyond the casinos, against the desert night sky, she could see the silhouettes of barren hills.

Sedonia's vision blurred, and her thoughts returned to Brad. She so wanted to be with him at that moment; she didn't see how she could wait for three days. And her business; she was anxious to get back and take charge. She turned and looked at her suitcase lying on the credenza. She didn't *have* to wait. She didn't *have* to continue in this tournament. She'd come here to confront Jimmy, and she'd done that. Playing him again tomorrow morning would mean nothing. She could get a flight out of here instead. She opened the desk drawer and withdrew the Yellow Pages to look up the Southwest Airlines number.

Then for reasons she didn't understand, a portion of a poem began to run through her mind, and she returned her gaze to the night outside. She'd learned the verse while in high school, before her mother moved away. She couldn't remember who had written it, or in what context. All she could remember were the concluding lines:

> *Let me do it now.*
> *Let me not defer or neglect it,*
> *For I shall never pass this way again.*

Her cue case lay on the desk. She unzipped it, withdrew her stick, and screwed it together. Simple elegance. It had brought her so far.

She returned the telephone book to the desk drawer. Then she again directed her gaze to the silhouettes of the stark hills that rose beyond the casinos. She would compete as hard as she could, for as long as she could, so she would never look back and wonder what might have been.

Chapter 22

Sedonia sat in a booth in Mel's Diner, lingering over morning coffee and killing time before her nine o'clock match with Jimmy. Sounds from the casino drifted through the open doorway and mixed with Elvis Presley's *Love Me Tender,* playing on the jukebox. A half-dozen waitresses worked the crowded room; their cheerleader uniforms complemented the diner's Fifties and Sixties decor. From their enthusiastic chatter, Sedonia gathered most attended the University of Nevada—Reno. She wondered if the universities here and in Las Vegas offered anything other than hotel management curriculums.

She redirected her gaze out the window to the hotel parking lot and listened to two middle-aged couples in the next booth discuss how they were going to pass the day. The wives planned to sightsee in Virginia City, which Sedonia gathered must be a former mining town. The husbands had tee times at a local golf course, although the weatherman had forecasted a high of 105. Sedonia was glad she'd be playing indoors today.

Past the parking lot and the adjacent street, a train rumbled by. An earlier one had awakened her a little after 4:00. After that, she'd been unable to get back to sleep, and finally had gotten up around 5:30 and worked out in the 17th floor fitness center. Sometime today, she'd need to take a nap.

She checked her watch: 8:40. She wanted to minimize any awkwardness with Jimmy, so she didn't want to arrive too early. On the other hand, she needed to get there in time to warm up. And, she'd never cared too much for Elvis Presley. She picked up her check and headed for the checkout register.

Sedonia glanced at her watch: 9:02. Still no sign of Jimmy. She spread the balls across the table and resumed shooting. Her shoulder felt tender, but the morning stiffness had loosened.

"Where's your opponent?" asked a man's voice.

Sedonia turned. The tournament director had walked up behind her. "No idea," she said. "Maybe somebody should call his room."

"It's not my responsibility to wake people up," the director said. "If he's not here by 9:10, he forfeits and is out of the tournament. That means he also finishes out of the money."

Sedonia shrugged and resumed shooting.

She was practicing bank shots when the director returned. "No sign of him. You're the winner. You play again at 1:00."

Puzzled, Sedonia unscrewed her stick. Moments later, as she exited the tournament room, she saw Snaggletooth crossing the foyer. "Snag!" she called out. He stopped, and Sedonia walked over. "Jimmy didn't show up for our nine o'clock match."

"He's gone," Snaggletooth said. "Left owin' me a dime."

"He left?"

"After you robbed him last night, nobody would stake him, so he hocked everything he had—watch, rings, even his cue sticks and case. Then he came back and lost it all in the casino. Jimmy's like most road players— a stone gambler. He thinks because he can gamble pool and win, it oughta work in a casino too. But in a casino, the house has too much weight."

Sedonia nodded. Snaggletooth had accurately described Jimmy.

"And a pool player hockin' his cue stick," Snaggletooth continued, "that's just plain dumb."

"That *was* dumb," Sedonia said. "The winner of our match was guaranteed to finish in the money."

Snaggletooth gave a dismissive shake of his head. "He knew there was no way he was gonna beat you. Now, I guess he's on the highway, headed back to Louisiana."

"I don't think so," Sedonia said. "Last night, he told me his car was in Carson City with a blown engine."

Snaggletooth responded with a braying laugh, obviously not sympathetic toward the man who owed him $1,000. "Come to think of it, last time I saw Jimmy was about 6:00 this morning. He left out of Mel's Diner, and was walking toward the railroad tracks."

Late that night, Sedonia leaned back in the fitness center's Jacuzzi. She was the only person in the 17th floor exercise facility, other than an elderly Latina attendant, who passed out towels at a station near the entrance. Sedonia repositioned herself so the water jet played against her right shoulder blade.

Despite having received a forfeit that morning, the day had been demanding. Her afternoon matches at 1:00 and 5:00 had been relatively easy; she'd won by scores of 9 to 4 and 9 to 2. During these matches, she'd noticed that her opponents were acting differently toward her. They were displaying the nervousness she'd felt in the past, when competing against renowned players. She'd recalled what Buster had told her long ago: striking fear in your opponent was worth three games on the wire in a race-to-9.

Her 9:00 p.m. match, however, had been a struggle. She'd played a top professional, and toward the end, she'd had to resort to a hard break and frequent safeties to eke out a 9 to 7 victory.

Now, the warm water felt good rushing against her sore shoulder. Her eyes began to droop. She hadn't taken the nap she'd planned. Instead, she'd enjoyed a long telephone conversation with Brad.

The fitness center attendant entered the room, and said in accented English, "You like another towel?"

"*Gracias,*" Sedonia replied.

The woman responded with a smile and raised her eyebrows. "You speak Spanish?"

"A little. *Un poquito.*"

"You tired from gambling?"

"I don't gamble," Sedonia said. "I play pool."

The woman frowned.

Sedonia said, "Uh . . . *juego . . . billar.*"

"*¡Ah, si!*" the woman said, and pantomimed shooting. *"Juega billar."*

Sedonia nodded and smiled, but felt too exhausted to struggle with a bilingual conversation. The woman seemed to sense it. She too smiled, and then returned to her post at the entrance.

Sedonia thought of Raul and the rest of her crew. She was surprised how much she missed them and looked forward to seeing them again.

She directed her attention out the plate glass window. The Jacuzzi overlooked the western side of the city. The other hotel-casinos were on the opposite side of the building, so from this vantage point, Reno appeared to be a quiet, sleeping town. Only a few cars' lights moved along nearby Interstate 80, which led to Northern California.

Sedonia's thoughts returned to the tournament. Her 6 and 1 record guaranteed her a 9th to 12th place finish, worth $10,000. However, she was barely halfway through the tournament. If she kept winning, tomorrow also would be a four-match day. Plus, the competition would grow even stronger, as lesser players were eliminated.

She slid lower in the tub to allow the water jet to rush against the back of her neck. Her eyelids again began to droop, then abruptly they opened wide and she sat up. Why was she thinking so negatively about tomorrow? She'd never done that before a golf tournament. She'd looked forward to competition.

She grabbed a towel and climbed out of the tub. She needed a good night's rest. Big day tomorrow.

Sedonia came out of the mezzanine ladies room. Across the foyer, a dozen fans stood near the tournament room doorway, smiling and waiting for her. As she approached, she had the feeling that Friday would never end. She'd had tough, grinding matches at 9:00 a.m. and 11:00 a.m., winning by scores of 9 to 5 and 9 to 7. Then she'd had a two-hour break, much of which she'd spent in the Jacuzzi soothing her aching shoulder. Fortunately, her 3:00 p.m. match had been a walkover, 9 to 2, but now she had to come right back and play again at 5:00.

"Would you sign my program, please?" asked an eager young woman.

"Sure," Sedonia said. "Be glad to." She leaned her cue case against one leg, and began signing whatever the fans thrust in front of her. After several minutes, when she'd signed the last one, she shouldered her cue case and glanced at her watch. She only had ten minutes to warm up before her last match of the day.

A pleasant deep voice behind her said, "Sign one more, please?"

Sedonia turned. "Brad!" In an instant, she was in his arms. "I don't believe it," she murmured, squeezing him as tightly as she could.

"I couldn't wait 'til tomorrow night," he said.

Tears filled Sedonia's eyes. Spectators on their way into the tournament room smiled as they passed. The tournament director walked by and said, "Somehow, Sedonia, I get the impression you know this guy."

Sedonia could only nod.

"You're up in five minutes," the director said over his shoulder as he passed through the doorway.

Brad gently extricated himself from her embrace. "Why the tears?" he said, as if uncertain whether to be amused or concerned.

"I don't know," she said. "Give me your handkerchief. She took a deep breath, and as she dabbed her eyes, she said, "How's the eyeliner?"

"You look great," he said.

"What are you doing here? When did you get in?"

"I just arrived about fifteen minutes ago. It sounds like you've got a game to play. Go ahead. We'll get caught up when you're done."

Sedonia looked back and forth between Brad and the tournament room.

He took her hand and led her toward the door. "Will my being in the crowd throw you off your game?"

"No . . . well . . . maybe."

"I'll wait for you out here, then."

"No. Well . . . come in. But if I start losing . . . then it's bothering me."

"And I'll leave."

As they entered the tournament room, the director began announcing the pairings for the five o'clock match. Sedonia gave Brad's hand a final squeeze, then headed for the playing area. During the day, eight of the original ten tables had been removed and replaced with additional seating. Still, the bleachers and reserved seats around table No. 1 were packed, and Brad would have to stand.

Sedonia scarcely had time to screw together her cue stick and take her position in front of her chair, before the director announced:

"Now ladies and gentlemen . . . we have our quarterfinal match. A young woman has graced our tournament this year. Just last week, she won the WPBA tournament in Los Angeles. From Nassau Bay, Texas . . . Sedonia—"

The crowd response drowned out her last name. Over the course of the past three days, Sedonia had become a fan favorite. She took a step forward, smiled, and gave a quick wave. Although this would be her fourth match of the day, seeing Brad and arriving late had her feeling disoriented. Everything seemed to be moving too quickly.

"And her opponent . . . three-time world champion . . . a member of the Billiard Congress of America hall of fame . . . Ronnie . . . Harriman!"

Harriman was in his fifties, and at least 75 pounds overweight. He heaved himself out of his chair, acknowledged the applause with a quick wave, and lumbered over to join Sedonia at the break end of the table. The exertion left him wheezing. He all but ignored Sedonia during their quick handshake, then leaned down and lagged in a single motion. Sedonia quickly leaned down and shot. Harriman won the lag.

Sedonia took her seat, irked that he'd sharked her out of the first break. *Concentrate, damn it!* she told herself. Then she frowned. The tournament director was racking the balls on their table, while Harriman stood at the break end, chalking his cue. Sedonia stood up, and walked over.

"Ronnie's had trouble handling the racking because of his . . . health," the director said. "I'll be racking for him this match."

Sedonia didn't respond for a moment. Hall-of-fame member or not, the man's only health problem seemed to be his diet. Finally she nodded her assent, and returned to her seat. Harriman had paid his dues in the world of pool. His attitude still irked her, though.

His break was only about three-quarters speed, but he made two balls. As he worked his way around the table, Sedonia saw for herself how he'd become a legend. His stroke was smooth and his position precise. He ran two racks and was shooting the 9-ball before he missed a relatively easy shot. As he came wheezing back to his seat, Sedonia sensed he wasn't worried. He gave the impression that playing her was a mere formality.

She got up and walked over to the table. He'd left an extremely long, thin cut down the rail, and since the 9-ball was the only ball on the table, there was no opportunity to play a safety. She carefully chalked her cue and allowed herself to enter into a now-familiar state of concentration. Her opponent and the spectators were partitioned out. Her world was the deep green rectangle, and two incandescent balls.

She leaned over. *One, two, three . . . stroke.* The applause exploded the instant the gold-striped 9-ball dropped. The score was 2 to 1.

"Let's hear it for Ronnie Harriman, ladies and gentlemen!" the tournament director said. "Ronnie's fourth place finish is worth $15,000!"

Sedonia joined the spectators in applauding the still wheezing hall-of-fame player. Harriman unscrewed his stick and ignored the crowd response, apparently still stung by his 9 to 3 defeat.

For the first time since the start of the match, Sedonia looked around and tried to find Brad. He waved to her as he worked his way through a crowd of spectators who were standing in an aisle.

"And now," the director continued, "let's hear it for the young lady from Texas . . . who came to play! Her win tonight guarantees that she'll finish no lower than third place. And . . . she may not be done yet!"

The crowed responded enthusiastically.

"Okay," the director said, "next will be the match-up you've all probably come to see. Our final competition of the evening will be between our last two undefeated players, Victor Morello and Ravan Kreig. The winner of that match will go on to the finals. The loser will play Sedonia at one o'clock tomorrow afternoon, to see who else goes to the finals.

As the director continued with the introduction of two players, Sedonia put away her stick, and then walked over and extended her hand to Harriman. He hesitated, then took it in his own soft grip. Peering at her through bushy eyebrows, he said, "You shoot good, kid." Then he released her hand, abruptly turned, and lumbered out of the playing area.

Brad came up. "Unbelievable!" he said as he pulled her into a hug.

"Do you have a rental car?" she said.

"Yeah?"

"I need to sign a few autographs here, and then run by my room to freshen up. Then, get me out of here!"

"I know just the place."

An hour later, Brad pulled into a shady parking lot. Sedonia climbed out and looked about. Towering pine trees swayed in the gentle evening breeze.

A hundred yards up the hill, stood the plush Hyatt Regency Hotel.

Brad came around the car. "Like it here so far?"

"It's beautiful," she said. He took her hand, and they started downhill toward a rustic, two-story building. A carved sign above the entrance read: Sierra Café. "And I see why they call this community, Incline Village. The slope of this parking lot must be at least 30 degrees."

A smiling hostess met them as they stepped inside. "Would you like to sit inside or outside?"

They agreed on outside, and followed her past a high-ceilinged bar area, and then through a large dining room, which featured a massive stone fireplace. Although it was still summer, the café had the cozy feel of a ski lodge.

"Oh, my God," Sedonia murmured as they stepped onto the wide veranda that overlooked Lake Tahoe. She followed the hostess to a table-for-two near the railing, unable to take her eyes off the panorama that lay before them. The late-evening sky had turned a deep blue, accentuating the surrounding gray mountains, which were capped with patches of snow. The magnificent lake lay still, reflecting the sky and extending past the horizon. Nearby, a man and a woman anchored a catamaran, then waded ashore. They seemed to move in slow motion as they crossed the beige sand and ascended the café stairs.

Sedonia reached across the table and squeezed Brad's hand. "When you get back to Nassau Bay on Sunday, liquidate my business and send all my things to me here in Incline Village."

"Hey," Brad said in mock alarm. "I wanted to entertain you, not lose you."

A waitress came over. Sedonia ordered Dewar's and water, and Brad decided he'd have the same. Sedonia resumed her silent enjoyment of the surroundings.

When their drinks arrived, she took a sip, and then asked Brad, "How did you know about this place?"

"Some clients brought me here a few years ago. We skied over at Squaw Valley."

Sedonia raised an eyebrow. "You're a skier?"

"Bunny slopes only," he said with a quick laugh. "Found I was more comfortable in the lodge."

"With the snow bunnies?"

Brad simply responded with a smile, then said, "I never was an athlete. I had to start working when I was a kid, and didn't have time for sports." His expression turned serious. "Listen, there's something I need to get out of the way. I want to apologize again for that lawsuit business."

"You don't need to—"

"Yes, I do," Brad interrupted. "There's no way I should have put that kind of pressure on you. Your dad was . . . my hero."

"Mine too."

For a moment, Brad seemed lost in recollections, then he said, "He was both a businessman and a sportsman. I focused on business. I wanted to impress him, to make him proud of the time and interest he'd taken in me."

"I know how you felt," Sedonia interjected. "For me, it was taking full advantage of the sports opportunities he gave me."

Brad smiled. "The only thing I knew about golf was that it was a country club game, and you were good at it."

Sedonia looked into Brad's eyes. "We both loved my father. You've developed one of his interests, and I've developed the other."

Brad reached across the small table and caressed her cheek. "We seem to complement each other, don't we?" He leaned forward and kissed her.

"Sorry to interrupt," the waitress said, "but are you folks ready to order?"

They both laughed. They decided on the fish of the day, which was trout.

When the waitress left, Brad said, "I saw something in you when you were playing this afternoon, which I don't know if you're aware of."

Sedonia frowned with interest.

"Your . . . intensity," Brad said. "Your focus. Do you happen to remember a photo of Joe Montana that your dad had in his den?"

Sedonia smiled. "The Cotton Bowl, between the University of Houston and Notre Dame. 'The look of eagles'."

"That's the one," Brad said. "You had that same expression this afternoon. To tell you the truth, you were kinda scary."

"Buster would be pleased to hear you say that. He's a believer of making an opponent fear you."

"Do you agree?"

"If it's a matter of them fearing me, or me fearing them, then I want them to fear me."

"Hmm," Brad responded. "Guess I see how that also could apply to business."

Sedonia opened her purse. "Speaking of business, and while we're getting awkwardness out of the way, here's something I owe you." She handed him her personal check for $22,000."

"Absolutely not!" he protested, and tried to hand it back. "That pool player's the one who embezzled it."

"While he was working for me."

Brad shook his head. "Have him thrown in jail. That's all the repayment I need."

"I want you to join me . . . in dropping charges against him."

A look of hurt momentarily showed on Brad's face. "Why? Is he that important to you?"

"Not important . . . in a romantic way." Sedonia looked out at the lake. It was important that Brad understand. She turned back. "I knew Jimmy was a hustler, and I willingly entered his world. Then I allowed him to enter mine. The fact that he's a crook, is *his* responsibility. The fact that he had the opportunity to steal from you, is *my* responsibility."

Brad looked as if he were about to debate what she'd said, but Sedonia cut him off. "Would you even have *thought* about arguing with my father over a situation like this?"

"Well . . . maybe not. But I can't see dropping charges, and letting this guy get off scot-free."

"That check is his money. Eight thousand of it came right from his pocket. Jimmy and I gambled last night, and I took him for everything he had. He left town this morning, dead broke. And the rest of it's also coming from him . . . indirectly."

"How's that?"

"I'm already guaranteed to finish no lower than third place in the tournament. That'll more than cover what Jimmy stole. I wouldn't have made it this far, except for what I learned from him."

"You learned not to trust people?"

Sedonia smiled. "That too. That lesson cost me $22,000. But that's not what I'm talking about." Again, she chose her words carefully, wanting Brad to understand what she'd only recently discovered. "I was blessed with natural hand-eye coordination. Then Dad and others taught me good technique, both in golf and in pool. But natural ability and technique aren't enough. Two women, who some might consider losers, taught me about 'heart'." Referring to Cissy and Audri, brought tears to Sedonia's eyes, and she paused, and again looked out at the lake.

Brad squeezed her hand and allowed her to recover. When she finally looked back with a sad smile, he said, "And Jimmy?"

"First he taught me about 'gamble'. In his world, they not only play continually for high stakes, they often play for everything they have. Sometimes, for *more* than they have, even risking their lives. But when he and I gambled last night, it wasn't about money. It wasn't even about revenge. It was important . . . *imperative* that I . . . *dominate*. Dominate. I don't know another word for it."

Sedonia paused, and Brad said, "And it sounds like you did . . . dominate. You sent him home empty handed."

Sedonia slowly nodded. "And in the matches I've played since then, I've discovered I can . . . call on that . . . emotion."

"The look of eagles."

Sedonia shrugged. "Whatever it is, if I hadn't come here and played Jimmy, I'd never have learned to marshal it."

Brad slipped her check into his wallet, then gave a wry smile and shake of his head. "God help your painting competitors when you get back home."

Later, they walked hand in hand up the hill to Brad's rental car. They'd been among the last patrons to leave, and the parking lot was almost empty. Night had fallen, and the lake breeze now felt chilly. Brad unlocked Sedonia's door, and she turned into his arms. They shared the kiss she'd longed for, throughout dinner.

"Thanks for a wonderful evening," she said, then hugged him again. "I'm so glad you're here."

"Wish we didn't have to go back," he whispered.

She leaned back so she could look into his eyes. "About ten years ago, I had a terrible crush on you, and you didn't even know I was alive."

"Not so," he said with a chuckle. "I noticed you back then. It just wasn't . . . appropriate, since I was in college and you were in high school. Not to mention, your father would have killed me."

Sedonia laughed. "He probably would have. But now, here we are."

"Here we are. Unbelievable."

They kissed again, and then got into the car. As Brad pulled out of the parking lot, he said, "Let's come back here sometime."

"And stay up there at the Hyatt," Sedonia agreed.

They were approaching the hotel driveway. "C'mon," Brad said. "Let's check it out."

"Okay."

A few moments later, they entered the elegant lobby. Brad guided her over to the casino entrance, and they looked inside. This gambling den didn't have the frenetic atmosphere of those in Las Vegas and Reno. Here, the lighting and sounds were subdued, and patrons seemed to wager at a more leisurely pace. Sedonia supposed the exclusive casinos on the Riviera must be like this.

"I love this place," she said.

"Would you like to come back tomorrow, after the tournament?"

She hesitated, then replied, "Yes."

Brad smiled. "Great. Let's see if we can make reservations."

The desk clerk smiled as they approached. "May I help you?"

"Yeah," Brad said. "We'd like to make reservations, beginning tomorrow, through . . ." He gave Sedonia an enquiring look. "Tuesday?"

"Certainly, sir," the clerk said. "Arriving tomorrow—"

"Make that *tonight* through Tuesday," Sedonia said.

* * *

"Are you nervous?" Brad asked as they drove east on Interstate 80. Ahead, the Reno skyline shimmered in the morning sun.

"After last night?" Sedonia said with a laugh. "I've never felt so relaxed in my life."

Brad reached over and squeezed her hand, then asked, "What do you plan to do between now and your next match?"

Sedonia checked her watch. "I've got almost three hours. Guess I need to get away from you, if I want to get back into man-killer mode."

He laughed. They exited the freeway, and made their way through downtown Reno. A few minutes later, hand in hand, they entered the Sands Regency through its side entrance.

Brad stopped and nodded toward Mel's Diner. "How about another cup of coffee?"

"You go ahead. I need to get ready for this afternoon." They kissed and she said, "I'll see you about 1:00, in the tournament room."

Brad headed for the diner, and Sedonia made her way into the crowded casino. Although it was mid morning, enthusiastic gamblers already occupied most of the slot machines and gaming tables. Sedonia picked up the pace. She planned to work out in the fitness center before reporting for her one o'clock match. She also needed to be sure the hotel cleaners had returned the slacks and shirt she was going to wear today.

As she started down the corridor that led to the hotel lobby, a woman's voice called out, "Miss Forbes!"

A young woman, dressed in jeans and a polo shirt, hurried out of one of the sundries shops, carrying a newspaper. She looked familiar, but Sedonia couldn't place where she'd seen her.

"I'm Karen Hughes," the woman said. "ESPN?"

"Oh, yes," Sedonia said, now recognizing the TV producer from Los Angeles. "What brings you to Reno?"

"Covering you. I've been trying to reach you all morning."

"Covering me?" Sedonia said.

"I need to talk to you. Can we go to your room?"

Sedonia gave an uncertain nod, and resumed walking toward the lobby. "What's going on?"

"Last week," the producer said, "I didn't realize who you were—that you were a former U.S. Women's Amateur Golf champion. You were the one who had a career-ending injury, right?"

Sedonia nodded. "Shoulder."

They crossed the lobby and arrived at the elevator bank.

"I'm a golfer, myself," the producer said, "and I watched reruns of your dramatic eagle on that final hole a dozen times. I *loved* the way you threw caution to the wind, and went with your 1-wood. Didn't you get into an argument with your caddy about it?"

Sedonia smiled at the recollection. "My college coach caddied for me that day. I was up by one stroke, so she wanted me to play it safe and tee off with a 3-wood. She probably was right, but I just had the feeling it was time to 'grip it and rip it'."

"Grip it and rip it," the producer said. "That describes it. But until yesterday, I didn't associate the golfer on TV with the pool player in Los Angeles."

"It's been a long couple of years," Sedonia said. *If this woman only knew.*

An elevator arrived and unloaded. Then Sedonia, the producer, and several other guests boarded. An elderly couple had been the last to get on, and as the elevator began its ascent, the man looked back and smiled. "We're looking forward to seeing you play again this afternoon," he said. "Good luck."

"Thanks," Sedonia said. The other passengers now looked at her with interest, and most smiled. Sedonia realized she was enjoying this new-found celebrity.

She and the TV producer got off the elevator on the 14th floor. As they started down the passageway, Sedonia said, "I need to get ready for my next match. What is it you want to talk about?"

"Last week's live telecast drew a larger share than any of the execs had anticipated. It started slowly, but then grew. By the time you and Margaret played that final game, our audience was five times larger than it's ever been for one of the regular, tape-delayed WPBA telecasts."

They arrived at Sedonia's room, and although she wanted to get ready for the match, she felt obliged to invite the woman inside.

The producer walked over to the window, glanced down, then turned and said, "Yesterday, the execs were reviewing the ratings and considering going live with the next WPBA tournament, when I learned you were here, winning against the men. I convinced them this battle-of-the-sexes could be bigger than when Billie Jean King kicked Bobby Riggs' ass in tennis. You're playing guys in their primes, not over-the-hill has-beens, like Riggs was."

"Listen," Sedonia protested, "I'm not here promoting women's rights. I'm just here to play pool."

"Too late," the producer said. "Have you seen this morning's paper?"

"I haven't read a newspaper in two weeks."

The producer handed Sedonia a copy of the Reno Gazette-Journal sports section. The headline over the lead article read "Lady defeats Legend." Featured was a photo of Sedonia shaking hands with Ronnie Harriman after her 9 to 3 victory. She scanned the article, which recapped her progress through the tournament so far, her previous week's victory in Los Angeles, and her past career as a world-class amateur golfer.

The producer resumed, "We already had a TV crew here in Reno, covering the International Olympic Committee contingent. So, we've preempted our scheduled programming, and we plan to carry today's matches, live. Obviously, we're hoping you're in the finals."

Sedonia suddenly felt a need to get down to the practice room and hit some balls.

"My crew's getting set up," the producer said. "I wanted to contact you and the other two players who are still in contention, so we didn't blindside you with the TV coverage."

The telephone on the desk rang. "I'll let you get that," the producer said, and started toward the door. "Good luck this afternoon. Personally, as well as professionally, I'll be pulling for you."

Sedonia nodded abstractly, then picked up the receiver. "Hello."

"Sedonia Forbes?"

"Yes?"

"This is Malcolm Oglesby, with Striker Cues. I'm down here in the lobby. I understand you don't currently endorse any equipment, and I'd like to come up and discuss your possibly representing us."

"Uh ... I'm sorry, I can't see you now. I have a match in a couple of hours."

"I realize that, but it's imperative we work out the agreement before these televised matches, so there's mention of our equipment."

"You want me to change cue sticks *today?*"

"Any offer I could make would be predicated on that."

Sedonia hesitated. Yesterday, she'd played the best pool of her life, followed by the most remarkable night of her life. Today, she felt as if she were being battered by a Gulf Coast hurricane. She opened her "genuine" Naugahide cue case, withdrew her faithful green Jerry Olivier stick, and screwed it together.

"Miss Forbes?" said the insistent voice.

"Goodbye, Mr. Oglesby."

Sedonia and Snaggletooth were playing One-Pocket in the practice room—$50 a game and $10 a point. Three railbirds had side bets and watched with interest, but otherwise the room was empty. Sedonia glanced down at her watch: 17 minutes before her semifinal match was scheduled to begin. Her opponent probably was already warming up next-door, but she'd opted to avoid as much of the pre-match ballyhoo as possible.

Snaggletooth had left her a cross-corner bank shot. She leaned down. *One, two, three . . . stroke.* The red-striped 11-ball rolled into the pocket. Moments later, she banked the green-striped 14-ball the length of the table for the win.

"Too strong for me, lady," Snaggletooth said. "You move like a ghost."

Sedonia smiled. "Move like a ghost" was a compliment to her defensive skill. Snaggletooth began counting out the $80 he owed her, and Sedonia said, "Keep it. Thanks for warming me up."

Snaggletooth re-pocketed the money, without argument. Then he said, "That German you're about to play? He's a snooker player. He's gonna try to play you safe. But don't worry about it; you're bankin' and kickin' real good. And later, if you get to play that Filipino, he'll shoot with you."

Sedonia nodded, and unscrewed her stick and slid it into its case. She made a final check of her attire. The hotel cleaners had done a good job removing the stains from the charcoal-gray slacks and the long-sleeve white blouse she'd worn in the Los Angeles finals. She'd try to keep the powder and chalk off them this time. She drew a deep breath, then said, "Time to go."

She noticed Snaggletooth didn't reply, and as she reached the door she turned back. "Snag, do you have anything riding on my next match?"

He responded with a look of chagrin. "Yesterday, I laid a dime on the kraut," he said. "But today, I think I fucked the duck."

"We'll see," Sedonia said. She opened the door and stepped into the mezzanine foyer. A knot of fans were blocking the tournament room entrance. A male spectator in front was arguing about reserve seat status. Sedonia waited patiently, her cue case slung over one shoulder. Finally the dispute was resolved, and as the congestion cleared, she heard a man in front of her say, "I heard some woman's kickin' ass."

His companion glanced over at Sedonia. "Her," he said with a grin and a nod. "Sedonia."

As she strode past them and into the crowded tournament room, she had to suppress a smile. There'd been no last name, just "Sedonia."

Spectators responded to her appearance with ripple of applause. The room had been rearranged again. This time only one pool table remained, additional reserve seats had been added, and an ESPN announcers' booth stood off to one side. A TV cameraman picked up Sedonia as she made her way over to the table. Karen Hughes, the producer, hurried over and waved him out of Sedonia's way.

Ravan Krieg was warming up. He acknowledged her with a curt nod, then returned his attention to the table. Sedonia screwed her stick together and waited while he completed running the rack. Then she walked over and picked up the cue-ball, indicating she was ready to practice. Without replying, he relinquished the table and took a seat.

Sedonia was already warmed up from her One-Pocket games with Snaggletooth. However, the tournament table had been moved, so she tried several long, slow shots to check for drift. There was none; the table mechanic had done a good job of re-leveling.

The cameras moved into place and the tournament director hurried over and called the two players together. The TV producer positioned the players on either side of the director, and told him, "Relax. You'll do fine." As she moved out of view of the camera, she whispered in an aside to Sedonia, "He's scared stiff. He's never been on TV before."

Sedonia smiled, realizing she was the veteran in this live TV business. They stood in silence for another minute, then the TV producer began counting backwards from ten. On zero, she pointed to the tournament director.

"Welcome!" he said. His voice broke and he had to start over. "Welcome to Reno, Nevada . . . for the *live* telecast of the semifinal match of the Sands Regency Open. From Hamburg, Germany . . . winner of numerous titles, including three world Snooker championships . . . Ravan Krieg!"

The crowd responded with a round of applause.

"His opponent . . . winner of last week's WPBA tournament in Los Angeles . . . from Nassau Bay, Texas . . . Sedonia Forbes!"

The crowd erupted with cheers and whistles, and Sedonia took a step forward and waved. She knew Brad was out there somewhere, but suppressed the urge to locate him, instead telling herself to remain focused.

As the director went over the rules for the benefit of the TV audience, Sedonia and Ravan moved to the break end of the table. The cameramen panned back and forth; Sedonia was never sure when she was on camera. She thought of Buster and Hannah, undoubtedly watching in Nassau Bay, and she experienced a pang of performance anxiety. She pushed it from her mind, taking several deep breaths and positioning herself for the lag.

Finally the director turned to the players. "Lag for first break."

Sedonia leaned down and in one motion hit her lag shot. Ravan was caught off guard and hit his ball too hard. Sedonia won the lag by more than a foot, and struggled to suppress a smile. Ronnie Harriman couldn't have stolen the lag any better.

The director nodded for Sedonia to begin play.

"You're supposed to rack," she said between her teeth, trying not to embarrass him.

The director responded with a sheepish smile and hurried back to the table. He told the spectators, "Sorry, folks. As the young lady has just reminded me, I rack for the TV matches." His hands shook as he fed the balls into the Sardo Tight Rack. Finally he stepped away, and again nodded for Sedonia to begin.

Sedonia placed the cue-ball on the right rail, and took a deep breath. She'd go with a hard break to open, and try to jump to an early lead. *Intimidation. One, two, three . . . stroke!*

* * *

Sedonia stood poised to break as the tournament director racked for the tenth game. She had run the first three racks in the race-to-9, then shoulder discomfort had warned her to revert to her soft break. The next six games had progressed slowly. When Ravan had finally gotten to the table, as Snaggletooth had predicted, he'd repeatedly resorted to safeties, trying to stop her momentum. Sedonia had either responded with safeties of her own, or managed to shoot her way out of poor position with kicks and banks.

Now the score was 8 to 1, and Ravan sat with the blank expression of someone who had witnessed a train wreck. Sedonia started to place the ball on the left side of the table for another soft break, then changed her mind and moved it to the right side. She'd risk another hard break, and try to close out the match right now.

Deep sigh. *One, two, three . . . stroke!* A stab of pain. Balls careened about the table. The gold-striped 9-ball rolled slowly toward the corner pocket.

"On the snap!" a leather-lung shouted from the bleachers.

Sedonia was in the finals.

Sedonia sat on the edge of the bathtub, stripped to the waist. Brad sat behind her, applying warm washcloths to her right shoulder blade. She checked her watch. The semifinal match had ended so quickly that ESPN had switched back to the studio for a forty-five minute edition of Sports Center. Sedonia needed to be back downstairs in twenty minutes.

"Is the Advil helping?" Brad said.

"Not yet. Sometimes they take a while."

"I'm not sure you should have taken four. I'm surprised you don't have prescription medication for the pain."

"I tried that," she said. "It . . . doesn't work for me."

He applied a freshly warmed cloth and gently massaged her shoulder. "I hate to see you hurting like this."

She patted his hand, then stood up, dried off her shoulder, and slipped back into her bra. "When things are important to you," she said, "sometimes you just have to play through pain."

As they crossed the expansive foyer, Brad handed Sedonia her cue case. She slung it over one shoulder, and they entered the tournament room. The crowd broke into spontaneous applause at her appearance. She gave Brad's hand a quick squeeze, then headed for the playing area, while he went off to find a seat in the bleachers.

Victor Morella was warming up. Attired in tailored black slacks, patent leather shoes, and a ruffled white tuxedo shirt, the trim Filipino was the epitome of a billiard champion. Only the unmanageable shock of straight black hair stood in contrast to his impeccable appearance.

As Sedonia approached, he interrupted his practice and looked at her with his dark, intense eyes. "So, you back, huh?"

"Go easy on me this time. I'm a girl, remember."

"Right," he said, with what may have been a trace of a smile. "I saw you torture Ravan an hour ago."

Sedonia pulled her cue stick out of its case and screwed it together.

"You want to hit some?" Victor said, offering her the table.

"No thanks." Her shoulder pain was only a dull ache now, but she didn't want to risk aggravating it unnecessarily. She pulled up a chair and looked around the room. Brad had found a seat at the top of the bleachers and was smiling at her. She returned his smile, and several men around him waved to her. She laughed.

A number of the professionals who had been eliminated earlier from the tournament had returned to watch the finals. The Philippine Islands were well represented. Seated nearby were pool legends Efren Reyes, Rudolfo Luat, and Francisco Bustamante. She felt a polite tap on her shoulder, and turned to see Florante, the Filipino she'd played at Tough Times in Bellflower.

"Good luck," he said. Then he whispered, "I got a dime bet on you with Efren."

Sedonia laughed. "Thanks."

The TV producer said something to Victor, then came over to Sedonia. "We need to get ready. They're switching back to us in three minutes."

Sedonia got up, and walked over to join Victor and the tournament director. One of the cameramen moved in for a tight shot. The TV producer took her position off to the side. Sedonia looked around, realizing that for some reason she didn't feel anxious. She again found Brad high up in the bleachers. He certainly added to her sense of tranquility. Would it take the edge off her competitiveness? She tried to remember how she'd felt before teeing off on the final round of the U. S. Women's Amateur Golf Championship. Confident. In control.

The TV producer began the backward count from ten. Then she pointed to the tournament director.

"Welcome to Reno, Nevada . . . for the *live* telecast of the Sands Regency Open Nine-Ball Championship! Our two finalists will be playing for $50,000! First, we have five-time World Nine-Ball Champion . . . currently ranked No. 1 in the world . . . undefeated in this tournament at 7 and 0 . . . from Cebu City in the Philippine Islands . . . *Victor Morella!*"

The crowd responded with an enthusiastic welcome.

"His opponent . . . a young woman who's taken the pool world by storm

. . . the WPBA's Los Angeles Champion . . . winner of the one-loss side of this tournament with a record of 11 and 1 . . . from Nassau Bay in Texas . . . *Sedonia!*"

The room erupted. There was no doubt as to the crowd's favorite. When the applause died down, someone in the far bleachers emitted a loud wolf whistle. Sedonia responded with a point in the direction of the whistler, and a broad smile. The crowd laughed and gave her another round of applause.

The tournament director continued, "This final match will be a race-to-11, with alternate breaks. Also, for this match there will be a 30-second time limit between shots, and players will be allowed one 30-second extension per game. Now, please turn off your pagers and cell phones, and no flash photography."

He turned to Sedonia and Victor. "Lag for first break."

They met at the break end of the table and shook hands. Sedonia took a deep breath. In the alternate-break format, it was extremely important to win the lag and get to the table first. They leaned down, and shot simultaneously. Victor won by less than an inch.

Sedonia took her seat while the tournament director racked for the first game. Victor looked intense as he waited to break. As in their first match, he broke hard and scattered balls all over the table. This time, however, none found pockets. Sedonia rose, surprised suddenly to find the break advantage shifted in her favor. She walked to the table, and took her time studying the layout.

"Ten seconds," announced the director.

"Extension," Sedonia replied, gaining another 30 seconds. She'd forgotten about the time limit. From here on, she'd need to pick up the pace. She followed her predetermined shot sequence and ran the rack without any problem. She heaved a sigh of relief; she'd gotten the first game out of the way.

It was her turn to break in the second game. The tournament director racked, and stepped back. Sedonia placed the cue-ball near the right rail, and took a deep breath. *One, two, three . . . stroke!* The pain felt as if someone had driven a nail into her shoulder blade. Two balls found pockets, the cue-ball came to rest in the middle of the table, and the yellow 1-ball offered a makeable cut in the side pocket. It had been a perfect break, but it had come at a price. She chalked her cue stick and appeared to study the table, while she waited for her shoulder throb to subside.

"Ten seconds," said the director.

Sedonia winced. Damn that clock! Rather than expend her extension, she leaned down and quickly shot. The 1-ball fell, but she scratched in the corner. Victor returned to the table, and Sedonia took her seat. A few minutes later, she sighed as Victor pocketed the gold-striped 9-ball in the corner. The score was 1 to 1 in the race-to-11. And, Victor had regained the break advantage.

Each ran their next three racks, making the score 4 to 4. Sedonia's shoulder ached. She grew concerned that if she continued to break hard, she might not be able to finish the match. Victor broke and made three balls, but after pocketing two more, he left himself in poor position on the green 6-ball in the side. Position was the one occasional flaw Sedonia had seen in his game during their earlier match. Now to recover, he played a safety.

Sedonia returned to the table. The 6-ball sat in front of one side pocket, and the cue-ball was near the other. The maroon 7-ball partially blocked the path between them. Sedonia could hit the 6-ball, but wouldn't be able to make it. She weighed the options. Prudence called for a safety. She glanced over at Victor, who gazed back with his usual, dark intensity.

"Ten seconds," announced the tournament director.

"Extension." Still undecided, Sedonia looked over at the TV producer, who was watching with interest. Sedonia smiled and said, "I think it's time to 'grip it and rip it'."

The producer frowned, then broke into a grin.

Sedonia lined up the shot, raised the butt of her stick, and drove the cue-ball into the slate. The cue-ball jumped the 7-ball and hit the 6-ball, but failed to make it. The 6-ball stayed in front of the side pocket, and the cue-ball came to rest near the far end of the table.

This time, the black 8-ball blocked a direct shot. Victor had the options of playing another safety, or trying a kick shot. He studied the possibilities, then looked over at Sedonia.

She stared back at him.

"Ten seconds," announced the director.

"Extension," Victor said. With the tip of his cue stick, he pointed to a place on the side rail. Then he deliberately chalked his cue, leaned down, and shot. The cue-ball kicked off the side rail where he'd pointed, rolled back across the table, and tapped the 6-ball into the side pocket. The spectators roared their approval, and Sedonia nodded hers. He made quick work of the remaining three balls, and received a standing ovation as the gold-striped 9-ball dropped into the corner pocket.

Sedonia now trailed 5 to 4, as she waited for the director to rack the balls for her next break. She'd issued a challenge, and Victor had answered it. From here on, the match promised to be an offensive shootout.

Moments later the crowd was back on their feet, when Sedonia slammed the cue-ball into the rack and made the 9-ball on the break. But as she returned to her chair amid deafening applause, the pain was so severe she felt nauseous. She sat down and looked across the room. Brad gazed back at her with a concerned expression. She managed a weak smile. For the rest of the match, she'd have to rely on her soft break.

Over the course of the next ten games, each player won when it was their turn to break. The spectators remained on their feet, applauding each shot and cheering the climax of each game. After twenty games, the match was tied, hill-hill. Victor, having won the initial lag, prepared to break for the twenty-first and deciding game.

Sedonia took her seat and rubbed her shoulder, hoping somehow to get to the table, one more time. This match reminded her of the final round at the U. S. Amateur Golf championship, except here, she was behind. And here, her opponent also was in dead stroke.

The tournament director finished racking the balls, then moved out of the way. Victor leaned down and prepared to break. Abruptly, he straightened, turned, and walked over to where Sedonia was sitting. She stood up, confused. He extended his hand and said, "Touch hands? Like boxers? Last round."

Sedonia smiled as they shook hands, and said, "Good luck." The crowd applauded their display of sportsmanship.

Victor returned to the break end of the table. He lunged forward with his hardest break of the match; it sounded like a thunderclap. Three balls fell, but the cue-ball rolled back to the break end of the table. Sedonia's hopes rose. Victor had a long cut shot on the blue 2-ball in the corner. Her hopes fell when he made it, but rose again when the cue-ball rolled back to break end of the table, leaving him another long cut shot, this time on the red 3-ball. He made it, and continued to improvise his way around the table. He drew repeated ovations, but each increasingly difficult shot caused progressively worse position.

Finally, he was down to the last two balls—the black 8-ball close to the near end rail, and the gold-striped 9-ball in front of the far corner pocket. The cue-ball was too close to the 8-ball for a makeable cut. The only possibility was a low-percentage kick shot off the side rail. Victor studied the shot, obviously trying to improvise a way to either make the 8-ball, or somehow knock in the 9-ball.

"Ten seconds," said the director.

"Extension," Victor replied. He continued to study the shot, then gave a resigned shake of his head, and settled for a safety.

Sedonia felt weak in the knees as she made her unexpected return to the table. Victor had left the black 8-ball frozen against the end rail, less than a foot from the corner pocket. The cue-ball had come to rest on the same side of the table, about three feet away. Sometime in the past—Sedonia didn't remember when—she'd been left with a similar shot: object ball frozen against the rail, requiring a cut of slightly more than ninety degrees. The rules of Nine-Ball required that she hit the 8-ball, and then either the 8-ball or the cue-ball had to touch a rail. If she failed to make a ball, the match probably would be over, since Victor should have no trouble making two balls on an open table.

The tournament director positioned himself for a good view of the 8-ball, to ensure she hit it. "Ten seconds," he said.

"Extension."

She heaved a sigh. She'd have to apply hard, low-left english, miss the 8-ball by the thinnest of margins, and hit the rail first. Then the english would spin the cue-ball off the rail and into the 8-ball ball. Having to hit the cue-ball so hard — possibly losing control of it — was her concern. She couldn't afford to scratch, since giving Victor ball-in-hand would certainly give him the match. Where was the cue-ball going to wind up when she hit it hard?

"Ten seconds," the tournament director said.

Then Sedonia saw it. She looked back at Victor and said, "Nine in the corner." He stood up for a better view of the shot, then smiled and nodded. Sedonia took a deep breath, released it, took another, released half of it, and leaned over the table and aimed the tip of her cue stick at the low-left side of the cue-ball. *One, two, three . . . stroke.* The cue-ball hit the rail precisely where she'd aimed, and the left english caught and spun it off the rail and into the 8-ball. As the 8-ball rolled slowly toward the corner pocket, the cue-ball sped down the table toward the 9-ball, sitting in the corner. The 8-ball dropped. The 9-ball dropped. The cue-ball stayed up!

The room exploded.

Sedonia's knees buckled, and she grabbed the table to keep from falling. Victor was the first to congratulate her. He raised her arm in triumph, and the din grew louder. Then he leaned over and said into her ear, "Gamble tonight in the practice room?" Before Sedonia could answer, he added with a smile, "But you gonna have to give me some weight."

The TV producer hurried them over to where the tournament director and one of the TV commentators were waiting to conduct the awards ceremony. Sedonia joined the applause for Victor, as he graciously accepted his $37,500 runner-up check. Then the room erupted again as Sedonia received the $50,000 check for first place.

Brad was standing in the midst of the spectators, and she waved him over. They shared a long kiss. Sedonia was vaguely aware of cameras going off around them. When they separated, she realized at least a hundred fans were hoping to get her autograph. She wanted to leave, but she remembered the consideration the women cueists in Las Vegas had shown their fans.

"Stay close to me," she whispered to Brad. "I'm afraid this is going to take a while."

"Take your time and enjoy it," he said with a smile. "You've earned it."

Finally the last autograph seeker had been satisfied, and Sedonia and Brad started toward the exit. Karen Hughes, the TV producer, came over and extended her hand. "Congratulations, Sedonia. Where do you play next?"

"This was my last tournament."

"You mean, last tournament this year?"

"No. My last tournament."

"You're kidding."

"It's been a marvelous two weeks," Sedonia said, "but I've got that shoulder problem, plus a business to look after." She glanced at Brad and smiled. "And more important things, which I've put off for too long."

The producer frowned. "I can't believe you're going to quit. Not now."

"Unlike my golf career," Sedonia said, "this time I'm quitting on *my* terms." The producer was still frowning as Sedonia turned to leave. She'd made her decision. Now she just wanted to check out of this hotel and head back to Incline Village. She interlaced her fingers with Brad's, and they started across the wide foyer.

"But how can you quit . . . *now?*" the producer called after her. "Now, when the International Olympic Committee has just announced that they're going to add cue sports to next year's competition?"

Sedonia took a couple more steps before the words registered. Then she stopped, and turned.

"Olympics?"

ACKNOWLEDGMENTS

I'm indebted to a number of people who have contributed to this novel. One afternoon, during the period when I was struggling through adolescence, a surrogate father took me into the smoky backroom of a neighborhood bar and grill. He spread pool balls across the faded green felt of an old Brunswick table, and he showed me how to hold a cue stick. That afternoon, he imparted skills that would prove to be a lifelong legacy. More than three decades later, I was still playing – leagues, tournaments, and socially.

Then in 1995, the Women's Professional Billiard Association (WPBA) came to Houston and held a tournament at the Westin Galleria. I arrived in time to watch the opening match, and through a friend, I met two aspiring young professionals, Deanna Henson and Bonnie Arnold. They, in turn, introduced me to many of the WPBA's featured players, including: Ewa Laurance, Jeanette Lee, Loree Jon Jones, Vivian Villarreal, and Belinda Calhoun.

I spent three days, perched on metal folding chairs, following match after match. These women were more than mere shot-makers. They were classy, accessible ambassadors of the game, with dreams and aspirations. They were professional women cueists. At some point while I sat watching, a seed was planted, the seed that would grow into this novel. I'm indebted to these women for the inspiration they provided.

I'm also indebted to dozens of longtime friends, family members, fellow writers, and pool players. Over the three-year period it took to complete this book, they were kind enough to review numerous iterations of the manuscript, offer their comments, and give me their encouragement.

And finally, I'm particularly grateful to my publishers, Sylvia and Steve Tomlinson, who were enthusiastic about this story from the onset, and who made the book a reality.